LDC-504

D0344461

WELCOME TO HIGBY

A Novel by Mark Dunn

MacAdam/Cage Publishing
155 Sansome Street, Suite 550
San Francisco, CA 94104
Copyright © 2002 by Mark Dunn
ALL RIGHTS RESERVED.

ISBN 1-931561-17-6

Manufactured in the United States of America.

Book and jacket design by Dorothy Carico Smith.

WELCOME TO HIGBY

A Novel by Mark Dunn

MacAdam/Cage

For my twin brother
Clay
who has been there for me since birth
and even nine months before that

1

But as for me, my feet were almost gone;
my steps had well-nigh slipped.
Psalm 73:2

LABOR DAY, 1993

"He ain't no daredevil. My opinion, the boy just ain't the *type*."

Avis didn't think Ray's statement merited a response, but he nodded anyway, his head cocked slightly back, his eyes squinting into the bright morning sun.

Ray's head was tilted much farther back. It looked to Avis like Ray was definitely risking a crick. "So, then, Avis, why you figure he does it?"

Avis shrugged. He made a visor with the plane of his hand against his forehead.

"I mean, a fourteen—what—fifteen-year-old kid climbin' all the way up to the top of a rickety ol' water tower just to sit. Just to sit and stare down at the world like that."

Avis nodded again. The boy seated on the catwalk of the water tower had now begun to remove his shoes.

"What's he doin' that for, I wonder?"

Avis shrugged and sniffed. Then he said, "Ray, did you have bowl of garlic for breakfast this morning?"

"Pizza."

The two men stood in silence for a moment. Then Ray spoke through his palm: "I tell you one thing: if that kid starts snipin' them shoes at folks, I ain't just gonna keep standin' here takin' in the scenery."

Avis gave his companion a long, weary look. "Y'know, Ray, I'm gettin' kinda tired of lookin' at Clint. I believe I'll get back to mornin' patrol."

Without waiting for Ray's opinion on this course of action, Avis started across the weed field to the cruiser, the thick, dusty green carpet of kudzu squeaking under his boots.

Ray hollered after him, "But what are we gonna do when all them

1

complaints start comin' in!"

Avis stopped to pick up a couple of Styrofoam drink cups that littered his path. "What kinda complaints would those be, Ray?"

"The ones we get ever time Clint goes up there." Ray made his voice sound high and naggy: "He's spyin' on me! That boy's invadin' my backyard privacy with high-powered binoculars!"

"I've never seen Clint with binoculars, high-powered or otherwise, Ray," Avis said. He scratched a little scaly place on his scalp. "You tell me now: You ever observed the boy totin' binoculars?"

Ray didn't believe he had.

"I'll call Reverend Cullen this evening."

"But you ain't even considerin' he might fall. You know how old and flimsy that railing is up there. He's liable to drop right down on top of somebody."

"That boy ain't gonna fall," Avis said, opening the door on the driver's side of the patrol car and sliding in. The seat was hot. He could feel the steamy warmth through his cotton twill uniform pants.

Avis was just turning the key in the ignition when, accompanied by sticks of brittle wooden railing, Clint began his unintended descent. It was Ray's pig-like squeal that brought the fall to his partner's attention. Together the two police officers watched as the shoeless teenager bounced off the top branches of Klaus and Abbadene Ostermeyer's side-yard oak tree and disappeared behind Johnny and Sheila Billows' stockade fence.

Sheila was sunning herself at the time, floating contentedly in her above-ground party pool on an inflatable raft that had been fabricated to look like a cartoon bear. The impact of Clint's splash-landing a few feet away sent a wall of water right over her head. It capsized her raft and doused the flames that had been spitting up from the coals of Johnny's hibachi.

All Ray and Avis could see from where they stood on the water tower property was the tip of the tidal wave of party-pool water forced up above the horizon of the Billows' fence.

For a moment neither Johnny nor Sheila spoke. Sheila had taken a considerable amount of water into her nose and was experiencing a painful sensation deep within her nasal passages. Johnny studied the humanoid creature that had just fallen from the sky into his pool and was now standing stunned and silent near his dramatically snorting wife. It bore an undeniable resemblance, at least in Johnny's mind, to the Cullen boy who lived down the street.

"Is that you, Clint?" Sheila finally inquired, sloshing over.

Clint didn't answer.

"I don't think he heard you," Johnny said. "I think the fall has popped out his eardrums." Johnny was on his way to assist Sheila when he noticed Muffin, the family terrier, racing from the miniature grill with a thick, choice-cut sirloin steak clamped between her teeth. Johnny abandoned his mission of aid and went for the steak.

As he pursued the little dog in a circular pattern around the swimming pool and then up and down the rows of beefsteak tomatoes and butterbeans in the sunny corner of the yard, Sheila yelled at her husband, "You quit chasin' that dog and get over here! There's a hurt boy in our pool!" Then she returned to the task of confirming the identity of the red-skinned teenager.

"You sure favor that Cullen boy," she said, blinking the heavily chlorinated water from her eyes.

"My face hurts," Clint finally said in a soft, half-whisper. "I think I broke my face."

By now Johnny had succeeded in trapping Muffin in the alley between the fence and a row of Sheila's prized tea rose bushes. He was about to lunge and take hold of the end of the steak that flapped from the dog's frothy mouth when Officers Avis Tomley and Ray Reese unlatched the gate to enter the backyard. Muffin seized this opportunity to make her getaway; she bolted for the open gate, scrambled through Ray's bow legs and scampered off down Deacon Lane.

Johnny gave momentary thought to going after her, then dismissed the idea, thinking it wouldn't look too good for him to leave the scene of an accident just to chase a dog through the neighborhood. "Clint Cullen fell into our pool," he announced, gesturing in the general direction of the partially emptied swimming pool.

"Yeah, we saw him come down," Avis replied. "How bad's he hurt?"

"I think he bruised his whole body," Sheila shouted over to the three men at the gate.

"Maybe you should call the hospital, Johnny," Avis suggested.

Johnny thought this was a good idea and went inside as Avis and Ray squished their way through wet nut-grass to the swimming pool.

"Where'd you come from?" Sheila asked Clint.

"I fell off the water tower," Clint replied. His hearing seemed to be improving.

Sheila took Clint's hand and began to lead him slowly to the side of the pool nearest Avis and Ray. "What were you doin' way up there on that old tower?" she asked.

"That's what I'd like to know," said Ray. His voice cracked a little on the word "I'd." Ray Reese's voice had been in the process of changing for the last twelve years.

Clint glanced up at the tower. Pigeons were now perched on the section of railing still intact.

"What I want to know," said Avis, as he speared the remaining raw sirloin steak from its platter with Johnny's two-pronged chef's fork, "is how in the name of God you survived that fall." Without waiting for an answer, the officer walked over and offered the steak to Clint. "Here. This'll make the swellin' go down."

Clint nodded his appreciation and pushed the sirloin strip up against his reddish-blue face. Sheila was happy she had bought the extra-large cuts.

2

*And let none of you imagine evil
in your hearts against his neighbor.*
Zechariah 8:17

"There's a funny-lookin' dog runnin' down the street with a big piece of meat in its mouth." Tula Gilmurray peeked over her shoulder; she wanted to see if her friend Flora Ludlam was listening. Flora wasn't. Tula pushed a few stray strands of her perspiration-dampened hair off her neck with the heel of her sudsy right hand.

"Why, I wouldn't think a dog that little could run half that fast if I hadn't just seen it with my own two eyes," she said in a slightly louder voice. Tula was determined to get Flora interested in this amazing event. But Flora didn't even look up. She was using a big wooden spoon to jab at a stick of margarine lying solid and stubborn at the bottom of her mixing bowl, her eyes fixed on the task before her.

Tula redirected her own gaze back out the window. Muffin had now disappeared behind an expansive gardenia bush.

"Why don't you give that oleo some time to soften up?" Tula offered, returning to her breakfast dishes.

Flora was in an irritable mood and saw no reason to pretend otherwise. "Excuse me, Miss Know-It-All, but this oleo has been sitting here for a half hour already."

"Well, you're goin' at it so hard, you're liable to knock the bowl off the table." Tula tried to say this as gently as possible considering the naked admonishment.

Flora took offense. "Do you want me to go home?"

"No, I don't want you to go home, honey. I'm just having concerns about that bowl. It goes clear back to the Depression."

Flora set down the wooden spoon and stared sullenly at her hands. Just as she was giving serious thought to calling her friend Liam to come drive her home, Tula's bachelor brother Hank appeared in the doorway. His kelly green snap-on bow tie was crooked and his lime green cotton slacks had crimps of wire-hanger crinkles across both legs along about the knees.

5

"I better iron those pants for you, Hank," Tula said.

"I don't have time. I have to get down to the VFW Hall. You seen my bazooka?"

Tula's hand flew to her mouth but the smile had already escaped. "You mean bassoon, honey."

"What'd I say?"

"Bazooka," Flora snorted. "You meant to say bassoon but you said bazooka."

Hank chewed on his lower lip for a little while.

Tula draped her dish rag over the sink divider and walked over to her older brother. "I do that all the time, Hank. You know, thinkin' one thing and sayin' something else. It's perfectly natural."

"Yeah, natural for a crazy man," Flora interjected. Flora was now scraping at the margarine stick with her spoon, pushing the yellow shavings into the sugar.

Tula led Hank out of the kitchen and into the front hallway. She opened the door to the coat closet. On the top shelf was a carrying case for a bassoon. As Hank pulled it down, Tula said, "Don't you pay any mind to what Flora says. She doesn't think you're crazy. She's just havin' herself a bad mornin'."

Hank nodded. Tula straightened his tie and brushed off the shoulders of his rust-plaid summer jacket. "You've got yourself a little hardenin' of the arteries, that's all. Nobody need be ashamed of *that*."

Hank nodded again. Tula kissed him lightly on the forehead and opened the front door. Calvin Gray waited in the driveway, sitting in his Regal eating prepackaged cheese and crackers, and reading *The Higby Star*.

"Mornin', Hank," Calvin said brightly as Hank opened the passenger side door. Tiny cracker crumbs sprinkled down from his beard as he spoke. "You ready to go jam a little?"

Calvin's clarinet sat out on the back seat next to an old cash register he'd picked up at a flea market six months before. Calvin's wife Edie had appropriated the clarinet's carrying case to make into a purse.

Hank patted his bassoon case and smiled. "I've been practicin' all week." Hank was about to get into the car when his neighbor Bowmar Stambler's fat black cat, Monty, caught his eye. Monty was lying on his back on Bowmar's stone walk, letting the sun warm his furry underside.

"Look at the funny old ignorant cat. I need to tell that cat about Christ."

Hank set his bassoon case down on the driveway and headed over to Monty.

"We're gonna be late, Hank!" Calvin hollered. He glanced over at Tula standing on her porch. She shrugged slightly. The cheery smile she'd been wearing just moments before had disappeared.

Tula raised her voice so she could be heard from her neighbor's walk: "Hank, honey, you don't want to be late for your band concert rehearsal. Why don't you tell Monty all about Jesus tomorrow?"

But Hank wasn't to be deterred from his mission. Ignoring Calvin and Tula, he knelt down next to the cat and proceeded to stroke the animal's furry belly while imparting great whispered truths. Bowmar's girlfriend and literacy tutor, Nancy Leigh, was observing all this from Bowmar's living room window.

"That Hank Grammar is witnessing to your cat again, Bowmar."

Bowmar didn't hear her. He was absorbed in a television nature program about meerkats. He was marveling at their ability to detect danger from many miles away.

"Just look at him."

"Look at who?"

"*Hank.* He's right down on his hands and knees tellin' your cat all about Jesus Christ of Nazareth." Nancy Leigh set down her bottle of Windex and turned to Bowmar. "This doesn't bother you the tiniest little bit?"

"I don't think it would be such a bad thing, Nancy Leigh, if my cat happens to wind up in Heaven."

"Your cat isn't goin' to Heaven, Bowmar."

Bowmar was in one of his argumentative moods: "Excuse me, Nancy Leigh, but I'd rather not go to Heaven myself if I don't get to have my cat and my bird-dogs with me." Bowmar began to work his right shoulder muscle with his left hand.

"Animals do not have souls," Nancy Leigh pronounced. "Humans are the only creatures with God-given souls."

"Well, I don't happen to agree with you on that point."

"If you believe in the scriptures then you can't believe that animals are gonna go someplace when they die," Nancy Leigh said. She was very sure of this fact and drove it home with a swift kick to the wooden footstool she'd been standing on to clean the top corners of Bowmar's smudgy windows.

"You certainly have a strong opinion on this subject, Miss Leigh, considerin' you once told me you didn't even think there *was* such a thing as Heaven."

"As usual, you got it all ass-backwards, Bowmar. I said I very much believed in Heaven. I just didn't think it would *look* like everybody thinks it'll look."

"So what do you think it'll look like?"

"Well, for one thing I imagine it'll be very colorful. And there's bound to be some paisley."

Nancy Leigh took a good long look at Bowmar. He was looking at her too, drinking everything in. Standing as she was, with legs akimbo, and hands placed squarely on her hips, Nancy Leigh looked to Bowmar like a wigged King of Siam.

"You know how much I love you, Bowmar," she said softly. "Movin' in with you was one of the best things I ever did, but don't you think it's time we maybe gave some thought to renting a house in some other neighborhood? There are, as you may have noticed, some very peculiar people on this block, and ever since my Aunt Sheba started settin' fires in other people's trash cans, I just can't tolerate peculiar people any more."

"I'm not so sure I like you talkin' about our neighbors that way, Nancy Leigh," Bowmar said. "Especially Ms. Gilmurrary and Mr. Grammar." Bowmar was at the window now, watching Calvin's car driving off down the street. Hank sat on the passenger side. Monty had moved to the turf of Bowmar's front lawn and was now batting at a little yard bug he planned to slay some time later. "You know that Tula Gilmurray has treated me with nothin' but Christian kindness ever since I got out of prison."

Nancy Leigh sat herself down on the footstool. Then, thinking it the most uncomfortable thing she ever sat on in her life, she got up, went over to the sofa and began to pick up a few Cheetos that Bowmar's fist had lost somewhere along its way from bag to mouth.

"I'm also thinkin' about that Carmen Valentine," Nancy Leigh said without looking up. "Some days that girl acts just as squirrelly as your friend Hank Grammar." Bowmar enjoyed watching Nancy Leigh's short black ponytail swish from side to side as she did a little dance step around the sofa while plucking Cheetos. Bowmar could watch Nancy Leigh all day long and never get bored.

"Excuse me, Miss Leigh," Bowmar said, his gaze now having moved to her curvy hips, "but I'm not gonna have you puttin' down Carmen Valentine. She's one of the nicest people I ever met." Bowmar decided that this might be a good time to clean the sofa of all stray party snacks, so he pulled off the cushions and went into the kitchen to find a trash bag.

Nancy Leigh stared at the landscape of the sofa's interior, strewn with chips and caramel corn, but was thinking mostly of Carmen and the funny way she had of looking only at people's chins when she addressed them.

3

And, behold, the angel that talked with me
went forth.
Zechariah 2:3

Carmen Valentine always made potato salad for Higby's municipally sponsored Memorial, Independence, and Labor Day picnics because Tina Louise Sperly had once told her she made the best potato salad in town. Tina Louise later learned that she'd been mistaken; it wasn't Carmen's potato salad she'd been savoring at the time of the compliment, but Abbadene Ostermeyer's. Abbadene used an old recipe that her husband Klaus's full-blooded German grandmother had left to Klaus and Abbadene in her will. Carmen was never informed of Tina Louise's error, though, and continued to contribute her potato salad year after year, noting with some puzzlement that it was hardly ever touched except by the husky, chronically hungry Pedloe twins, Harold and Carold, and usually then only after most of the other potato salads were gone.

Carmen was this way about certain things. There were facts about herself that she preferred not to face up to. She even had difficulty admitting to her correct age. She was twenty-eight but hardly anybody knew it. Only a few days before, she had told a telephone pollster that she was twenty-two and had graduated from Vassar College with academic honors.

Then there was the matter of Carmen's guardian angel. If she'd thought about it long enough, logic probably would have convinced her that what she'd heard on the railroad track that warm spring afternoon five years before had been merely the product of an overactive imagination. The voice she claimed to have heard could very well have been the engineer's whistle, garbled and distorted as it traveled from her eardrums to her brain. What had been interpreted by Carmen as "Get off this track, girl! There's a big train bearing down on you," could have been, simply, one great big "toot toot." But this notion didn't explain Carmen's other encounters with her guardian angel, most often at the supermarket.

"In addition to having saved my life on at least one occasion," Carmen would sometimes tell those who showed an interest in these

11

sorts of revelations, "my guardian angel likes to help me stretch my shopping dollar. She saves me a pretty penny at the checkout counter."

"And how does she do that?" Azalea Jeffcoat had politely asked one day as she and Carmen worked to pry apart the locked front grillworks of their two grocery carts. Carmen had only moments before become distracted by an eye-catching toilet bowl cleaner display on her trip down the soap and cleanser aisle, and smacked Azalea's cart head-on.

Carmen shrugged. "She just talks to me. Now and then. Reminds me of the weekly specials so I won't miss 'em."

Carmen usually didn't mention to anyone that her guardian angel was a large, robust African- American woman named Arnetta. Too many people would wonder how she knew. Carmen didn't know, herself. Maybe it came to her in a dream one night; she wasn't sure.

Muffin was stretched out on Carmen's hand-laid brick patio now, gnawing contently on the boney remains of the purloined beefsteak. Carmen would surely have seen the little dog had she not been busily rearranging the contents of her overstuffed refrigerator, making room for her freshly-prepared potato salad.

At first Carmen hadn't wanted to go to this year's Higby, Mississippi, Labor Day Picnic. The reason was that Tie Gibbons would be there. Tie had moved to Higby from Chattanooga in late May to take a job at the Pomeroy Lumber Company. As the summer progressed Carmen had found herself falling desperately in love with him. She'd first noticed him at her church, Calvary United Christian, usually sitting in the back next to his best friend and roommate, Stewie Kipp. Sometimes while running an errand or doing her marketing Carmen would drive a little out of her way in hopes of catching a glimpse of Tie through the lumberyard fence. Only once was she successful, and then all she really got for her trouble was a snatch of sunburned forehead. This was just as well. She had a plan—one that required great patience and care.

Carmen had already begun to put her plan into effect. Each Sunday morning she would move one pew back from her traditional spot in the front of the sanctuary. According to her calculations, she would reach the back pew—that very same pew occupied by Stewie and Tie—by the second Sunday in December. Carmen had marked this date with a big gold star on her kitchen calendar. The back pew would place her in convenient enough proximity, she hoped, for Tie to take special notice, lean over and invite her out for a club sandwich and Coca-Cola following the worship service.

A picnic just wasn't a suitable place to meet a popular guy like Tie Gibbons. And yet Carmen Valentine had never missed a Higby Labor Day Picnic. It was her favorite picnic of the year. She didn't have to walk around all day with her ears plugged with wax as she often did on the Fourth of July. And Memorial Day was always too sad a reminder of a favorite uncle who suffered a reproductive wound in the Vietnam War.

"I've really got to do somethin' about this," Carmen said to herself as she poked around inside the refrigerator. "There's enough old food in here to pack a landfill. Of course, what kinda person spends her Labor Day mornin' doin' labor?"

"Clean it out, honey," she thought she heard her guardian angel say. The voice was faint; Arnetta was apparently quite some distance away, having, no doubt, just departed for her long-overdue vacation.

"I'd rather not," Carmen said aloud.

"Suit yourself, child," she thought she heard Arnetta reply. "It ain't life and death anyway. Besides, I'm goin' skiin'.'"

Carmen shut the refrigerator door and switched on her kitchen radio. She was hoping to hear a few minutes of her favorite talk show personality Jewel Connell who had overcome personal hardship through the balm of laughter. She thought that Jewel's bright radio voice might put her in the right spirit to get the most out of a festive holiday picnic. But first the station aired a commercial for Higby Presbyterian Hospital that featured an earnest doctor barking the word "stat" over the urgent beeping of an active heart monitor.

Carmen tried hard to push back thoughts of Tie lying stricken on an operating table. She was assisted moments later when Jewel started to accept phone calls from listeners who looked like their pets.

4

Peace to him that is far off,
and to him that is near,
saith the Lord;
and I will heal him.
Isaiah 57:19

Ponce Humphries didn't venture down to the E.R. unless he absolutely had to. Not that Higby Presbyterian Hospital's emergency room was such a terrible place to be. You'd hardly ever see the kind of grisly things you'd see in the big-city hospitals. But Ponce was chief hospital administrator now, and as such didn't have to look at even the occasional broken limb or deer-season gunshot wound unless he really wanted to. Ponce came down this particular morning because he'd heard that Reverend Cullen's son Clint had just been brought in. According to head E.R. nurse Maxine Armbrust, Clint fell from the old Higby water tower and landed in Johnny and Sheila Billows' backyard pool. The boy was apparently so bruised in the face, legs and arms that Priscilla Rood, one of the newest members of the hospital's nursing staff, had declared upon first sight that he looked just like "somebody who'd been beaten up by everybody he'd ever met."

Maxine wondered where Clint's father Oren might be. It was two police officers who had delivered the boy to the emergency room. Ponce guessed that the Reverend Cullen had probably gotten a late start from Bible Methodist Church Camp. Oren Cullen had just completed a two-week tour of duty there as camp administrator. Clint hadn't accompanied his father this year. Ponce thought it might have been a mistake to let Clint stay home.

Ponce Humphries and Oren Cullen had been friends for many years. Ponce was the Cullens' family physician at the time of Oren's wife Alice's illness; after Alice's death he had persuaded Oren to join the Dads Without Moms support group to which he belonged.

Ponce and Oren, both in their mid-forties, made a very odd pair: Ponce the former wrestler, large-boned and authoritative; Oren small and lean and unassuming. Neither was a big talker, but Oren even less so

15

than Ponce. Except for Sunday morning services during which Oren made every attempt to keep his sermons as brief as possible, he spoke only when absolutely necessary, using an economy of words very rare for this part of the country. Those infrequent exchanges that actually reached the status of true conversation almost always involved Ponce, and were more than likely of a theological nature. Ponce was an unabashed atheist, and this fact troubled Oren to no end.

"Hi there, sport," Ponce greeted Clint as he approached the examining table. "They tell me you took a pretty bad fall."

Clint nodded. It was difficult for him to make out Ponce's face with both his eyes nearly swollen shut.

"We don't think there've been any internal injuries, but we're going to run a few tests just to be on the safe side."

Clint nodded again. "Is my dad back yet?"

Ponce shook his head. "But I'll stick around till he gets in, if that's okay with you."

"All right."

A short silence passed before Ponce said, "So, I understand these last couple of weeks you've been staying at your friend Pauly's."

"Pauly isn't my friend. He's just somebody whose house I *had* to sleep at while Dad's been off at camp."

"I see."

"My mouth hurts to talk. I'm gonna be quiet now, okay?"

"Sure," Ponce answered softly.

"Dr. Humphries?"

"Yes?"

"Could you let me know if they're gonna come back and poke at me?"

"Can do."

Clint closed his eyes.

"Son?"

"Huh?"

"Don't drift off quite yet. We need to make sure there hasn't been any head trauma."

"Head trauma?"

"I doubt if you have any. But let's not take any chances. I don't think it would be a good idea for your dad, first thing back in town, to hear that you'd lapsed into a coma while he was away. What do you say?"

"No. Not too good."

Out of the corner of his eye Ponce could see nurse Rood and intern Craig Stonebreaker rolling over a gurney. "Okay," he said, "time for a little damage assessment." To Craig, Ponce said, "Let's start with a head scan with and without contrast."

"Hello, Bruise Boy," Priscilla greeted Clint sunnily. Something about the young nurse's melodious voice reminded Clint of his mother. Suddenly he felt good and bad at the same time.

5

Be not forgetful to entertain strangers:
for thereby some have entertained angels unawares.
Hebrews 13:2

Despite the invitation, Oren wasn't going to sit in the Far East House of Massage and make phone calls all day. It seemed easier to simply hike the six or so miles into town. Surely, somewhere along Table River Highway he and his busload of ten-, eleven-, and twelve-year-olds would run into somebody they knew who could send back word of their breakdown. This was very strange, the phone not being answered in the church office. Unless Nina Lewis and all the parents had chosen to wait for their children at the Labor Day picnic. Maybe she put up a sign: "We're all at the picnic! Come on over!"

Even with all of Oren's serious Christian doubts about entering the establishment, suspected by almost everyone in town of being the site of some very un-Christian activity, Desiree Parka, its red-headed proprietress, had worn him down with kindness. "What's the harm in just comin' in to use the telephone?" she had asked.

I suppose there isn't any harm in *that*, Oren thought to himself, so long as the children remain safely outdoors, beyond the masseuse's potentially negative influence.

Inside, though, Oren found Desiree to be the perfect southern hostess. After serving Oren a tall glass of iced tea, tastefully garnished with a mint sprig and a slice of lemon, she excused herself to carry a pitcher of Kool-Aid out to the kids, who were now tossing Frisbees on her gravel drive. She returned to share his consternation over not being able to reach anyone on the phone, then offered to shuttle into town as many of the kids as she could fit inside her mobile massage van.

"Thank you anyway, ma'am, but I just don't think that would be proper."

"I'm not a bad woman, Reverend Cullen."

Oren was surprised to hear such a frank retort. He stumbled a little in his reply: "Oh no, Ms. Parka—I don't—certainly don't think you're bad—no, no, of course not."

"Then why won't you let me help you out?"

"You did help me out. You let me use your telephone."

Desiree pursed her very red lips into a quivering pout. "A big help that was—you couldn't reach anybody."

"I just don't think these youngsters' parents would understand if some of them came riding up to the church in the back of that van."

"Oh, I wish people wouldn't be that way. This really galls me." Desiree sank down into her sunshine orange vinyl couch, and folded her arms.

Oren didn't know what to say. It felt very strange being inside a house of massage with a beautiful masseuse who was galled. He started to think of how he might make a polite exit. In the process, a very strange notion popped into his head. How nice it would be before I left, he thought, if Ms. Parka would give me a massage—a professional foot massage. He wondered if she could massage feet as well as Alice could. At the thought of his deceased wife, a wave of sadness washed over Oren. Before he even had time to do anything about it, his eyes became moist and his throat tight.

"Are you all right, Reverend Cullen? My perfume's not makin' you allergic, is it?"

Oren shook his head. He wasn't about to speak. He didn't know what weird kind of sound might emanate from his constricted throat.

"Well, I really wish you'd tell me what's the matter. I hope I didn't offend you in any way." Desiree pulled herself up from the couch and walked over to her favorite lumpy armchair, where Oren seemed to be half-sitting, half-poised for sudden flight.

He shook his head again and cleared his throat. "I was thinking about my wife."

"Well, if she's as sweet as you are, she's not gonna care one bit you came in here."

"No, I mean she's gone. She died."

"I'm so sorry."

"I was thinking, well, she used to give me foot rubs."

Desiree grinned. "I can give foot rubs! That's one of my specialties!" Desiree dropped to her knees and began to unlace Oren's shoes. "And I'm not even gonna charge a nice man like you."

Oren shook his head and stood up. "Maybe some other time."

Desiree didn't hide her disappointment. "Some other time, all right. In fact, next time you're here, I won't just stop at the feet. I'll give you a nice full-body massage."

"Thank you," Oren said. "That would be nice." He helped Desiree to her feet, pulling her up by her hands. They held the clasp for a moment, neither speaking. A Frisbee struck Desiree's front picture window, a gaggle of children appearing a moment later to retrieve it.

"They're probably trampling your flower bed."

Desiree shook her head. "Nothing grows there anyway. Reverend Cullen, I would be happy to report your predicament on my way to the picnic."

This seemed, to Oren, to be a good compromise.

As Desiree led Oren to the front door she said, "And I'm serious about that massage."

Oren nodded and smiled.

Oren and the children had walked less than half a mile down the highway when their rescue party arrived: a small caravan of moms and dads in pickups and station wagons.

"When you didn't show up on time we guessed that your bus probably had itself another breakdown," Veneece Cobb said.

Veneece's husband Germaine added, "I guess it's time to shoot that ol' bus and put her out of her misery."

The sun was starting to give Oren a headache; he was relieved that he wouldn't have to hike the remaining five and a half miles into town.

Oren looked at the line of cars and trucks now parked along the gravelly shoulder of the blacktop, their glistening metallic finishes reflecting a string of brilliant miniature sunbursts. Half-obscured behind the wall of glare was Porter Grogan standing next to his old rust-blotched white Rambler, waving Oren over. Even though the Grogans' Rambler hadn't had a working air conditioner for years, Oren didn't mind riding with Porter, Edith, and their son Cubby because the Grogans, all deaf, never put great conversational demands on their passengers.

Oren was about to join the Grogans for the ride into town when he noticed Mikey Rood flagging him frantically in the opposite direction toward his pickup. Oren signaled Porter to go on without him, and crossed the steaming asphalt to where Mikey was standing. Mikey looked pale.

"I'm supposed to take you straight to the hospital, Reverend. Your boy, he fell off the catwalk of that old water tower."

Oren felt a jolt. For a moment Mikey's face became the face of his best friend Ponce. For a brief moment Oren was taken back to the morning Ponce delivered the news that Alice had finally lost her fight to live. The empathetic, apologetic deliverer of tragic news.

Oren climbed into the cab. At the same time he tried to swallow. His throat had almost totally closed up. "How bad, Mikey? How bad is he hurt?"

"Priscilla says they don't think there've been any internal injuries. Dr. Humphries, he don't even think Clint broke any bones, but he's bruised up pretty bad. Fell into a swimmin' pool if you can believe it. Smacked that water like it was hard ground."

Clint was alive. Oren closed his eyes and sent up a short prayer of thanksgiving. When he opened them the first thing he saw was the Grogans' ancient Rambler. It was being passed by Mikey's truck. Through the Rambler's windows Oren could see Cubby signing happily away about his fun-filled weeks at church camp, his parents smiling and attentive.

6

They are all dumb dogs…
sleeping, lying down, loving to slumber.
Isaiah 56:10

Talitha Leigh watched a convoy of pickups, station wagons and a white Rambler that had seen better days roll past the tiny bathroom window as it sucked in motor exhaust and two flies the size of small grapes. She closed the window and returned her attention to the shower diverter knob that had a few minutes earlier come off in her hand. She tried to figure out how to reattach it so she wouldn't be forced to take a bath in a tub that didn't seem all that clean. "Oh shit," she mumbled to herself. "I just hate this place."

Now, even the idea of a shower was losing its appeal. Talitha generally hated taking showers in strange places—especially motels—and most especially low-rent establishments like the Dollar Econo Motor Court. The shower in her bathroom at home was perfect, and she didn't know why she wasn't there at this very moment enjoying the soothing spray of the Shower Massage attachment, which her older sister Nancy Leigh had given her a week and a half earlier for her thirtieth birthday. The trouble was, Talitha really hated saying goodbye to a date while he was still asleep, and despite it being early afternoon, this particular hard-drinking trucker companion from the night before didn't seem anywhere near waking up.

She caught a glimpse of herself in the large mirror over the sink vanity. *That frown is very unbecoming,* she thought. Then, working her mouth into a sultry smile, she posed. She threw her chest out and rolled her shoulders back. She held her arms out to the sides to check for underarm flab. Talitha liked the way her body looked. She never had to diet like her sister Nancy Leigh whose low fat dinners often sent her boyfriend Bowmar out on late night forages for Cheetos and canned Vienna sausages. Talitha could pretty much eat whatever she wanted and still maintain a figure that very few of her dates failed to compliment her on. Although she'd always felt her nose was a tad too wide for the shape of her face, none of the men she went out with ever agreed, and several said it made her look a little exotic ... even Nubian, which, she supposed, was a good, sexy thing to be.

"BODGER, GET IN HERE AND HELP ME WITH THIS DOO-JIGGY THING SO I CAN TAKE A SHOWER!"

Talitha sat down on the edge of the tub and listened for any sign of stirring from her bed partner.

"HEY! WAKE UP! YOU'VE BEEN ASLEEP FOR TEN HOURS!"

From the other room came the sound of a man moaning in pain.

She tried another approach: "I'M STANDIN' HERE NAKED. WANNA COME DRINK IT ALL IN?"

"Quit yellin' at me," replied a muffled, anguished voice. Too softly for Talitha to hear, the voice added, "I feel like somebody done run over me with one of them Monster Macks."

"Well, I'm not gonna take a bath in this undisinfected tub," Talitha said. She tried one last time to reconnect the shower knob to the top of the spout. Giving up, she got herself dressed and marched into the bedroom where Bodger, his head hidden inside a teepee of pillows, was groaning.

"Oh just look at you," she said. "You're no fun at all. Well, you give me no choice. I'm just gonna have to leave you here to nurse that hangover all by yourself." Talitha waited a moment to see if Bodger would at least acknowledge her departure with a wave of the hand. When he seemed incapable of even this tiny exertion, she opened the door to the motel room and left.

As she walked home in the bright early afternoon sunshine, her driver's license having been suspended five months earlier due to an accumulation of seven speeding tickets in a three-year period, Talitha thought about how drab and dull her life had been lately and how much she'd like to spice it up. Even if this meant getting herself into a little trouble. A person can't get herself into too much trouble in this town, she thought to herself.

She passed the Hoffbrau Tavern, which had only been open for a couple of months and which she had vowed to visit following an offhanded remark by her friend Vondelle Chatelaine. Vondelle had said that brawny, angular-faced "chocolate soldiers" from the army base over in Yashoba County sometimes liked to drop by the Hoffbrau for a change of pace to listen to the beer hall music, slap each other a lot on the back and shout "Prost!" in happily inebriated voices. Neither she nor Vondelle knew what the word "prost" meant, but it sounded like the kind of place for Talitha to shake herself out of the late-summer doldrums. Even if it wasn't always Black USO night, there was still no telling what kinds of interesting non-trucker people she might meet there.

7

She openeth her mouth with wisdom;
and in her tongue is the law of kindness.
Proverbs 31:26

Carmen Valentine passed B and Q Barbecue, The Giant Loom, and the Hoffbrau Tavern, then slowed to let a slender, rumpled young woman with rebellious hair vacate the crosswalk. Her mind wasn't on the woman or the local scenery, though. It was Tie and the 1993 Higby, Mississippi, Labor Day picnic that continued to consume her thoughts. Carmen was determined not to let her enjoyment of the picnic hinge on whether Tie Gibbons noticed her. If he happened to be in attendance, and if he, well, just happened to amble her way and strike up a nice, friendly conversation, that would just be perfectly fine with her. It would certainly spare her from a dozen more Sunday mornings of pew-shifting. But if this *didn't* happen Carmen was determined to have herself a good time anyway. Carmen Benelda Valentine had long ago accepted the fact that her looks weren't going to open any doors for her, including the doors leading to men's hearts. "I know I'm not beautiful," she once admitted to her guardian angel Arnetta who cheerfully countered with, "Of course you're beautiful, honey. But most of your beauty is *inside*. You keep it in this special sunny little place where it blossoms oh so pretty every time you think a kind thought or do a good deed." Carmen liked hearing Arnetta say this. In fact, this would have been the perfect day to hear it again. Unfortunately, Arnetta was on vacation.

"I can't find a place to park," Carmen remarked to the baton-wielding teenaged boy who seemed to be in charge of finding parking places for all the picnickers with cars. The boy's incipient blond mustache reminded Carmen of her bristly-lipped cousin Claude who lived down in Clancy Point and who at the age of fourteen started eating Spaghetti-O's at every meal and didn't stop, even after psychological counseling.

"Go look over by the playground." the boy said. "There might be a few spots left over there." Carmen thanked him and drove around the southern perimeter of the park to the children's playground. Passing a

27

cluster of baby pine trees, she spotted Tie and his roommate Stewie Kipp lifting a large barbecue grill from the bed of Stewie's truck. Tie wore a T-shirt that read, "Never hate a man for the color of his neck." He was laughing so hard that his whole body was shaking; in fact, Carmen didn't think she'd ever seen a man laugh so hard. His whole face seemed to radiate happiness.

"I'm sure that Tie Gibbons could make me very happy," she said to herself, swerving just in time to keep from running right into the jungle gym.

***

"I give up."

Tula glanced at the large sunburst clock over her kitchen window. "It's almost noon. You can sit there and stare at the floor for as long as you like, Flora, but *I* need to get ready for the picnic."

"I'm not goin'."

"You've already told me that, dear."

Tula was mounting the stairs to her bedroom to change into her picnic clothes when Flora added, her voice raised to be heard from the kitchen table, "I have told you what I think of Labor Day! I don't believe such a day should be honored, let alone celebrated!"

Tula refused to allow her oldest and dearest friend to have the final word: "Labor Day is a very good holiday," she declared, returning to the kitchen. "One of the best we have. There is absolutely nothin' Communist about it."

"It was dreamed up by Communists and Communist sympathizers."

Flora glared at Tula. Tula wanted very much to respond to this angry face by noting how much Flora's personality had changed since her stroke six months before, but chose instead to give brief thought to what Jesus might do if he found himself in a situation such as this.

After taking a deep, calming breath, Tula addressed Flora in a softer, more considerate, and decidedly more Christian-like voice: "Honey, you and I both know what's put you in this grumpy mood. It's because Euless forgot to call you on your birthday yesterday."

"That's not true."

Both Tula and Flora knew that it was.

Tula sat down across from Flora. She studied the unfriendly expression on her friend's face. "I just wish you could see what you look like right now."

"Well, you make me so mad sometimes," Flora shot back.

"I'm sure that he just got too busy with all he's been doin' for Mr. Pomeroy these days. I just know that fine boy of yours would never have forgotten your birthday if he didn't have good reason."

"He is a good boy, isn't he?" Flora said, softening. She wasn't scowling anymore.

"If I'd had children, I would want them all to be just like Euless."

"You would?"

Tula nodded.

"I think you're right about him workin' too hard," said Flora, eager to talk about her son. "Why, between Mr. Pomeroy and that car fix-it place I'll bet he puts in about seventy hours a week."

Tula wanted very much to leave for the picnic, but wanted even more for Flora to come with her. The two women sat talking on for a while about Euless, and about how proud he made his mother, holding down two jobs, earning Mr. Pomeroy's favor even though he had always been a slow child who most thought would never amount to much. Finally, Flora, with a great show of reluctance, agreed to stop by the picnic, but only for a few minutes; she did, after all, want to see if anybody liked her sugar cookies. She had used a new, untried recipe.

8

An evil disease, say they,
cleaveth fast unto him:
and now that he lieth he shall rise up no more.
Psalm 41:8

Conwell Pomeroy had cancer throughout his body and was supposed to be dead by Easter. No one knew why he'd been able to hang on for so long but there were theories. Perhaps it was because of all the money he'd accumulated. Conwell, was, after all, the richest man in Higby, and as such had certainly bought himself the best medical care around. Then there were some, Euless Ludlam among them, who preferred to think that Conwell's survival might be the result of pure willpower; that, as sick as he was, Conwell Lucius Pomeroy II had simply willed himself to keep on living.

Euless watched from across the room as the withered old man slept fitfully in his bed. This was Euless's job for the moment: to monitor Conwell's rapidly deteriorating condition. What was entailed in "monitoring" beyond simple observation Euless wasn't quite sure, but "monitoring" was definitely the word Nurse Ringfinger had used in her instructions to him before she left to take her afternoon break.

Euless didn't mind; it was an opportunity for him to sit and think. Euless Ludlam had a lot of thinking to do, mostly about his future—a future that didn't seem to hold much promise at the moment. Mr. Pomeroy had been the best employer Euless had ever had; the old man had paid Euless a more-than-decent wage to keep his prized collection of Case touring cars polished and running. Mr. Pomeroy had paid him so well, in fact, that he was able to retire almost all of his debts and even make a respectable down payment on a small mobile home. Now Euless's employer was dying, and Euless's term of employment here was coming to an end. Without the extra income, Euless would be hard-pressed to find enough money to continue the mobile home payments *and* keep up his monthly installments to the IRS for the five years of back taxes he owed. Either he'd lose his new house and have to go back to sleeping on the office couch in Saul Joseph's We-Fix-It Auto Repair Shop, or get a visit from federal marshals ready to haul him right off to jail. Neither prospect seemed much to look forward to.

Conwell woke with a start and cried out something that Euless couldn't understand. Euless bounded from his chair and rushed to the old man's bedside.

"What's that, Mr. Pomeroy? I didn't get what you said."

Conwell blinked his rheumy eyes a few times and tried to get a fix on where he was.

"It's me, Mr. Pomeroy—Euless Ludlam."

"Hello, Euless. I was having a bad dream. Where's Nurse Ringfinger?"

"She's out in the garden gettin' herself a little fresh air. You want me to fetch her?"

Conwell shook his head. "You don't have to sit with me, Euless. I'll be all right."

"The nurse thought you might want another pain shot when you woke up. You sure you don't want me to go get her?"

"What time is it?"

"About one."

"You aren't at the picnic."

Euless shrugged. He wasn't a big one for picnics.

Conwell smiled and glanced out the window. Irmene Ringfinger was in full view down in the vegetable garden, placing ripe red tomatoes in a pouch she had made in the fold of her apron. The bright white of the private duty nurse's uniform she was wearing reflected the sun so strongly that she seemed to be shimmering. "She's a funny one, gardenin' with her little nurse's hat on," Conwell chuckled. Euless smiled in agreement.

Euless noticed that the corners of Conwell's eyes crinkled a little when he laughed; with his bushy white beard he looked to Euless like a very gaunt and sickly Santa Claus. Conwell coughed twice, then remarked with quiet sobriety, "There were people chasing me, Euless."

"What's that?" Sometimes Conwell mumbled.

"In my dream. People were chasing me. Everybody was chasing me. I couldn't get away from them."

"Nobody's chasin' you now, Mr. Pomeroy. You got nobody comin' after you that I can tell."

Conwell nodded and patted a spot on the bed next to where he lay. Euless obligingly sat down, half on, half off the bed because he hadn't been left much room. Euless caught a glimpse of his reflection in the pane of the nearby window. He was a little surprised by his own haggard appearance. His face sported about two day's worth of dark beard growth, making him look a little like Fred Flintstone. His eyes appeared tired and bloodshot. His hair was unkempt, and apparently, given his rapidly receding hairline, falling out in great clumps.

"You like it down there at that repair shop?" Conwell asked in a casual conversational tone that belied the fact that he was now down to his last hours on earth.

"It's an okay job," Euless said. Euless liked it that Conwell felt like talking; he only wished that his employer would move over just a tad to give him more room on the bed. In his present groggy state he could easily see himself nodding off and then toppling right to the floor.

"My grandfather was a mechanic," Conwell said. "Pretty good one. He was a tinkerer too. Could fix just about anything. You give him the right tools and the right parts, and, why, he'd have whatever it was whirring and purring in a matter of minutes."

Conwell swallowed hard a couple of times. Euless poured him a glass of water from the pitcher on the nightstand. Slowly he brought the glass up to the old man's parched, cracked lips. Conwell took a couple of small sips, some of the water dribbling out of the corners of his mouth and onto his beard. He nodded for Euless to withdraw the glass, then said, "I look at your hands, son, and I see my granddaddy's. He had big, strong hands just like yours. No tellin' the things he could have made for himself with those hands if he'd had a little money. Could've been another Edison. But Granddaddy was a poor man, you see. Father—now *he* was the one who made things happen. *He* was the wheeler-dealer, uh-huh."

Euless nodded. He was trying to pay close attention to what Conwell was saying, but it wasn't all that easy; he'd just caught a glimpse of Conwell's nurse out the window, and had become distracted. Irmene was putting on a real show: dancing about and swatting at the air around her head with her free hand. She was being pestered, it seemed, by some sort of troublesome flying insect, and appeared to be on the verge of losing her apronful of tomatoes and ladypeas.

Conwell reached over and touched Euless's right hand. Euless was surprised to find the old man's fingers so cold; Conwell had been burning up with a high fever through most of the morning. "You've got my granddaddy's hands, all right. Those exact same hands. I used to watch him working with those hands when I was a boy. Wanted to grow up to be just like him. Course I didn't. I grew up to be like my father."

Euless took another quick glance out the window. Irmene had just collided with a fencepost and knocked all the wind out of herself. Euless wanted to go to the window and holler down to find out if she was all right, but Conwell, his eyes closed now, was holding onto him, two of his fingers hooked around Euless's thumb, squeezing like a little baby.

A moment or so passed, and Conwell drifted back off to sleep. Euless could hear the rattly, wheezing sound of the old man's breathing. The fingers loosened around Euless's thumb, and he was able to get up from the bed and return to his chair at the other end of the room. Soon Irmene would return from her adventure in the garden, and he could go home and get a couple of hours rest before heading for the auto repair shop to begin his night shift.

Euless couldn't remember the last time he'd felt so depressed.

9

A man that hath friends
must show himself friendly:
and there is a friend
that sticketh closer than a brother.
Proverbs 18:24

Carmen Valentine found a nice spot beneath a loblolly pine and made a comfortable pallet for herself out of the fallen brown needles. She drew a large, rose-colored cloth napkin from the side pocket of her crushed-leather shoulder bag, and spread it across her lap. She set her Chinette plate carefully down on this makeshift tablecloth, then began the formidable task of selecting which of the various dollops of cold salad she'd assembled for her tasting pleasure would have the privilege of going into her mouth first.

A few yards away, a group of young men who worked at the Pomeroy Lumber Yard, their T-shirts freshly spotted with mustard and barbecue sauce, were tossing horseshoes until such point as their overtaxed digestive tracts might withstand a strenuous game of power volleyball. Carmen was happy to discover Tie Gibbons among them. Unfortunately, he'd been teamed up with Coot Malloy, a musclebound, former Mississippi State linebacker from Vicksburg who hadn't had much experience pitching horseshoes and was consistently overthrowing by several yards.

"You might wanna move back a ways," Carmen heard a voice behind her say. "They're probably gonna switch sides in a minute and you'll be right in Coot's line of fire."

Carmen turned and looked up into the familiar face of her friend Stewie Kipp. She had always thought that Stewie's was a nice-looking face, but not really her type. It was quite obvious, at least to Carmen Valentine, that Stewie needed more protein in his diet; everything seemed to cave in a little too much just below the cheekbones. At times Stewie looked to Carmen like a twenty-seven-year-old Abraham Lincoln. She did, though, give him points for being so trim.

"Thank you for the advice," Carmen said. Without hesitation she picked up her shoulder bag, plate, napkin, and can of Diet Coke, and car-

35

ried them to the base of another pine a little more removed from the horseshoe pit. As she eased herself down she discovered that this wasn't nearly as comfortable a spot as the one she'd just abandoned; the ground was lumpy, and the sun would now be shining right into her face. Nonetheless, she wasn't in the mood to move again, so she accepted her lot and made her peace with it.

Stewie followed her over. He took a big swig of his A&Wroot beer, then crumpled the now empty can with one of his large but slender, Lincolnesque hands.

"You want this, Mr. McElhaney?" he called out to a stoop-shouldered man dragging a fat, dimpled garbage bag through the picnic table area nearby. The man nodded and started over.

"He lives in a car," Stewie said matter-of-factly. "I think it's an Impala."

Mr. McElhaney accepted Stewie's can, deposited it in the bag, then turned to Carmen. "You done with that there beverage can?" Mr. McElhaney was eagerly eyeing the cola can now resting against a tree root jutting up next to where Carmen was sitting.

Carmen shook her head. "There's still some liquid left in it."

"Take your time. Take your time. I'll be back directly." As Mr. McElhaney headed for a group of sunbathing high school girls, each well on her way to finishing her third Diet Sprite of the afternoon, he began to whistle a tune which neither Carmen nor Stewie had heard before. It was a pleasant little tune, and it immediately put Carmen in a cheerful mood.

Stewie leaned back against the new pine, watching the horseshoe game for a moment. Then he said, "That Tie, he's a pretty good shoe pitcher, don't you think?"

"I suppose he is. I don't know that much about horseshoes."

"You'd probably like to meet him, wouldn't you?"

Carmen craned her neck to look up at Stewie. It was an unnatural position for her, and she could feel a protest from her vetebral column. "Now what makes you think I'd be interested in meetin' Tie Gibbons?"

"I don't know. I just got myself a feelin'."

"And where would you get a feelin' like that?" Carmen took a gulp of Diet Coca-Cola. Some of the fizz escaped through her nose.

Stewie squatted down next to Carmen and lowered his voice, even though there wasn't really anyone around within earshot. Pinning her with his deep-set eyes, he said, "Well, for one thing, I notice how you've been moving one pew closer to him every Sunday morning."

"How do you know it's Tie I'm trying to get closer to? Maybe I just wanna be near all the mothers with their cute little babies."

Stewie shook his head and grinned. "It's Tie all right. I can tell."

"All right, all right. So what if it is? I don't think that's such a bad thing for a person to want to do." Carmen immediately regretted sounding so brusque with Stewie who always made an effort to sit next to her in their young adults' Sunday School class, and who, she discovered not too long ago, was also her birthday twin.

Stewie didn't seem to mind. He kept right on smiling. "No, it's not a bad thing at all. I only mentioned it because I thought I might be able to save you a little trouble."

"What do you mean?"

"Okay. Forget about church and forget about this picnic since it looks like Tie's gonna be spendin' the whole afternoon playin' horseshoes and volleyball. Come to my place tonight. I'm gettin' some folks together, Tie included. We're gonna play Tripoley."

"I love Tripoley," Carmen replied with just enough enthusiasm, she hoped, to mask the fact that she at that moment could not think of a more boring card game played by adults.

"Good. Most everybody's comin' around seven-thirty. If you give me a little piece of paper from your purse there, I'll write down the directions."

Carmen dug around in her shoulder bag for a scrap of paper, and finally settled on a postcard recently sent to her by Higby Presbyterian Hospital reminding her not to miss its upcoming Women's Wellness Fair and Heart-healthy Bake Sale. She was so happy and excited about finally getting to spend time in the company of the man of her dreams she almost didn't notice when an iridescent blue dragonfly lit right on her knee.

10

Thou hast showed thy people hard things:
thou hast made us to drink the wine of astonishment.
Psalm 60:3

Ponce found Oren sitting next to Clint's bed staring at an arrangement of miniature roses and baby's breath that Charday Hollings had dropped off a half hour earlier on behalf of the office volunteers at the church.

"I know young boys don't much favor flowers," Charday had said somewhat apologetically, "but Mr. Mews at the florist's shop said this particular arrangement would be all right because there are a lot of manly ferns in there. Boys like ferns, he said, because it makes 'em think of trampin' through the woods huntin' bears and other creatures of the wild."

Oren had thanked Charday in a whisper because he didn't want to wake Clint. She left quietly after telling Oren how much she and Nina Lewis, the church secretary, and everyone else at Bible Methodist would be praying for Clint's speedy recovery.

"Why don't we go on down to the coffee shop for a few minutes?" Ponce asked Oren.

"You aren't off for the holiday? Who's looking after Donnakaye?"

"Had some paperwork to catch up on. Little Miss T-Rex is spending the day with Petti Jean and the kids."

Oren looked over at Clint, who was still sleeping soundly.

"He's going to be fine, Oren. Come on."

Ponce led Oren down the hall toward the elevators. As the two men passed the open door to Hazel Dursten's room, Oren noticed Mrs. Dursten sitting up in bed eating custard and watching Andy Griffith.

She noticed him too. "Why, Reverend Cullen!" she exclaimed.

Oren stepped inside. Ponce followed.

"I thought you did your visitation on Sunday afternoons."

"I usually do, Ms. Dursten," Oren answered politely. "My boy's in the hospital."

Hazel's face fell. "Oh, I'm so sorry to hear. I hope it's not real serious."

"He had an accident, but Dr. Humphries says he's going to be all right."

"That's good news. You wanna see my toy?"

Hazel searched through the clutter of items on the swing tray beside her bed, finally plucking up a small metal elephant. She held it out in the palm of her hand.

"It's all right to touch it, Reverend Cullen. It's been sanitized."

Oren picked up the walnut-sized elephant and examined it. All of the paint had been dissolved away. Except for its long trunk the elephant had absolutely no identifiable features.

Oren passed the miniature elephant to Ponce who gave it a brief inspection, then placed it back on the tray. "And you say it had been in your stomach for how long?"

"Since I was three, Dr. Humphries. Lordee, that's fifty-seven years."

"Dr. Coffin tells me it was a fairly simple operation," Ponce said. "He probably could have gotten it out for you years ago."

"But see, years ago I didn't have the money. And my insurance man wouldn't pay because he said that elephant wasn't doin' any harm down there. He said it would have to be elective surgery which my policy doesn't cover."

Ponce shook his head. "I'm not so sure he was right about that, Ms. Dursten."

"Well, that's what he said. Anyway, this is the first year Farley hasn't had to use his big spring sales bonus check to catch up on his child support. So guess what he did? He gave all that money to me. Just walked in and plopped that check right down on the breakfast table. 'Here's three thousand dollars to do with whatever you want, Mama,' he said. 'Buy yourself a mink coat, go to Paris.' I told that boy, 'Now you know I can't take a plane trip with this thing in my tract settin' off all those airport metal detectors. I'll just spend that money to have it removed, that's what I'll do!' Which is exactly what I did, and I cannot begin to tell you what it's done for my spirits." Hazel spooned up the last puddle of custard from her dessert bowl.

Oren felt like he'd visited with Hazel long enough, especially since she wasn't even a member of his congregation. He wished he knew an easy, polite way to take his leave.

"Well, glad to see that Dr. Coffin is taking good care of you, Ms.

Dursten," Ponce said, coming to Oren's rescue. He patted Hazel on the leg, then stepped away from the bed.

"But wouldn't you like to stay and watch the rest of this Andy Griffith program with me, Reverend Cullen? My son and his new girlfriend won't be by for another thirty minutes or so." Hazel had a very hopeful look on her face. She reminded Oren of the way Desiree had looked when she extended her invitation for him to come back for a full-body massage.

"You better rest now, Ms. Dursten," Ponce said. "You shouldn't be too tired for when your son gets here."

"Oh, Farley doesn't tire me out except when I have to watch him luggin' around that big tuba. And I cannot tell you how much I hate the sound of the thing. It's like some big ol' ape or something sittin' in the room with you, just burpin' himself silly. They wouldn't let him bring that noisy thing into the hospital, would they, Dr. Humphries?"

"I wouldn't think so," Ponce answered.

"Of course that new girlfriend of his, that Tammy Van Winkle, she's a real chatterbox. She could wear me out in a minute."

"Good-bye, Ms. Dursten," Oren said. "You should come visit our church some time."

"You know, I've been thinkin' about it. Choctaw Hill Southern Baptist just hasn't been the same since that young man started playin' the guitar during the Sunday night worship service. It puts me in mind of one of those hippie Jesus cults."

Oren and Ponce were out the door before Hazel could get revved up on this topic. Ponce led Oren past the nurses' station. One of the younger nurse's hands was sandwiched between two frozen gel bags. She was moaning and squirming as a male orderly stood by, his thumb poised over the start-and-stop button of a stopwatch.

Ponce gave the two a look of mild disapproval; they immediately suspended their game and returned to their stations.

One of the doors opened just as Oren and Ponce reached the elevator bank. A beautiful blond-haired young woman with puckery red lips stepped out. She was carrying a large basket of fruit and humming a Wynonna song. She smiled and nodded at the two men, then proceeded down the corridor, her hips straining against her tight black leather skirt.

Oren and Ponce watched her move down the hall. Ponce held his finger on the "door open" button on the elevator panel until she disappeared into one of the rooms.

11

His countenance is as Lebanon,
excellent as the cedars:
his mouth is most sweet: yea, he is altogether lovely.
Song of Solomon 5:15-16

"Forget that stupid hospital show. Why don't we watch this scary movie with wolves?" Marci Luck set down the television remote. With her newly freed hand she stabilized the bowl of onion dip she'd procured for herself, then used her other hand to scour the bottom with her whole-wheat party cracker.

"No more TV, Marci," Stewie replied. "I've got the table all set up for the game. And besides, there's only one person we're still waitin' on. Now go wake up Euless."

Euless Ludlam had showed up on time for his night shift at Mr. Joseph's automotive repair shop but was promptly sent home, Saul expressing concern that in his present sleep-deprived state Euless might have an accident and lose a bodily appendage. "I don't know why I agreed to let you come to work on a holiday evening, anyway. For Heaven's sake, go back home and get some rest. You look like a zombie man and you're scarin' my dog."

So Euless went home and fell asleep at his kitchen table, his head pillowed on an overturned roll of paper towels right next to a bowl of Campbell's bean with bacon from which he'd taken only a couple of bites. After a nap of about twenty minutes he was awakened by the telephone. It was Stewie: "You're home. Great. Come on over and play Tripoley. I know you love the game."

"I'm pretty sleepy, Stewie."

"The party'll wake you up. It's a really rowdy bunch. Marci's here, and you know Tie. And Ray Reese, and he's brought this new friend of his, Tanyette."

Euless made it safely to the party but was asleep within minutes of his arrival. Marci walked over to where he sat slumped on Stewie's sofa, his head tilted so far down that his slightly cleft chin rested wholly against the crew collar of his Ole Miss T-shirt. Marci placed a hand on his

43

shoulder. He lifted his head and struggled to open his eyes.

"Oh, let him go upstairs and lay down for a while," Marci said to Stewie. "He looks like he hasn't slept for weeks."

"You're right about that," Euless said, fighting the urge to drop right back off again.

"We need you for Tripoley, Euless," said Stewie. "Why don't you get up and move around a little bit?" Stewie was in the kitchen alcove making queso with Velveeta. It was a recipe he'd jotted down from a popular daytime talk show where the celebrity guests discussed their latest television and film projects, then put on aprons and cooked things.

"Just look at him," Marci said to Stewie. "I told you we shouldn't have dragged him over here."

Tie Gibbons came out of the bathroom, then remembering that he hadn't flushed, went back in, and shut the door.

Ray Reesé was sprawled out on the floor in front of the television next to his date for the evening, Tanyette Spencer. Tanyette had had one too many Sea Breezes at the Sunset Tavern earlier in the evening and was now watching all the furniture in the room go rubbery and shimmy about.

Ray said, "I could wait a little longer on the card game, Stewie. Looks like this movie's getting to the good part." A woman on the screen with flaming red eyes and sharp fangs was just clamping into the unprotected neck of an elderly cemetery caretaker.

"I invited you all over here to play Tripoley," Stewie said. "I thought everybody liked it."

"It's a fun game, Stewie," Marci replied, "but it gets kinda boring after a while. I mean, either you have the pay cards or you don't."

"There's more to it than that," Stewie responded, a little hurt by Marci's ready dismissal of his favorite card game. The queso now seemed just about the right consistency. He turned down the burner.

"You makin' pizza fondue?" Tie inquired, emerging once again from the bathroom. "I love pizza fondue."

"It's Mexican cheese dip," said Marci Luck, "and psst! your fly's open."

Tie zipped up on his way into the kitchen. Marci noticed that Tie walked a little bowlegged. Either he had a strong interest in horseback riding, Marci thought, or he hadn't gotten enough calcium as a child.

Marci used to be the dietician at Higby Elementary School, and sincerely believed that most of the world's problems were the result of insufficient vitamin and mineral intake.

"Who'd you say we were waitin' on?" Tie asked Stewie.

"Carmen Valentine. From church."

"Yeah. I think I can picture her. She's got straight black hair, kinda hangs in bangs?"

Stewie nodded. "She's been wantin' to meet you. Here, stir this."

"She's nice?"

"Yeah. A little shy, though. Doesn't look you right in the eye too often."

Marci crouched down next to Tanyette Spencer.

"Tanyette, you okay?"

"Oh sure. Ray's takin' very good care of me." Tanyette gave Ray a slobbery kiss that landed partly on his jaw and partly on his neck. It went almost unnoticed by Ray, who was caught up in the fanged woman's pursuit by snarling rottweilers.

"Who's the most handsome man here tonight?" Marci asked Tanyette in a half-whisper. "Give me your honest opinion."

"Ray. Ray Reed."

"Reese," Ray corrected his date for the evening. "My last name is Reese." He didn't take his eyes off the TV screen.

"You go in that bathroom with me and be honest," Marci said.

Tanyette frowned. "I can't do that. The minute I get up, I'll fall right down and make a big drunk fool out of myself."

Marci looked at Ray's bulbous chin, and then at his close-set eyes, and then she glanced over at Tie Gibbons, standing with Stewie in the kitchen nook. Bow legs or no bow legs, Tie Gibbons had to be the most handsome man ever to move to Higby. He looks like some kind of Greek statue, she thought. A Greek statue in jeans.

"I'd do anything to get Tie to ask me out," she found herself saying to Tanyette.

"Would you call off your wedding to Stewie?" Ray asked. Ray was arching an eyebrow and staring right at Marci even as the rottweilers on the TV screen were tearing the wolf woman to shreds.

12

My soul is full of troubles.
Psalm 88:3

"And before you know it, everybody in the movie goes and turns into werewolves, except it's not as scary as you would think because the children all look like furry puppies." The waitress, having completed her movie review, turned from a table of hamburger-chomping teens, to the two men in the booth directly behind her.

"Just the coffee, fellas? You don't want a slice of pie or crispy pecan roll?"

"Just the coffee for me, Janice," Ponce said. "Oren?"

Oren was looking out the window. He was watching a hefty man in a checkered blazer pull a big brass tuba out of the back of an old Country Squire station wagon.

"You sure you don't want something to eat, Oren?" Ponce asked.

Oren shook his head. "I'm not that hungry."

The waitress named Janice made a few scratches on her order pad and returned to the counter.

"You feel like talking a little bit?" Ponce asked. Oren shrugged, and picked at the small eczema patch under the lobe of his phone ear.

Ponce started flipping a sugar packet over and over in his hand. "Clint's a good kid, Oren."

Oren nodded. He folded his hands in front of him.

"I don't think he means to worry you the way he does."

"I know he doesn't."

"Have you thought about taking him to see somebody?"

Oren slid forward on his booth cushion. "What do you mean?"

"I have a friend in Memphis who's really good with kids."

Oren was almost too afraid to ask: "A psychiatrist?"

Ponce smiled and shook his head. "Sort of a family counselor. That's all."

"I don't know—" Oren didn't feel much like talking about this right now. He knew that Ponce was only trying to help, but somehow the conversation only served to remind him that as a father, he wasn't doing the

47

greatest job in the world by Clint.

Janice returned with the coffee. "Now y'all just give me a holler when you're ready for refills," she said.

As Janice moved on to tend to a group of four young women dressed in pink bowling outfits, Oren said sharply, "I'm a counselor of sorts myself, Ponce. I ought to be able to counsel my own son." Oren was surprised at the angry tone to his voice. He hadn't meant for it to come out like this.

After a moment Ponce said, "I'm a doctor of medicine, Oren, but that doesn't mean I'd have an easy time taking out Donnakaye's appendix."

Oren's gaze had become fixed once more on the parking lot outside the window. The moon was creeping up over a trio of crepe myrtles at one end of the lot. "I know I don't talk to Clint enough. You're right. Sometimes I just don't know what to say. Ever since Alice died, it's been hard for me to look at him and not think of her."

"The last time he climbed that water tower, did you ask him, Oren? Did you ask him why he went up there?"

Oren shook his head. He blew on his coffee. Then he said, "I thought he was just being adventurous. You know the mischief that boys get into."

"I think he goes up there for some reason that has nothing to do with adventure, Oren."

Ponce was the first to notice Johnny and Sheila Billows approaching the booth. He smiled and nodded at the couple. Years ago Sheila had been one of his very first patients; he had treated her for a damaged cochlea. She had been sunbathing on the beach at Chickasaw Lake when a teenaged girlfriend came up behind her and inexplicably slapped her ears. Sheila couldn't hear anything for several days except for sounds of very low frequency such as the humming of heavy industrial machinery and Johnny Cash.

Sheila was the first to speak: "Hello, Dr. Humphries. Hello, Reverend Cullen. Johnny and I came by to see how Clint's doin'."

"He's doing very well," Ponce said. "He was a very lucky kid to have that pool to fall into."

"Do you think it would be all right if we went up to see him?" This question was directed at Oren.

Ponce didn't give Oren a chance to answer: "I think he'll probably be sleeping for the rest of the night, Ms. Billows. Why don't you come by tomorrow?"

"All right."

Johnny sighed and shook his head. Very solemnly he said, "I hate to think about what would've happened if we'd put that pool where we had it last year."

"I think the Lord spared him for a reason," Sheila said. "Now you know I'm not a very religious woman, Reverend, but I do truly believe that."

Oren didn't know how to respond, so he just nodded and took a sip from his cup. The coffee was still very hot and scalded his tongue.

Sheila and Johnny said good night and squeezed past the group of female bowlers whose number had now grown to six.

"I'm going to stay over tonight," Oren said. "Who should I call to get a cot brought up to Clint's room?"

"I'll take care of it for you."

"Thanks."

"Will you at least think about the suggestion I made?"

"All right."

"It has nothing to do with your abilities as father or minister, Oren. You suffered a great loss when Alice died—both of you. It takes a long time to make the necessary adjustments after that kind of loss. You remember what they told us in Dads Without Moms."

"It's been two years. You'd think that after two years—"

"Sometimes it takes *ten* years, Oren. Sometimes you *never* get over it—completely. It's always there. Always that feeling that something's just not right. But at some point you have to accept it and move on. Because you can't spend the rest of your life with that cloud casting a dark shadow over everything you do."

Oren wanted to say something, desperately wanted to give voice to something that had been troubling him for months. Ponce could sense that Oren needed to talk, but could find no way to let his best friend know that it would be all right.

In the kitchen somebody dropped a plate. It didn't break but spun around in a tight circle, making a loud, hollow, whirly sound until it finally came to rest. One of the lady bowlers delivered a punch line to a joke that drew screams of laughter from her friends. When the laughter had subsided, Oren cleared his throat and in a quiet, steady voice said, "I don't think God hears my prayers anymore, Ponce. I don't think He's listening to me at all."

Then Oren began to cry.

***

On the drive back to their home on Deacon Lane, Sheila Billows told her husband Johnny that she was very worried about Clint Cullen. "He's gonna be fine," Johnny said, casually steering the car with one finger the way he always did when he was feeling relaxed or relieved.

"I'm not talkin' about the fall," Sheila replied. "I'm referrin' to his state of mind. Clint is a very troubled young man."

"Well, I guess he is, but there's not too much you can do about it." Johnny had two fingers on the wheel now.

"What if I ask Reverend Cullen if it'd be all right for Clint to go down to Gulf Shores with us over the Thanksgiving weekend? I'll bet you the salt air and the soothing sound of the surf would be a good salve for his spirits." Sheila didn't say it but she was also thinking that it wouldn't hurt for Clint to spend a little time in the company of a woman like herself, somewhat close to Alice Cullen's age. After all, there'd been hardly any female presence in the boy's life for the last two years, and this just couldn't be a good thing.

Johnny said he wouldn't mind if Clint came with them so long as he didn't throw himself off a pier or something, but he didn't see how Oren Cullen would allow his son to go off for several days in the company of near-strangers.

"Then we'll just have to get to know the Reverend a little better. He really seems to be a nice man, although I know you complain a lot about how he keeps his yard."

Johnny was about to say something about how you can read a person by the look of his lawn, when he noticed a little dog sitting next to an overturned trash can nibbling at something white which was spilling out of a plastic garbage bag. He slammed on the brakes. Sheila pitched forward into her loosened seat belt strap and groaned.

"It's Muffin!" he cried. "Right there, eating refuse."

"That isn't refuse. Here, Muffin! Come over to the car, honey."

Muffin looked up from her meal and began to wag her tail. She was wearing a little white goatee made of hominy.

Johnny opened the car door and crouched down for Muffin to come to him. Instead, she ran off down the street.

"I hate that dog," he muttered. Sheila didn't hear him. She was too busy inspecting her chest for safety belt burns.

13

I opened my doors to the traveler.
Job 31, v.32

Carmen Valentine unfastened her shoulder belt, which had worked itself into a coiled pinching device that she could very well do without. Carmen needed no uncomfortable distractions at the moment. She was having difficulty finding Stewie Kipp's apartment. She knew where the complex was; she'd passed its front entrance on Market Street hundreds of times. But locating the apartment itself seemed to demand a major amount of detective work because none of the identical red-bricked, mansard-roofed apartment buildings had numbers on them. The addresses were stenciled on the mailboxes, but the numbers had faded to the point that many were nearly illegible. "Well, isn't this a bother," Carmen said to herself as she puttered through the complex in her dusk blue Skylark, studying each building for some sign that a Stewie Kipp might reside within. "I wish Arnetta weren't off skiing somewhere. I'll bet she has special angelic radar that could come in quite handy right now."

Carmen also would have liked having Stewie's phone number. It was presently unlisted due to a phone company error, and Stewie had neglected to give it to her when he'd dictated his very nearly useless address.

The door swung open. A man who looked to be in his early thirties and who was dressed in swimming trunks and a white tank top appeared.

Carmen had thought through what she was going to say but it still came out hurried and confused: "Hello. I'm tryin' to find—there's a guy named Stewie Kipp who—do you know him?"

"Stoogie what?"

"Stewie. Like Stewart. Kipp like ... Kipp."

"What does he look like?"

"He's about your height. Blond hair."

"A lot of guys livin' in this complex look like that."

"He drives a red Chevy pickup."

"A lot of guys livin' in this complex drive red Chevy pickups."

53

Carmen was about to thank the man in the white tank top for his time and move on to another apartment with perhaps a more helpful occupant, when a young woman suddenly appeared next to the man. She was wearing a child's space helmet. It was a very tight fit for her large head. She was holding something in her left hand—an onion it looked like to Carmen—and in the other hand, a small kitchen knife.

The woman raised the visor of the helmet and addressed her visitor: "Are you sellin' beauty products? I hate to admit it but I'm pure near out of everything."

"She ain't a saleslady," the man snapped. "She's lookin' for somebody. What'd you say his name was again?"

"Stewie. Stewie Kipp."

"I know him," the woman said matter-of-factly.

"Really?" Carmen was so happy to hear this that she made brief inadvertent eye contact with the woman.

"Yeah. He lives in that building over by —" Carmen couldn't make out the rest of what the woman had to say; the visor had suddenly slipped back down over her face.

"This guy's a secret friend of yours?" the man asked the woman while helping her pull the helmet off her head.

"No. I just say hello to him at the mailbox now and then. He's a Christian man, Drew. And he's engaged. And he helped me change a flat one night when you was workin' late at the hardware store."

Carmen didn't want to seem rude but she was already forty-five minutes late for her very first Tripoley party. "But where does he live? That's all I need to—" She stopped herself before her voice began to sound too fretful.

The woman pointed across the street and up a small hill. "The building over yonder to the right of the pool. See that hedge? It'd be the door on the end."

"Thank you. I really appreciate this." Carmen turned and started down the walk to her car. Along the way she tripped over a break in the concrete where part of the walkway had settled and part hadn't. Losing her balance, she fell forward, landing halfway on the lawn and halfway on the broken concrete walk, her left hand skidding along the rough texture of the hard surface, her arm buckling under the weight of her body, and without its support, permitting her face to come in abrasive contact with the punishing concrete. Within seconds the whole left side of her face came to feel as if it had been slapped repeatedly by an angry hand.

Maybe they didn't see it, she thought to herself. Maybe they'd already closed the door before —

"You poor thing!" Carmen now heard the woman cry. "You poor accident-prone girl!"

***

"... all fall down." Irmene Ringfinger turned the teeny handle on the miniature Victrola that lived on a knick knack shelf below Conwell Pomeroy's telephone table. Here in Conwell's large, dual-turreted, Victorian gingerbread house just off the square, Irmene, phone receiver pressed to ear, listened to the tiny music box's one-note rendition of "Ring Around the Rosey; Pocketful of Posies" while waiting for Euless Ludlam to pick up his phone. She caught herself singing along but only by rote and without any feeling.

It wasn't a night for singing.

"Hello? Euless Ludlam's residence."

The voice was female, definitely not Euless's.

"Hello, who is this?"

"Euless's mother. Who is *this?*"

"Irmene Ringfinger. I'm Mr. Pomeroy's nurse—*was* Mr. Pomeroy's— is Euless there?"

"No. He's out. Were you singing 'Ring Around the Rosey?'"

"I could have been. It's been a very long day. I was attacked by yellow jackets for no good reason."

Flora yawned. "They'll sting you as soon as look at you."

"Do you know when Euless might return?"

"No. In fact, I don't even know where he is. I just got here about thirty minutes ago. I brought over a bacon and swiss cheese pie which is one of his favorites, but he isn't here to enjoy it. The good thing about a bacon and swiss cheese pie, though, is that it refrigerates quite well without substantial flavor loss."

"Mrs. Ludlam, I called to tell Euless that Mr. Pomeroy passed away a little while ago. I thought he'd want to know."

"Yes. I'm sure he would. That is so sad."

"Mr. Cochran is taking care of everything. He says he'll have a check for Euless in a day or so."

"I'll tell him. Do they know when the funeral will be?"

"They haven't set the date yet. Maybe Thursday."

"Well, I suppose the doctors did everything they could."

"He hung on a bit longer than was expected."

Flora Ludlam thought she detected a slight catch to Irmene's voice. "Are you all right, dear?"

"Yes. I'll be fine."

"Are you still there at Mr. Pomeroy's house?"

"Yes."

"Well, you go right on home, dear, and turn on some real funny show on the television, and you try to get your mind off the demise for a while, you hear?"

"All right. Good-bye, Mrs. Ludlam."

"Good-bye, Ms. Ringfinger."

After Flora hung up she settled back into Euless's old patched-up black Naugahyde recliner. Fighting the urge to drift back off to sleep, she recalled the time Conwell Pomeroy, in his capacity as precinct judge, had helped her open the curtain to the voting booth when the switch came off in her hand. Flora was never quite sure if her vote had counted that year, but she didn't want to make an issue of it at the time. Conwell Pomeroy had been most helpful and courteous, especially given his net worth of about twenty-four million dollars.

"Where are you, Euless?" she wondered aloud, sleep slowly enveloping her. "I have pie."

14

It is better to dwell in the wilderness,
than with a contentious and an angry woman.
Proverbs 21:19

"Well, it looks like Carmen's not comin'," Stewie proclaimed in a raised voice to compensate for Euless's amplified snoring.

"Qué será, será," Tie replied, pouring himself another tumbler of cola drink. "I guess I'll just see her in church." Tie took a big drink of cola and wiped his mouth with the back of his hand. Marci watched him out of the corner of her eye from her seat at the kitchen bar counter. Marci would usually seize every opportunity she could to look at Tie, but was careful not to be too obvious about it.

"You know, it's gettin' kinda late, Stew," Tie added. "Maybe we oughta forget about playin' Tripoley tonight."

"I second the motion," Marci said. "Look, half your guests are fast asleep."

Stewie didn't have to look; Ray's protracted breathy exhalations created an obvious counterpoint to Euless's snorts and snuffles. Tanyette had drifted off even earlier, long before the end of the wolf movie, and was now wrapped around Ray, mumbling nonsense words and gurgling a little like a baby.

"Maybe we oughta give it another shot next weekend," Tie said to Stewie. "I like gettin' to meet all your friends."

"Well, I don't know if I'm invitin' those two over there," Stewie said, indicating with a nod Ray and Tanyette whose arms and legs were provocatively intertwined.

"I like Tanyette. She's real funny," Marci said, reaching for the nacho bowl.

"She's really drunk, Marci," said Stewie.

"She's not hurtin' anybody and she really spiced things up, I mean before she fell asleep. Your parties sometimes need a little cinnamon and spice, Stewie."

Stewie turned away from Marci and Tie, and started hunting through his kitchen hardware drawer for a screwdriver.

"What are you doin'?" Marci asked.

"I noticed there's a loose screw on this can opener."

"Well, if you're gonna start fixin' things around here then I'll just go swimmin'. Would you like to go swimmin' with me, Tie?"

"Sure. You wanna come swimmin' with us, Stewie?"

"No. I think I better help all these sleepy folks get home. I'm sorry the party went bust, Tie."

"It's not your fault everybody got tuckered out."

Tie went upstairs to change. Marci glared at Stewie for a few seconds. Then she said, "You know, Stewie, ever since you accepted Christ as your personal savior you just haven't been any fun at all."

"Why? Because I don't drink like a fish anymore?"

"You don't do *anything* anymore. And worse than that, you've become very judgmental about other people. You never used to be that way."

Stewie used the screwdriver in his hand to point with. "You think I'm bein' judgmental, not wantin' that drunken girl nobody even knows to come into my home and drape herself all over Ray like she's gonna die if she can't do the nasty with him right there on *my* rug?"

"She wasn't doin' any harm, Stewie, and you know it. And what in the world possessed you to invite Carmen Valentine over here? You hardly even know her. Don't answer that question. I just figured it out. It's because you think she's the only girl who's *Christian* enough for Tie. Well, you wanna know somethin' funny, Stewie? I don't think Tie's all that Christian himself. I think he only pretends to be because he thinks that's gonna help move him up at the lumber yard."

Stewie put the screwdriver away and sat down at his kitchen table. In a solemn, cheerless voice he said, "I don't know why you're comin' out with all these opinions right now."

"Maybe because lately you've got me thinkin' really hard about whether we oughta be gettin' married. Maybe because ever since last fall when you went and got born again I don't think I know you anymore."

Stewie had no idea what he should say in response to such a candid, troubling admission. He was spared by the return of Tie, who just that moment could be heard coming down the steps using a very heavy tread. The loud foot thumps woke Tanyette, who sprang up into a seated position from where she lay, thrust her palm into the air, and sang out, "Stop!

In the name of love, before you break my heart!"

Euless's eyes flicked open and he let out a tiny moan. He had been dreaming that he was the owner of a classic car museum, and at that moment was comfortably stretched out on the back seat of a '39 Packard, being hand-fed grapes by a beautiful blonde in a tight-fitting dress. The woman who now sat directly within his sleep-fuzzed line of vision wasn't a blonde nor was she wearing a tight-fitting dress; her hair was, in fact, brown with oddly placed frosted highlights, and she was wearing a pantsuit from another era. She was also doing a very bad impression of Diana Ross.

"Think it o—ver!"

15

Ointment and perfume rejoice the heart.
Proverbs 27: 9

The woman with the space helmet and onion half whose name was Alaura Trumble dabbed ointment as gingerly as she could onto Carmen's reddened cheek. "Do you like the Supremes? If you don't, I can put on somethin' else."

"No. The Supremes are fine." Carmen winced and bit her lip.

"It ain't supposed to sting," Alaura said apologetically.

"I have a very low tolerance for pain," Carmen said. "Sometimes when it rains I feel like somebody's pokin' me over and over again with a ballpoint pen."

"Then I suppose you're experiencin' some genuine discomfort right now," said Alaura. She closed the cap on the ointment tube. "I'm afraid that's gonna scab up, sugar. You ain't gonna be all that pretty to look at for a few days."

"That's okay. I was never all that pretty to look at to begin with." The stinging on Carmen's face made it hard for her to even think. She waved her hand back and forth next to her cheek like a fan, but this didn't seem to help much.

"Of course you're pretty. Don't you agree, Drew?" Drew was now in another room watching TBS. Alaura called out, "DREW?"

"WHAT?"

"DON'T YOU THINK CARMEN'S PRETTY?"

"WHO THE HELL IS CARMEN?"

"OUR GUEST HERE. STEWIE KIPP'S FRIEND."

The voice from the other room sounded a little annoyed. "YEAH. PRETTY AS A PICTURE. I'M WATCHIN' THE BRAVES GAME NOW."

"Are you a doctor?" Carmen asked her hostess.

"No. But I'm plannin' on bein' a nurse. Is it really noticeable, my love of healin'?"

Carmen nodded.

"It's my callin', actually. It's all I ever wanted to be."

"I think you're gonna make a good nurse," said Carmen. Alaura had taken over fanning duties for the time being. She was gently parting the warm air next to Carmen's face with a copy of *Fisherman's Paradise Magazine*, which she'd picked up from the coffee table nearby.

"Oh, I'll be a good nurse, all right. That is, if I ever survive nursin' school."

"Is it really hard?"

"Yeah, but that's no problem. I'm very disciplined in that area." One of the Braves players hit a home run, and the crowd began cheering wildly. Alaura went to close the door to the TV room. When she returned, Carmen was standing at the window looking up the hill to the fourplex where Stewie Kipp lived.

"I guess I won't be meetin' Tie Gibbons tonight," she said wistfully.

"Who's Tie Gibbons?" Alaura asked, joining Carmen at the window. The moon, now perched high in the evening sky, was bathing all the parked Chevy pickups in a soft, cool light.

"He's a friend of Stewie's. Stewie was gonna formally introduce us tonight."

"Is the guy cute?"

Carmen nodded. Her face still smarted and she felt as if she ought to be getting home, but it was kind of nice talking to a real person like Alaura. Not that she didn't enjoy conversations with her guardian angel. It was just that Arnetta didn't usually have much to say about herself. Carmen would ask her questions: What's it like up there where you live? Do you have any favorite movie stars? And Arnetta would usually reply, "You know I'm not allowed to answer questions of a personal nature, child. I'm only here to see that no harm comes to you, and to make sure that you get the best value for your shopping dollar." Sometimes whole days would go by with Carmen saying little more than "hello" or "good morning" to another human being, and receiving little more than a "hello" or "good morning" in return. But here Carmen was, gabbing away with Alaura, like two old friends, Alaura taking a sincere, personal interest in her health and love life. Despite the stinging on her face, Carmen was beginning to feel quite comfortable and easy with this onion-scented woman.

"I'm sorry things didn't work out," Alaura said. "Maybe Stewie can set up another time for you to meet this Tie guy."

"That's okay. I really don't want him to see me like this any time soon anyway."

"Oh, pooh," Alaura said. "My first date with Drew he'd gotten himself into a brawl the night before. His face was all blue and green, and he had this tiny little railroad track of stitches right above his left eye. I was actually kinda turned on by it. I find hot-tempered men with wounds very sexy."

"Hot-tempered men are different from girls who fall on their faces, Laura."

"*Ah*-Laura. You know: Laura but with an 'a' out front."

"Oh. I didn't hear the 'a'."

"That's all right. I probably just slurred right over it. I do that. Drew says I sound like a drunken sailor sometimes."

Alaura now led Carmen away from the window and over to the sofa, which had images of pheasants and game ducks quilted into its cushions. Alaura sat down on one of the arms, her chunky pink legs spreading out slab-like over the chocolate brown upholstery fabric. Carmen couldn't help noticing a bright red "X" stenciled onto Alaura's left thigh.

"What's that for?" Carmen asked.

"Oh, *this*." Alaura circled the "X" with her right pinkie. "This is what just might keep me from graduatin' from nursin' school."

"What do you mean?"

"We got this important practical tomorrow—that's like a test where you have to *do* somethin'. What we gotta do is give ourselves injections. Right into our very own legs. I've always had this major fear of shots. I don't like to get 'em, and I get all nervous thinkin' about havin' to give 'em. And guess what? Tomorrow mornin' at nine o'clock I gotta do both." There was genuine fear in Alaura's soft, charcoal gray eyes. It had been a long time since Carmen had seen someone who looked so scared.

"I know exactly what you mean."

"You're afraid of shots too?"

Carmen nodded. "And lucky me, because of my allergies I have to get a lot of them." Carmen was staring at the "X" on Alaura's leg and starting to feel a little light-headed. She tried to focus on one of the poorly stitched pheasants. She took a couple of deep, calming breaths.

"Oh Carmen, I wish I could find the courage somehow, but ever since Dr. Etter made that announcement in class I've been in a major panic.

Drew don't understand. He says I'm just bein' silly. I say, 'Drew, ain't there nothin' *you're* afraid of?' and he goes, 'You know I'm fearless, babe. That's why you married me.' I, of course, don't bring up the fact that he won't go anywhere near an escalator on account of this story he once heard about a woman in Florida who got pulled down inside one of them things and got all chewed up by the gears. One time when we was shoppin' at Penney's up in Memphis, I found him sittin' off by himself among fancy men's dress socks just shiverin' and shakin'. I knew exactly what he was thinkin' about but I didn't let on. I just wish he'd pay me the same courtesy."

Carmen wanted to help Alaura. She wondered what she could do. Whatever she came up with would have to have some element of sacrifice to it. This would assure Alaura that even though their friendship was young, it was being constructed on solid ground. Finally Carmen said, "Give *me* the shot."

Alaura flashed Carmen a look of surprise.

"Because if you're able to give it to me, that would mean at least you'd be over your fear of *givin'* shots, right? And how often does a nurse have to give *herself* a shot, anyway? I mean, unless you're a diabetic or drug addict or somethin'."

Alaura shook her head in happy astonishment over Carmen's offer. "You'd really do this for me?"

"I think you'd make a good nurse, and I'd hate for you to lose the chance on account of this."

Without warning Alaura flung her arms around Carmen and gave her a big hug. Then she dashed out of the room to get her medical supply bag. Carmen felt good about what she had volunteered to do. She felt very warm and very good. Then within seconds all the blood seemed to leave her head, and she had to lie flat on the floor with both her legs up in the air to keep from passing right out.

16

As a jewel of gold in a swine's snout,
so is a fair woman which is without discretion.
Proverbs 11: 12

Not five hundred yards away Marci Luck caught a glimpse of Stewie's truck as it pulled out of the parking lot. From her vantage point on the apartment complex swimming pool diving board she could just barely make out the dark figures of Ray and Tanyette nestled against one another on the passenger side of the cab.

Unbeknownst to Marci and Tie, who could have been of some assistance, Stewie had had a little trouble getting Ray and Tanyette out to the truck. For a moment Stewie had thought he'd have to pick Tanyette up and carry her slung over his shoulder mountain-man style. When he finally did succeed in coaxing her legs to move by themselves she kept stopping along the way to inquire in a sleepy yet cheerful childlike voice, "We gonna see Grammy? We gonna go Grammy's house and get M and M's?"

Euless, who'd fallen into a deep sleep, couldn't be roused, and Stewie had thought it best to let him spend the night on the sofa.

"I'll be back in a while," Stewie had informed Tie and Marci. "I gotta stop at the all-night Handy Mandy and buy some bacon and eggs for breakfast."

"Take your time," Marci had shouted from the deck chair where she'd plopped herself down to remove her sandals. Tie was already in the water and was pretending to be a European fountain sculpture. He waved goodbye to Stewie while squirting a thin stream of water out his mouth and straight into the air.

Moments after the truck disappeared from view Marci executed an abbreviated, yet precise swan dive into the deep end of the pool.

"Where'd you learn to dive like that?" Tie asked.

"Took a few lessons," Marci replied as she swam over to Tie with her head completely out of the water like a movie star without her bathing cap.

"I can't do much more than a cannonball," said Tie, his arms sweeping slowly back and forth across the surface of the water.

"You should've been a professional swimmer," Marci said, looking Tie over unabashedly. "I'll bet with those shoulders and arms you could've wowed everybody with your butterfly."

"What's a butterfly?"

"It's a stroke. A swimmin' stroke." Marci was standing right next to Tie now. She threw her head backwards into the water to get her long chestnut brown hair out of her face.

"This is fun," Tie said. "I can't remember the last time I went swimmin' at night."

"I love swimmin' at night. In the cool moonlight. It's so hot in the daytime. And crowded. And there's always this thick film of suntan oil on the top of the water. It's really disgustin', especially if coconut has never been one of your favorite scents."

Tie swam a few strokes away from Marci, then swam right back. "How long have you and Stewie been goin' together?"

"About three years. After I got fired from my dietician job, I worked for a while at the lumber yard in the accounting office. That's where we met."

"Is it gonna be a big wedding?"

Marci realized she'd gotten a little water in her ear and tilted her head to one side to let it drain out. "We haven't decided yet."

"My parents gave my sister Cora Eileen a big wedding. They had a champagne fountain and about four different kinds of shrimp."

"Do you come from a wealthy family?"

"No. We're pretty much middle class. Why do you ask?"

"You have very nice, straight teeth."

"Thank you. I had to wear braces for two years."

Marci's face lit up. "Me too. Didn't you hate it?"

Tie smiled and nodded, then scooped up a beetle that was floating in front of him and tossed it from the pool.

Marci moved over to the side and hooked her arms around the concrete overhang. She began to kick her legs for exercise. Looking over at Tie's straight, very white teeth, she suddenly declared, "I should be truthful with you: I don't think Stewie and I are gonna get married."

"Really? How come?"

"It just isn't workin' out. Tell me somethin', Tie, and I hope you don't mind me askin' you a personal question —"

"Course not."

"Are you as religious as Stewie thinks you are?"

"What do you mean by 'religious'?"

Marci stopped kicking her legs and allowed the water to get very still and unripply. "I mean, is your faith the most important thing in your life? Even more important than, say, the needs of a fiancée?"

"But I don't have a fiancée."

"But if you did, who would be the most important person in your life—Jesus, or her?"

"Well, it would depend on how pretty she is."

Marci waited a few seconds to lend an element of drama to her next question: "Do you think *I'm* pretty?"

Tie let himself sink slowly beneath the surface of the water, a big grin bowing his lips. Marci waited for him to re-emerge. She wore a curious smile on her face.

After a few seconds Tie popped back up several feet away in the vicinity of the diving board. Marci was about to swim over to him when she noticed a figure—it seemed to be a man—moving through the shadows between the pool and the tennis court. This wasn't such an odd picture in and of itself—it was a warm night and there were quite a few late-evening strollers about—but there seemed to be something not quite right about the man's gait; it was halting, uneven, as if he were disoriented or lost. And something else made it hard for Marci to turn away: the stranger was carrying something with him—something big, something that looked—well—looked very much like a bassoon.

17

Therefore I will not refrain my mouth;
I will speak in the anguish of my spirit.
Job 7: 11

"Oh please pick up. Please, please." Tula considered praying but hated to trouble the Lord with something that wasn't a clear-cut life and death matter.

Click. "Hello?" It was Flora's voice on the other end. She sounded sleepy.

"Flora, this is Tula."

"How'd you know I'd be over here at Euless's house?"

"You weren't at home, so I called Mr. Haas. He said you asked him to drive you over."

"I got to thinkin' about Euless, wonderin' how he's doin'. He isn't here, by the way. What's wrong?"

"I'm really worried about Hank. He never came home from the picnic. Nobody seems to know where he is."

Flora's legs had cramped all up on her as she slept curled in her son's recliner, and now it hurt to stretch them out. "This isn't the first time he's stayed out late, you know."

"I know."

"Like those nights when his band practice runs over or—doesn't his men's Bible study group sometimes go over to Donut Boy after their meeting?"

"Yes, but those times I usually know who he's with, and somebody always makes sure he gets home okay."

"Maybe he and Calvin Gray went to play pool or somethin'. Did you call Calvin's house?"

Tula said she had. There was no answer.

"Well, see, that's a possibility. Or you know what? Maybe he just decided to walk home from the park after the fireworks. That's a long walk, you know."

"Hank has a very poor sense of direction, Flora. He could be halfway to Dogwood by now. You know, I'm of a mind to call the police." Tula was

69

pacing back and forth in her kitchen. Years earlier when Hank still had sharp skills as a handyman, he'd replaced Tula's old kitchen telephone cord with one he'd patched together that was about five times the standard length. This allowed Tula to do all manner of household chores while speaking on the phone; once she even walked to the end of her driveway and picked up the afternoon mail while listening to every detail of her friend Frances Vaughn's pilgrimage to Eureka Springs, Arkansas, to see the Passion Play. Tonight Tula made use of the extra long cord by moving about her large kitchen and making periodic checks out each of the three windows to satisfy herself that if Hank were anywhere in the vicinity she'd be able to spot him in an instant.

"Well, you could call the police, I guess, but they're liable to suggest that you put him in a home for mental incompetents."

"They can make any suggestions they want to. I'm not sendin' my brother to any place like that." Tula was upset with herself now for having sought any assistance from Flora. This was just like her, Tula thought, playing devil's advocate in the midst of a crisis. "I think I'll go out and look for him, Flora. You go back to sleep."

"You know you can't be drivin' at night. You have a restricted license."

"I'm not gonna drive. I'm gonna walk."

"Oh Tula, dear, you're just gonna get *yourself* lost."

"I am not. I know this town like the back of my hand."

Flora released a long, exasperated sigh. "Can't you wait long enough for Euless to get home? I'll send *him* out to look for Hank."

"You don't even know when he's supposed to get back."

"I guess I don't."

Tula studied the dark shapes in her front yard. She thought she detected movement. "Wait a minute. I think there's somebody out there."

"It could be a prowler. Oh Lord, honey, hang up and dial nine-one-one."

"But it might be Hank."

"No, it's probably a prowler. Oh, I fear for you, dear."

"I don't think it's a prowler. But if it is, I'll just run over to Bowmar's house."

Flora couldn't believe her ears. "I just don't understand you at all, Tula. If some strange man is skulkin' around your yard in the middle of the night—a possible criminal, mind you—you'd go to an ex-convict for protection?"

"Bowmar is one of my very best friends. He's a fine young man who I am certain just fell in with the wrong crowd."

Flora pulled herself up from Euless's recliner, took a handkerchief from her purse, and began to wipe dust from a nearby reading lamp. Flora hated dust, and couldn't understand how her grown son could live with thick layers of it covering most of his furniture and household items. "Bowmar robbed a hobby shop, Tula. He's a convicted felon."

"He paid his debt to society. Besides which, he felt he had a good reason."

"There's no good reason for robbery."

Tula wasn't about to give in on this point. "There was a young sick boy in his hometown whose days were numbered. He only stole a few baseball cards for that sick boy."

Flora sighed again, this time longer and more vocal.

"I have to go and find Hank now," Tula said. The dark, shadowy figure in Tula's yard materialized into her other next-door neighbor, Fred Cowls, who was taking his Great Dane for a bathroom walk. Tula regretted having mentioned in casual conversation to Fred that manure made the best fertilizer for her vegetable garden; Fred seemed to have interpreted this statement as license to let Champ make as many deposits as he wanted to on her front lawn.

"What about the prowler?" Flora asked.

"It isn't a prowler, after all," Tula answered. "It's Mr. Cowls."

"Good. Now why don't you just stay put till Euless gets back?"

"Because Hank may be lost and I should find him and bring him back home. Now let me go on, so I can do what I have to do, Flora."

"Oh, I didn't even tell you, Tula: Mr. Pomeroy died tonight."

"Oh, that's a shame."

"I talked to his nurse. She was callin' to inform Euless."

"Did she say when the funeral will be?"

"Thursday, she thinks. She's not sure."

"He was a pillar of the community."

"Yes, he was."

There was a long silence and then Flora said, "I wish Euless would get home."

18

And he shall put off his garments,
and put on other garments.
Leviticus 6:11

Bowmar didn't feel like talking. All he really wanted to do was hold Nancy Leigh quietly in his arms, breathe in the sweet fragrant scent of her shampoo, and listen to Johnny Mathis crooning softly on his bedside clock-radio. But Nancy Leigh was worried and needed somebody to talk to.

"Talitha is too much of a good-time girl is her problem. She just seems to want to spend her whole life zippin' from one party to the next. Sometimes she stays out all night long. I don't see how she can even keep her eyes open some days."

"You used to be just like that yourself, Nancy Leigh, and you turned out fine. Oh, he's singing 'The Tennessee Waltz.' Let's be quiet and listen."

Nancy Leigh wriggled out of Bowmar's snuggle. "I'm really worried about my sister and all you wanna do is listen to some old white bread Patsy Cline song."

"It reminds me of my youth. I grew up in Memphis, you know."

"Okay, so we'll put on some Isaac Hayes a little later. Right now I have a real concern about my sister that you're just passin' off like it was nothin'."

Bowmar ran his hand once more along the silky contour of Nancy Leigh's back, then leaned over and kissed her neck.

"You're ticklin' me," she said through a half-smile.

Bowmar smiled back. "Quit thinkin' about Talitha and think about me."

"I told you: I'm worried about her," Nancy Leigh said, scooting off the bed.

Bowmar watched as Nancy Leigh put on the robe he had given her for her last birthday. He had planned on taking her to the Hungry Kitchen for their new barbecue pizza, and then surprise her with a gift certificate for an afternoon of indulgence at the Pamper Pretty Chinese

Spa, but the burgundy velour bathrobe seemed to have her name all over it. At least this is what her friend Janet Goslair who worked in the bed and bathwear department of Johnston's Department Store had said. So he ended up getting her the robe instead.

Bowmar rolled over onto his stomach and spoke almost into his pillow, "You know Talitha never listens to anything you say, Nancy Leigh."

"Then maybe *you* should be the one to talk to her." Nancy Leigh began to brush her hair, which had become mussed during love play.

"Baby, what makes you think she'd listen to *me?*"

"I think she looks up to you."

"Nobody looks up to me, Nancy Leigh. Much less your sister." Bowmar's romantic mood was pretty much gone now, so he got out of bed and started to get dressed.

"Oh don't wear that smelly old shirt," Nancy Leigh said. "You've worn it for a week."

Bowmar sniffed the shirt he was now holding in his hand. It was of the flannel plaid lumberjack variety. Bowmar counted it among his most favorite.

"Here. I'm gonna do a wash. Let me have it." Nancy Leigh yanked the shirt out of Bowmar's hand. "You don't know how silly you look wearin' this heavy winter shirt in the hottest part of the summer. No wonder it's so smelly. You must just sweat buckets in it."

Bowmar wondered to himself how Nancy Leigh, so soft and pretty and sexy and desirable just five minutes earlier, could become transformed so quickly into an unhappy woman in a coverall burgundy robe who now only seemed interested in talking about men's apparel and dirty laundry and everything that was wrong with her footloose younger sister.

"Talitha must think there's somethin' excitin' and dangerous about you because of the time you spent in prison," she said.

"Oh." Bowmar hadn't considered this before. "Well, I can't help what people think about me." Bowmar shrugged, then said, "Why don't you take off that robe and do me a funny booty dance?"

Pretending not to hear him, Nancy Leigh walked out of the bedroom. She was carrying the laundry basket under her arm, and looked to Bowmar like a European peasant woman in an old painting. Bowmar found another flannel shirt in the closet and quickly put it on.

19

The spirit of a man will sustain his infirmity;
but a wounded spirit who can bear?
Proverbs 18:14

It took a little coaxing but Ponce eventually succeeded in getting Oren to accompany him to the Hungry Kitchen restaurant about half a mile from the hospital. Ponce had hoped that a change of scenery and a tasty barbecue sandwich might take Oren's mind off his son for a while. Clint was actually doing quite well for someone who had just taken a fifty-five-foot tumble, and Ponce just didn't think the boy needed to be attended by a fretful father every single moment of his hospital stay.

But it soon became apparent to Ponce that Oren was going to fret no matter where he was. This fact became abundantly evident to Ponce during their visit to the restaurant. Upon arrival Oren took little notice of the Hungry Kitchen's down-home décor, which had been praised by *The Higby Star* as well as by Julienne Fry's weekly radio restaurant review program, "Champs in Chow." When the food was served, Oren ate only a few bites of his pork barbecue sandwich, and registered hardly any interest at all when several of the waiters and waitresses began singing "Happy Birthday" in loud and raucous voices to the woman in the booth behind him.

For a few minutes the men discussed Oren's most recent stint as director of Bible Methodist Church Camp. Then Ponce steered the conversation around to the Cardinals and whether they had any chance of going to the playoffs. This topic was exhausted after a minute and a half. The remainder of the hour the two dined in silence. By the time the check arrived, even Ponce was eager to get back to the hospital.

But Oren appreciated the thought.

Clint was still asleep as the two men entered his room. A nurse was taking his pulse.

"It looks like he's probably gonna sleep through the night," she whispered, "although I got a little concerned he might wake up a few minutes ago when Mr. Dursten started playing that tuba."

75

The nurse wrote something on Clint's chart and went out.

After a short silence, Oren, who was standing by the window, turned to Ponce. Keeping his voice low so as not to wake Clint, he said, "I don't know where He is."

"Where who is?"

"God. I used to be able to feel His presence. I used to be able to draw from His strength. Now, it's like He's hiding from me."

"Did you ever stop to think that maybe He was never there in the first place?"

Ponce Humphries knew that this was hardly the time to mount the atheist's soapbox, but it seemed to him that no small number of Oren's problems might be solved by his simply discarding a crutch that had not served all that useful a purpose anyway.

"Of course I've thought about it," Oren replied. "I wouldn't mention this to anyone but you, but I've got to say that lately I've been thinking about it a lot. It's a scary thought too."

"I know it is."

Ponce settled into a chair at the foot of Clint's bed. Oren leaned against the pane of the room's solitary window. Every now and then he'd glance down at Getwell Street three floors below. There was very little traffic—just a few late-night revelers straggling home from their post-fireworks tailgate parties at the park. "To think that when it comes right down to it, Ponce, without a God, without a great loving, benevolent being looking after us, we're pretty much—alone. We—we sink or swim based on our own devices. I don't like that setup. If I have to be alone, I'd just rather not be."

"You learn self-reliance. It's not such a bad existence."

"I don't know if I want to be self-reliant."

"Look, Oren, it boils down to this: without total, one-hundred-percent assurance there's a God, you've got no guarantee there's going to be anything waiting for you after you die. No afterlife: no chance to see Alice again. False hope, that's what it is. Okay, so it's kept you going for these last two years. I wish I'd had something to cling to after Vicki died. But maybe it was only a matter of time before—"

"Just because a person has doubts about the existence of God doesn't mean that he should start living his life as if there isn't one."

Ponce laughed. "And what kind of life would that be, Oren? A totally amoral one? Do *I* live a totally amoral life? Even atheists can be good citizens, you know."

"I just want to believe that we're not alone. That's all, Ponce. That's all I'm talking about. And I think Clint wants this too."

Ponce got up from his chair and went over to stand next to his friend at the window. "Clint isn't alone. He's got you."

"I don't think he wants me," Oren said softly.

Getwell Street was almost totally deserted now. It looked quiet, desolate. Oren was glad he'd be spending the night here at the hospital. He didn't embrace the thought of driving down dark, empty streets to a dark, empty house.

No, he wouldn't have liked that at all.

20

My cogitations much troubled me,
and my countenance changed in me;
but I kept the matter in my heart.
Daniel 7:28

Carmen didn't like this at all.

But she would never tell Alaura. Alaura was her new friend. Alaura was depending on her. Still though, it wouldn't hurt, she thought, to hear the game plan again. "So you just swab the area and put it in as quick as you can, and it's a small needle and I'll hardly even feel it."

"Hardly even feel it." Alaura gave her grapefruit a couple of extra jabs with the practice syringe to bolster her confidence. Then she picked up the syringe designated for Carmen and brought it into the vicinity of Carmen's thigh.

"Did you swab the area?"

"I already swabbed the area."

"Are you gonna tell me right before you do it?"

"I'm about to do it."

Carmen shut her eyes tight and gripped the arm of the sofa. She tried not to think about the prick of pain that was soon to visit her leg. She focused her thoughts, instead, on Tie Gibbons—specifically on the way he had looked the second time she ever saw him: it was on the occasion of his second visit to her church—the visit which confirmed for her that he was to be more than just a one-time guest there. Tie had just entered the narthex a moment before, and, as Carmen recalled, was being handed a Calvary United Christian Church bulletin with that Sunday's order of worship printed inside. She noted the respectful, almost reverent look on his face as he browsed through it.

It was a look that would have been appropriate on any other Sunday but this one. Because this particular Sunday Faye Wallace had been enlisted to type the bulletin due to a several day absence by the church secretary Virginia Catheil who had been called out of town to dissuade her daughter from naming her newborn baby Aureola. Faye, while a speed typist, wasn't very accurate, and there were several comical mis-

79

spellings, from the common "Cavalry" for "Calvary" to the less common "Gordon Wedgerke" for "the Reverend Gordon Wedgerly." It was hard for many who had just opened their bulletins after claiming their pews not to snicker at the mistakes, but Tie didn't even crack a smile. Carmen remembered thinking at the time that he either possessed a great degree of self-control or else just didn't find typographical errors to be all that humorous. Now, sitting on Alaura's sofa and trying not to think about what her new friend was about to do to her leg, Carmen came up with another reason for Tie being so straight-faced that morning: he couldn't read.

Her neighbor Bowmar Stambler couldn't read either. Bowmar was being tutored by his girlfriend Nancy Leigh, who Carmen understood was employing the popular each-one/teach-one method. Only every now and then would she take a break from, for example, offering up all the variant pronunciations of the letter combination "ough" to suggest other ways for her boyfriend/pupil to improve himself. Carmen knew all this because Nancy Leigh would often tutor Bowmar in the couple's kitchen, with its window, conveniently situated only a few feet from Carmen's backyard patio, invariably wide open. In fact, it was during such a digression that Carmen learned that Bowmar had a bad habit of chewing whole mouthfuls of food as few times as possible, thus inviting indigestion with every meal.

"Okay—now," Alaura announced. Carmen gritted her teeth; her whole body tensed up, but there followed not even the slightest sensation of being injected. "False alarm, sorry," Alaura said. "But this time it's a go." Again Carmen reflexively tightened all the muscles in her body and waited, only to receive, moments later, another apology. "Okay, now I *really* mean it," Alaura said. This time Carmen, having been tricked twice before, merely sighed. The pain in her leg that ensued felt like the sting of a dog-sized hornet.

Carmen bit her lip. She sometimes wished that she wasn't such a nice person.

***

Euless woke suddenly to the sensation of someone's hand covering and blocking the air to all of his breathing orifices. "Somebody is trying to suffocate me in my sleep," was the terrifying thought that followed a microsecond behind Euless's collision with consciousness. Almost as quickly, he knocked the hand away from his face and sat straight up on Stewie's sofa. He swung around, prepared to face the evil intruder head-on, but found no one there. He searched the shadows. He was apparently alone.

And yet it seemed too real to have been a dream, Euless thought. I must be going mad. He wondered why he had thought the word "mad" rather than the regular "crazy." Maybe it was the Vincent Price movie he'd watched a couple of nights before.

The prickly feeling in his right hand finally solved the mystery. My own hand, he laughed to himself. I tried to suffocate myself with my own numb, slept-on hand. Euless rubbed the hand briskly, hoping to shorten the amount of prickle time. He looked about the dark, empty room. He decided that everyone had gone home, and Stewie, always the good host, was happy to lend him a sofa for the night. But now that I'm awake, Euless thought, I might as well go on home to my own bed.

Euless pulled himself up and padded, still slightly groggy, into Stewie's kitchen. Remembering the jar of Tang he had noticed sitting on a shelf in Stewie's pantry earlier in the evening and which he could never find in his own supermarket, he proceeded to make himself a glass. Between gulps of his favorite breakfast drink, he scrawled a note to Stewie on the magic pad velcroed to the door of the refrigerator, then took one parting look inside Stewie's aquarium. The goldfish with all the tumors must be hiding in the grotto, he thought. Or else it died. Stewie said the fish didn't seem to feel any pain from the tumors—one on its face so bulbous and strategically placed that it could have been taken for a third eye—but remembering this only got Euless to wondering how a fish would be able to tell you if it was in pain.

Tumors reminded Euless of Mr. Pomeroy.

It wasn't going to be a very pleasant drive home.

21

Behold, I go forward, but he is not there;
and backward, but I cannot perceive him.
Job 23:8

Tula was thinking of Conwell Pomeroy. She was thinking about the year her brother Hank worked for him as a lumber salesman, and how Conwell later fixed him up with a company that sold portable outdoor buildings. He didn't seem to mind losing his best salesman. Maybe he minded, but he never showed it.

And now a good man is dead and another good man is wandering around Magnolia County, unable to find his way home. Tula knew that her chances of finding Hank close by were slim at best. If he'd been able to make it this far, she thought, it just stood to reason that the familiar landmarks and street names would guide him the rest of the way. And yet it still felt better for her to be out and about, conducting her own search, even if it *did* happen to be on foot, and even if it *was* limited to a five-block radius of her house. At least she was doing *something*.

Tula remembered the last time she had to go looking for Hank. It was after he'd failed to return home following an afternoon of watching the tennis team practice at Higby High School. It didn't take Tula long to discover her brother snoozing away safe and sound beneath Germaine and Veneece Cobb's ancient front yard oak tree. As Hank later explained, it had looked like a very comfortable place for a person to take a nap, so he had just lain down and closed his eyes. After Tula woke him he realized to his horror that he'd rolled over onto Veneece's little thrift bed and had uprooted and mashed down almost every one of the dainty little purple flowers. Veneece wasn't very happy about this, and Hank and Tula both felt simply terrible.

Sometimes, at such a moment of frustration, Tula would regret that Hank had ever come to live with her. But these moments usually didn't last long. After all, it had originally made a lot of sense for him to move in. Tula had a comfortable-sized house with two spare bedrooms. She often got lonely, having buried her husband Theo not long before, and had always been very fond of her older brother. When Hank had decided to retire from a lengthy career as a very mobile traveling salesman Tula invited him to come stay with her. After giving the offer some very serious thought, he came to agree that maybe it was time for him to put down roots somewhere. Tula could never have guessed how soon after becoming a daily fixture in her life he was to become a daily burden as well.

"Ms. Gilmurray? Tula Gilmurray?"

Tula turned. Through the dark fuzziness of her night blindness she could just barely make out the face of Gordon Wedgerly, the pastor of her church, as well as that of another man who was unfamiliar to her, approaching from a few yards down the sidewalk.

"What are you doing walking around all alone at such a late hour?" Gordon inquired, taking Tula's hand.

"Hank still isn't back from the picnic yet. I was hopin' I might find him out here somewhere." Tula was looking at the other man now and trying to determine if she knew him.

"Oh, this is my brother Dell. Dell, this is Tula Gilmurray. She and her brother are members of Calvary."

"It's nice to meet you," Dell said, taking Tula's other hand.

Tula began to see some resemblance between the two men. Both had jaws that disappeared into their necks and big bushy eyebrows. Tula had always thought that her pastor looked very British, like somebody out of a Sherlock Holmes mystery story. Now she was getting the same feeling about his brother.

"Have you called the police?" Gordon asked solicitously.

Tula had now had enough of these men holding onto her hands; she retracted first her right, then her left, and tucked them into the big front pockets of her detergent-faded green plaid housedress. "No. I thought I'd wait a little bit longer. Sometimes when Calvin gets in one of his impulsive moods, he goes off and does the craziest things, draggin' Hank right along with him."

"What kinds of crazy things does he do?" Dell asked.

"One time they went night fishin'," Tula said, "and on several occasions Calvin's taken Hank over to Tunica to play the nickel slots"

"Gambling?" Dell's face registered more than polite interest.

This drew a frown from Gordon; his big caterpillar-like eyebrows turned downward at forty-five degree angles. "The Bible Belt has, I'm afraid, Brother Dell, a growing tarnish in the buckle. And that tarnish has a name: riverboat gambling."

"Lighten up, Gordon. It ain't Armageddon." Dell had been tossing back Budweisers for most of the afternoon and early evening, and was in no mood for, as he sometimes referred to it, "pious pronouncements from the white sheep brother."

Dell ran his hand over his mouth a couple of times as he slipped into thought. "Tell you what you do, Ms. Gilmurray: you go on home and give ol' Hank, let's say, another hour or so to make it home on his own, and if he still doesn't turn up, you place yourself a purely precautionary call to the police. And in the meantime, the Reverend and I will continue our stroll through your lovely neighborhood and keep on the lookout ourselves."

"Thank you," Tula said. This time it was she who took Dell's hand. "And thank you too, Reverend. I'm sure he's off with Calvin somewhere. It was nice to meet you, Dell. Are you just visitin' or will we be seein' more of you?"

"Visiting for now. But I hope to move here with my family in a couple of months to set up a dental practice."

"That's good to hear. Although all I have are dentures."

Walking back to her house, Tula felt a little better. Of course Hank was all right, she told herself. He just wasn't ready to come home yet, that's all.

22

I will go along by the high way.
Deuteronomy 2:27

Euless was trying to remember the frequency of his favorite country station. Earlier in the evening, on the drive over to Stewie's apartment, he had tuned his truck radio to a twenty-four-hour hip-hop station. Euless found that whenever he was in his truck and feeling the urge to nod off, if he switched to a station with a musical format he wasn't all that partial to and cranked the volume up as loud as he could stand it, and then set the air conditioner on high, and aimed the vent right at his face, and then composed in his head a list of all the people whose alternators he had replaced that month, the desire to sleep would usually diminish. Now he was pretty much awake and ready to hear something with a soft southern twang. Unfortunately, the tuning knob and the preset buttons had fallen off the radio back in the days when the truck belonged to his father, so Euless had to scan the band with tiny turns to the metal screw protruding from the left side of the console. He was concentrating so hard on this task that he almost didn't notice the dark, slightly hunched figure moving slowly within a small grove of sweet gums just a few yards up the road.

"Glow little glow worm, glimmer, glimmer." The voice, though tinny and hollow, did not seem to be coming from the truck's old Philco. Euless applied the brakes, pumping a couple of times to get the fluid flowing.

Through the passenger window Euless could barely make out the outline of the hunched person as he moved in short, halting steps from tree to tree.

Experience had taught Euless to be wary of strangers exhibiting strange behavior. Once he had stopped just north of the Higby town limits to assist a young man he'd come upon who was dancing in circles around the Higby Jaycees' "Welcome to Higby, a friendly town with good neighbors" sign. At first Euless had thought the man might be mentally retarded; Euless had worried that someone had simply grown tired of caring for him and decided to drop him off at the first town they came upon that was friendly and had good neighbors. But as Euless moved in for a closer inspection the man began to chuck large rocks at him, coupled with angry invective. It turned out that the stranger was a fugitive from a northeast Mississippi private mental health facility, and Euless received as reward for playing the good Samaritan eight stitches over his left ear.

Euless parked the truck. He turned off the motor and got out. The man stopped singing. He stopped moving as well. Euless had been noticed.

"Excuse me, sir, are you all right?" Euless kept his distance.

"Who wants to know?" the man replied. He seemed to be squinting at Euless, one arm resting uneasily on the large musical instrument carrying case he'd set down next to him.

"My name is Euless Ludlam. Is everything okay?"

"Euless Ludlam—do I know you?"

"Well, I don't know. Who are you?"

"I'm Hank Grammar."

"Tula Gilmurray's brother?"

"Yes. I believe so."

"I thought you looked a little familiar. You know, Hank, it looks like you might have gone and gotten yourself lost."

"I have?"

Now satisfied that this was somebody he knew—although it had been quite some time since he had last stopped by the Gilmurray house despite Tula being his mother's best friend—Euless walked over to Hank and placed a friendly hand on his shoulder.

"Where do you think you are, Hank?"

"I'm on my way home."

"Well, I have to tell you, you're a pretty long way from home."

Hank smiled, embarrassed. "Would you know what time it is?"

Euless poked the light button on the liquid crystal display digital watch that everybody told him not to buy. "About ten till eleven."

"Good Lord, my sister Tula's bound to be worried sick about me."

"Come on, Hank. I'll give you a lift."

Hank nodded and took Euless's arm. A large patch of soggy grass and mud lay between the sweet gums and the road, and Hank felt that Euless would be better at navigating around it than he. "How far am I from home, Euless?" he asked.

"Slightly north of town. I took a wide detour to avoid all that work they've been doin' on the Pomeroy viaduct."

"I'm *north?*"

Euless nodded.

"Oh," Hank said, a little sad.

Carmen could see the truck all right. The problem was that she thought it was moving, speeding carelessly down the darkened country road without its lights on. With a drunk fool for a driver, Carmen imagined. She braked a little to put some distance between her Skylark and the suicide-mobile ahead of her. Then she braked a little more. Then when it became terrifyingly apparent that the truck in front of her wasn't moving at all, she pressed the brake pedal all the way to the floor. By then it was too late. With Euless and Hank still a few paces away, Carmen's Skylark, accompanied by the squeal of locked tires streaking pavement, smashed right into the rear of Euless's truck.

The impact of the collision slammed the truck into the trunk of a stately oak tree standing just off the road's shoulder. As splintered bark flew in all directions the Skylark met the truck again, crumpling up against it.

Hank threw his hands up over both eyes. For a long moment he stood like this, peeking through picket fence fingers.

Euless was in such a hurry to get to the Skylark and rescue whomever it was inside who might at any moment be engulfed in flames (Despite Euless's familiarity with automobiles and their unlikely potential for sudden combustion on level surfaces, he always preferred to err on the side of caution.) that he slipped on a slick spot in the wet grass and fell flat onto his knees. "Hang on!" he cried out, picking himself up. "I'm comin'!"

"Euless is coming! Euless is coming!" Hank shouted, trying to be of some assistance.

By the time Euless reached the mangled car, Carmen had already extricated herself through the front passenger-side window. "Get away from that car!" he barked. With the sound of screeching and scraping and buckling frames and fenders still reverberating in her ears, it was impossible for Carmen to understand what Euless was saying to her, and so she just stared at him, puzzled and dazed. Euless didn't repeat himself; he seized her by the arms and began to drag her forcefully from the wreckage.

"You're hurting me!" she cried. Euless ignored this, and pulled her cha-cha style all the way to the sweet gums.

Hank followed. Carmen appeared to Hank more than a little shaken by her ragged experience.

Euless was looking Carmen over now too. "Are you hurt, ma'am?"

"A little. Not bad." Carmen's hearing seemed to be returning.

"Nothin' feels broken?" he asked, touching her lightly on the arms. She shook her head. "You're a little cut up, though. You have a pretty bad scrape on your face."

"I got that earlier tonight. I'm so sorry about your truck, but I thought it was movin'. I didn't realize it was parked until it was too late."

"No, it was my fault. I should've left my hazard lights on." Euless continued his diagnostic interview: "You sure you don't have any broken bones? No bone pain at all?"

"I don't think so." Carmen was now beginning to feel a little light-headed. "I just need to sit down for a minute, that's all."

"Here. You can sit down on my beluga case," Hank offered.

"Are you two men hunters?" Carmen asked as she tried to get comfortable on top of the awkwardly sloping bassoon case.

"Hunters?" Euless glanced over at the scene of the accident. Both cars appeared totaled. "I hunt when I have a free weekend," he said. "I can't really speak for Hank here." It seemed strange to Euless that this young woman was acting so calm and conversational following such a traumatic event. He inspected her eyes.

"Why are you lookin' into my eyes like that?"

"You might be in shock."

"Why would you say that?"

"Well, you asked if we were hunters," Euless replied. "That question isn't very relevant to the moment."

"I don't know why I asked that. It's just something that popped into my head."

"Maybe you should lay down."

Carmen didn't want to lie down on the wet, gum ball-knotted grass. She shook her head, then glanced over at Hank who was studying the night sky. "I know you, I bet," she said.

"This here's Hank Grammar," Euless said.

"Yes. I knew I'd seen you before. You and your sister go to my church: Calvary United Christian."

"Then you must know my mother," Euless said. "She goes there too. Flora Ludlam."

"Of course I know Ms. Ludlam. She makes cinnamon apple buttons for the potlucks. Are you Euless?"

Euless nodded. All of a sudden Carmen felt wobbly and a little nauseated.

"What's wrong?" asked Euless.

"I don't know. I'm startin' to feel very unstable."

"Why don't you put your head between your legs?"

Carmen did as instructed. The bassoon case had an old leathery smell that reminded Carmen of cowboy saddles. For a minute or so Euless didn't say anything. The crickets were chirping enough for the three of them. A deep-throated bullfrog croaked off in the distance. Hank was still looking up at the sky. And he had begun to hum, quietly, "Moon River," Euless thought.

"You didn't tell me *your* name," Euless said.

Carmen didn't lift her head. This position actually did help her feel more equalized. Her voice came out a little muffled: "Carmen. Carmen Valentine."

"You're not by any chance the same Carmen Valentine who was supposed to be at Stewie Kipp's house tonight, are you?"

"Yes I am," said the muffled voice. "How'd you know that?"

"Because I was there tonight."

Carmen pulled herself up. "Are you a friend of Stewie and Tie's?"

Euless nodded. "Everybody missed you at the party."

"Really? I wish I could have been there, but I fell down on a sidewalk on my way over." She pointed to her scraped cheek. "I guess I didn't want to gross everybody out."

A short silence passed and Carmen added, "I'm not having a great night."

Euless was curious: he wanted to take a closer look at Carmen's facial wound, but decided it might be more polite to keep his distance. At just this moment Hank waved at him, then pointed to the sky. Euless looked in the general direction of Hank's pointed finger. "What is it, Hank? I don't see anything."

"It's bats. A very large number of them."

Euless now noticed a small portion of the dark sky that seemed a little darker than the rest. "I don't know that much about bats," he said, "but I suppose we have no reason to fear them."

"I believe they are good and helpful free-tailed bats," said Hank. "I think they're goin' off to dinner."

Carmen didn't know whether to be frightened or not. She had seen pictures of bats up close, and while they certainly weren't the most handsome creatures she'd ever met, they did have a kind of rodent cuteness to their faces, like little field mice with wings, she remembered thinking to herself. "What do you think we should do?" she asked.

"Oh we're all right," Euless replied.

Hank waved at the bats. "Bon appétit!" he shouted.

23

And I also have given you cleanness of teeth.
Amos 4:6

After dropping off Ray and Tanyette, Stewie Kipp decided to check out the new twenty-four- hour Mammoth Mart that had just opened a couple of weeks earlier about a mile south of town. "You wouldn't believe their inventory," Marci had breathlessly reported after her initial visit. "Think of just about anything and they probably have it in stock."

Stewie imagined it might be kind of relaxing to walk down the store's wide, brightly lit aisles without a lot of people around to jostle him or ask him to pull things down from the high shelves for them. Maybe if he stayed there long enough, Marci would be gone when he got back home, and thus unable to tell him that she wanted to break off their engagement, this being something he knew she'd been preparing to do for some time now.

Lately Stewie had begun to wonder if Marci still loved him, especially now that he'd given his life over to the Lord. For one thing, Marci had always been suspicious of religious people. "I don't think they're all that sincere," she had once said. "I like to be around people who say exactly how they feel about you. To your face. Not behind your back."

As Stewie steered his truck into the large, nearly empty Mammoth Mart parking lot he was thinking about the night he told Marci that he had decided to dedicate the rest of his life to Christ.

"I thought your life was already dedicated to Christ," she had said. "Why do you have to go and do it again?"

"I'm not dedicated to Christ, Marci. I hardly even *know* Christ. Like I just found out last week that he was a carpenter. See, I didn't even know a simple thing like that."

"Big deal. Jesus wore a tool belt. I guess this means we're not goin' drinkin' on the weekends anymore. I guess this means we don't get to go to the Punt 'n' Whistle anymore."

"I was gettin' kind of tired of the Punt 'n' Whistle anyway, Marci," Stewie had replied.

"Are you givin' up all alcoholic beverages?"

"I suppose I should. I like the taste too much. It's liable to make me stray from the path."

"And what path is that?" Marci had asked, knowing full well the answer.

"The path to eternal salvation."

This response had prompted Marci to roll her eyes in a very exaggerated way. Her back was turned to Stewie and she had assumed he hadn't seen her reaction, but it happened that he'd been looking at her reflection in the glass pane of one of his double French patio doors, and so at that moment came to know a sad truth: a pure Christian love between Stewie Kipp and Marci Luck would probably never be.

Stewie tried to get his mind on something else now as he walked through the automated opening door and into the coliseum-sized interior of Magnolia County's brand-new Mammoth Mart. As he suspected, there were very few people inside. Only three of the fifteen checkout stations were staffed, and one of the women standing behind her shiny new computerized cash register didn't have a single customer; she was leaning casually against a bright red concrete pillar, reading a paperback romance novel and chewing on the Tootsie Roll center of a Tootsie Pop.

I will think about that girl with the lollipop stick coming out of her mouth, Stewie thought to himself. I will think about how pretty she is, and how we would look sitting next to each other during faith-sharing hour on Wednesday nights at Calvary United. He considered the woman for a moment and decided that she was more than merely pretty. She was, in fact, beautiful. She had all the features that he found most attractive in a woman: thick shoulder-length tawny-colored hair, long accented lashes, full pouty red lips and an ample chest. Marci possessed none of these things. He had to admit it. Marci was cute, perhaps even pretty in her button-nosed, twinkly-eyed way. But if beauty was represented by the woman who now stood, slightly slouching, before him, then Marci was not, truth be told, beautiful. This sudden realization made Stewie feel strangely ambivalent.

He was still looking at the Tootsie Pop woman when she glanced up from her book. She immediately caught his gaze.

"Who do you think *you're* lookin' at?" she nearly shouted given the distance between them.

Stewie shrugged and shook his head. He suddenly felt like a little kid who'd been caught stealing a peek inside a girly magazine at the Handy Mandy.

"Come over here," the woman commanded. "Come right over here and tell me why you're lookin' at me like that."

Stewie felt a sudden urge to run straight out to the parking lot and make a mad dash for his pickup. But the desire quickly passed. He hadn't done anything wrong. He'd simply looked at a pretty checkout clerk. There was no crime in that. He walked over to her station.

"I wasn't really lookin' at you," he said. "My mind was wanderin' and you were in front of my eyes." Now he was lying. He was a Christian man standing before a beautiful woman, out and out lying.

"I think you were lookin' at me all right. Do I maybe resemble somebody you know?"

"You don't look like anybody I know," Stewie said, this time telling the honest truth.

The woman dog-eared the page of the book she'd been reading, and set it down on the little conveyor-belted counter in front of her. Stewie noticed the title of the book: *Stolen Desire*. These words were superimposed over a colorful illustration of a handsome, brawny, shirtless man clutching a ravishingly attractive woman. The woman was wearing a full-flowing peasant dress. Stewie wondered, as he usually did when he passed such books in their carousels at the drugstore, why the men on the covers always had on fewer articles of clothing than the women.

"You're not some kind of pervert, are you?" the woman asked.

Stewie shook his head vigorously. "I assure you I'm not a pervert."

"Then what are you doin' at the Mammoth Mart at eleven o'clock at night just standin' over there starin' at me for?"

"I thought you were pretty." There. He said it.

"Oh."

"I was gonna buy a new hammer and I noticed you, and I guess I was just taking my time getting to that hammer." This wasn't a total lie because Stewie *had* thought about comparing prices on various tools during his visit. And a hammer *was*, after all, a tool.

"I'm Jeannie Plough. Who are you?"

"Stewie. Stewie Kipp."

Jeannie smiled and removed the Tootsie Pop stick from her mouth. Stewie noticed that she had very pretty, polished-white teeth for someone who seemed to really like her candy. "Stewie—is that short for Stewart?"

Stewie shook his head. "No, it's just Stewie. It's even on my birth certificate that way. I don't know where the name came from. My parents never told me."

"It's an interesting name. You know, I have a theory that only lonely people come to the Mammoth Mart late at night."

"I'm not lonely," Stewie said. "I just hadn't gotten over here yet. I thought this would be a good time."

Jeannie nodded. "It was a mob scene last week. I couldn't even get my breaks. Twice I almost peed my pants."

"That's pretty bad." Stewie was suddenly struck by the stark blueness of Jeannie's eyes. He hadn't noticed them before, but now he believed that *they* were her most winning feature. Stewie often found himself attracted to blue-eyed women. Marci had blue eyes, although hers weren't nearly so saturated with blueness as Jeannie's.

A large woman with a grocery cart full of Pampers appeared behind Stewie. She didn't stop her cart in time and it bumped him in the leg. "Beg pardon," she said.

"I should ring this lady up," Jeannie said.

Stewie nodded. "I should go check out the hammers. It was nice to meet you, Jeannie."

"It was nice to meet you too," Jeannie replied. "You can come back later and stare at me some more if you want to," she laughed.

Stewie couldn't tell if she meant this or not. He squeezed past the overweight woman who was now piling the large packages of disposable diapers onto Jeannie's counter, and headed off to find the home tools. He wanted to take a parting glance over his shoulder to see if Jeannie was watching him, but chose not to. He'd rather not find out that she'd gotten all caught up in the large woman's diaper purchase so soon after this nice little moment they'd spent together.

24

I am my beloved's, and my beloved is mine:
he feedeth among the lilies.
Song of Solomon 6:3

Marci Luck still had some water in her left ear canal and was having a difficult time draining it all out. "Okay, tilt your head all the way to the side and kinda tap it with the palm of your hand a few times," Tie instructed.

"I already tried that," Marci said, straightening up. She shrugged. "Oh well. Guess I'll just have to learn to live with it."

She popped up from the lounge chair and grabbed hold of Tie's hands. "It's such a beautiful night, but I've simply got to get out of this pinchy ol' bathing suit. Shall we go inside and slip into something more comfortable?"

"It's gettin' kinda late," said Tie. "Maybe I should turn in. I have to be at work at seven-thirty."

"I wouldn't say it's late at all," Marci countered. "I'll bet it isn't even midnight yet. Aren't you enjoyin' my company?"

Tie was actually enjoying Marci's company very much. "Yeah. But, you know, I was also thinkin' about, well, you know—you and Stewie."

"Oh for Heaven's sake, Stewie's yesterday's news. We are as good as broken up, believe me."

Tie shifted his weight from right leg to left and then back to right leg again. "Since when?"

"Since tomorrow mornin'. I plan on havin' a long talk with him. I'm gonna break the engagement."

Tie sort of knew this. He let his gaze rest for a brief moment on the subtle V of Marci's understated cleavage. Then he looked away.

"I have a wonderful idea," Marci said, clapping her hands together like her maternal grandmother used to do when she was trying to excite her grandchildren out of their Sunday visit doldrums. "We go over to my place and I pop some airpop popcorn and make us a couple of rum and Cokes, and we get to really know each other a little better. What would you say to that?"

"You don't wanna wait till after you and Stewie have made things official?"

"No." Marci was getting a little impatient. "What I *want* right now is to spend some more time with *you*, Tie. I'm really enjoyin' your company right now, and you don't look all that bored yourself."

Tie thought about this for a moment. He was definitely feeling something for Marci. He couldn't quite put his finger on what that something was, but it was certainly worth exploring. The only problem, if it could be called a problem, was Stewie. Tie was very much indebted to his best friend, and even if Marci and Stewie were never going to speak to one another again, it still might not be right, before things were formally ended between the two of them, for Tie to go running off in the middle of the night with Stewie's lame-duck girlfriend to drink rum and Cokes and "get to know each other a little better."

On the other hand, he had been wondering for some time now what it would be like to have sex with Marci Luck.

So that pretty much settled it.

"We could be at my house in five minutes. You sure you don't wanna come over for just a little while?" Marci gave Tie her best pretty-please look.

Tie had already made up his mind, but pretended for his own amusement to be giving the offer some careful thought. He scratched his jaw— angular, slightly jutting, and late night-stubbled. A handsome jaw line for such a handsome face, Marci observed. A most un-Stewie-like face.

"And if you're worried about what he's liable to think when he gets home and finds us gone, we'll just say I was havin' car trouble, so I asked you to escort me home. Stewie knows how undependable that old Maverick of mine is. It stranded me on the interstate not two weeks ago as you may remember."

Tie allowed Marci to cajole him for a moment longer, then consented to go with her. She didn't conceal her delight over his decision.

Assuming that Euless was still asleep on the living room sofa, Marci opened the front door as quietly as she could. When she saw that the sofa was unoccupied, she called out Euless's name. Receiving no response, she turned to Tie, who was now looking even more appealing to her through romantic half-shadow. "I guess Euless has gone on home. Hey, you know what? Let's not go to my apartment. Let's stay right here."

"I don't think Stewie has rum."

With a mischievous grin Marci replied, "That's okay. It just so happens that I'm not all that thirsty anymore." Without warning, Marci unfastened the clasp of her bikini top and let it drop to the floor. Purring softly, she pressed her still damp breasts snug against Tie's still damp chest. As the scent of chlorine hung in the air and a puddle of pool water expanded around their feet, Tie responded to Marci's overture by tilting her head back with the heel of one hand. Then he kissed her squarely on the lips.

Marci didn't close her eyes.

25

I will return unto you.
Malachi 3:7

Carmen closed her eyes, then opened them, closed them, then opened them again. She would never tell anyone but she had always feared that one day, as the result of some stressful event, her tear ducts would dry up and she would have to devote the rest of her life to keeping them artificially moistened.

As Carmen blinked, Euless bounced, the locked bumpers beneath his feet refusing to uncouple.

"Well, that's enough of *that*," he announced to Carmen, standing nearby. Jumping down to the ground he added, "And besides, I'm gonna need a tow truck for your car anyway."

"So what do we do?" Carmen asked.

"Maybe there's a pay phone a little closer to town." Euless gave the bumpers one last bounce, then jumped down. "If not, well, it can't be more than a forty-minute walk to the auto repair place where I work. You'll be okay until I get back?"

Carmen nodded. "Hank'll serenade me."

Hank had taken out his bassoon and was polishing all of its metallic components with a greasy rag he kept with him for this purpose.

"And you're positive you weren't hurt in the crash? I don't wanna go off and leave you here if you've got internal bleedin' or somethin'."

"My stomach hurts a little bit, but I think it's because I didn't eat anything tonight. I have a little peptic ulcer."

"You want a candy bar? I think I have a Butterfinger in my glove compartment."

"How long has it been in there?"

"A few months. Maybe a year."

Carmen declined.

Euless touched Hank's arm. "You look after Carmen till I get back."

"Yes, I'll do that," Hank replied, enjoying the funhouse reflection of his surroundings in the shiny parts of the bassoon.

Carmen watched as Euless started his hike down the darkened road into town.

"Be careful!" she suddenly cried out.

Euless turned and nodded, then continued on. Carmen could swear he was smiling.

Euless's trek took him past several houses—more like estates they seemed to him—country club-sized ranch styles and columned Tara-like manors which couldn't be more than three or four years old, because it was only five years earlier that Mr. Biggers decided to stop growing soybeans and sell all of his 250 acres to a developer from Memphis who wanted to give the county's wealthiest citizens a little room to sprawl just north of town. This area, called Biggers Pool after Mr. Biggers' cow pond, which had been expanded into a small recreational lake, had become the subdivision of choice for most of Higby's doctors, dentists and lawyers, not to mention the owners of its five major automobile dealerships. Euless imagined, though, as he walked the considerable distance between each house, that it must be a very unpopular neighborhood for trick-or-treating youngsters on Halloween night.

Ten minutes into his journey, and with no pay phone in sight, Euless began to debate with himself over whether he should disturb any of the now sleeping residents of Biggers Pool. Most people wouldn't take too kindly to being awakened in the middle of the night by an almost stranger—much less the guy who tuned up their Lincoln Continentals and Mercedeses—unless it was a life-or-death emergency. And he was pretty sure this wasn't life or death. Besides which, the repair shop was now less than a brisk half hour's walk away.

So Euless forged on, his mind a jumble of thoughts. He wondered how hard it was going to be to uncouple his truck and what was left of Carmen's Skylark. At the same time he wished that somebody had thought to offer Hank a lift home after the Labor Day picnic band concert and fireworks show. He tried to predict Carmen's response when he asked her if she might like to have dinner with him on Saturday night, his one free night of the week. He also wondered if werewolves could drive cars, and if so, which would they prefer: automatic or stick? All these thoughts jockeyed for Euless's full, undivided attention.

Carmen soon won out.

26

And why wilt thou, my son
be ravished with a strange woman,
and embrace the bosom of a stranger?
Proverbs 5:20

Stewie couldn't believe his good fortune; just when he had been feeling despondent over the fact that his Tripoley party had put Euless and Ray and Tanyette into a deep sleep, and that his long engagement to Marci Luck was about to come to a sorrowful end, here he was at one o'clock in the morning at the all-night Burger-Hop sitting across the table from a sassy, blue-eyed, large-chested single woman about his age named Jeannie Plough who was telling him funny stories about 4-H club livestock show mishaps she'd witnessed growing up the daughter of a county agent in rural Georgia.

"But I got tired of all that farm stuff, so I moved to Atlanta and went to secretarial school. You have a piece of hamburger meat or booger or somethin' stickin' to the corner of your mouth."

Stewie quickly snatched a napkin from the metal dispenser and gave his mouth a thorough wiping. "Thanks. So how'd you wind up in Higby?"

"I enrolled in the Mammoth Mart assistant manager trainee program. They transferred me here. Then they realized they had too many manager trainees around the country so they demoted a bunch of us, including yours truly. We've got some kind of lawsuit in the works since it was pretty much only women that got pushed downstairs, but hell if anybody knows where that's at right now. For the time bein' anyway, Mammart's got me workin' as cashier supervisor for the graveyard shift. Real impressive job, right? I get to supervise three other cashiers five nights a week. How're we doin' on time?"

Stewie looked at his watch. He was immediately struck by the abnormally large number of moles on his left arm. He wondered if this sort of thing turned a girl off. Marci had never complained. "Oh, we're about halfway," he said. "You know, I'm really enjoyin' talkin' to you. I wish you didn't have to go back to work."

"Maybe I don't. I've already mentioned to tell Stephanie that I might have to leave early tonight on account of sinus problems."

"Great."

Jeannie took a couple of bites of her heavily ketchuped fried onion ring, then asked Stewie if he lived nearby.

Stewie was pretty sure that it was more than casual curiosity that prompted Jeannie to inquire. "Not too far," he said.

"That's convenient." Jeannie dabbed at a spot of ketchup on her chin with her napkin.

Suddenly Stewie found himself faced with a major dilemma: if he didn't invite Jeannie back to his apartment—something he was now feeling fairly certain she was hinting that he should do—she might end up being very disappointed and maybe never want to see him again. On the other hand, he hardly even knew her; Jeannie Plough was still very much a woman of mystery to him. And on top of this, his newfound Christian faith would not permit him to go to bed with Jeannie outside the bounds of marriage, although he and Marci did seem to get around that stricture fairly easily. Of course, he justified his and Marci's sexually oriented relationship by invoking a grandfather clause: since he was having sex with Marci before he became born again, what would be served in suddenly cutting that relationship off or pretending that it never happened? With Jeannie, however, grandfather clauses weren't applicable. Stewie's faith was about to be tested.

"Would you like to come over to my place, I mean, you know, later?" Stewie said this very quickly—so quickly, in fact, that for a brief moment he wondered if Jeannie had understood him.

"You mean later this evening or later like tomorrow or somethin'?"

"Whenever you like." Stewie took a quick, nervous drink of what turned out to be Jeannie's Coca-Cola.

"Did you mean to drink my Coke?" she asked. "It's all right. I was just wonderin'."

"No, I didn't mean to at all. You want a drink of my root beer to even things up?"

"No, that's all right. Stewie Kipp. Stewie Kipp. I don't think I've ever met a Stewie *or* a Kipp."

"I don't think I ever met a Jeannie before either. But once I did work for a man named Plough. He put in bathroom fixtures. That's back when I thought I wanted to be a plumber."

"So you like lumber better than flushometers?"

Stewie shrugged. "I suppose."

Jeannie adjusted her bra strap, which had been itching her for the last five minutes. "If you're not too sleepy, we could go over to your place. My house isn't gonna work. My roommate gets all weird on me when I bring guys home in the middle of the night."

"All right."

"I just need a couple of minutes to Stephanie I'm havin' an allergy attack of the first magnitude. Then I'm all yours."

"That'll be good," Stewie said. He tried to sound sincere. He nodded a couple of extra times to punctuate his interest.

Jeannie summoned the waitress for the check, which Stewie insisted on paying. As the two were walking out to the parking lot, Stewie suddenly remembered his own roommate, Tie Gibbons. Tie would sometimes stay up all night long watching talk shows and infomercials. What if he was still awake? How would Stewie even begin to explain Jeannie?

Well, Tie did seem a little tired when I left, Stewie thought. And Euless is usually a pretty sound sleeper. I'm sure if Jeannie and I are quiet ... Suddenly Stewie panicked. Quiet doing *what?* In an instant his face and hands began to tingle and his heart began to race. He'd felt this way only a few times before—this mixture of fear and excitement—like the first time he tried to buy condoms.

"You ain't gonna fill those things with water and drop 'em on folk's heads, are ya, sonny?" the drug store clerk had clucked.

"No, I—I got a different use in mind," Stewie had stammered while dropping his voice as low as it could go to offset his youthful looks.

Jeannie stepped over the concrete divider that separated the tiny Burger-Hop parking lot from the stadium-sized parking lot for Mammoth Mart. "Be out in a jiffy. Why don't you drive your truck around back to the employee parking area? I'll meet you there and then I can follow you home."

Stewie agreed that this was a good idea. He watched Jeannie as she hurried across the expansive parking lot, her bright red Mammoth Mart apron imprinted with a happy mastodon appliqué flapping to one side, her long, wind-blown hair lifting slightly off the back of her blouse. Stewie wondered what Jeannie's hair might smell like if he got his nose close enough to sniff it; Marci's hair always smelled clean and floral. Was it possible for hair to smell even better than that?

Of course it was.

Stewie believed he was in love.

27

Come, let us take our fill of love until the morning:
let us solace ourselves with loves.
Proverbs 7:18

Tie was cupping Marci's breasts in his hands and kissing them in a circular pattern that Marci found interesting when the phone in Stewie's room began to ring. "Who could that be at such an ungodly hour?" Marci exclaimed, glancing over at Tie's Little Ben alarm clock. The luminous dial read 2:15.

Tie lifted his mouth from Marci's left breast, which had become a little red and chafed from all the attention. "Maybe we oughta just let it ring," he suggested, a little annoyed at the distraction.

"No. It might be Stewie. He's been gone an awfully long time. I hope he hasn't had some kind of accident."

"Guess you're right," Tie said, releasing Marci, then vaulting right over her. Marci heard Tie's feet hit the floor with a loud slap. She giggled. It was funny seeing Tie running out of the room without a stitch of clothing on. Stewie didn't do this sort of thing anymore. It was something she really missed about him. Marci immediately recalled their "nudist weekend," a fun idea she had read about in *Cosmopolitan*. For two days she and Stewie had confined themselves to his apartment, shedding all their clothes and inhibitions like monkeys at the zoo. In the old days Stewie was up for just about anything in the "dirty and daring" department, Marci thought, pulling the sheet up over her slightly chilled breasts. She missed those days.

It took a moment for Tie to figure out how to get Stewie's phone to work. It didn't look anything like a telephone, resembling, instead, a miniature Jaguar sports car; since Tie had never had opportunity to use it before, he had no idea what you had to do to answer a call.

"Hello? Hello?" Tie pressed the underside of the tiny Jag to his ear, flicked open the hood, closed the hood, poked the teeny tires, then finally thought to tap the equally teeny steering wheel.

"Hello?" came a woman's voice from inside the little car. "Is that you, Stewie?"

"No, it's Tie. I'm a friend of Stewie's."

"Oh, yes, I believe I know you from church. This is Flora Ludlam. Do you know my son Euless?"

"Yes ma'am. He was over here earlier. Stewie had a party." Tie felt a little foolish standing in the middle of Stewie's bedroom without any clothes on, talking into a miniature car to Euless's mother in the middle of the night, but there wasn't a lot he could do about the situation now. He pulled a piece of quilt lint from his thick nap of chest hair and watched it float to the floor.

"I'm very worried about him. He never came home and I don't know where in the world he might be."

"We thought he was gonna spend the night on the sofa, ma'am, but when we came in from the pool, he was gone."

"I see." Flora yawned. She immediately examined the mouthpiece for the presence of unhygienic saliva beads.

"Maybe he just stopped off somewhere to get a sandwich," Tie offered.

"You could be right. The boy doesn't even know I'm at his house right now or I assure you he'd be more considerate. I'm sorry I woke you up, Tie."

"That's all right. You didn't wake me up," Tie said.

"You're all such good boys. I don't know why we worry about you at all. It's just that Euless has been so overworked lately and—oh, you don't want to hear this. I'll just see him when I see him. The good Lord, I trust, will keep him safe in the meantime."

"Put it in the hands of the Lord, that's what I always say," Tie said, imagining how Marci must be looking at that moment with the moonlight spilling in across her powder-white, sun-starved hips and bottom. He hoped she wouldn't be asleep by the time he got back to her.

"Sorry to disturb you," said Flora. "Bye-bye." Tie set the Jaguar phone down in exactly the same place he had found it so Stewie wouldn't think somebody had come into his room and been using his things without permission.

Marci was still very much awake as Tie climbed back into bed. "That was Euless's mother. Seems like everybody in town's decided to stay up late tonight." Tie locked his arms around Marci's waist.

Marci smiled blissfully. "Hold me tighter. I like to be held very close."

Just as Tie began to kiss Marci again, the couple suddenly became aware of the sound of a motor vehicle pulling to a stop and then idling just outside the window. Marci became very still, even as Tie shrugged and continued to kiss her. Her eyes darted over to the door to the hallway to make sure it was closed. "Sounds like Stewie's truck," she said. "What should we do?"

"You got me all worked up now, Marci. I'm not gonna just let you sneak out of here."

"What if he finds us in bed together?"

Tie rolled onto his back and cupped his hands behind his head. "Stewie respects a guy's privacy. But I'll lock the door if that'll make you feel better."

"Yeah. If you don't mind. I really don't want him to find us like this, Tie. I mean, that's not the way I wanted it to end."

"Sure. Okay," said Tie, getting up to go lock the door.

"Now go check out that window. Tell me if it really is him."

Tie did as instructed, confirming that it was, indeed, Stewie. He also reported a car pulling up behind Stewie's truck. In fact, Stewie seemed to be expecting it.

"What kind of car?" Marci asked. "Who's in it? Anybody we know?"

"Why don't you come look for yourself?"

"I don't want to take a chance he might see me. So tell me! Tell me!" Marci began to bounce impatiently on her knees.

"I don't recognize her. She's pretty. She's got long brown hair. She's wearing a Mammoth Mart uniform or apron or something. The car's an Excel. I can't tell what year."

"Well, I don't understand this at all!" With this, Marci jumped out of bed and moved quickly but cautiously to the window. She wrapped the curtain around her head like a heavy veil, leaving only a small space for her eyes. Then she took a peek out the window herself. Tie immediately pulled her to his side; he wanted to feel the smoothness of her legs against the roughness of his own. Marci wriggled away; she was preoccupied with the strange woman accompanying Stewie to the front door.

"Where did he find *her*!" Marci scoffed.

"Judging from the apron, I'd guess Mammoth Mart," Tie said. "Let's go back to bed and make love."

Marci ignored the suggestion, and now brazenly pressed her face right against the window pane. Then in an angry whisper she declared, "He is such a hypocrite. Just look at him."

"I don't wanna look at him. I wanna look at *you*."

Marci could feel one of Tie's hands gently caressing the curve of her left bottom cheek. She turned around, caught his affectionate gaze, and smiled. "I guess I'm bein' rude, aren't I? Well, it was over between Stewie and me anyway. What difference should it make what kind of trash he picks up in the middle of the night?" Marci allowed herself one parting glance out the window. "Except that he goes around tryin' to pass himself off as Mr. Pure-as-the-Driven-Christian-Snow."

Tie had begun to give Marci little tugs in the direction of the bed. He was also making little whimpering sounds, like a hungry puppy. Pulling her down onto the mattress he said, "He's only human. Stop worryin' so much about it." Tie said this very softly, then added, "We're all human, when you come right down to it."

"You're right," Marci replied, thinking Tie could sometimes, when you least expected it, be very profound. She was determined to get her mind off Stewie and onto Tie even though she could now distinctly hear the sound of the front door creaking open downstairs. She tried to concentrate on Tie's very well-developed arms and chest. She imagined that he must lift a great amount of lumber on any given workday. She wondered if he ever got splinters in strange places like Stewie sometimes did.

The two lay still for a moment. Stewie and the woman could now be heard conversing down in the living room, though it was hard to tell through the closed bedroom door what was being said.

This is very distracting, Marci thought. Then remembering the night she made love to Paul Varney beneath the bleachers in Higby High School's gymnasium with the district championship basketball game in noisy progress just yards away, she suddenly became determined not to let anything—including the sound of Stewie entertaining his trampy late-night date—ruin her evening of passion with Tie Gibbons. She began kissing Tie deeply and forcefully, her fingers squeezing his arms and shoulders like little lobster pincers.

Downstairs Stewie was pouring Tang Screwdrivers for both Jeannie and himself, Jeannie having volunteered the bottle of vodka that she kept under the front seat of her car.

"I don't really drink that much these days," he said apologetically, "so I don't keep the house very well stocked."

"I guess that Tie person you live with must be asleep," Jeannie said, moving about the room, examining things.

"I suppose he is," Stewie said, handing Jeannie her drink. "And this note here—it's from Euless—looks like he went on home."

"Was it a fun party?"

"I suppose. It would've been more fun if *you'd* been here, though." Jeannie was peering into the aquarium now.

"That was sweet. Did you know your goldfish has a big growth on him?"

"It's a tumor. Can I kiss you?"

Stewie's question caught Jeannie by surprise. Her eyes grew big and she smiled reflexively. "Why not?"

Stewie took hold of both of Jeannie's arms. He leaned in and gave her a long, probing kiss. He remembered that Marci always liked tickly tongue flicks, so he threw in a couple of these for Jeannie.

Catching her breath, Jeannie said, "That was quite a kiss." She set her Tang Screwdriver down on the coffee table, then offered her lips for an instant reprise. Stewie wanted to sweep Jeannie Plough up into his arms that very moment and carry her upstairs. He couldn't remember the last time he'd felt like this: wild and crazy with desire. Marci still turned him on, but Marci hadn't made him crazy for some time.

"I have to tell you somethin'" he said.

"What?"

"I accepted Jesus Christ as my personal savior about eleven months ago."

"I did too," Jeannie Plough said. "Last year."

"You did?"

Jeannie nodded, then began to suck on Stewie's chin.

Upstairs Tie was whispering, "I love you," over and over again into Marci's ear.

"You're ticklin' my ear," Marci said.

"I'm glad you decided to stay the night," Tie said sleepily.

Marci had been straining without success to hear what Stewie and Jeannie were saying downstairs. Now it had become very quiet. "Do you hear anything?" she whispered. "I can't hear anything."

Tie didn't answer. He had drifted off to sleep. Marci studied his face for a moment. She just couldn't understand it: Tie Gibbons was ten times more handsome than Stewie. With sweet tenderness he had just whispered, "I love you" following an extremely intimate and passion-filled three minutes of love-making. He was, hands down, much more her type than Stewie was: the kind of man who, unlike her former lover, could easily give in to an impulse and address the consequences later; the kind of man who simply liked to have himself a good time. So why couldn't she relax and enjoy his company? Had she become so attached to Stewie that it would take major emotional surgery to sever the two of them? And who in God's name was this woman Stewie was being so very quiet with down in the living room? She would have a lot of questions for Mr. Kipp in the morning.

Marci closed her eyes and tried to fall asleep. But her brain wouldn't cooperate. He doesn't even snore, she thought, listening to Tie's soft, barely audible breathing. What in the world is wrong with me?

28

Commune with your own heart upon your bed,
and be still.
Psalm 4:4

Oren was having his own trouble sleeping. The cot that one of the orderlies had brought in was very uncomfortable; the mattress was much too thin, and there was a metal bar, situated right where the frame folded up, pushing directly against his tailbone. Almost as bothersome was the ambient hospital noise penetrating the room from the corridor outside the door: doctor's paging bells going off, elevator doors rattling open and rattling closed, nurses speaking to one another in anything but hushed tones. Oren was amazed at how soundly Clint seemed to be slumbering through all of this.

It was nearly three o'clock before Oren finally managed to drift off. He immediately fell into a deep sleep and dreamed that Desiree Parka was massaging his back and shoulders.

"Farther down my back," he instructed. "It's very tight near the bottom of my spine. It feels like something hard and metallic is pushed up against it."

Desiree seemed happy to oblige. "Your next trip, I'll give you a freebie. The works. I'm very good. Ask any of my clients."

Then Oren dreamed that Desiree kissed him. Right on his back. A tiny, delicate kiss like one you'd give a little child after tucking him into bed at night. "Thank you," Oren dreamed he said. Then, just as she seemed about to respond, a familiar voice intruded: "Dad? Are you awake, Dad?"

Oren woke to find Clint sitting up in bed looking at him. Clint's face was still swollen; he resembled a squirrel with too many nuts in its mouth.

"How are you doing?" Oren asked, swinging off the cot.

"I hurt all over, Dad."

"Do you want me to get the nurse? Why don't you lie back down?"

Clint lay back down—slowly. Even the slightest movement seemed to hurt. Oren pushed the nurse's call button.

113

"I've been havin' crazy dreams," Clint said.

"Well, you've been through a lot." Oren felt a sudden desire to take hold of his son's hand, which lay on top of the sheet very close to where his was resting, but before he could act on the impulse Clint rolled over onto his side so he could look at Oren without having to turn his head.

"In one dream I thought I was flyin'," Clint said with a half smile. "Like Superman. It was weird."

Oren didn't really know what to say to this. He simply smiled and nodded.

"My other dream, I was underwater. I know why I dreamed that. Did Dr. Humphries tell you?"

Oren nodded again.

"I can't believe I landed in that pool. I guess I could've been a dead man."

"We won't think about that," Oren said.

A male nurse came in and addressed Clint: "You need somethin' for the pain?"

Clint nodded. "No shot, though. A couple of Tylenols, I think."

The nurse smiled. "Two Tylenols it is. I'll be right back."

After the nurse left, Clint picked up the remote control and switched on the TV. "I've always wondered what kinds of shows come on at three-thirty in the mornin'," he said.

Oren wanted to tell Clint that maybe he shouldn't be watching television at such a late hour, but decided to let it go. He was actually a little curious himself. "Better keep the sound low, though," he suggested, "so you don't disturb the patients in the other rooms."

Together, in silence, father and son watched a couple of minutes of an old *Barnaby Jones* show. Then the nurse came back in. With his attention divided between patient and television, he gave Clint his medication. "You should probably get some rest," he said to Clint. Then he mused aloud, "I wonder why they never gave Lee Meriwether her own series."

After the nurse left, Clint and Oren watched a few more minutes of the program. Buddy Ebsen was being held hostage by a trio of thugs. Meanwhile, Lee Meriwether was trying to convince several men who appeared to be law enforcement authorities that her boss's life might be in grave danger. Oren thought to himself that Lee was very good at appearing concerned and distraught.

Clint turned off the TV. "I'm gettin' kinda sleepy again," he said. "Are you gonna stay all night?" Oren nodded. "Good." Clint eased back and closed his eyes.

Oren sat down on the cot. He watched his son breathing for a moment, then lay back down. After several minutes of trying unsuccessfully to get comfortable, Oren gave up on sleep and began to think. He had a lot to think about.

29

Beware of dogs.
Philippians 3:2

Euless had made it to the repair shop in slightly better time than he'd predicted. This was due in part to an angry, territorial German shepherd who had jumped her fence at the corner of School and Court, and had chased him all the way to the Town Park baseball diamond at Court and Church.

Saul, who sometimes slept in the back office following nocturnal altercations with his wife, was snoring away on the tattered sofa that butted against his work order- and invoice-cluttered desk. On the wall above one end of the sofa hung a calendar still turned to August and its full-color photo of an attractive, seemingly carefree woman lounging on a beach. The woman was wearing a string bikini and clutching a lug wrench. Sometimes Euless would stare at these beaming young women, always dressed in bikinis regardless of the season, and wonder where they lived and what kinds of cuisine they liked.

The jangly sound Euless made when he reached for the tow truck key hanging on the key rack next to the door woke Saul up. Not bothering to put on his glasses he squinted up at Euless and said groggily, "I told you not to come in tonight."

"I didn't," Euless said. "There was an accident. A woman hit my truck over near Biggers Pool."

Saul stretched his neck, which always got stiff and cricked whenever he had to sleep without sufficient support for his head. "What woman?"

"She's from here in town. Her name is Carmen Valentine."

"I know her," Saul said. Euless could detect a little grouchiness to Saul's voice. "Or at least my wife does. Carmen was one of Rebecca's students."

"That's pretty amazing."

"What's pretty amazing?"

"That your wife could remember a student she taught years and years ago."

"Not so amazing," Saul said, scratching his ear. "They've stayed in

117

touch. Sometimes Carmen makes candles which Rebecca takes up to the Hadassah store in Memphis."

"I didn't know Carmen was Jewish."

"She isn't." Saul was wide awake now and sitting up. "She just likes to make candles. And weird paintings fabricated out of spaghetti and whatnot. You know the girl hears voices, don't you?"

"No, I didn't know that."

"Angelic voices." Saul reached for his glasses among a cache of spark plugs on the desk, and hooked them behind his ears. "You want some coffee?"

Euless shook his head. "I have to go get Carmen and Mr. Grammar. I left them kinda stranded."

"Mr. Grammar?"

"Hank Grammar. I gotta go."

"Go. Go," said Saul, waving Euless out the door.

After Euless had gone out into the customer service area Saul suddenly remembered something. He went to the door and found Euless buying cheese and crackers from the snack food machine. "Oh, Euless. Mr. Pomeroy died."

"When?"

"Earlier this evening. Your mother called here lookin' for you."

"Thanks for tellin' me."

"I guess I'll close the place for the funeral. I'd kinda like to go myself. The man loaned me some money a few years back. The bank wouldn't give me a red cent but he extended me a low-interest personal loan. I'd imagine everybody in town'll probably go. What do you think?"

"Most everybody, I expect," Euless said, stuffing a package of cheese and crackers into one of his jeans pockets.

"You're not gettin' any of the ones with peanut butter," Saul observed through a yawn. "More than likely one of them two is gonna want peanut butter."

"This'll be fine," Euless said. "Oh, would you do me a favor, Saul? Would you call Tula Gilmurray and tell her that I found her brother Hank and I'll be bringin' him home directly?"

"All right."

Through the large glass panes of the customer service area Saul watched Euless as he strode over to the parked tow truck. Saul's gaze drifted over to a familiar Spanish-style stucco bungalow hunched in darkness across the street. How he wished he could sleep in his own bed, soft and snug and smelling sweetly of whatever fragrant night cream Rebecca happened to be using that evening. The sofa in the office was dusty and lumpy and had an unpleasant motor oil smell, and ever so often Saul would get a whiff of where somebody had spilled a cup of coffee. But Saul Josephs was not the sort of man to crawl back to his wife when she had definitely been the one in the wrong. He tucked his arm behind his head and closed his eyes.

On the drive to Biggers Pool Euless couldn't stop thinking of Conwell Pomeroy and how nice the old man had been to him. He felt sad for Mr. Pomcroy, not because he was dead, but because he had been so unhappy during his last years on earth. People always disappointed him, and he was never sure, he once told Euless, whom he could trust. "I don't mean *you*, of course," he quickly added. "Of course I trust you ... oh, and Ricky. But that's about it."

Ricky Day was Conwell's personal barber. Ricky had cut Conwell's hair on a business trip Conwell had made to New Orleans a few years earlier. The old man had been so happy with the somewhat flamboyant hair stylist's success in hiding Conwell's bald spot that he invited Ricky to move to Higby and open a barber shop on the square. "I'll stake you," Conwell had said, "because you're a good barber and you have an honest and friendly way about you."

Ricky had declined, but agreed to drive up to Higby once every five or six weeks to cut Conwell's hair and give him a professional beard trim. Conwell paid Ricky very well for his trouble, and the two of them became good friends. Conwell had even once made a special return trip down to New Orleans just to see Ricky do his Audrey Hepburn tribute at a club in the French Quarter.

"Don't get me wrong," Conwell had confided to Euless upon his return from the jaunt. "The boy and I are just friends. But he does make me laugh so."

When Euless finally pulled up behind Carmen's Skylark, Hank was playing "Born Free" on his bassoon and Carmen was combing her hair with short, angry strokes. "A bat got in my hair," she announced to Euless as he approached. "He got all tangled up. It took forever for him to work his way out and all the time he's flappin' his hairy wings in a panic. But I remained calm, didn't I, Hank?"

"She remained very calm," Hank replied. "I've never seen a woman so calm and composed with a bat in her hair."

Euless nodded and handed Carmen and Hank each a package of cheese and crackers. They tore into them hungrily.

30

We shall not all sleep,
but we shall all be changed.
I Corinthians 15:51

Tula sat patiently on her living room sofa, flipping without interest through a recent issue of *Prevention* and listening to a man on an all-night radio talk show discuss low-risk, high-yield investments. She tried to think back to the last time she had stayed up so late. It might have been the night of Flora's stroke; it had been well past three o'clock before Tula accepted Euless's offer to drive her home from the hospital so she could get some sleep. She didn't know whether to glean fate or mere coincidence from the fact that once again Euless would be responsible for sending her off to bed after a crisis-filled night.

After hearing from Saul that Hank was all right, Tula had prayed for a very long time, asking the Lord to watch over Hank in the days to come. Now she set her magazine down and prayed again: "Dear Lord, give me the wisdom to do the right thing by Hank. I am having, as you know, such difficulty takin' care of him. Lead me, Lord, to some way to keep him safe but not confine his spirit. In Jesus's heavenly name I pray, Amen."

Tula was about to get up and make herself another cup of instant coffee when Euless's borrowed tow truck pulled up, its headlights illuminating one of the living room walls. Tula hurried to the front door and opened it; she could see Hank and Euless coming up the marigold-bordered flagstone walk that curved from the driveway to the front porch.

"Euless, thank you so much for finding Hank and bringin' him home. I was only moments away from goin' to the police when Mr. Josephs called."

"No trouble, Ms. Gilmurray. I'm happy to help out."

Hank climbed the steps to the porch. Euless waited on the walk. "I had a little trouble gettin' home from the picnic, Tula," Hank said sleepily, handing his sister his bassoon case.

"Could I make you some coffee or somethin', Euless?" Tula asked. Then she noticed someone sitting in the cab of the tow truck, and added,

"Would the young lady like to come in too?"

"That's Ms. Valentine," Hank said, studying the moths that flitted around the porch light just above his head. "Caramel Valentine."

"My goodness," Tula exclaimed, and waved at Carmen.

Carmen waved back. Then Hank said, "Ms. Valentine's hair is messed up due to a bat. I think she'd prefer to go home and wash her hair."

"Thank you for the offer, Ms. Gilmurray," Euless said, "but I've still got a couple of hours worth of work ahead of me, and like Hank said, Ms. Valentine needs to get home. So I guess I better say good night." With this Euless turned and started back down the walk.

"Thank you so much," Tula said again, ushering Hank inside. After she shut the front door she looked at Hank for a long time without speaking.

Hank broke the silence: "I'm sorry I kept you up so late, Tula."

"That's all right," Tula replied. "It was just one of those things that happen."

Later as Tula lay in bed, listening to her antique walnut clock on the mantel downstairs strike four, she began to cry.

She cried for a very long time.

***

As Euless was walking Carmen to her door he said, "I'll give you a call sometime tomorrow with a report on your car."

"Do you think it can be fixed?" she asked. "It's the only car I have."

"I'll let you know after I've had a chance to look 'er over. But you probably shouldn't get your hopes up." Euless took a few steps back, then said, "Well, good night."

"Good night. Thank you for not bein' mad about me crashin' into your truck."

"I should've had my hazard lights on. It was my fault."

"Will it take you a long time to get them unhooked?"

Euless shook his head. "Not too long, I guess. I do this sort of thing about two or three times a week."

"That's good. Well, good night."

"Good night."

As Carmen was getting ready for bed she wished that Arnetta had been around so she could tell all the things that had happened to her that night. She's always gone when I need her, Carmen thought. And—oh no!—what if she never comes back?

Thinking about life without Arnetta suddenly made Carmen very sad. Then she thought about how considerate Euless had been bringing back cheese and crackers for her immediate nourishment, and this lifted her spirits somewhat. Euless is a sweet and gentle man, she thought. Maybe he was tired and upset about his truck, but I wish he had shown me some spontaneous affection. Carmen had not experienced spontaneous affection since being grabbed and kissed by a visiting Marine during her ex-friend Edna's last "Come One, Come All" New Year's Eve party. Although the handsome, buzz-headed Marine had also kissed three other women in quick succession, Carmen believed that his lips had touched hers the longest.

I guess it would have been awkward for Euless to just snatch me up and kiss me like that for no reason, especially after the bat got in my hair and I wasn't looking my best, she thought as she slipped her cotton lace nightgown over her head. But even with those prominent circles under his eyes he is still very cute and I wouldn't have minded one bit if he'd asked me out.

Carmen pushed her large menagerie of stuffed animals over to one side of the bed and slid under the sheets. She could see the earliest light of dawn peeking through the gauzy lace curtains of her bedroom window, and for some reason she couldn't quite put her finger on, this made her very happy. She released a tiny sigh of contentment and closed her eyes. Then suddenly Euless's pickup truck appeared before her. It loomed large and dark and menacing and unusually stationary. She choked back a scream, opening her eyes just in time to avoid revisiting the collision. She took a couple of deep breaths, then went into the kitchen and toasted herself a couple of strawberry Pop Tarts.

Carmen Valentine did not go back to bed.

31

This day is a day of trouble.
Isaiah 37:3

Nancy Leigh dropped her half-eaten strawberry Pop Tart into her brushed-leather slouchy tote and gave her sister Talitha's front door another round of knocks. She was going to be late for work again, and as usual, it would all be Talitha's fault. Nancy Leigh regretted having offered to give Talitha a daily lift to and from the county courthouse where the two women worked in the county clerk's office registering marriages, births, and deaths. In fact, Nancy Leigh was starting to regret having ever recommended her sister for the vacant "clerk to the clerk" job in the first place, although it seemed like the right thing to do at the time: Talitha had grown tired of waiting tables at the Hungry Kitchen and needed, as she put it, "a heavy-duty career change." Talitha promised Nancy Leigh that she would behave herself at her new job and stay out of trouble during her off-hours. This staying-out-of-trouble part included being ready for her ride to work every morning at precisely 7:45—stone-sober and not even the slightest bit hungover.

Nancy Leigh knew exactly what she was going to say when Talitha finally tottered yawning and half-dressed to the front door. Nancy Leigh's words would, no doubt, serve as a preamble to a major showdown between the two sisters: "You better straighten up and fly right, Talitha Leigh, or you can just find yourself another sister. Why, I can't believe I'm related to someone so selfish and irresponsible. If Mama was still here she'd be cryin' her eyes dry."

And Talitha would become defensive, and lash back, and after they'd both had their say, the two wouldn't speak to one another for several days; as a rule it was Nancy Leigh who usually swallowed her pride and mended things between the two of them because she knew in her heart that this is what their mother would have wanted. But this time Nancy Leigh intended to hold her ground. Because, after all, Talitha had just turned thirty, and that was far too old, Nancy Leigh believed, for a person to continue in such a pattern of careless and undisciplined behavior. Hadn't she herself given up this sort of lifestyle at the age of twenty-seven?

But Talitha never came to the door. And Nancy Leigh, fearing that something terrible may have taken place, had to let herself into the house with a spare house key that she had made Talitha give her for just such an emergency as this, and which she kept on her dyed-pink rabbit's-foot key chain along with all the other important keys of her life.

"Talitha! Talitha, are you here?"

There was no answer.

Nancy Leigh walked all the way to the back of the small, narrow duplex. The air conditioning seemed to be off, the rooms warm and stuffy. As she neared the closed door to Talitha's bedroom, Nancy Leigh could hear the faint sound of music coming from inside. She knocked, waited, then opened the door. Apparently, Talitha's clock radio had clicked on, but Talitha hadn't been around to turn it off. And even though Talitha never made up her bed, it still didn't look as if it had been slept in recently.

Maybe she spent the night over at the Hospitality Inn with one of her trucker boyfriends, Nancy Leigh thought, remembering, if not their names, then at least Talitha's physical descriptions of several truck drivers with whom she spent, in Talitha's words, "occasional evenings of grand passion." More than likely Talitha planned on going directly to work from the motel, and Talitha being Talitha, hadn't thought to call her older sister to inform her of the alternate commuting arrangements.

There was nothing left for Nancy Leigh to do but get on to work herself. She stepped into Talitha's bathroom and ran some cool water into her hands from the faucet of the room's ancient pedestal sink, then blotted her perspiration-beaded face with her wet palms. She dried her face and hands with one of the carnation rose-colored towels that she'd given Talitha Christmas before last. As she had imagined, they looked just perfect against Talitha's black and silver speckled, azure-tinted bathroom wallpaper. Now she opened the mirror-door to Talitha's medicine cabinet to check for evidence of drug abuse. She was relieved to find nothing overtly suspicious. "Since I'm already here," Nancy Leigh said to herself, "it wouldn't hurt just to ..." Nancy Leigh soon found herself peering inside Talitha's bedroom closet. The time had come for her to find out once and for all if her sister had lied to her several summers before when she said she'd ruined Nancy Leigh's favorite peach organdy evening dress in an embarrassing boating accident, and tossed it out rather than return it all in shreds. Should Nancy Leigh find the dress hanging in that closet, or even worse, should the dress look as if it had never been anywhere near the propeller of an outboard motor, why, Nancy Leigh just didn't know what she'd do.

Thankfully, the dress wasn't there. Nancy Leigh smiled. Talitha had unknowingly redeemed herself. At least when it came to theft or suspected drug use.

Nancy Leigh returned to her car and began to back out the parallel concrete-runnered driveway, the grass and weeds in the middle section having grown so high and thick you could hardly even see the old and cracked concrete strips. I'll give her until ten o'clock, Nancy Leigh said to herself as she slowly negotiated her way to the street. Then I'm going straight to the police.

Sometimes Nancy Leigh wished she'd been born an only child.

***

Talitha Leigh opened her eyes and suddenly wanted to scream. She had no idea where she was or how in the world she had gotten there. Nothing in the room into which she had just awakened looked even remotely familiar to her—not the bed with its faded rose blossom-patterned sheets, nor the brown-and-gold-dotted, greenish short pile rug on the floor nor the slightly soiled yellow-green curtains over the windows, nor the eight-by-ten-inch framed black and white photograph of the strange young man that hung on the wall. It was as if she had just entered her own private *Twilight Zone* episode.

Then slowly things began to come back to her. A night of drinking too many steins of authentic German lager at the Hoffbrau Tavern, a lot of silliness and dancing on the tops of heavy wooden picnic tables: "Look at me! I'm a crazy German wench girl who likes to dance in a frenzied way to German beer hall music!" The room had spun off its axis, and she had spun with it, and all of her new friends had spun and danced and laughed and sung, and she remembered thinking that this was the happiest night of her life. Then she met the pale white girl with the orange-colored hair who said that Talitha's life was vacuous and without any moral center whatsoever, and who escorted her out to the parking lot and coaxed her into the back of a van and drove her several miles out from Higby to a secluded farmhouse where she was tucked beneath the faded pink sheets.

There was an elephant sitting on top of Talitha's head. She was sure of it. She climbed out of bed, and moving very slowly, and steadying her head with both hands lest the elephant become unnerved and begin to trumpet loudly right into her ears, she made her way across the room toward the closed door that seemed to lead to the rest of the house. She turned the knob and pulled. The door didn't open. She jiggled the knob, then slapped loudly on the wooden face.

"Somebody help me! I'm locked in this room!" The elephant was standing now, all four legs balanced on Talitha's head as if upon some circus stunt ball. Talitha stumbled backward, her head pounding.

Within seconds came the sound of a key clicking in the lock. The door was opened by the girl with orange hair. "Good morning," she said brightly.

"Why'd you lock me in here?"

"We were afraid you might sleepwalk in the night. We didn't want you to get hurt."

"Do you have any aspirin? My head is killin' me."

"We don't use drugs here."

"Aspirin isn't a drug. It's a mild, over-the-counter analgesic."

The girl with the orange hair smiled politely and shook her head. "It's still a drug. We use no drugs here. I'll make you some happy wake-up tea. How would you like that?"

The girl stood in the doorway looking at Talitha, waiting patiently for an answer.

"What's your name?" Talitha asked. She wasn't in a very pleasant mood and her voice sounded gruff.

"I am called 'Joy.'"

"Joy what?"

"Just Joy. I was named by Valor." Joy nodded in the direction of the photograph on the wall.

"What kind of place is this?" Talitha asked.

"This is our home. It will be *your* home too from now on."

"Come again?" It was at this point that Talitha noticed she no longer had on the clothes she had been wearing the night before at the tavern.

Instead, she discovered a purple kimono with gold lamé trim clinging to her sweat-moistened skin. "Have you flown me to Japan?" she asked.

Joy laughed, walked over to the bed and began to make it up. "I'm going to straighten up your room while you get dressed; there are some pretty flowery shifts in the closet there. But tomorrow you will be expected to do this for yourself. A clean life begins with a clean room."

Talitha folded her arms across her chest. "I don't plan on bein' here tomorrow. I'll be home. And if you don't *let* me go home I'll have you arrested for kidnappin'."

Joy laughed again, her slightly upturned nose crinkling. "We didn't kidnap you. You came with us of your own accord. Your 'contract for a life worth living' is lying right there on that dressing table."

Talitha walked over and picked up her "contract for a life worth living." She read it quickly: "I, Talitha Leigh, hereafter called Blithe— 'Blithe'? What kinda fool name is—do renounce my former dissipated life, and pledge to do only good as a humble servant of the Lord in the company of the Brothers and Sisters of Redemption, Magnolia County, Mississippi Chapter. Signed: Talitha Leigh, a.k.a. Blithe. Witnesses: Joy, Hope, Valor and Pud, September 6, 1993."

"I don't remember signing this."

"That isn't your signature there?"

"I guess. I don't know. Hey, don't plump up my pillows so much."

"That piece of paper makes it official, Blithe. You are now an official member of our loving family."

Talitha sat down on the corner of the bed, the contract clutched in her trembling hand. "But I don't want to be part of your family. I want to go back to Higby."

"You cannot return to your former debauched lifestyle. You have signed the contract and you will live a good life among us."

"Who named me Blithe?"

Joy sat down next to Talitha. "We all thought it would be a good name for you. All except Pud. Pud voted for 'Ecstacy.'"

Talitha's neck hurt from the twisted way she had scrunched her body in sleep. She looked sideways at Joy and asked, "Why's he called Pud?"

Joy smiled, and brushed a few stray strands of Talitha's black hair away from her eyes. "If you must know, it's because Pud says there aren't any good manly qualities he'd like to have for a name, and if he gets slapped with a sissy one like Patience or Humility, he'll have trouble keeping his mind on the Redeemer. Now, I think you and I should get down on our knees and pray to the Lord that you will grow and take nourishment from your communion with us, and that your body will be forever clean from the stains of sin we plan to wash away right after breakfast."

This said, Joy took Talitha's hand and pulled her down to the floor beside the bed. Joy bowed her head. Talitha bowed hers too but didn't close her eyes. She just stared at a bit of fuzz on the coverlet, and wondered if she would ever get to see her sister Nancy Leigh and her hard-drinking friends again.

32

Thou mayest look on their nakedness!
Habakkuk 2:15

Marci Luck woke up on the floor next to Tie's bed. Given the fact that Tie was still in bed, sprawled spread-eagle across the mattress, it became instantly apparent to Marci that she had been inadvertently kicked or pushed right off some time during the night. She wondered for a moment why the fall hadn't woken her, then noticed that she was lying on top of all four pillows which had preceded her to the floor. Tie, she thought, is a really active sleeper.

Marci got to her feet. She stacked the pillows neatly next to Tie's head. She located her clothes all balled up in one corner of the room, and got dressed. For a couple of minutes she just stood at the foot of Tie's bed, watching him sleep. He has such a peaceful, angelic face, she thought. I wonder if he's dreaming about me.

Marci waited for the same rush of affection that came when she watched Stewie sleeping some mornings. She liked to know there were times when he was totally vulnerable—not that she wanted Stewie this way all the time. She actually preferred that he be well-rounded: cuddly and vulnerable some days, strong and sure-footed on others. Lately he'd been neither. He'd just been, well ... *Stewie.*

Marci wondered how Stewie looked at that very moment. She wondered whether she might get the desire to climb right into bed with him. She remembered certain Sunday mornings when the two of them would lie in bed for hours wrapped around each other listening to music on the radio or watching videos they hadn't been able to finish the night before because Stewie never liked to leave a video store on a Saturday night with fewer than four current action-thrillers under his arm, even if this meant having to see something he'd already seen a few weeks before.

Marci waited for a similar rush of affection for Tie, but it didn't come. She wasn't happy about this. But maybe it would come in time.

The sheet and blanket were wadded at Tie's feet; she covered him up. He shifted his body a little but didn't open his eyes.

She went over to the door that opened onto the upstairs hallway, unlocked it, and slowly pulled it open. She checked her watch; it was almost eight. She started out into the hallway, thinking about her cat, Falana, who would be hungry and cross with her for staying away all night. She also thought about Jory Adams, the State Farm agent for whom she worked as secretary. Jory had mentioned that he probably wouldn't be able to get to the office until at least eleven this morning; even though Marci had plenty of time to beat him in, she didn't wish to risk running into him on the street. For Marci the most chilling moment in the movie *Psycho* had nothing to do with knife-wielding mayhem; it was that terrible instant when Janet Leigh was spotted by her employer away from the office when she wasn't supposed to be.

Marci started down the short carpeted hallway to the stairs; then something froze her right in mid-gait. The door to Stewie's room had blown open in the night as it sometimes did when the air conditioner kicked on. This gave Marci a clear, unobstructed view of Stewie's bed and its two occupants: Stewie and his overnight guest. "Oh m-my God!" Marci stammered. These words, though originating deep in her throat, were clearly audible to anyone who might have been awake at the time.

Jeannie Plough, who was not only awake, but thinking seriously about going down and making Stewie a three-egg cheese omelet as an early-morning surprise, now opened her eyes to find Marci staring right into the room. "Who the hell are *you*?" she asked, simultaneously startled and vexed. Jeannie nudged Stewie in the side. He woke in an instant but it took a couple of seconds for him to realize where he was. Finally he said to Marci in a hoarse and husky voice, "What are you doin' here?"

Marci didn't answer. She just continued to stare at Stewie and Jeannie who, though discreetly covered by the bed sheet, which had a pattern of wagon wheels and old camp lanterns on it, were probably, Marci imagined, totally naked underneath. This very strong possibility Marci found puzzling since, as far as she was aware, Stewie hardly ever went to bed shirtless, let alone without any pajamas on at all.

"I thought Tie was a *guy*," Jeannie said with a sarcastic edge to her voice.

"That's not Tie," Stewie said. "It's my—friend, Marci."

"That's all I am to you—just a friend?" Marci blurted out without really thinking. She didn't feel very pretty at the moment; her lips felt dry and slightly chapped, her hair hung all limp and tangled from rolling about with Tie shortly before retiring. She also wished she had brushed her teeth; she was sure her odorous morning breath could be detected from several yards away. Stewie's bed companion, on the other hand, was a vision of morning loveliness. Marci imagined that the woman's breath even smelled fresh and minty.

"We were gettin' ready to break up, Marci," Stewie said, a little sadly. "You knew it was comin'. I thought it was what you wanted."

"Maybe it was. Maybe it wasn't. We should have had a long talk about it before you hopped into bed with the first floozy who crossed your path."

"I am *not* a floozy!" Jeannie protested. Turning to Stewie she said, "You tell that Marci person that I am not a floozy!"

"Of course you aren't," Stewie replied, giving Jeannie's soft, only slightly frizzy hair a couple of affectionate strokes. "Marci, could we maybe talk about this later? Let's talk about this tonight."

"Not tonight, Stewie," Jeannie said, scooting up into a seated position against the headboard of the bed. Jeannie made a point of not taking the sheet along with her so that all who were interested might now have a clear view of her large, perfectly rounded breasts. Marci could tell by the contemplative look on Stewie's face that he was at that very moment making the inevitable mental comparison between the obvious endowments of the woman sitting next to him and the boyish chest of his former girlfriend.

As Stewie tucked the sheet carefully under Jeannie's armpits, she continued, "Don't you remember? You said you'd come hear me sing at that club I was tellin' you about."

"Yeah, I guess I did say that. Marci, I have to do this thing with Jeannie tonight. Maybe I could drop by your office around lunchtime."

"You can drop dead for all I care," Marci shot back with growing fury. "You're unfaithful and mean and a hypocrite, and if there *is* such thing as hell, I hope you go there and fry like bacon!"

Marci was crying now. Stewie could not think of what to say in response, so he sat dumbly, grimacing, scratching the back of his neck. Jeannie wondered why Stewie hadn't been a little more up front with her about this former girlfriend of his with the bad temper and the flat chest.

Oblivious to all that was taking place in Stewie's bedroom, Tie now shuffled drowsily out of his bedroom on his way to the bathroom. Seeing

Marci standing in Stewie's open doorway, he glanced inside. "Good mornin', Stew," he said. "Did you know we're late for work?" Noticing Jeannie, he added, "Oh—good mornin' to you too, good-lookin'." Then he gave Marci a peck on the cheek, sniffed her hair, said, "Smells nice," and proceeded into the bathroom.

"I guess *that* was Tie," Jeannie said.

Stewie nodded.

For what it was worth, Marci wished that Tie had at least been wearing his underpants.

33

Joy cometh in the morning.
Psalm 30:5

Carmen sat out on her brick backyard patio blowing on her hot herbal tea and listening to all the sounds of the morning. She wished she could identify birds by their songs the way her fifth-grade teacher Miss Davenport used to do on nature hikes with her class through the woods. She also wished that Bowmar would turn down his radio. It was resting on the sill of his open kitchen window blaring out unwanted sports scores not ten feet from her head.

"Bowmar," she finally called out, "your radio is very loud I have to tell you."

Bowmar's face appeared in the window. He had been shaving over the kitchen sink, assisted by Nancy Leigh's little portable vanity mirror. Earlier in the summer the mirror door on his bathroom medicine cabinet had fallen off its hinges and shattered on the tile floor, the result of a bout of roughhousing that had taken place between Bowmar and his brother Russell who had been visiting from Gary, Indiana.

"Sorry," Bowmar said affably, one side of his face and most of his upper neck still hidden under thick lather. "That tea smells good. What kind is it?"

"It's a mix: Orange Blossom and Strawberry Surprise. You want some?" Carmen shifted her chair so she wouldn't have to keep talking to Bowmar sideways. The large scab on her face now came into full view.

"Thanks, but I don't—hey, what happened to you there?"

"I tripped on a sidewalk."

"I'll bet that smarted. Nancy Leigh has some Vitamin E cream if you'd like to use it."

"Thank you, but I've been applying an ointment of my own. You're sure you don't want any tea? It'll only take me a minute."

Bowmar declined with a shake of the head. "I only drink Almond Pleasure. When I was in the slammer it was the only tea my cellmate would drink and I got kinda used to it."

"What was he in prison for?"

"Grand theft auto. He said he was also doin' time for carryin' grenades around and threatening salespeople with 'em, but it's hard for me to buy that one."

Carmen emitted a gasp of shocked disbelief, then in the next breath she suddenly declared, "You know, I'm just in the best mood this mornin'. Which is odd when you think that I didn't get a minute's sleep last night."

"Me neither." Bowmar was talking a little louder now to make up for the fact that he had ducked his head back inside to resume shaving. "Nancy Leigh was pretty restless last night. She does this kicking thing with her legs sometimes. I finally just gave up tryin' to sleep and went into the TV room and watched the last half of *Ben Hur*. I got to see the chariot race and that scene with all the lepers."

"Yes, I know that scene," Carmen said. For someone who supposedly had her mind on lepers, Carmen looked strangely cheerful and contented. Bowmar didn't understand this at all; usually when the two of them would speak, regardless of the topic of conversation, Carmen would seem to Bowmar, if not a bit shy and uneasy, then at least slightly formal and solemn. Bowmar liked this change in his next door neighbor's personality. He hoped it would be permanent.

A phone began to ring.

"Yours," Bowmar said.

"Excuse me," Carmen said. She set her cup down on the wrought-iron table next to her wrought-iron backyard patio chair and stepped inside.

Bowmar waited a moment, then turned the volume on his radio back up. Nancy Leigh didn't like to listen to the radio in the morning, and Bowmar always had to wait until she left for work before switching on his favorite show where the moderator accepted only sports-related calls and was very opinionated and derisive toward his listeners. Bowmar hoped that Carmen would stay on the phone until the show was over.

Carmen picked up the receiver on the fourth ring. "Hello?"

"Hello—Carmen?"

"Yes?"

"This is Euless Ludlam. Did I wake you up?"

"No. I never went to bed." Carmen sat down at her kitchen table and began to build a miniature tower out of a pile of restaurant packets of Sweet 'n Low she'd been collecting.

"I wanted to catch you early. I didn't have your work number." Euless was calling from the bedroom of his trailer home. He was trying to keep his voice low so as not to wake his mother, who was asleep in the recliner in the next room.

"I work in my home," Carmen said.

"What do you do?"

"I make candles. I also make tactile paintings with macaroni."

"Oh. Well, I bet they're really pretty."

"You can come over some time and see 'em if you like. And touch 'em too. The macaroni is attached pretty securely."

"Thank you. I just might do that. The reason I called is to give you a damage report on your car."

"Okay."

"You want details or just an overall assessment?"

Carmen decided that Euless had a very pleasant telephone voice, which she wouldn't mind listening to for a while. "Details, please."

"Well, let's see—startin' from the front, your entire bumper, grill, and headlight assembly's destroyed. Your hood and your front fender are pretty much beyond repair—I mean, it's gonna be impossible to bend those suckers back into shape."

Carmen emitted a sad little peep, which Euless didn't hear.

"The radiator and radiator supports are crushed up against the motor. The motor mounts on the frame and the frame itself's all bent up. And the motor—it's kinda crunched up against the fire wall. I guess that's it. Oh—and the door jambs are popped."

"What does that mean?"

"You mean about the door jambs?"

"No. I mean what does that mean about my car?"

"It basically means you're gonna need a new car."

Carmen let out another little peep and toppled her sugar packet tower with a flick of the finger.

"I got an old Chevette down at the shop I keep running pretty good. You can use it like, you know, until you can get a new car."

"Thanks, but I think I'll get a new one right away," she said.

"I guess those macaroni things sell pretty good."

"No. I mean, I just don't have a lot of expenses in my life."

This was only partly true. Following the deaths of her parents in a traffic accident five years before, Carmen learned that she'd been named the sole beneficiary of no less than eight different life insurance policies her overly prudent parents had taken out over the years. All totaled, the death benefits amounted to enough money to keep her from having to be employed for the rest of her life. But this just wasn't the kind of thing you should go around relating to people who have to work hard for a living, Carmen thought ... and so she didn't.

"Well, that's about it, I guess."

"Yes," Carmen said, "I suppose I'll just have to go buy me a new car."

"I can come, you know, kick the tires for you if you want me to," Euless said with a little bashful hesitancy to his voice.

"I'd like that."

"Just give me a call when you're ready."

"All right," Carmen said.

"Bye. Sorry about your car. Bye."

"Bye."

Carmen didn't know whether to be unhappy about having to buy a new car or happy about the fact that Euless Ludlam had offered to help her make the selection. She sat, her hand still resting on the phone receiver, waiting to see which feeling would win out. It seemed, at least for the time being, an even match.

34

For he seeth that wise men die ...
and leave their wealth to others.
Psalm 49:10

Euless was angry with himself for not asking Carmen if she'd like to have lunch with him. He thought he might like to see her macaroni paintings too, because it was hard for him to visualize what something like that would look like. But halfway into the conversation, he noticed his mother sitting with her eyes open; he just knew she was listening to every word he was saying.

He hung up the phone and went into the living/kitchen/dining area of his small mobile home. "You awake, Mama?"

"Yes. I have a very stiff neck from this chair."

Euless went to the coffeemaker and pulled out a paper filter from the box beside it.

"What are you doin' here?" he asked.

"I brought you over a bacon and swiss cheese pie. You weren't home, of course, so I decided to wait for you. I got sleepy waitin' and must have just drifted right off. Oh, some bad news, hon': Nurse Ringfinger called to say that Mr. Pomeroy died."

"Yeah. I heard from Saul."

Flora got up out of the chair, holding one hand on her neck like an improvised neck brace. "You shouldn't stay out all night like that. I can understand when you have to work the late shift at that car repair shop. But on nights you have off you really ought to be home restin'."

"I'm makin' coffee. Want some?"

Flora was standing next to her son, now. "All right. What if you fell asleep driving your truck and had a bad accident?"

Euless took a furtive glance out the window over the sink. His white Ford pickup had the unmistakable look of having been in a bad traffic accident. Euless hoped that Flora wouldn't make this discovery any time soon. He wasn't in the mood to listen to his mother go on and on about how traffic mishaps can usually be avoided by spending quiet, restful evenings at home alone, or in the company of a loving, protective mother.

139

There was a long silence. Then Flora said petulantly, "You forgot my birthday."

"I did?"

She nodded.

"I'm sorry. I'll get you somethin' today."

"I don't need a present. I just would have liked it if you'd remembered."

"You know I'm not good at rememberin' things, Mama."

"I just like to know that you think about me every now and then, that's all."

Using her fingers as a comb Flora made a couple of passes through Euless's thinning hair.

"I think about you, Mama. It's just that I have a lot of other stuff on my mind right now."

Flora started to tidy up around Euless's tiny kitchen. "Will this hurt you—not bein' able to work for Mr. Pomeroy anymore?"

"You mean money-wise?"

She nodded, momentarily horrified by a patch of mold growing at the bottom of one of Euless's coffee cups.

"I guess I'll have to get another job. I don't want the IRS to throw me in jail for stoppin' my payments."

"No, we wouldn't want that. Maybe I can loan you some money until you can find more work."

Euless shook his head. This movement made the pain of his low-grade no-sleep headache intensify for a brief instant. "I'm not gonna take your pension money, Mama. I'll get by."

A dog started to bark outside the trailer. "Why, that sounds just like Shadow," Flora said, remembering the black labrador retriever that had jumped the Ludlam's backyard fence when Euless was twelve, and which Flora continued to hope might one day return.

"It isn't a lab, Mama," Euless said, looking out the kitchen window at a medium-sized Heinz 57 mutt lifting a hind leg over the right front tire of Euless's truck.

"Are you sure?" Flora said, and moved to the window to check out the dog herself. "Oh my Lord, what happened to your truck?"

"I had an accident. Did you know Hank Grammar got himself lost again?"

"You didn't run over Hank Grammar, did you?" Flora asked, frightening herself with this possibility.

Euless shook his head. He was about to explain exactly what had happened when the telephone began to ring. "When the coffee's finished, pour us a cup," Euless said as he started into the bedroom to take the call on the extension.

"Hello?"

The voice on the other end of the line was only vaguely familiar: "Is this Euless Ludlam?"

"That's me."

It was a man's voice, but it had an unmistakably feminine quality. "Euless, this is Ricky Day. Remember, I used to come up to cut Mr. Pomeroy's hair?"

"Yes, I remember you, Ricky."

"I just heard the sad news from Ms. Ringfinger. Euless, there's something very important that I must talk to you about. Do you have a moment?"

"Yes." Euless sat down on the bed. His look of concern drew Flora's interest.

"The last time I cut Connie's hair—oh, I called him Connie. He didn't mind. Do you?"

Euless said that he didn't.

"The last time I cut his hair Connie and I, we had a very serious talk about his illness and about what he wanted to leave behind, you know, after he'd gone." Ricky was speaking very quickly and excitedly, and had to take a breath before proceeding. "Anyway, we spoke of intangibles for a while—his hopes for a better world, that sort of thing. Then he got very specific. I mean, specific regarding how he wanted his fortune, you know, distributed. He had certain charities he supported, and he mentioned them, and then he said—oh God, Euless, I'm hyperventilating!"

"He said, 'Oh God, I'm —' what?"

"Not *him*. Me. Euless, are you sitting down?"

"Yes, Ricky. I am."

"It appears that you and I are about to become millionaires!"

"We are?"

"He's leaving us half his estate. That's what he said. He never told you—I mean, never even hinted —?"

"No. I think I'd remember if he had."

"Well, it doesn't matter. He told *me*. Now, of course, nothing's going to happen right off the bat. You know, the attorneys will have to do whatever it is attorneys do when that much money is about to change hands, but we're in the will, I have Connie's word on that, and we're in that will to the tune of about six million dollars apiece, you rest assured."

"I just don't understand —" Euless had such a puzzled look on his face that Flora began to get worried.

As she walked into the bedroom to stand at her son's side, Ricky said, "What's not to understand, Eulie? He didn't have any kids. What relatives he had he didn't much care for. He liked *us*. So we're each getting six million dollars. Look, I'm coming up for the funeral, then the attorneys will probably want me to stick around for the reading of the will. If you need to reach me I'll be residing in the presidential suite of the Hotel Peabody in Memphis. Come on up and we can have a drink by the fountain and watch the ducks."

"Sure. Okay." Euless had never been to the Peabody before; Memphis was over an hour's drive from Higby, and the only times he went up there were to check in with the IRS agent who had helped set up his back tax payment plan, or to play dominoes with his high school buddy Jimjay McKissick who had lost an arm in a freak demolition derby accident.

"Well, congratulations, and I'll be seeing you real soon. Ms. Ringfinger says the funeral will be on Thursday. Bye now."

Euless hung the phone up slowly. He had a very grave look on his face.

"Oh my Lord, what's the matter?" Flora asked.

"No, it's nothin' bad," Euless said quickly, not wishing to distress his mother. It had pretty much been decided that fear and gnawing anxiety had played at least small roles in bringing on Flora Ludlam's last stroke.

"Then what is it, honey?"

"I believe I'm about to become a millionaire."

Flora thought about this for a moment, then said, "I need some new shoes."

35

There is no fear in love;
but perfect love casteth out fear.
I John 4:18

Flora's best friend Tula needed some advice. Since this was somewhat of a medical question, she decided to call Dr. Ostermeyer's office. Klaus Ostermeyer had been Tula's family physician for the last twenty years. Klaus's wife Abbadene, who served as his nurse and receptionist, answered the phone. It wasn't a busy day and Abbadene had a few moments to chat. She talked to Tula about peonies and a recent Valerie Bertinelli movie-of-the-week in which she lost her baby to its birth mother and then became a senator. The conversation eventually turned to all the difficulties Tula was having with Hank. Abbadene suggested that Tula make an appointment for a private consultation. In fact, there was an opening that very afternoon. Tula liked talking to Abbadene. She had a positive outlook and was always quite chipper.

After irrigating her colostomy bag and getting dressed for the day, Tula went to Hank's bedroom door and knocked. "Hank, it's after ten. Would you like some breakfast?"

"Yes, I'd like some breakfast." The voice sounded small and distant.

"May I come in?" Tula asked.

"All right."

Tula opened the door to find her brother seated at the foot of his unmade bed. He was wearing his pajamas and holding his robe all bunched up in one hand. His silver hair hadn't yet been brushed. It was pushed into a flat plane an inch or so above the scalp. His eyes were moist. It looked to Tula like he'd been crying.

"Are you all right, Hank?"

"I am now."

"Did you have a bad dream or somethin'?" Tula walked over to Hank. She touched him tenderly on the arm, allowing her fingers to linger there for a moment.

"No." Hank looked around the room. He looked down at his feet. He was wearing worn-out canvas house slippers, which Tula had tried to get

143

him to throw out, but without success. Then he looked up at the ceiling. Tula looked up there too.

"There's nothin' up there," Hank said. "I'm just lookin' around."

"Did you forget where you were again?" Tula asked softly.

Hank nodded. "I was in the bathroom doin' my business and I forgot. Tula, I forgot whose bathroom I was in. I thought for a while that I might be doin' my business in *your* bathroom, and that you might come in and wonder why I was in there."

"Hank, you can use my bathroom whenever you want to. I wouldn't think anything of it."

"Then I thought I might be in Calvin Gray's bathroom. I was tryin' to remember how I got there."

Tula sat down on the bed next to Hank. "Oh, but honey, you know that Calvin and Edie have those fancy European bidet things in their bathrooms. Did you see one of those bidet things on the floor next to you?"

Hank shook his head. He had forgotten about the fancy bidet.

"Do you know where you are right now?"

"Yes."

"Good. Let's go down and get us some breakfast. I cannot believe how late I slept. The day's half over."

Hank smiled. He was already tasting Tula's buttermilk pancakes.

36

She was a woman of good understanding,
and of a beautiful countenance.
I Samuel 25:3

Desiree Parka sprinkled a little of the Bisquick flour into her hand and poked it with her forefinger. "Why are you weevils always picking on my pancake flour?" she said. She brushed her hands over the sink.

Confrontations with pesky weevils notwithstanding, Desiree Parka had recently arrived at an important truth about herself: she was a morning person. Not to say that she didn't enjoy her evenings too; after all, you had to be somewhat of a night owl to make a living in the massage business. But if Desiree had to pick a time of day as her most favorite, it would probably be the morning. Mornings are quiet and cool. Mornings are about waking, rising, opening up—"the earth reborn with each new day" was how one of her former clients, also a morning person, used to put it. Rebirth. Fresh new start. The symbols of the morning held special meaning for Desiree who had been working very hard for several months to get her life back on track after years of, as her perceptive morning client liked to call it, "skittering along the shoulder of the Highway of Existence."

Turning over a new leaf—going "legitimate"—hadn't been all that easy for her. Most of the residents of Magnolia County still believed the Far East House of Massage to be just as waist-deep in sin and debauchery as it ever was, despite the fact that its proprietress and head masseuse was now a fully licensed massage therapist who'd even spent three weeks in Stockholm learning how to Rolf. Desiree had to agree, though, that old habits do sometimes die hard: Ling Sue and Bibi Francois, her two live-in employees at the Far East House, would still get frisky with their favorite customers from time to time in spite of their employer's orders to the contrary, and especially if the price was tempting.

Desiree turned down the blaze under her skillet of pan fries and sausage, and turned up the volume of the grease-spattered transistor radio she'd hung from the ventilation hood over the stove. Dolly Parton was singing one of Desiree's favorite songs: "Rocky Top." Despite the fact that

145

Desiree had heard this song hundreds of times since it first came out, it always seemed to brighten her day. For some reason that she couldn't explain, it now reminded her of Oren Cullen. Oren had been on her mind off and on ever since she'd said good-bye to him the afternoon before. "He is such a good man," she said to herself. "So filled with the lovin' spirit."

Desiree gazed wistfully out at the unattended cotton field that adjoined her property. Sometimes wispy white fibers from the unpicked bolls would blow right up to her window and affix themselves on the screen like bunched snowflakes. "You know, I think I'm just gonna call that Reverend Cullen up and see how his boy's doin'," she said to herself.

The evening before, during the band concert in the park, Desiree had heard the news about Oren's son falling off the water tower. There were several stories circulating through the crowd, though, and it was late into the night before she got the true account from her cousin Annabelle Ruberi who worked in the records office of Higby Presbyterian Hospital. Among the more far-fetched scenarios reported to Desiree was one which had Clint landing squarely in the middle of the Willifords' backyard trampoline and being spring-propelled all the way back up to the top of the tower.

Desiree now became aware of her three-legged half cocker spaniel/half mystery dog Bubbles whimpering at her feet. She dropped a link of pure pork breakfast sausage onto the floor. The little dog gobbled it up and tidily licked the grease spot it left behind. "Now that's enough people food for you, Bubbles. Go on now—go eat your Purina and quit slobberin' all over my slippers. GIRLS! BREAKFAST IS ALMOST READY! RISE AND SHINE!"

Desiree slid the spatula under the clump of hash browns and dumped them into a serving bowl. Then she thought a little more about how Oren had reacted when she'd invited him to return for a full body massage. Coupled with the obvious trepidation, there seemed to be—dare she believe it?—a tiny spark of interest.

***

"I don't see why we can't go ahead and send you home, Clint," Ponce said cheerfully, touching Clint gently on the arm. "Sure, you'll probably hurt like hell for a couple more days, but at least you'll be in familiar surroundings, right?"

Clint nodded. Ponce stood next to Clint's hospital bed, taking his patient's pulse. Oren was over by the window letting the morning sun warm his stiff back.

"So, Clint, I guess you can get yourself dressed and we'll go on home then," Oren said. He couldn't believe that Ponce was discharging Clint so soon. He had assumed that his son would be kept under observation for at least another day or so.

Detecting a little concern in Oren's voice, Ponce turned to Oren and said, "We have no indications of internal bleeding. There doesn't seem to have been any neurological damage. And I know you've got lousy family hospitalization coverage from that denomination that employs you. So let's just get Clint into his own bed and keep our eye on him there for a while."

"If you think he's going to be all right."

"I think he's going to be fine."

Clint smiled, in spite of the pain. He had generally hated his hospital stay except for those brief few moments when he and his father had watched *Barnaby Jones* together.

Just as Clint began to get dressed someone knocked on the door. "Who is it?" Oren called out.

"Sheila and Johnny Billows," Sheila announced from behind the door. "We came to see how the great flyin' boy is doin'."

"The great flying boy is dressing," Ponce replied bluntly.

"Well, just let us know when the coast is clear," Sheila said.

There was a brief silence on both sides of the door as Clint labored to pull his jeans up over his bruised legs. Oren wanted to give him a hand, but there really wasn't any way for him to help. Ponce walked over to the door and opened it.

Sheila entered the room first, followed by Johnny, who was carrying a Stratego board game with a red bow stuck to it.

"Up and around so soon!" Johnny declared. He noticed Clint eyeing the game and said, "We know how much teenage boys like Stratego. At least I did when I was your age." He set the box down on the bed.

"Thanks," said Clint, grimacing as he pulled his T-shirt down over his head.

Sheila looked at Clint while frowning empathetically. "I think it's a miracle, Reverend Cullen," she declared. "I said it yesterday. I'll say it again."

"Yes, it was," Oren said politely. "Well, it looks like we're about ready to leave. Clint was just discharged by Dr. Humphries." Oren directed the first half of this news to Sheila, the second half to Johnny.

"Good to hear," Johnny said, taking a few steps back to allow sufficient berth for the Cullens' exit. "Hope you enjoy the game, Clint."

Johnny looked poised to depart himself, but Sheila still had something she wanted to say: "Reverend Cullen, Johnny and I are gonna be spendin' the Thanksgiving weekend in Gulf Shores, Alabama. We like to go there for the holidays because everyone usually stays home eating turkey, and we get to have the whole lovely beach to ourselves."

Oren let out a tiny, hardly noticed sigh of impatience, wondering where Sheila was going with this. Clint, however, maintained steady interest.

"We thought perhaps Clint might like to join us." Turning quickly to include Clint, she added, "If, of course, you like the ocean that time of year. Which I know some people don't, it really not being tanning or swimming season, you know."

Johnny wasn't happy that his wife had suddenly begun to sound like a rambling crazy woman. And he especially wasn't happy that she had chosen this particular moment to bring up her idea of taking Clint to the beach, because all it did was put Oren on the spot. What if Oren and Clint had other plans for their Thanksgiving holiday weekend? Sometimes Johnny wished that his wife wasn't so impulsive, although this character trait did come in handy about a half hour earlier when she had made him pull over on the way to the hospital so she could investigate a ball of fur she'd glimpsed beneath a parked pickup. The fur ball turned out to be Muffin, who was resting after her twenty-four-hour adventure, and who allowed Sheila to pick her up and put her in the car without complaint.

Oren was about to thank Sheila kindly for her offer and request that he and Clint be given some time to think about it, when Clint spoke up; he said it sounded like a lot of fun and yes, he believed he'd like to go. Clint's response caught Oren totally by surprise.

"Good," said Sheila. "We'll have so much fun. In the meantime you just concentrate on gettin' better. Oh, and when you're feelin' like your old self again, we'll have you and your dad over for a pool party. How would you like that?"

"That'd be great." Clint was thinking about how Sheila had looked in her bathing suit the day before. It hadn't made a tremendous impression on him at the time because of all the other stuff that was going on, but now he faintly recalled a very shapely chest with curves. He wouldn't mind seeing those smooth curves again—the sooner the better.

37

Be filled with the Spirit;
speaking to yourselves in psalms and hymns
and spiritual songs,
singing and making melody in your heart to the Lord.
Ephesians 5:18 & 19

Talitha took a spoonful of bran flakes into her mouth but the taste was strange, and it took a concentrated effort to follow through with a swallow. "This milk tastes weird," she confided to Joy who was sitting across from her at the communal dining table.

"It's soy milk," Joy replied. "You'll get used to it."

"I prefer real milk on my cereal, if you don't mind."

The young man whom Talitha recognized from the photograph hanging on the wall in her room spoke up: "We are strict vegans, Blithe." Talitha didn't think the man was all that bad looking but she didn't much care for his pale and pasty complexion—an obvious sign of deficiencies in the diet.

"You don't have to kill a cow to get milk," Talitha said, plucking a couple of grapes from the communal fruit bowl in the middle of the table.

"Milk is for calves, Blithe," said a pretty, waxen-looking girl with almost powder white hair.

"I don't think I'm gettin' enough protein from this meal. I must have my protein." Talitha tried to sound as querulous and demanding as possible. "I cannot turn my life around if you're plannin' on starving me to death first."

The waxen-skinned girl who had introduced herself to Talitha as "Hope" but whose name Talitha had immediately forgotten because of its abstract nature said in a very sweet and accommodating voice, "If you'd like, we can make you a hardy bean soup for your lunch. There's plenty of protein in legumes."

Valor agreed with an enthusiastic nod.

Talitha shook her head. "Sorry, folks. This just ain't workin' out." She pushed her chair away from the table and was ready to leap to her feet and make a mad dash for the door that she had earlier decided

151

seemed the most likely to lead to the outside world when she felt a hand on her shoulder. Slowly and apprehensively, Talitha shifted her gaze to the hand. She reminded herself of a character in a B horror movie, certain that some sort of perilous creature was lurking behind her, yet too paralyzed by fear to flee for her life.

The hand was smooth and pink and chubby. Talitha's eyes worked their way up to the face by way of a wrinkled khaki work shirt. The face was also smooth and pink and chubby. "You must be Pud," she said.

The short, stocky man grinned and nodded, then declared in a raspy, slightly nasally voice, "And you must be that drunk, drugged-out girl who needs to reorder the priorities of her life."

"I'm not drunk or drugged-out anymore," Talitha retorted, then added somewhat pleadingly, "And I promise to reorder my priorities, but you just cannot keep me here against my will. It isn't right. Besides which —" She now set her jaw in defiant indignation. "I absolutely refuse to live in a house without any people of color. You're all way too white for me, I'm sorry."

"We have a person of color here, Blithe. It's you," said Hope. "And someday we'll have people of all colors and nationalities in our joyous family, all doing the wondrous work of the Lord. 'Red and yellow, black and white—all are beautiful in His sight!'"

Hope clasped her hands together in a display of silent rapture.

"And I'm going to remind you once again, Blithe," said Joy, "you are *not* here against your will. You signed the contract for a life worth living."

Hope nodded in agreement. She had just finished taking a big drink from her glass of soy milk, and wore a white mustache.

Pud picked off a few of the grapes from the bunch in the fruit bowl, and put them between his lips and teeth so that he looked like a funny gorilla man. Everybody but Talitha laughed. "You'll like it here," Pud said, although all Talitha heard was, "You—loo-hoo." As Pud spoke, a couple of the grapes shot out of his mouth and across the table.

Valor gave Pud a look of mild disapproval, then said, "Of course she'll like it here. This is a happy, caring place. Now, we should go into the fellowship room. It's time for Bible study."

Talitha didn't want to go into the fellowship room and study the Bible. She wanted to cry. This was a horrible thing to happen to a person. She'd read about cults and their success at brainwashing people. Unless she could find some way to escape, the life she knew and loved (despite all its crimps and wrinkles) might truly be over.

"Be happy. Rejoice in the Lord," Joy said, sensing Talitha's despondence.

"I'm concerned about my sister—my sister Nancy Leigh. She's probably very worried about me right now. She probably thinks somethin' terrible has happened to me."

Valor thought about this for a moment, then said, "You will have to write her and let her know you're all right."

"I'd rather give her a call. Where's your phone?"

Valor shook his head. "We try to minimize our contact with nonbelievers." Valor got up from the table and carried his breakfast dishes off into the kitchen, which Joy, for some reason not revealed to Talitha, called the "galley." From the door to the galley Valor said, "No phone. No fax."

"We don't have a radio or television either," Hope added. Everyone was clearing the table now except for Talitha, who had suddenly become very depressed and was staring listlessly into her bowl of bran flakes in soy milk. Apparently Pud had eaten breakfast earlier while Talitha was still in her room. Given his girth, it looked to Talitha that Pud was in the habit of eating very large breakfasts.

After the table was cleared, Joy gave Talitha a piece of canary yellow stationery and a pen. "Here, you write a letter to your sister, and we'll take it to her."

"You won't, like, censor it or anything, will you?" Talitha asked, her eyebrows raised expectantly.

"Well, it depends on what you plan to say." Joy patted Talitha on the back and went to fetch her Bible for Bible study. Left alone for the moment, Talitha divided her gaze between the blank piece of stationery, and the door. Then, suddenly sensing that someone was watching her, she turned to discover Pud, who was now regarding her curiously. He was also picking at his teeth with the fingernail of his right pinkie.

"I was just like you about six months ago," he said confidentially. "Now look at me, praise the Lord."

"You mean you were also kept in this place against your will?" Talitha tried to keep her voice low so that no one but Pud could hear.

"I wouldn't say *that*. I'm just sayin' I was as mixed up as you were. But none of that matters now. Because now I get to come and go as I please, and I've decided to stay. This is a nice place. You'll do just fine here." Pud paused for a moment, then added, almost as an afterthought, "In case you're thinkin' about leavin': it's pretty easy to get outside, but you really wouldn't want to unless Valor's tied up the dobermans. They don't take to strangers too well."

Talitha suddenly felt a little sick to her stomach. This may have been partly due to her hangover, or to the soy milk, or it might very well have been due to the fact that she had always had an intense fear of angry dogs growling and salivating and baring their teeth. She tried to cover her queasiness with a weak smile.

Pud wasn't fooled. It was like he said: he'd been there.

38

Read this, I pray thee.
Isaiah 29:11

Oren pulled his Duster into the back parking lot on the Bible Methodist Church grounds and parked it in the spot reserved for "Pastor." Then he turned to Clint, who was sitting next to him. "You sure you'll be okay if I run in for a minute?"

"I'll be fine, Dad." Clint was drumming his fingers on the game box in his lap. Oren couldn't tell if he was in pain or simply making percussive accompaniment to some song playing in his head.

Oren had wanted to take Clint straight home but got to thinking that there might be things of timely importance at the church he needed to see to—things that the church secretary wasn't about to call him up and worry him about since he seemed to have enough to worry about already. Nina was very protective of Oren.

Nina was surprised to see Oren standing in the doorway leading into the church administrative office—so surprised, in fact, that her fingers lost their placement on the office computer keyboard where she had been updating the church membership roster. As a result of this slip she accidentally changed the sex of choir director Brandon Holbrook.

"What are *you* doin' here?" she declared.

"I'm on my way home with Clint."

"Oh, they're lettin' him go home. That's wonderful!"

"Yes, he's a very fortunate young man. Nina, I was just wondering if there was anything you thought I should attend to before tomorrow."

Nina shook her head. "It's been pretty quiet the last two weeks. I paid Mr. Maslow for plastering that water spot in the ceiling in the eight- and nine-year-olds' Sunday school room. The plumber—what's his name—Mr. Novik said you should be expectin' a bill from him for fixin' the sink in the ladies' rest room. Madeleine had her baby. It's a seven-pound little girl. Livia wants you to continue to remember her mother in your prayers; the poor thing was just diagnosed with a prolapsed lung."

"I don't know what that is."

"I don't either, but it sounds serious. Oh, and this came for you—

155

hand-delivered this mornin' by a girl from the Orient." Nina held out a sealed envelope on which were written the words, "Personal for Reverend Cullen."

"The girl didn't look troubled or anything," Nina continued. "Maybe she's got a friend in need of counselin'."

"Thank you, Nina," Oren said, stuffing the letter into one of his back pockets. "Clint's out in the car. I'm going to take him on home. Call me if anything comes up, all right?"

"All right. You got some sun, I see, out there at the children's camp."

"I guess I did," Oren said.

"I know they say sunshine's not supposed to be good for you, but I don't care. I just think a good tan makes a person look healthy."

"I guess you're right about that," Oren said. Then he nodded a couple of times and moved toward the door. "Okay, well, I'll see you tomorrow."

"See you tomorrow mornin', Reverend Cullen."

After Oren left, Nina sat for a moment thinking about how lonely it was in the church office when the Reverend Cullen wasn't around. Leonard Mitchell, the church custodian, wasn't good company because all he ever wanted to talk about was how overworked he was, and how much he'd like to take off and go fishing for crappie.

"I'm pretty sleepy," Clint said when he and Oren got home a few minutes later. "I'm goin' to my room and lay down."

Oren agreed that this was a good idea. He asked Clint if there was anything he needed. Clint said no. Oren said he'd check in on him a little later.

Oren gave his still unpacked suitcase, which he'd dropped right by the front door, a long, disdainful look. "Get to that later," he mumbled to himself as he moved to his antique roll-top desk and prepared to tackle the small mound of mail Clint had deposited there over the course of the previous two weeks. As he sat down, though, he could feel the corners of the small envelope Nina had given him poking into his thigh. He pulled it from his pocket and opened it. The letter inside was written in pencil and signed, "Your friend Desiree." He read it with great interest:

Dear Oren,
    I sent Ling Sue to the church with this letter after I

lost the nerve to call you. I heard about what happened to your son and was very shocked and saddened by the news. I hope he is doing better and nothing was broken that could not be mended. I realized as I sat by that phone wanting to call you that I have more reason to speak to you than just an interest in the health of your son.

Oren, I would like very much to have you for a friend. I have known very few men in my life who did not look at me in a certain way. I think you know the way I'm talking about. Not to say that with some of these men I didn't want to be looked at or felt about in that way. But there are times when I also want a friend. I am not one of these people who think that men and women cannot be good friends.

Please understand that this does not have to do with the fact that you are a minister. In other words, I do not seek a friendship with you as a way to guide me down the right path. I happen to think my life today is not all that dissolute regardless of what some may say. My faith is not all that strong, I'll admit it, but I am making some definite changes for the better. I just refuse to believe that I am doomed to spend eternity gnashing my teeth and renting out my clothes.

If you'd like to take me up on my offer of friendship you may drop by my house of massage on any Tuesday night when I am sure to be home because this is the night we are closed, and I always insist that Bibi and Ling Sue leave me the house to myself so that I may curl up in bed and relax with a glass of white wine and one of my racy novels or one of my favorite Elizabeth Taylor movies.

Your friend?
Desiree

Oren read through the letter two more times, then slid it back into its envelope and locked it safely away in the bottom drawer of his desk. Then he went outside to pick up the scatter of small broken branches that had blown into his front yard during the windstorm that had hit Higby while he was away. Oren considered himself lucky; some of his neighbors had lost much larger branches and even a few saplings. In Clancy Point a few miles south of town the storm had downed power lines and flipped over at least one trailer home, coincidentally while its occupants were watching a program on the Discovery Channel called "Angry Skies: Clouds of Woe."

Oren always thought best while doing yard work. The more mindless the labor, the better.

And he *did* have something that needed long and serious thought: the letter he'd just received from Desiree Parka.

Well, of one thing he was certain: a Tuesday night meeting with Desiree Parka was totally out of the question. Tuesday was his adult Bible class night.

39

*If I justify myself,
mine own mouth shall condemn me.
Job 9:20*

Marci couldn't keep her mind on her work. She had a stack of automobile insurance claim forms that needed to be filed away, but all she could think about was Stewie. She felt very guilty about what she had said. Especially the part about Stewie burning in hell for sleeping with another woman. After all, it wasn't as if Marci and Stewie were married. And the relationship was pretty much "dead in the water," as her friend Naomi Sailor liked to say.

Or was it?

Marci wished that she hadn't stormed out of Stewie's apartment without even saying anything to Tie. She should have at least waited for him to come out of the bathroom so the two of them could talk. Then she'd have a better idea as to how he felt about her. And if it turned out that he was madly in love with her, then maybe how she felt about Stewie being with other women wouldn't matter so much.

Or would it?

Marci sighed. She dropped all the unfiled forms into her overburdened "in" box. Then she closed the file cabinet drawer, hearing it latch with a satisfying metallic clack. A moment later she was poking her head into Jory's private office and saying, "I'm gonna take a little break. I'll be next door if you need me."

Jory nodded his consent. He was tied up on the phone, listening with flagging interest to a policyholder describe the hail damage which her Range Rover had sustained during a recent road trip through Oklahoma.

Marci stepped out onto the concrete walk that connected Jory Adams's State Farm Insurance Office with the offices of Vanity McElroy's Real Estate Professionals. The air was thick and warm. She could feel the heat steaming up into her cream- and taupe-striped dress slacks. Her friend Naomi Sailor waved at her through the large real estate office window. Naomi was one of Vanity's two secretaries. Unlike her counterpart Trish Brashears, who was currently on vacation, Naomi was studying nights to become a real estate professional herself.

Naomi opened the door and ushered Marci in. "How was your weekend?" she asked merrily. "I didn't see you at the picnic."

Marci moved a pile of colorful apartment complex brochures from the chair next to Naomi's desk, and sat down. "It started out fine. It ended in disaster."

"What do you mean?" Naomi looked very concerned. Marci knew she had come to the right place, and related the events of the previous twenty-four hours in great detail. She was careful to omit, however, certain intimate particulars, her belief being that private physical moments between a man and woman should be kept in sacred confidence.

Naomi was an eager vessel for everything Marci had to say. Her summer had been a fairly uneventful one and she was regretful. "Does Tie love you?"

Marci said she wasn't sure.

"You said he was fun and thoughtful and good-tempered. Maybe he *does* love you. And I'll bet you love him too. He's really cute, Marci. Forget about Stewie. Stewie's yesterday's news."

"I am *tryin'* to forget about Stewie, but it just isn't all that easy." Marci noticed that Naomi had a few tiny white hole-punch circles static-clinging to strands of her frosted bangs. She flicked them off for her.

Naomi thanked Marci and then said, "You've told me a million times how tired you are of Stewie and that religious way he's been actin'."

"But maybe it's just a phase. What if he's comin' out of it? Naomi, I already told you: he slept with this woman—a total stranger. I don't believe born-again, Christian men are supposed to do that."

Naomi smiled, her lips curling back enough to display a mouth full of only slightly tobacco-yellowed teeth. "All men are weak in that department—the bad ones *and* the good ones. Look, forget about Stewie's faith for a minute. You also said he was boring. You said he had no adventurous spirit whatsoever. Did you change your mind about that too?"

"No." Marci thought about this important point for a moment, then said, "But Tie's kinda boring too. Actually, most of the men I've ever been out with have been boring."

"Welcome to the real world, girl," Naomi said. "Most guys have the personalities of houseplants. So what you do is you just dismiss personality altogether, and go for looks. And I gotta tell you, if there was a Miss America Pageant for guys, Tie would win hands down. Stewie wouldn't even take Magnolia County."

Marci took moderate offense at this: "Excuse me, but I think Stewie Kipp has some very nice features."

"Yeah, for a horse. Hey, suit yourself. I just think you're kidding yourself, is all. You don't feel anything for him, be honest. You just got comfortable havin' him around. He's like some ratty old house slippers you can't bring yourself to throw out. I also think you're maybe just a little bit jealous."

"Jealous?"

"Yeah, because you're the only woman he's been with for the last three years, and now all of the sudden you find him in bed with that silicone queen. Let go of it, girl. Let him have his fun, and you go have *your* fun. See what develops with Tie, and if nothin' does, well, no big loss. Just make sure you give him my number." Naomi winked.

Marci was ready to end the conversation and go back to work but Naomi didn't feel like getting back to work just yet. She suggested, instead, that the two go for coffee and little nutbread squares at the Singing Kettle two doors down from Vanity McElroy's Real Estate Professionals. Naomi knew that Marci could never pass up the Singing Kettle's tasty nutbread squares. Suddenly Marci was glad to have Naomi for a friend, even though Naomi didn't always say the things that Marci wanted to hear.

While the two women continued their discussion over cups of steaming hazelnut coffee, Stewie, who had walked into Jory Adams's State Farm Insurance Office just moments after Marci's departure, was listening with growing impatience to Jory's generous golf tips—tips that would have been much better appreciated if Stewie had ever played the game.

40

Let no man therefore judge you.
Colossians 2:16

"Is that your friend Stewie in there with Jory Adams?"

"I can't tell."

"Wonder what kind of insurance he needs. Slow down. This car is a death trap as it is."

Euless tried to keep his eyes on the road, but every now and then felt obligated to check on his mother. She seemed to be sinking right down into the other gutted bucket seat of the Chevette. Euless had officially put the car into service the night before. Among its many problems was a left front tire with an erratic leak and bucket seats that had fed numerous rodents during the car's many years of disuse.

As for Euless's truck, it was still operable, but just barely; being rear-ended had thrown everything out of alignment. The axle and frame were now all bent up, the warped drive shaft scraping so loudly against the undercarriage that Euless was convinced he'd woken up half the town of Higby during his extended hobble home.

"So what did you decide? Can I tell Tula or not? She's my best friend." Flora found a sticky spot on the dashboard and began to fish a premoistened towlette from her purse.

"Just make sure she keeps it to herself."

Flora was about to respond when the Chevette's right front tire dipped into a pothole. The jolt caused the glove compartment to pop open. Several very old Esso and Sinclair courtesy road maps expanded accordion-like onto the sticky compartment shelf. "I've got 'em! I've got 'em!" Flora exclaimed, shooing Euless's hand away. As she stuffed the maps back where they'd been, Flora guessed, for the last fifteen years, she declared, "Well, I just don't understand it. If I was you, I'd just be bustin' to tell everybody in town about my good fortune."

"First of all, Mama, that Ricky Day may have gotten it all wrong. You know, there were times when Mr. Pomeroy wasn't really of a right mind."

Flora interrupted her son: "Now you stop right there. Mr. Pomeroy had a real fondness for you. It was plain to see. Now he probably didn't

163

enjoy your company as much as he did that Ricky boy, because not to speak ill of the dead, but I do think there was somethin' a little funny goin' on between those two, or else he wouldn't have gone all the way down to New Orleans that time to see the boy do that Katharine Hepburn tribute."

"It wasn't Katharine Hepburn, Mama. I think it was *Audrey* Hepburn."

"Mother, daughter, what's the difference?"

Euless was ready to say how he hated it when his mother jumped to conclusions about people when he spied his surviving employer Saul Josephs crossing Church Street about half a block ahead. Euless slowed down and stuck his head out the window. "Hey, Saul!"

Saul walked a little crooked as if one of his legs was out of joint. "Mornin', Euless," he responded grumpily.

Euless pulled to the curb and waited for Saul to shuffle over to the car. "Okay for me to come in a little late?" Euless asked. "I gotta get my mama home."

"Take your time. I'm goin' home myself and take a nap. That is, if Rebecca hasn't changed all the locks. Good mornin', Ms. Ludlam."

"Good mornin', Mr. Josephs," Flora said formally. Flora had a habit of always being polite and respectful toward all of Euless's employers; this way she hoped to help her son stay employed longer.

Saul asked what was to be done with the Skylark, and Euless said he'd check with Carmen to see if she wanted them to sell it to Mr. Galvin for parts over at the scrapyard. Then Saul asked Euless if he knew there'd been an old mangy dog living in the Chevette. (Euless wasn't aware.) Before departing for his nap Saul complimented Flora on her new hairstyle. It really wasn't all that new; she'd had this slightly looser, less blue and more silvery perm for at least two weeks now, but she appreciated the friendly comment nonetheless.

When Euless had pulled back into the light traffic on Church Street Flora said, "Anyway, I believe you're gonna get that money so I don't see any harm in lordin' it over some people."

"What people?"

"All the folks in this town who thought you'd never amount to much."

Statements like these coming from his mother didn't usually sit well with Euless. "Mama, I never got the impression that people were thinkin' about me one way or another."

"Oh, you just weren't paying a lot of attention, honey. Why, I remember when you were a little fellow, Mr. Percy down at the grammar school almost didn't let me enroll you in first grade because he thought you were a retarded child in need of special schooling. I had to make a real stink."

"I never knew that."

"Well, I hadn't planned on ever tellin' you because I thought it would hurt your feelings, but now that you seem to have all this money comin' and a wonderful future in commerce ahead of you, I don't think it would do any harm for you to know a few things."

"What did Daddy think about me?"

"Your father loved you very much."

"Did he think I was retarded?"

"Why, of course not! Maybe he didn't think you'd turn out to be as successful as he was, but never for a minute did he think you were slow. Only different. Not slow."

"I don't know what that means."

"It doesn't matter. Watch the road."

As Euless pulled into Flora's driveway, Liam Haas, who was watering his rose bushes, greeted his favorite neighbor and her son with an exuberant wave. It was Liam who had driven Flora over to Euless's mobile home the night before. Flora didn't own a car, and what's more, didn't know how to drive. Most of the places she needed to go—to the supermarket or her friend Tula Gilmurray's house, for example—were in easy walking distance. But whenever the weather turned inclement or she felt inclined to visit her son Euless on the other side of town, she'd have to get Liam to give her a lift.

He didn't mind. Liam Haas, unlike most of the other people Flora knew in town, enjoyed her company. The more sour her mood, the more he wanted to be with her. Sometimes he'd ask her straight out to belittle and denigrate him. She'd shake her head bemusedly and say that he was the strangest man she knew.

Then she would obligingly call him unflattering names.

"Good-bye, Mama," Euless said, after Flora had gotten out of the car. "I hope your neck gets better."

"The stiffness is gone already. Do you want to come in and have some coffee cake?"

"No, I really better go."

"Look at this. I have dog hair all over my dress."

"Yeah—sorry."

"That's all right. I'll just use the lint roller when I get inside. I can't believe you're gonna be a millionaire."

"I can't either. Well, I'm gonna go now."

"All right. Do you think I can have a white rabbit fur coat?"

"If you want one." Flora was holding the passenger door open, not letting Euless pull it shut. She had a thoughtful expression on her face; she was considering how she'd look in a new rabbit fur coat. "I really have to scoot, Mama." Euless tugged on the door until Flora finally had to let go.

"Bye. I'll call you later."

As Flora was watching her son's car turn onto School Street and disappear from view, Liam walked over, his garden hose still dribbling water. "I wore these red and green striped pants just for you, Flora," he said. "I know red and green are your two favorite colors." The water quickly began to make tiny rivulets in Flora's driveway.

"Well, you shouldn't have bothered," Flora said, making no effort to be polite. "Those pants are old and out of style. You look like an overgrown Christmas elf."

"I thought you'd like 'em."

"Well, think again."

"I guess that was a pretty stupid assumption on my part. I guess I'm a pretty stupid man, aren't I, Flora?"

"Yes you are. I don't know anybody stupider than you, Liam. Would you like to come in for some coffee cake?"

"Yes, I believe I would. I do love coffee cake."

41

Make haste, my beloved,
and be thou like to a roe
or to a young hart upon the mountains of spices.
Song of Solomon 8:14

"Is there somewhere we can go to talk?" Stewie asked Marci upon her return to the State Farm office. "How about we get some coffee cake at the Singing Kettle?"

Marci noticed that Stewie had a very earnest look on his face—even more earnest than usual. "I just had my break. Besides, I was just at the Singing Kettle. They'll start to think I have an eating disorder." Marci said this while trying to dislodge a little sliver of walnut from between two of her upper front teeth.

"Then you name the place. Jory says it's all right. I asked him."

Marci sat down behind her desk and flicked her IBM Selectric type-writer on and off in an intentionally lackadaisical manner. "I guess we could sit in your truck for a few minutes."

Once the two were inside the cab of the pickup, Stewie's expression grew even more grave. He took off his John Deere cap and mopped his moist, high forehead with the sleeve of his work shirt. "I'm really sorry about this mornin'."

Marci nodded. After a brief, uncomfortable silence she said, "Well, I'm sorry I said I wanted you to burn in hell. I didn't really mean it. Did you really mean what you said about us breakin' up?"

Stewie took a long breath and closed his eyes. He'd been rehearsing all morning what he was going to say to Marci when the two of them were finally alone; he hoped to be able to express in a very gentle and thoughtful manner that it was time for them to go their separate ways, that they'd had something very special at one time, but at this juncture in their lives—he liked the word "juncture" and wished that he had the opportunity to use it more often—they no longer had anything in common, their needs being so different now. And it would be best if they could part as friends.

However, what came out, much to Stewie's chagrin, was, "I don't think I love you anymore."

Suddenly Marci was seized with the desire to throw open the door and flee. Fighting the impulse, and looking right at Stewie, the pain transparent in her pale blue eyes, she said softly, "In what way do you not love me anymore?"

"I don't know. I just don't think I have the feelings I used to. And I bet you don't either. Admit it."

"I thought I didn't. But then this mornin' after spendin' the night with Tie, I found myself thinkin' about you a lot."

Stewie said in a quiet voice, "I think about you a lot too, Marci. But that doesn't mean we should stay together. There's so much about me that you don't like and there are things about you, you know —"

"That *you* don't like? Like what? Tell what it is that you don't like about me. If it's somethin' other than my cup size, maybe I could change."

"You shouldn't have to change. Not for me, not for anybody. You should stay just the way you are. Because that way somebody'll come along, you know, like Tie for example, who'll accept you and love you for who you are."

"That was very sweet, Stewie."

"Well, I mean it."

"I'll miss you."

"I'll miss you too, Marci."

"I guess you really like Jeannie."

"Maybe I do. Tie's a pretty good guy."

"I suppose so." Marci slid a few inches closer to Stewie and then said, "Can we kiss good-bye?"

Stewie nodded. Then he took hold of Marci's shoulders and drew her face close to his. He looked into her eyes for a moment. He could see his own reflection, his face looking a little distorted, kind of pear-shaped. Marci closed her eyes and let her head tip back a little.

"I'll always have a special place in my heart for you," he said with sincere, whispery affection. Marci wished that she had put on more lip gloss as Stewie began to kiss her. Also, her chin and cheeks had become substantially chafed from contact with Tie's rough beard the night before, making her skin very sensitive to Stewie's touch.

It wasn't the best kiss she'd ever had, but Marci, caught up in the heady passion of the moment, allowed certain feelings to swell up inside her. "Make love to me, Stewie Kipp!" she erupted. "Make love to me once more before we part!"

Stewie pulled back. He gave Marci a quizzical look. Things had been going so well, he thought. He'd been right on schedule with his plan to say goodbye to Marci, then swing by Jeannie Plough's apartment on his way back to work and surprise her with a good afternoon kiss and a Filet-o-Fish sandwich which she'd mentioned liking the night before.

Now Stewie didn't know what he was going to do. Because he very much wanted to make love to Marci Luck one last time. The last is always the best, Coot Malloy, one of his buddies and coworkers at the Pomeroy Lumber Company, had once said. This was, of course, before Stewie met Marci and long before he became a born-again Christian and banished all thoughts of having himself as many short-term, sexually charged relationships as possible.

Marci offered Stewie her sexiest look, which included making her eyes into narrow slits, opening her mouth slightly and rolling her tongue around in an unpredictable pattern.

"There isn't time to take you to my apartment, and yours is even farther away," he finally replied.

"Then we'll just have to make do with some place closer by."

Stewie tried to recall if he and Marci had ever made love somewhere other than their two apartments; he drew a blank.

"Oh God! For the first time in our relationship we're gonna be daring and adventurous!" Marci felt a squeal coming on but suppressed it. "I know! I know! We'll go to that dental office at the other end of the shopping center. Naomi says they still haven't gotten a new tenant since Dr. Washburn lost his license for unsanitary practices."

"Does she have the key?"

Marci nodded excitedly.

"Is there *furniture* in there?"

Marci nodded again.

Stewie couldn't quite believe what he was agreeing to do. Never in his life had he been so sexually aroused—not even the night before when Jeannie had made him so crazy and desirous.

"You meet me in front of the dental office. I'll get the key from

Naomi." Marci was out of the truck before Stewie could say a word.

Naomi was more than willing to give Marci the key to the vacated dentist's office but first she had a couple of other things she wanted to say about Stewie Kipp.

"I've already heard your opinion on the subject of me and Stewie," Marci said testily, while snatching at the key which Naomi dangled playfully from its chain and kept yanking just out of Marci's reach. "And besides, I'm not tryin' to revive our relationship. I just wanna say goodbye in a way Stewie will always remember."

"I'll bet you do," Naomi replied with a leer.

"And I would thank you, Ms. Sailor, not to tell anybody where we are."

"Yeah, yeah, yeah." Now Naomi let the key chain drop from her hand. Marci caught it deftly right in midair, and breezed out the real estate office door. Naomi watched her friend make a hard right in the direction of the dental office. Several seconds passed before Naomi remembered something important; all the working dental chairs had been picked up by a furniture reseller the week before. All that was left behind was an old chair with a snapped center spring. She debated with herself for another minute or so over whether she ought to warn Marci away from it, then decided the odds of the couple wanting to make love in a worn-out old dental chair were pretty remote, especially with a big, inviting corduroy couch right in plain sight the moment you opened the front door.

"This couch looks pretty comfortable," Stewie said, holding Marci's hand as if the two were a happy young married couple picking out their first living room suite at a bargain furniture store.

"Oh we can do better than that," Marci responded, and pulled Stewie along with her through the waiting room and down a short corridor. She stopped at the door to the hygienist's room.

"Remember that movie we rented a while back about all those people in that ancient castle, you know, havin' feasts and makin' love all over the place?"

Stewie nodded. He remembered the movie well. He also remembered a certain throne in a certain scene in the movie, and the strange, almost acrobatic things that a beautiful young naked princess did with an equally young and handsome unclothed stable attendant.

"Could I pass for a princess?" Marci inquired with a wink as she stepped into the room.

Stewie nodded again. "You could be a queen."

As Marci reached for the buttons on Stewie's work shirt, Stewie began to kiss her excitedly on her lips, cheeks, and neck, all the while slowly easing her down into the broken dental chair.

Now Stewie was certain that Jeannie Plough wouldn't be getting a Filet-o-Fish sandwich that afternoon ... but suddenly he didn't seem to care anymore.

42

Children, obey your parents in the Lord:
for this is right.
Ephesians 6:1

"I made you a grilled cheese sandwich and some noodle soup. You getting a little hungry?"

Clint took off his headphones and looked up at his father who was standing in the doorway to his room. Oren was wearing a plaid apron. Clint thought it looked funny—kind of like a kilt.

"Yeah, I guess I could eat somethin'."

"Should I bring it back here or would you like to come join me in the kitchen?"

"I can eat in the kitchen. Oh, I was thinkin' I might go for a walk when I get through with lunch."

On their way to the kitchen Oren told Clint that it might be better for him to keep to the house for a couple of days. "And Ponce thinks it wouldn't hurt for you to put off starting back to school until next week."

Clint carefully pulled his body up onto one of the two stools at the kitchen counter. He picked up his grilled cheese sandwich with both hands. Clint liked the way Oren made grilled cheese sandwiches: he used lots of butter. The grilled bread always had a very rich flavor. Clint took a big bite. Before his next bite he said, "I won't go far. I've just been layin' around so much, I really need to get out and use my legs a little bit."

Oren looked at his own sandwich. Suddenly he didn't feel much like eating. "Well, I still think it would be best if you stayed here."

Clint didn't respond. He didn't feel like pushing it. For the next five minutes he ate his grilled cheese and soup in silence, his eyes directed down. Oren stood at the sink, looking alternately at his son sitting opposite him at the counter and out the nearby window at some wasps building a nest under the eaves. His sandwich grew cold in his hand.

When Clint was finished, he excused himself and returned to his room. Oren could hear the sound of his son's bedroom door being shut. Oren set his sandwich down on his plate, rinsed his hands under the kitchen faucet, then went out to the storeroom to look for the hornet and wasp killer. He remembered having bought an extra large-sized aerosol can earlier in the summer.

It took about twenty minutes for Oren to exterminate just about every bee, mud wasp and yellow jacket on his property. The next chore he could think up for himself offered an even greater challenge: straightening up the storeroom off the carport. Oren couldn't even remember the last time he'd tried to bring order to this tiny, dusty room filled with rusting tools and mice-gnawed cardboard boxes. Could it have been while Alice was still alive? That would have been over two years ago.

"I thought we gave you away," Oren said to Clint's child-sized bicycle, training wheels still attached. The bike was peeking out from behind an old weather-rotted screen door. Oren saw Clint proudly pedaling his new bicycle up and down the driveway. He rolled the bike out and looked it over. It was in sorry shape, the fenders bent and rusted, both tires punctured and deflated. He doubted that even Goodwill would take it. Clint didn't ride a bike anymore. He walked. Clint took lots of walks.

Oren decided he'd think about something else—*someone* else. This wasn't a difficult task.

If this were some magical fantasy world, he thought, where consciences were never consulted, and people did just what their selfish hearts desired—especially on Tuesday nights—life would be far easier, and infinitely more gratifying. Bible classes would be cancelled, friendly neighbors named Sheila and Johnny Billows would be summoned to come over and look after sons named Clint, and *then*, after having relieved oneself of the two biggest responsibilities of the evening, a person would be free to hop into his poky old Duster and drive to wherever he wished. Even if that destination happened to be Desiree Parka's Far East House of Massage—where, upon entry, one would most certainly find ... Heaven on earth.

But not in this world. And not given everything that was expected of Oren as both a father and a minister. Oren Cullen had come to the sad conclusion that these were two of the toughest and most thankless jobs in the world. He sometimes wished that he could take a long vacation from both—from a congregation that never seemed to appreciate the things he did for them, coming to him with only fears and complaints, and from a son who seemed to neither want nor need a father at all.

Oren pulled out a dusty old lawn chair and opened it up. He brushed away a swirl of sticky cobwebs from the seat and sat down to think. He was in a rebellious mood. Life had lost its pleasure for him. He took little joy and comfort from his faith. He couldn't remember the last time he'd truly been happy.

And six miles out Table River Highway lived a woman who wanted very much to make him happy.

Not in this world. Never in this world.

For the first time in months Oren laughed out loud. It felt good to laugh.

43

Blotting out the handwriting ...
which was contrary to us.
Colossians 2: 14

Talitha was having a hard time concentrating on the scriptures that were being read and discussed in afternoon Bible study. For one thing, she was gnawed by the fact that her bath hadn't gone well at all. She had flatly refused to remain in the tub for the length of time required for proper spiritual cleansing after she noticed that her fingers were beginning to prune up. Both of the attending Sisters of the Blessed Redeemer had withdrawn from the bathroom distraught and dismayed over the possibility that some of Talitha's sins might not have gotten completely washed away. And neither had thought to leave her a fresh towel.

Talitha was also unsettled by the inordinate amount of time it was taking Joy to get ready to go out and deliver the letter she had written to Nancy Leigh. Neither of the distaff members of the Brothers and Sisters of the Blessed Redeemer, Magnolia County, Mississippi Chapter, was permitted to wear makeup, and just how long does it take, Talitha wondered, for a person to throw on an ugly floral housedress?

Just as Talitha had finished reading aloud, at Valor's request, First Corinthians, Chapter 13, verses 11 through 13, Joy strolled into the fellowship room wearing a different ugly floral house dress than the one she had been wearing earlier. Her hair was pinned severely to her head. She looked to Talitha like a woman who was preparing to put on a wig. Yet there didn't seem to be any wig in sight. Talitha remembered how Hope had responded earlier in the Bible study session when Talitha had asked her, irrelevantly, why neither she nor Joy wore any makeup: "We do not believe that women should adorn themselves excessively. We are all naturally beautiful in God's eyes."

To this Talitha replied, "Well, I certainly wouldn't call a little base, a hint of blush and maybe some lipstick in a muted color 'excessive'"

"*We* do, and we happen to believe that God does too."

"What about lip gloss?"

"The point is that beauty comes from what we are, not from what we do to ourselves. Besides, men do not feel such a need to change their appearance."

This statement made Talitha laugh out loud. "You're tellin' me, girl! I'll drop dead the day I meet a guy who takes the time to make himself look halfway presentable to a woman. You wouldn't believe some of the slobs I've been out with."

"Our newest member asks a lot of questions," Valor observed with a curious smile. "Questions are fine, Blithe, and we'll try to answer them whenever possible, but you must learn to pose them in a more respectful way. Now, Pud, I believe it's your turn for scriptural interpretation. Tell us what Paul meant by 'I see through a glass darkly.'"

Talitha noticed that Joy was still holding the letter for Nancy Leigh in her hand. Pud had read it first and struck through two lines that he felt might be a little alarmist: "Help! Help! I've been kidnapped by a religious cult and am being brainwashed even as you read this!" and "There are bloodthirsty doberman pinchers who will eat me alive if I try to escape!" At first Pud had merely been troubled by the misspelling of the word "pinschers." Then he had second thoughts and scratched through the whole sentence before passing the letter along to Joy.

Joy had wasted no time in making a few deletions of her own. She was particularly troubled by the sentence, "They only eat fruit, and I am not getting enough protein even as you read this!" Now the big question was whether Valor, too, would have to look over the letter before Joy took it away to be delivered to Nancy Leigh at the County Clerk's office.

"Well, I'll be going now," Joy said cheerfully. Joy welcomed any opportunity to go into town; there was always the chance she'd meet another Pud or Talitha—someone in desperate need of spiritual reclamation.

"Maybe I should take a look at Blithe's letter before you go," Valor said, extending to Joy an upturned palm. Talitha's heart sank.

"What's left of it, anyway," Pud laughed. He was holding his Bible in a careless way. It slipped from his grasp and fell to the floor. This gave Joy a little jolt.

"I'm just so glad that wasn't the King James Version you were so negligent with," she said. Joy wasn't alone in thinking that Pud still had some distance to go in his spiritual development.

Valor read the letter to himself, took a pen from his shirt pocket and inked through a few more lines. "All right. I guess you can take it now."

As Joy slipped the letter back into its matching canary yellow envelope Talitha reminded her that she'd left off the return address.

"You're a funny one," Joy said, and started out to the communal van. Talitha wondered what there could possibly be left for Nancy Leigh to read. Of course, if Nance is as bright as she wants people to think she is, Talitha thought, then maybe she'll be able to read *between* the lines.

Talitha surely hoped so. It would be nice to be rescued in time to make her Thursday night date with Vinny Greco; Vinny had phoned a couple of days earlier from Jersey City, New Jersey, to say he'd be hauling his rig through Higby on his way to New Orleans along about then and wouldn't mind seeing Talitha. The shipment was mostly women's undergarments, and Talitha had Vinny's permission to try on as many as she liked. Or, if she preferred, she didn't have to wear anything at all.

44

And the eyes of them both were opened,
and they knew that they were naked.
Genesis 3:7

Stewie couldn't speak. He'd never experienced pain and nausea this intense before.

"Are you all right? Stewie, honey, tell me you're all right."

Stewie wanted to answer. He *tried* to answer. But when he opened his mouth the only thing that came out was a squeak.

Hearing this, Marci's concern for Stewie's well-being rose to something just short of raw fear. She rolled over onto her side, and, preparing herself for the worst, tried to focus her contactless eyes on the fuzzy, fleshy mound that she assumed to be Stewie lying a few feet away. The linoleum floor felt cold against her hand and forearm.

Stewie lay on his back, his eyes open, staring up at the ceiling. He had a strange, almost unhuman grimace on his face. Marci noticed but did not dwell on the fact that both of his hands were cupped over his crotch.

"What's broken, honey? Your ribs? Did you snap your spine? Oh God, Stew, tell me you didn't snap your spine!"

In a pained voice that sounded like air being slowly released from a balloon, Stewie was finally able to say, "It's not my spine, Marci."

Marci began to extricate herself from the jumble of dental hardware that had rained down on top of the two of them after the chair in which they had been making love collapsed and pitched them naked and unprotected onto the floor of the hygienist's room, pummeled and pelted along the way by all manner of dental paraphernalia: flying drills, hand pieces, spongy bits of an old ripped headrest, as well as—among other things—a metallic instrument tray, ceramic cuspidor, and a broken saliva ejector. It took a moment for her to shake off all the equipment, the clanging and clatter echoing through the half-empty rooms of the dental office, and scramble-crawl over to where Stewie lay.

"Can I do anything? Please tell me what I can do to help!"

"You can look and tell me if it's all still there."

"If what's all still there?"

Stewie uncovered his groin. A surge of pain shot all the way up to his abdomen.

"You're all still there. I guess that really smarts," Marci said with a sympathetic frown. "As we were fallin', I sort of remember you bouncin' up and down on that arm rest like you were ridin' a buckin' bronco or somethin'."

Marci didn't think she'd ever felt more affection for Stewie than she did at this moment. It had to be the vulnerability thing—she was sure of it now. In fact, Marci wondered if maybe this was the reason she was having such a hard time getting turned on by Tie. Tie seemed too sure of himself, although in a naive, almost blundering sort of way. Marci kissed Stewie on the forehead.

"We sure took a fall, didn't we?" she said with forced buoyancy.

Stewie tried to smile. Marci was looking very attractive to him at just that moment, despite the waves of intense pain. Her hair was wet and tangly from perspiration, and hung down like dangling vines, tickling his chest. Her cheeks were red—hot-looking—like she'd just completed a long race in the summer heat. He reached over and touched one of her smooth thighs. It was cool from the floor.

"You're gonna be black and blue tomorrow," she laughed, "but I'll be the only one who knows it."

A moment later Naomi Sailor, with great clamor and fanfare, unlocked the back door to the dentist's office and escorted the Reverend Gordon Wedgerly and his dentist brother Dell inside. In an artificially loud voice she said, "WELL, HERE WE ARE, DOCTOR WEDGERLY—COMING RIGHT IN THROUGH THE BACK DOOR AND NOT THE FRONT DOOR. WHY DON'T WE START OUR LITTLE TOUR HERE IN THE HYGIENIST'S ROOM, SAVING, OF COURSE, THE WAITIN' ROOM FOR LAST."

Before it could even register with Marci and Stewie what was happening, the couple found themselves confronted by Marci's best friend, Stewie's pastor, and Stewie's pastor's dentist brother from Lansing, Michigan.

Naomi diverted her eyes, as did the Reverend Wedgerly. Brother Dell, however, took in the whole scene: flesh, rubble and all. Then he turned to Naomi and said matter-of-factly: "I don't lease the place unless you fix that chair."

With his back now turned, Gordon said in a grim, slightly uneven voice, "Stewie, I think that we should have ourselves a talk this evening. Can you come by my office around seven?"

"Yes sir," Stewie said. His voice sounded small and choked.

"I'll be waiting outside," Gordon announced to Dell and Naomi before fleeing the building.

Marci began to gather up all the clothes that had been flung wildly about the room during impetuous foreplay. Stewie, for the present, chose to remain right where he was. He wished that Naomi and his minister's brother would follow Gordon's example and depart as well.

"Naomi, I swear—if you did this deliberately, I'll never speak to you again!" Marci glowered at Naomi as she pulled her bra off the tube head of the x-ray machine.

"I thought you'd be in the waitin' room, Marci," Naomi said apologetically. "I brought 'em around back to give you time to escape out the front."

"I don't know if I believe you or not," Marci snarled. She was now feeling underneath the metal supply cabinet for Stewie's short-sleeved cotton work shirt.

"I did everything I could, Marci! I didn't know they were comin', and then when they *did* show up, I had to absolutely beg Vanity to let me be the one to bring 'em over here. I was afraid she'd take 'em right through the front door and into the waitin' room, and there you'd be—you know, kind of like you are now, except not all bruised and cut up."

Marci now found it difficult even to look at Naomi. She tossed Stewie his underpants. He was putting them on slowly and with great care when Dell announced that he'd seen enough of the hygienist's room and was ready to check out the rest of the suite.

Just prior to his departure Dell addressed Stewie: "I doubt it was worth it, champ, but I gotta admire you for trying."

"Look, I'll call you," Naomi said to Marci. "Oh no—who's gonna pay for all this?"

Marci didn't answer. Naomi shrugged and slipped quietly out of the room.

45

Cast me not off in the time of old age;
forsake me not when my strength faileth.
Psalm 71:9

Tula thought that Dr. Ostermeyer's office had an impressive number of diplomas and certificates on its walls, and she told him so.

"But you'll notice that not all of them are related to my education and accreditation, Ms. Gilmurray."

Tula examined the framed certificate hanging nearest her chair. It said, "For participation in the 'Save Our Trees' Benefit Bowling Tournament, February 13, 1987, sponsored by the Higby Arbor League."

"Oh, I remember this tournament," Tula said. "It was for a very worthy cause."

Klaus smiled and nodded in agreement. Then he cleared his throat and leaned forward across his desk, almost touching his forehead to the framed photograph of his wife Abbadene and fourteen- year-old daughter Micah next to his Rolodex. "So, Ms. Gilmurray, Abbadene said you wanted to talk about Hank."

Tula nodded.

"There's been a decline in his condition since I saw him last?"

"Yes. He seems to be losin' touch more often."

"That is unfortunate, although we had discussed the possibility that such mental deterioration might come sooner than we would like."

"I just didn't realize it would happen *this* fast." Tula was now picking nervously at the tiny bullets of colored glass that formed abstract patterns on her leatherine purse.

"Can you give me some examples—things he's said or done that make you think he's losing touch?"

Tula didn't have to think too hard: "Twice now in the last two days he's forgotten where he was. Last night he tried to walk home from the town picnic and got very lost."

"Well, I certainly recommend that you bring Hank in for another checkup, Ms. Gilmurray, and I wouldn't throw in the towel just yet. But at the same time, it wouldn't hurt to start thinking in terms of some form

185

of outside care for Hank."

"I don't think he's ready for a nurse, Dr. Ostermeyer."

"He *is* fairly ambulatory," Klaus said with an understanding nod. Then he smiled. "Maybe a little *too* ambulatory."

Tula accidentally pulled one of the bullets right off her purse. She held it tightly in her hand so she could glue it back on as soon as she got home. "Flora says that Medicare can give you an aide who visits your home about twenty hours a week. But they're really only there, as I understand it, to do basic things like bathe and feed a person, and Hank's still perfectly able to do those kinds of things on his own. What he really needs is somebody just to watch after him—you know, when I'm not able to—to be around to assure him that everything's all right when he forgets where he is or gets scared by something he doesn't understand. Is there such a person, Dr. Ostermeyer?"

"That you could hire? I don't think so, Ms. Gilmurray."

"I feel terrible sayin' this, Dr. Ostermeyer, but I just can't spend my whole day followin' him around to make sure he isn't alone when he gets disoriented like he does. And he wouldn't even let me if I tried. He'd just give up on wantin' to live if he thought he'd have to stop takin' his mornin' walks or goin' out to the garage by himself to work on his bird houses. But sometimes he has the scaredest look on his face when I walk in and everything's suddenly become so unfamiliar to him. I'm really stymied, Doctor. I just don't know what would be the best thing for him."

"*And* for you." Klaus said this with a gentle, knowing nod; it was important, he felt, for Tula not to feel the least bit guilty about expressing her own needs. "Now, I certainly understand how Hank values his independence, especially having spent so much of his life on the road, but he's going to have to be made to understand that his condition requires certain lifestyle adjustments—if for no other reason than for personal safety. You said he got lost last night. How long was he out there by himself?"

"About five or six hours."

"Not that you haven't already thought about it, Ms. Gilmurray, but any number of things might have happened to him in that period of time."

Tula nodded. This meeting with Dr. Ostermeyer, far from lifting her spirits, was making her feel worse than ever.

"I suggest that you start looking into a few of the nursing homes in our area."

"Oh, I couldn't possibly put Hank in a nursin' home!"

"It's just an option, Ms. Gilmurray."

Tula stood up. She was squeezing the colored glass bullet so tightly that it made her hand throb. "I could not put Hank in a place like that. In addition to which, I don't think he'd go. No, I'm *positive* he wouldn't go."

Now Klaus was standing too. "I understand how you must feel, Ms. Gilmurray."

"I'm sorry. I know I should be grateful for your advice. I am at my wit's end. You must understand this."

Klaus nodded. "You just give some thought to what I've said. I'll be happy to see you again whenever you wish."

"Thank you." Tula spoke in a tiny, tired voice.

"And don't forget to schedule an appointment for Hank on your way out."

Tula was so upset she didn't even acknowledge Abbadene as she hurried past the reception counter to the front door, let alone stop to schedule an appointment. Abbadene was on the phone and didn't look up until Tula was already gone.

46

Then shalt thou call ...
and he shall say, Here I am.
Isaiah 58:9

Every time Nancy Leigh called the Pomeroy Lumber Company she had to wait about five minutes for somebody to hunt Bowmar down. She could never understand why the Pomeroy Lumber people didn't employ a loudspeaker paging system like the ones used at all the car dealerships.

"Bowmar, I've been sittin' here tyin' up this taxpayer-paid-for telephone line for five whole minutes."

"I'm sorry, baby. I was helpin' Tie and Brady load up a shipment of yellow pine. The tongue and grooves are about as far away from this telephone as you can get."

A few minutes earlier Nancy Leigh had spilled her morning coffee all over Julian and Betty Jo Francescini's marriage license. She had tried to scrub the stain away with a homemade recipe offered by Pamela Lowden, the Magnolia County Clerk. It hadn't worked; it had, in fact, left one whole corner of the embossed document brown and unsightly. Nancy Leigh turned the license over so she wouldn't have to look at it. Bowmar now had her full attention. "I'm really worried about Talitha. She wasn't at home when I went by to pick her up this mornin'. No note. Nothin'."

"Did you call the Hospitality Inn?"

"Yes. She wasn't there either. *Or* at the Dollar Econo Motor Court. I'm just imaginin' horrible things, Bowmar."

"Yeah, I'll bet you are." Bowmar was using the phone on Grinnette Hubble's desk. Grinnette was sorting account payables and pretending not to listen, but Bowmar knew she was getting every word.

"Do you think it would be all right for me to call the police? Have I waited long enough?"

Bowmar turned away from Grinnette whose thick-lensed glasses made her eyes look equine. "I guess so. Just promise me that Ray Reese dude isn't gonna drive straight over here and harass me the way he did that time your aunt's purse got stolen out of her car at Holmes Food Village."

"You *are* an ex-convict, Bowmar. This happens to make you a prime suspect whenever a crime takes place."

In a slightly whiny voice that wasn't like him at all Bowmar said: "Now just how fair is that—a guy pays his debt to society —"

"I don't have time to talk about this right now, baby," Nancy Leigh interrupted. "I have to find out what's happened to my little sister. I'm gonna call Officer Tomley."

"Good. I like Avis. Call me back when you know somethin'."

Suddenly Bowmar found himself addressing a dial tone. "Conversation terminated," he mumbled to himself.

As he was returning the phone receiver to its cradle, Grinnette said, "Do you think Nancy Leigh's sister has met with some sort of foul play?"

"Now how do you know that's what this call was about?" Bowmar asked, a little irritated by Grinnette's eavesdropping.

"I can put things together. I wasn't born yesterday. I was born in 1947."

"Well, I'm pretty sure it isn't foul play, Grinnette, but just to be on the safe side, it's probably a good idea that Nancy Leigh's goin' ahead and callin' the police."

Grinnette agreed, then asked Bowmar if he wouldn't mind walking her home that night after work.

"It doesn't look like we're going to get that stain out, Nan," said Pamela, "so you'll have to call up the Francescinis and apologize. I just hope they weren't planning to buy an expensive frame and hang that license up over their mantel."

"All right," Nancy Leigh said, preoccupied with dire thoughts about her sister. Pamela went back into her office cubicle. Nancy Leigh was about to pick up the phone and dial the police when a woman with pinned-down orange hair, wearing a faded and aesthetically uninteresting floral print housedress approached the counter.

"May I help you?" Nancy Leigh asked mechanically.

"Yes. Will you please give this to Nancy Leigh? I believe she works here." The young woman placed an envelope on the counter.

Before Nancy Leigh could say that *she* was Nancy Leigh, the woman turned and trotted out the door. Nancy Leigh opened the envelope and quickly read the letter that was folded up inside. There wasn't much to read:

Dear Nancy Leigh, my loving sister:

XXXX! XXXX! XXXX XXXX XXXXXXXXX XX X
XXXXXXXXX XXXX XXX XX XXXXX
XXXXXXXXXXX XXXXX XX XXX XXXX XXXX!
XXXXX XXX XXXXXXXXXXXX XXXXXXXX
XXXXXXXX XXX XXXX XXX XX XXXXX XX X XXX
XX XXXXX! XXX XX

XXXXXXX XXXX XXXX XXX XXXXX XXX X XX
XXX XXXXXXX XXXXXX XXXXXXX XXXX XX XXX
XXXX XXXX! Now I don't want you to worry. X XXXX
XXXX XXX XX XXXX XXX XXXXXX XX, XXXX, X
XXXXXXX XXX XXX XXX XXX XXXX?

I love you very much. Did I ever tell you that? Give my
best to Bowmar. XXX XXXXXXX XXXXX. XXX XXXX
XXXXXXXXX XX XXXXXX XX X XXXXXXXX
XXXXXXXX.

Your loving sister,
Talitha.

Nancy Leigh was so disturbed by Talitha's letter that her body suddenly went limp. She had to lock her knees to prevent her legs from
giving way. Meanwhile her torso, with a mind of its own, propelled her
forward in a pronounced slump, splaying her upper body across the
counter, tipping over her coffee cup and spilling what was left of the hot
brown liquid onto yet another pristine marriage certificate.

"Oh shit!" she cried. This outburst brought Pamela from her cubicle.
"Oh Nancy Leigh! You simply must be more careful!"

But Nancy Leigh wasn't even listening to Pamela. She was flying
through the gate at the end of the counter and toward the door through
which the mysterious orange-haired courier had just made her hasty exit.

Nancy Leigh pushed open the large ornamental doors of the courthouse building. She squinted and blinked, trying to adjust her eyes as
quickly as she could to the bright afternoon sun. She surveyed the

southern perimeter of the square, looking for some sign of the woman in the unattractive dress. Just as she was about to give up, an odd-looking van appeared from beyond the west corner of the square. It sped past the front of the courthouse, then, with tires squealing, careened around the square's east corner and quickly disappeared. The vehicle, Nancy Leigh noted, had a curious picture painted on its side; it depicted a quartet of joyous young people in colorful exotic garb—two men and two women— their hands joined above their heads as if they were either shouting praises to the Lord or engaged in some sort of jubilant ethnic dance. Although tinted windows prevented Nancy Leigh from getting a look at the van's driver, the recognizable caricature of the redheaded woman in the picture told her exactly what she needed to know. The only problem was the license plate. It was hanging from a loose wire and swinging so wildly that Nancy Leigh couldn't read the numbers. Maybe it can be traced some other way, Nancy Leigh thought. In any event, it was defi-nitely time to involve the authorities.

47

She will do him good and not evil.
Proverbs 31:12

Over a tasty lunch of tuna salad on toast, Frito chips and a Bartlett pear with only one tiny bad spot on it, Carmen made an important decision: she would get herself another car. And the sooner, the better. Without a car she would be seriously inconvenienced. After all, Higby didn't have a public transportation system, and Carmen just didn't feel right about imposing on her neighbors or members of her church whenever she needed to get across town. Higby did have a taxi service but its primary driver bore too uncomfortable a resemblance to Mr. Tazewell, a family friend who, when Carmen was a young child, sought to amuse her by rearranging the folds of skin on his craggy face with his elderly twig-like fingers and ended up frightening her nearly witless.

And walking was simply out of the question; any distance over half a mile usually produced painful tendinitis behind Carmen's knees.

The more she thought about it, the more Carmen became convinced that it was best not to put off the purchase. In fact, it was important for her to start comparison shopping that very evening. That is, if Euless really meant what he said about coming along with her. Was he just being polite, she wondered, or was he sincerely interested in helping her get the best car for her money?

"Euless cain't come to the phone right now."

Carmen didn't recognize the crackly teenaged voice on the other end of the line. "Are you Saul?"

"No, I'm Wayne Biddle. I assist Euless with transmissions." Euless had just requested that Wayne fetch him a three-quarter wrench from the Snap-On set when the phone rang. Saul was in the rest room where he usually spent about a half hour after lunch, and had hollered for somebody to "please get the damned phone because I don't wanna have to start all over again!" Now Wayne was flipping the wrench in his hand, wondering if Carmen might be Euless's girlfriend.

"Could you ask him to give me a call when he's free?"

"Sure. Who are you?"

"Carmen Valentine. I'm a friend of Euless's."

"Okay. Hey, are you that lady what talks to the angels? My mother says there's this lady here in Higby named Carmen who —"

"No. I don't talk to the angels. He has my number. Good-bye, young man."

Carmen hung up. She was not at all happy about being asked if she talked to angels. First of all, she only talked to one angel: her guardian angel. And second of all, she didn't plan on even talking to *her* again. Right before lunch and after much careful thought Carmen concluded that it was time to say good-bye to Arnetta. So she sat down and wrote her a long letter. In the letter Carmen explained that while she appreciated everything that the heavenly spirit had done for her in the past, she'd reached a point in her life when she just didn't feel she had to be looked after anymore. In fact, if Euless became a permanent fixture in her life, she was afraid that Arnetta might even start to become somewhat of a nuisance.

It felt good to write the letter which she tucked into the Bible that lay on her night table right on top of her latest issue of *Southern and Sassy Magazine*. If felt good because of what it meant. Arnetta had been a real helpmate to Carmen after her parents died, but now that Carmen's emotional health had improved, her needs were different. "Not that I don't welcome the shopping tips," she had written, "but surely there are people down here with bigger problems than mine you could be helping."

She signed the letter, "Your Christian ward, Carmen," and then added a P.S.: "You will be pleased to know that I have been making quite a bit of eye contact lately. Especially with the aforementioned Euless. He is really something to look at."

Euless rolled out from under Tina Louise Sperly's Pontiac Grand Prix. His face and neck were smeared with so much grease and motor oil that Wayne thought he looked like an old timey-minstrel singer. "Hand me that towel over there," Euless said.

While Euless was wiping his face, Wayne said, "You got a call from a woman named Carmen Valentine. She said she's a friend of yours."

"Yes, she *is* a friend." Euless sat up and stretched his shoulders back. He felt a familiar crackle in his spine. Although Wayne couldn't tell, Euless was smiling—inside. He liked it that Carmen had referred to herself as "his friend." That was much better than "the woman who plowed into his truck last night."

Saul was out of the bathroom now and, as was usually the case following a successful postprandial bowel movement, in a breezy mood. Wayne took advantage of Saul's ebullience to ask if he could take off the upcoming weekend to drive up to Memphis to attend a rock concert.

"A rock concert don't last a whole weekend," Saul replied. "If it's a Saturday night, I'll let you leave a little early that afternoon."

This seemed good enough for Wayne, who went over and sat himself down on top of a stack of tires in one corner of the work area. Using his teeth, he tore open a small package of barbecue-flavored potato chips he'd just purchased from the vending machine in the customer service area.

As Wayne was crunching on his chips and noodling on an imaginary guitar, Saul drilled Euless about Tina Louise's car.

"'Be done with it by this afternoon," Euless responded, thinking about how good barbecue-flavored potato chips would taste with the ham and cheese sandwich his mother had made for him to take to work that morning. Euless didn't tell Saul that the reason Tina Louise's Grand Prix wasn't ready yet was because he had fallen asleep under it; Euless figured he'd probably been napping for about the last forty-five minutes.

During that time Euless dreamed that Ricky Day was actually a girl with long blond hair who spelled her name "Ricki" and that Conwell Pomeroy was just about to marry her when he died. Euless was supposed to be the best man, and Audrey Hepburn had been chosen for maid of honor. Euless didn't recall much more of the dream than that except that Ricki seemed to be in tears most of the time and said, given a choice, she'd prefer to have Conwell back and forget about all the money the old man was prepared to leave her.

Euless wondered why he hadn't dreamed about Carmen, who had definitely been on his mind prior to his learning that he was going to be a millionaire, but then he remembered what somebody had once told him about dreams: given a choice between dreaming about love or dreaming about money, you'll dream about money every time.

48

*Be not soon shaken in mind or be troubled,
neither by spirit, nor by word,
nor by letter.*
II Thessalonians 2:2

Avis switched on his desk lamp and held Talitha's letter up to the bulb. "Well, no doubt about it: they're holding her against her will."

"They are?" Nancy Leigh asked anxiously, sliding forward in her chair. Avis nodded. "You mean you can read the parts they crossed out?"

"A six-year-old could read 'em." Avis handed the letter to Nancy Leigh. He twisted the flexible neck of the lamp so she could see for herself. All the words Talitha had written came through clearly and legibly against the back light.

"Oh no!" Nancy Leigh exclaimed. "She's not getting enough protein! What are we gonna do?"

"You said they drove a van?"

"Yes, but I couldn't get the number off the license plate."

"Do you remember what the vehicle looked like?"

"I can draw you a picture. Or do you want me just to describe it to you?"

"Why don't you just describe it?" Avis pulled a pack of Camels from his uniform shirt pocket. Almost as an afterthought he asked Nancy Leigh if she minded if he smoked.

"Not if you blow it in the other direction."

Ray Reese walked up with an affidavit for Avis to sign.

Nancy Leigh closed her eyes and tried to picture the van. "It had faces on it. More than faces—more like busts. Painted on the side. One man and three women. No—two men and two women. They were all holdin' hands."

"I've seen that van," Ray said.

Nancy Leigh's eyes popped open. Avis turned and gave Ray a long stare, his forehead corrugating a little deeper than usual. "You're not just sayin' this to get attention, now are you, Ray?"

"No sir. I've really seen it. 'Couple of times. Funny-lookin' thing. At

197

first I thought they was maybe just passin' through town, but by the second time I figure it's gotta belong to somebody here in the county."

Avis asked Ray if he happened to get a look at the license plate. Ray shook his head. "I don't generally look at license plates, Avis, not without I got a reason."

"Thank you for the information, Ray. Why don't you give a call to Motor Vehicles and see if they can do anything for us without a tag number. Otherwise, all we can do is check out vans by sight. It might take a while. Magnolia ain't a small county."

"Sure thing, Avis—but don't you think since we're talkin' possible kidnappin', we oughta maybe bring in the F.B.I.?"

"Technically, it may not *be* a kidnapping. There hasn't been a ransom note, has there, Ms. Leigh?"

Nancy Leigh shook her head. Avis took a long draw off his cigarette, then blew the smoke out his nose. Nancy Leigh turned away; she hated to see cigarette smoke escaping from nostrils.

While glancing in the general direction of the large framed street map of Higby that hung on the wall behind her, Nancy Leigh said, "But you know, Officer Tomley, now that I think about it, she does state in her letter, 'Help! Help! I've been kidnapped by a religious cult and am bein' brainwashed even as you read this!'"

"The lady has a point," Ray said, resting his hand on the top of Avis's swivel chair and making it bend too far back for Avis's comfort.

Avis shook his head. "I don't read this as a textbook kidnapping. What I think has happened here, is that Talitha has fallen in with some religious zealots —"

"Who are holdin' her against her will!" Ray said excitedly.

"Ray, let go of my chair. You're pullin' me down to the floor."

As Ray moved a safe distance from Avis's chair, Nancy Leigh said, "I think Ray's right. I think maybe we *should* treat this like a bona fide kidnapping. Now, I won't make trouble if you don't wanna bring in the F.B.I. right off the bat, because this religious group, they probably don't intend to harm her—I mean, physically. But please just promise me you'll give this case top priority, because there's no tellin' what kinds of religious misinformation they're feedin' her right now. Plus, she's a very independent-minded girl, and for her to be kept in a situation where she has no free will, it'll totally destroy her spirit."

Avis nodded and said, "We'll find your sister, Ms. Leigh. Just give us a little time." Avis's voice, while far from sounding sufficiently paternal and understanding to Nancy Leigh's ears, at least had a ring of sincerity to it, and this made Nancy Leigh feel a little better.

"Ray, go on now and make that call. Ms. Leigh, I need you to give me a picture of Talitha so we'll have somethin' for identification purposes."

As Nancy Leigh was slipping a small photo of Talitha from the picture and credit card section of her wallet-clutch, Ray added, "In case they got her drugged or somethin', you know, and deny that she's Talitha."

Nancy Leigh didn't like to think that her sister might be drugged and unable to speak for herself. Not that Talitha hadn't on certain occasions found herself too intoxicated on tequila shots or Cuervo margaritas to even form coherent sentences. But these instances were always of Talitha's own making. This would be quite a different situation entirely.

Thinking about Talitha lying in a strange bed with her eyes rolled back and her tongue hanging limply from her mouth made Nancy Leigh shudder. Avis noticed, and for lack of anything better to do, offered Nancy Leigh a box of Kleenexes.

49

Faithful are the wounds of a friend.
Proverbs 27:6

Tula set her purse down on the small table in her front entry hall, then smoothed back her hair, which had been blown about on her drive home from Dr. Ostermeyer's office. "Hank? Hank, dear, I'm back. Are you upstairs?"

Tula waited a moment. She was just about to call out again when Hank answered: "I'm here. I'm in my bedroom."

Tula moved to the foot of the stairs. In a loud voice she said, "I just wanted you to know I'm home now if you need anything." Hearing no response Tula went into the kitchen. From the cookbook shelf of her pinewood cook's hutch she pulled down one of her least consulted recipe books, *Cooking on the Edge*. Tula was in the mood to prepare something exciting for dinner. Lately her meals had been a little on the unadventurous side. Without even realizing it she had made oven-baked chicken twice in the past ten days, and hadn't even varied the seasonings. Although Hank never complained, Tula was sure he would appreciate something exotic for a change.

Tula was sitting at the kitchen table leisurely turning the glossy pages of the amply illustrated cookbook, lingering over its brightly colored food-filled photographs, when the telephone rang.

She caught it on the second ring. Tula usually tried to answer her phone by the second ring; she considered this just good manners.

"Hello?"

It was Flora: "I'm glad to hear that Hank got home safe and sound thanks to my son Euless."

"Yes, I was so happy that it was Euless who found him."

"Tula, if I tell you somethin' wonderful will you promise not to breathe a word of it to another livin' soul?"

"Not breathe a word of *what* to another livin' soul?" Tula was about to sit back down, but now changed her mind.

"You have to promise me, Tula."

"All right. I promise."

"Euless is gonna inherit part of Conwell Pomeroy's ungodly fortune."

"How do you know?"

"That gay young hairdressin' man told him."

"What hairdressin' man?"

"That Ricky Day who Mr. Pomeroy used to pay to come all the way up from New Orleans to cut his hair. He said Mr. Pomeroy said the only two people he was leavin' his money to were him and Euless."

Now Tula sat down. "How do you know that boy is tellin' the truth?"

"Well, why would he want to lie about somethin' like that? Oh Tula, why are you tryin' to spoil my happy moment with doubts?"

Tula sighed, then said, "I didn't mean to spoil your happy moment. I just—well, I'm very happy for you, Flora. And for Euless too. I can't think of anyone who deserves that money more."

"I just had to tell you or I'd bust. I'm already thinkin' of things I've always wanted to buy but could never afford. Because I'm sure Euless will want to share it. I mean, the boy can't possibly spend all that money on himself even if he wanted to."

"Are you bein' practical, Flora, or are you dreamin' up things you don't really need?"

"I am bein' *very* practical if it's any of your business." Flora's voice had suddenly lost all of its cheer. "You know, Tula, I would have never thought you'd be so jealous."

Now it was Tula's turn to get angry. She slammed the cookbook shut. It had been opened to a large double-page photograph of a juicy, steaming shrimp casserole. The picture had only served to remind her that Higby grocery stores never carried shrimp that wasn't either popcorn-tiny or outrageously expensive. She was so tired of scrimping and cutting corners in her food budget to make Hank's and her pension and Social Security money go farther, and here Flora was calling her up just to gloat that the Ludlams were about to become rich beyond anyone's imagination. "I am not jealous," Tula protested between clinched teeth.

Tula sometimes wished that she were the kind of person who could hang up on somebody and not feel guilty about it for weeks. Flora often hung up on *her*, sometimes without any provocation at all.

"You *are* jealous, or else you'd be tellin' me how happy you are for Euless and me."

"I already told you how happy I am. How many times do I have to say it?"

"Well, you certainly sound like somebody who got up on the wrong side of the bed."

"No. But I *did* get up to find Hank cryin' in his room because he didn't know where he was. Now if you'll excuse me, Flora, I have to start dinner. Bye."

Tula didn't exactly hang up on Flora; she did, after all, say good-bye. But it was close enough for her to feel that she'd just taken one important step toward some new level of assertiveness.

"Tula?"

Tula turned to discover Hank standing in the doorway that connected the kitchen to the utility hall. He was wearing an old tweed jacket. A bright green clip-on tie hung crookedly from his shirt collar. In one hand was the familiar bassoon, in the other a suitcase.

"I'll be goin' on now, Tula."

"Going?"

"Yeah. Believe so."

"Where are you goin', Hank?"

"I think it's time I hit the road again."

"But Hank, you're retired. You retired several years ago. You don't sell portable out-buildings anymore."

"I know that." Hank set his suitcase down on the floor so he could scratch his nose. "What I mean to say is: I'm leavin' to go live somewhere's else."

"Where?"

"I have a place in mind. It's all planned."

Tula walked over to Hank and took his hand. "*This* is your home, Hank. This is where you live."

"This is *your* home. It isn't mine. I am becomin' a burden to you, Tula. That's why you went to talk to Dr. Oscarmeyer."

"How do you know I went to Dr. Ostermeyer?"

"I walked over there and saw your car in the parkin' lot. I have to go, all right?"

Tula now reached up and brushed Hank's cheek affectionately with the back of her hand. Then she held his face, letting his chin rest in her palm. He seemed to be making a point of not looking at her. "Hank, you really shouldn't be goin' off like this. You'll get yourself lost again."

"No I won't. I know how to get to where I'm goin'. It's not far."

"Where are you goin', Hank? Please tell me."

After a short silence Hank answered, "I'm movin' in with Calvin Gray."

"Does he know you're comin'?"

"No. But I'm sure he won't mind. He's my buddy."

"What about Edie? Do you think it will be all right with her for you to live there?"

Hank shrugged.

"Hank, honey, can you do me one favor? Can you wait a day or two and think this over? Please? For me?"

"I've already thought it over."

"Can you think about it some more?"

After a very long silence Hank said, "All right. I'll think about it a little bit longer." Then he turned and climbed the stairs back up to his bedroom.

For a moment Tula just stared at the old suitcase Hank had forgotten and left behind. Then she knelt beside it and snapped the two rusty buttons on the identical latches. She opened it slowly. She knew it was wrong to violate Hank's privacy in this manner, but she was too curious about its contents not to take a look.

Inside she found all of Hank's most cherished worldly possessions: a favorite pipe from the days when he used to smoke, a fishing trophy, an old tarnished harmonica, photographs of Hank and Tula's mother and father, and faded snapshots of some of his old girlfriends. There was also a snapshot taken of Tula when she was sixteen. She was sitting on a fence squinting in the sun. Her hair was light brown and waist-long. She seemed happy, confident and carefree.

It didn't take Tula long to notice something special about the contents of Hank's suitcase: everything had labels—little white labels taped or glued to each of the items, each label carrying a few scribbled words in Hank's handwriting. On the bottom of the trophy was one that read, "Chickasaw Lake Bass Tournament, 1967. You did well. Donna Royce stood on the bank and watched you and laughed when you nearly fell out of your boat." And with the pipe, "You smoked this pipe from January, 1961 to about March, 1974. Your favorite tobacco was Prince Edward." And on the back of the picture of Tula were the words, "This is your sister

Tula just after she turned sixteen. She was very beautiful all through her life."

Tula had to go out on the back porch to keep Hank from hearing her cry. She stayed out there for a long time.

***

"Hello?"

"Hello, is this Irmene?"

"Yes it is."

"This is Flora. Flora Ludlam."

"Hello, Ms. Ludlam. How are you this mornin'?"

"I'm fine."

Flora was sitting at her kitchen table, the phone receiver in one hand, the handle grip of her Hoover upright vacuum cleaner in the other. She had been vacuuming up all the coffee cake crumbs left on her kitchen floor by the untidy Mr. Haas. He had been reluctant to sit down and eat over a plate like any normal person, preferring instead to stand inches away from Flora as she scrubbed her counters, and drop cake crumbs and tiny almond half moons all over kingdom come. As Flora vacuumed, Tula's doubts about Ricky's news had begun to vex her. It suddenly became very important for her to hear from somebody else that what Euless had been told was completely true. Having to wait in suspense until the official reading of the will would unnerve her to no end.

"Irmene, forgive me if I seem to be pryin' too much."

"It's true."

"What's true?"

"What you're about to ask. Please don't tell anybody I told you this, but Mr. Pomeroy showed me a copy of the will not two days before he died. Euless and that girl-boy are each gettin' six million dollars."

"Oh goodness." Flora's heart began to race. "And what did he leave *you*, dear?"

"I didn't know him all that long, Ms. Ludlam. I really shouldn't be gettin' anything. But Mr. Pomeroy was such a thoughtful man. I guess that's why I'm gettin' his collection of blue willow china."

"Do you want the china, dear?"

"Why, of course. It's very beautiful," Irmene replied. "He must have noticed me admirin' it on a couple of occasions." Flora couldn't tell from Irmene's voice whether she was speaking honestly about the china or not, but it didn't matter; Flora had found out what she wanted to know and now could rest easy, assured that her son wouldn't have to work two jobs anymore. He wouldn't have to work *any* jobs unless he wanted to.

Flora didn't return to her vacuuming after saying good-bye to Irmene. Instead, she placed another call. She decided to hire herself a maid.

50

Depart ye, depart ye,
go ye out from thence, ...
go ye out of the midst of her.
Isaiah 52:11

"What kind of car does your mother drive?"

Euless was talking to the youngest of the Pinckney sons. "She doesn't have a car, Paul. She never learned to drive."

"That's an unfortunate situation," Paul said. "Of course that one over there; *she* can drive all right. Drove herself right into the back of your truck you said." Paul laughed, his bared teeth attesting to the spinach salad he'd had for lunch.

Carmen was on a mission to find at least one customer courtesy dish in the car showroom that wasn't filled with dietetic candy. Carmen hated dietetic candy and wished they had put out some Hershey's Crackles or good old-fashioned sugary Gummi Bears. Empty-handed, she made her way back to Euless and Paul Pinckney.

"That Sable's a real good car, Euless. No doubt about it. Oh, there she is. Did you get yourself some candy, Ms. Valentine?"

"It was all dietetic." Despite the heavy makeup, the scabby place on Carmen's face was still quite noticeable; she'd been fairly successful, though, in keeping the offending cheek turned away from the two men, and was now speaking to Paul while gazing raptly across the showroom at an array of bright, multicolored balloons tied to a silver Grand Marquis.

"Wouldn't you know it? See, it was Pete's wife Georgeanne's turn to fill the candy dishes. Georgeanne's a diabetic. Next year I'll get Piper to do it."

"And tell her to get some Crackles. They're a real crowd-pleaser." Carmen began to fan herself with a glossy, oversized Mercury Sable buyer's companion. Despite the fact that the sale was scheduled to go on until midnight and despite the presence of dozens of twinkle-star and crescent moon mobiles hanging all about, Carmen just didn't feel that the dealership looked or felt all that nocturnal at the moment. After all, it wasn't even five-o'clock yet, and bright sunlight seemed to be invading every corner of the large windowed showroom.

"Crackles. I'll write that down," Paul laughed. He stepped back from the Mocha Frost Clearcoat Sable LS which he'd been showing to Euless so that Carmen could now get a good look. Carmen stepped up to the car and ran her hand along the smooth outer body panel.

"It's very sleek," she said.

"The lady knows her stuff," Paul said in mock confidence to Euless. "Ms. Valentine, may I show you some of the features?"

Carmen agreed to be shown some of the vehicle's more appealing features. She was impressed by the standard air bag supplemental restraint system for both driver and right front passenger, but not so impressed by the variable assist speed-sensitive power steering, and four-wheel independent suspension, although the fact that Euless was nodding a lot as Paul explained them meant that these were probably good things to have.

"Would you like to take 'er for a test drive, Ms. Valentine?" Paul asked.

"Yes, I believe I would. Will you come with me, Euless?"

Euless nodded...and relaxed. He'd been worried that Carmen for whatever reason might prefer to take the test drive by herself. That would be a definite sign that whatever was developing between the two of them had already run its course. Now he still had a good shot at winning her heart.

The drive was not as enjoyable as Carmen had hoped it would be; she became so intimidated by the electronic instrument cluster and all the other various controls, and so overwhelmed by the smell of the leather and vinyl, not to mention Euless's liberally applied Chaps cologne that she had to pull the car over not five blocks from the dealership and trade seats with him. Euless watched with concern as Carmen lowered the passenger side window and breathed deeply to get fresh air into her lungs.

"I like the car a lot," Carmen reported to Paul upon the couple's return to the dealership showroom. "I still need a little time to think about it, though."

"Tell you what—why don't you sleep on it and come back and see us tomorrow? We'll run some more numbers by you and see if we can't get you in this car A-S-A-P."

Carmen agreed that this sounded like a good idea. Euless thanked Paul for his time. As Euless was walking Carmen out to the Chevette he asked if she might want to visit the Chevrolet dealership across town.

"No. I think I've seen enough cars for one afternoon. Would you like to come over to my house for a cool beverage and maybe a bite to eat?"

Euless nodded ... and relaxed yet again. This was exactly the invitation he'd been hoping for.

"Please make yourself comfortable," Carmen said, indicating with a sweep of her arm the sofa near the spinet piano, which, despite five years of lessons, she hadn't touched since her parents died. "So what would you like to drink?"

"You got any beer?"

"Yes, I do." Carmen smiled to herself. Moments before Euless pulled up in her driveway to take her to Pinckney's, she'd remembered his saying something the night before about liking beer. Not seeing any possible way to get to the store and back before he arrived, she'd stolen into Bowmar's kitchen via their adjoining back yards and his unlocked door, and taken a couple of cans of Budweiser from his refrigerator. Under a refrigerator magnet that looked like a miniature hobby horse she'd left a big note.

Carmen was already halfway back to her house before she remembered that Bowmar, though making steady progress under Nancy Leigh's patient tutelage, still wasn't all that proficient of a reader, and might have some trouble, should he get home first, making sense of such a hastily scribbled note. So she returned to Bowmar's kitchen, crumpled up and tossed the original note away, tore another sheet from the pad on the counter next to the refrigerator, and drew a cartoony picture of two cans of beer next to an arrow pointing to a big heart (for Valentine), then printed at the bottom in quite legible block letters as if by a first grade teacher, the words, "Thank you, thank you."

"I like your house," Euless said, looking about. Carmen had just returned to the living room with one of the purloined cans of beer for Euless and a legally purchased can of Fresca for herself. "This used to be your parents' place?"

Carmen nodded. "I grew up here. Most of this stuff was theirs. Except for that end table there. I got that little table at an antique show. I refinished it myself."

"You did a good job."

"Thank you. Oh, would you like to see one of my macaroni pictures?"

"Sure." Euless's eyes followed Carmen as she set her Fresca down on a ceramic coaster bearing a tiny hand-painted map of the state of Mississippi, excused herself and left the room.

All of the sudden Euless experienced a very strong desire. First it puzzled him. Then he became downright alarmed by it—frightened by its intensity. And just as frightening: it seemed to come right out of nowhere. One minute he was feeling perfectly fine, enjoying Carmen's pleasant, undemanding company. The next minute he found himself in the thrall of a dangerous, possibly uncontrollable craving.

Then it hit him; in a split second he knew exactly why he was feeling the way he was. And there was only one thing for him to do: leave. And he had to leave Carmen's house as quickly as possible—before any harm could be done.

And so while shouting, "I have to go, Carmen. I'm sorry. I gotta go," Euless did just that: he bolted right out his hostess's front door.

Carmen returned to the living room just in time to see the dilapidated Chevette speeding off down School Street, its tires squealing, gravel spewing in its wake. Carmen was carrying one of her favorite pasta paintings: "Bird of Paradise, Number Three." The shock of Euless's sudden departure loosened her grip on the frame and it slipped from her hand. Little pieces of dyed macaroni and rigatoni and orzo and egg noodles broke off and crumbled upon contact with the hardwood floor.

"Honey, I'm here if you need me," came a small voice from far away. "I just have to unpack."

"I don't need you," Carmen replied. She picked up the painting and gave it a long look. It had ceased to make any visual sense. She propped it up against the sofa, then knelt over the bits of dried pasta and began to sweep them up in her hand. She addressed Arnetta in a steady, cheerless voice: "It was a good thing you were here for me after my parents died, but I am quite capable of handlin' moments of grief and crisis on my own now, thank you. Not that this is exactly a moment of grief or crisis."

"But child, he ran out of the house like a crazy man—and for no apparent reason."

"I'm sure he had a good reason." Carmen was fighting back tears now. "Maybe he had diarrhea and didn't want to trouble me for use of my bathroom. My father, as you remember, was very prone to episodes of diarrhea and nausea which would strike without warning. Especially in demanding social situations."

"Well, I just wanted to let you know that I'm here."

"Thank you," Carmen said, her voice growing in volume. "But you can just go back to where you came from. Didn't you read my letter? You really should read people's letters when they take the time to write you." After saying this, Carmen sat down on the floor. She could feel the dry macaroni crunch beneath her. Her throat had become tight and now began to ache. Euless didn't have diarrhea; she was only fooling herself. Euless was running away, fleeing a woman who looked much fatter and uglier in the daylight than she did in the dark of night. Yes, that's what she now believed. She would face these cold facts, because only then could she move on.

Euless had the air conditioner turned up full blast but was still wet and sticky with sweat. He glanced at his speedometer; the Chevette was doing about sixty-five. Even fifty was sometimes too fast for Table River Highway with its twists and turns, and farm roads feeding in without proper warning.

Euless slowed down to sixty. The maples, ashes and pin oaks still blurred dark green in his peripheral vision. His eyes were focused on the blacktop now, but he was thinking of Carmen, thinking about what he had wanted to do to her.

Seeing Carmen in her parent's house had triggered a memory in him. He was seventeen. So was Melanie Rupert. Melanie's parents had left for a camping weekend in Ouachita National Forest. Melanie had talked her father and mother into letting her stay home. Within an hour of her parents' departure Melanie had invited Euless over. Soon he was kissing her—urgently, frantically. Melanie was equally ravenous, equally consumed by hormonally fueled adolescent desire. By Sunday night the two teenagers had made love in every room in the house. They had broken expensive fixtures. Never in all the years that followed had Euless felt such a strong, overwhelming sexual attraction to another human being. That is, until he walked into Carmen's living room.

If I don't leave now, Euless had thought to himself, I won't be able to control myself and I'll try to kiss her and she won't understand and she might become frightened or think I'm some kind of molester—or even worse, I might accidentally brush that tender place on her face and bring her pain or discomfort.

And Euless didn't want to make Carmen hurt. Carmen was sweet and gentle and pretty in a special kind of way. Euless often found himself attracted to girls like Melanie and Carmen—girls with warm hearts and ample figures. He had trouble relating to the flashy types with the svelte glamour bodies and the toothy smiles. In Euless's opinion this second group of women gave far too much attention to their looks. Euless never gave a great deal of attention to his own appearance and didn't think a woman should have to either.

The problem for him now was explaining to Carmen why he'd had to leave her house in such hurry. Maybe there *wasn't* any good and easy way to tell her. After all, how do you make a person understand that on occasion, maybe once every fifteen years, certain men get overpowering urges to take certain women in their arms and kiss them with a fervor so intense that even a sexual release isn't sufficient to quell the desire—that a total emotional, even spiritual catharsis must take place with tears and laughter and singing and dancing, and at least in the case of Euless's memorable weekend with Melanie Rupert, even a couple of larynx-taxing Tarzan yells.

So Euless decided he *wouldn't* tell her. He wouldn't even call her. Not that he didn't plan to make proper amends for walking out on her. The minute he got his six-million-dollar check from the executor of Conwell Pomeroy's will, he'd give about a million of it to Carmen Valentine. She could use the money to buy all the macaroni she wanted.

51

For it is a day of trouble, …
and of perplexity.
Isaiah 22:5

People were staring.

Nancy Leigh had been driving around Higby for almost an hour in search of the strangely painted van, and people were definitely starting to look at her a little funny. "Who is this distraught woman in the blue Corolla who keeps circling the block?" she could easily imagine them asking themselves. And the looks of those who actually knew her seemed equally inquisitive: did a box of important court papers fall out of that poor, overworked Nancy Leigh's car?

"Well, this is silly," Nancy Leigh finally said to herself. "I'll bet they've got her somewhere out from town. Maybe I should just go on home and wait for a call from Officer Tomley."

Monty was lying between two grease spots on the cool cement slab floor of Bowmar and Nancy Leigh's carport when Nancy Leigh pulled into the driveway. He was cleaning his face: licking his right front paw, then brushing the black fur around his mouth and whiskers with it. He seemed so caught up in this important activity that he didn't notice Nancy Leigh's car creeping up the driveway. She had to toot her horn a little to get him to move—which he did with a great show of reluctance.

Nancy Leigh entered the house through the door from the carport. She went straight to the den to check the answering machine. There was nothing from Avis. In fact, the only message on the machine belonged to a hair product saleswoman who'd been trying for several weeks to get Nancy Leigh to host a Charisse Sheen Hair Fantasy Party. "Oh go to hell, you money-grubbing bitch!" Nancy Leigh bellowed at the answering machine. The little blinking light had really gotten her hopes up.

Nancy Leigh kicked off her shoes and went into the kitchen. She was about to open the refrigerator door and get herself some grape juice when she noticed the rebus that Carmen had posted there about an hour earlier. "Two cylinder thingees, an arrow and a heart. Then 'thank you,

213

thank you.' Oh, I don't understand what this means at all!"

Nancy Leigh picked up the phone and dialed the number for the Pomeroy Lumber Company. It took a record seven minutes for Bowmar to come to the phone, during which time she was sure she'd had at least two petit-nervous breakdowns from worry. Nancy Leigh tried her best to describe the cryptic message to him; first, though, she had to define what the word "rebus" meant.

"Okay. Okay. I think I got it." Bowmar said, doodling out his own version of the hieroglyphic-like message on the back of a cancelled work order he'd pulled from the wastepaper basket next to Grinnette Hubble's desk. Grinnette looked on snoopily, ignoring all the other calls coming into the lumber company office.

"It says somethin' about Talitha. I just know it," Nancy Leigh said anxiously.

"You could be right."

"Maybe somebody is tryin' to drop us a hint as to her whereabouts."

"Like maybe a fellow captive escaped and is tryin' to help us find her."

Now Grinnette spoke up: "Why wouldn't they just put it all in English? Or better yet, why wouldn't they just call you up on the phone?"

"Who's that with you, Bowmar?" Nancy Leigh asked.

"Oh, it's Grinnette Hubble. She's askin' why this person wouldn't just—oh, you tell her Grinnette." Bowmar handed the receiver to Grinnette who asked what all three thought was a very valid question.

While Nancy Leigh was thinking this over Bowmar came up with two possible explanations: first, whoever left the coded message was, like him, functionally illiterate; second, the person might have been so thoroughly brainwashed that he or she had simply lost all grasp of the English language.

"Except for a few simple words like 'thank you'" Grinnette added helpfully, having relayed Bowmar's two theories to Nancy Leigh over the phone.

"Maybe now all they can speak is one of those religious languages like Hebrew or Greek so they decided to just take their chances with the universal language of pictures," Bowmar elaborated.

"That still doesn't explain what the message means," replied Nancy Leigh impatiently. "Grinnette, could you put Bowmar back on the line?

Hello, Bowmar—listen, baby, I'm gonna take this down to the police station. You pick up some KFC or somethin' on your way home. It might be late before I get back."

"All right. Nancy Leigh, you be careful now. If there's a bunch of crazy people out there pickin' up young women and brainwashin' 'em with scriptures, you just better be on your guard."

"I will. Love you. Oh, I don't have time to feed Monty. Don't give him any tuna because it gives him bladder trouble."

"Okay. Bye." Bowmar hung up the phone. He glanced over at Grinnette. Her glasses were slightly askew and Bowmar thought this made her look a little bit crazed herself at the moment.

"You know, Bowmar, it makes me so mad when people do bad things and then try to make out like it was all done in the name of Jesus. Jesus was nothin' but pure love and kindness. It's about as simple a fact as there ever was. I just don't understand how some people can twist it all up."

Generally, when Grinnette got herself worked up about something she would acquire a coating of phlegm on her throat, and would start to sound as if she were underwater. Such was now the case; Bowmar could still understand what she was saying but the gargly quality to her words was a little annoying.

Bowmar cleared his throat exaggeratedly in hopes that Grinnette might consider doing the same, then said, "Back when I was a little boy and had that cross-eyed problem that kept me from learnin' how to read, my grandmother used to read passages out of the Bible to me. And I know there was a lot of not-so-great stuff that went on—especially with the Israelites and all the problems they had, you know, on account of being the chosen people, and I guess all the Hittites and the Amorites and all those other peoples bein' a little jealous of this fact—but anyway, I think overall the Bible has a lotta good lessons to teach, you know, if you don't take it the wrong way or screw it all around to make it say what you want it to say."

"That's exactly right, Bowmar. Sometimes you talk just like a preacher and not an ex-convict. By the way, you promised me when you first started working here that some day you were gonna tell me what crime it was you committed that you had to go to prison for."

Bowmar walked over to the water cooler and filled himself a paper cone of chilled spring water. "I already told you, Grinnette. I stole some baseball cards for a kid."

"I thought you were jokin'."

"I wasn't jokin'. They were expensive cards. I broke into a hobby shop. I only took about five. I took 'em to this little boy I knew who had one of those tragic childhood cancers."

Grinnette finally cleared her throat, much to Bowmar's relief, and said, "But you told me you were in prison for three years. That seems like an awfully long time to be incarcerated just for stealin' a few little pictures on cardboard."

"Well, see, during the trial the prosecutor said some things—really out-of-line kinds of things about me and this boy. I was real fond of that boy, I admit it. He was kinda like my son I guess you could say, because I was, well, datin' his mother at the time and he didn't have a father and so I was kinda like his father. But this prosecutor was makin' wild reflamatory—no, *de*flamatory statements about my relationship with the boy like there was somethin' else goin' on—somethin' bad between me and that boy just because I liked him so much. And I just couldn't sit there and listen to any more of that mean and crazy talk of his so after, like, I think the third insinuendo I just got up outta my chair, walked over to his table and knocked him sideways cross the room. Trouble was, I broke his neck in the process."

"Oh my Lord!"

"I didn't kill him, you understand, but he ended up pretty much paralyzed from the waist down. Felt pretty bad about that. Didn't really put up much of a fuss when they handed down my sentence."

"Sweet Jesus in Heaven. Let me have a drink of that water."

"Anyway, the little boy died while I was doin' my time. They didn't let me out to go to the funeral."

"Do you still see his mother?" Grinnette took a little sip. Being told frightening things always made her mouth dust-dry.

"No. After I got out we tried to pick up where we left off, but it just didn't work out. She wanted us to have a child together, but I really couldn't oblige her."

"You didn't want a baby or you didn't have enough sperm?"

"I didn't have enough sperm."

"Oh."

"So we just kinda drifted apart. I guess I better get back to work now,

Grinnette."

"I hope Nancy Leigh gets her sister back in one piece, I mean, with her mind intact. Well, you know what I mean."

"I know what you mean."

"Oh—one more thing —"

"Uh-huh?"

"Do you ever hear anything about that lawyer you crippled?"

"Matter of fact, I see him every now and then. He's a Christian man. He forgave me for what I did. I hooked him up with this wheelchair-basketball league I know about. He really likes that."

Bowmar took his time returning to Section 17 where he'd been loading up two-bys for a customer in Southaven. Bowmar was thinking about little Davey Hambridge and the look on his face when he saw the '58 Topps Willie Mays. It was a picture Bowmar never wanted to forget.

52

I am troubled;
I am bowed down greatly.
Psalm 38:6

Carmen wasn't expecting a male voice to answer the phone. Her surprise registered as silence. The other party responded by promptly hanging up.

It took her about five minutes to get up the courage to call again. This time she blurted out, "Is Alaura there?" before the other party even had a chance to say hello.

"Who wants to know?"

"Carmen Valentine. I'm the girl who fell down outside your apartment last night."

"Well, if you're callin' to say you're gonna sue us you can just save your breath, because we don't own that cracked old cement walkway. It belongs to the apartment complex."

"No, that isn't why I called. Is this Drew?"

"Who else would it be—the butler?"

Carmen was so taken back by Drew's abominable telephone manners that she seriously considered—this would indeed be a first for her—giving the man a piece of her mind. She didn't have time to go through with it, though, because Alaura got on the line from the bedroom extension and beat her to the punch. "Drew, why do you talk so rude to everybody that calls? Is this the World Book man?"

"No. It's Carmen Valentine."

"Oh hi, Carmen. I was gonna call you but I didn't know your number."

"I'm not gonna listen to this girly gab!" Drew muttered. Then he hung up.

Carmen, sitting at the table in her breakfast room, glanced out the window and across her patio. She could easily see right into her next-door neighbors' kitchen, where Nancy Leigh was now gulping down a glass of what looked to be grape juice. Carmen hoped that Nancy Leigh wouldn't get a sudden hankering for a cold beer; she didn't recall seeing any left in the fridge after she borrowed the two cans for Euless.

"Drew's in the worst mood," said Alaura. She had been curled up in bed reading the new issue of *Vanity Fair* she'd just received in the mail. It was only the second one she'd gotten since she started the subscription, but she was already hooked on the erotic ads and photographs of glamorous celebrities. "He just got laid off from his job. He works at the David Davis Hardware Store. When the Mammoth Mart opened up they started losin' a lot of their customers, so now they're cuttin' back on their employees."

"Last hired, first fired, I guess." Carmen said, trying to sound sympathetic.

"No. Smart mouth, treat the customers like shit, first fired. He brought it on himself. And to top it all off —" Now Alaura raised her voice; this last statement was clearly meant for Drew's ears as well: "HE'S ABOUT TO GET HIMSELF THROWN IN JAIL IF HE DON'T RETURN THAT VAN OF THEIRS!"

"HEY, THEY KNOW WHERE I LIVE," Drew shouted back. "THEY WANT THEIR DAMNED VAN, THEY CAN COME THE HELL OVER HERE AND GET IT!"

"Anyway, like I said, I tried to call you but your number wasn't in the book."

"I'm in the book. But I'm listed as 'Valentine, Henry and Ruth.' I just never got around to changing it after my parents died."

"Oh. Well, the good news is: thanks to you, I passed my test. In fact by the end of the day I was pretty much jabbin' that needle into anything that moved. I almost had to be restrained."

"That's wonderful." Carmen tried to sound excited.

"So how's life been treatin' you since last night?" Drew was now standing in the doorway to the bedroom, rubbing his stomach like a parody of a hungry man. Alaura shooed him away.

"Well, as you know, Alaura, I don't have all that many friends."

"Yeah. You told me last night. Can't understand it, but then I can't understand why Drew sometimes hits his customers either."

Carmen didn't want Nancy Leigh to think that she was a Peeping Tom, so she got up and closed the curtains of her large picture window. The breakfast room and kitchen suddenly became very dark. She switched on the chandelette which hung over the table. "Last night under some very strange circumstances I met this man. I was really beginning to like him, and I thought he was starting to feel something for *me*. Then late this afternoon he drove me over to the Pinckney Lincoln-Mercury Moonlight Madness Sale and afterwards we came back over here, and while I was back in my studio gettin' one of my macaroni paintings to show him, he ran out the front door and drove away."

"Maybe he don't much care for macaroni."

"No, I think it's *me* he doesn't much care for."

"Were you actin' any different than the way you acted last night?"

"Yes. But that was only because last night was so unusual. See, I plowed into the back of his truck."

"Carmen Valentine, you have more accidents than anybody I ever met. Oh well, I wouldn't lose any sleep over it. He sounds pretty weird to me. What about that guy you wanted to meet at the party, what was that fella's name?"

"Tie. Tie Gibbons."

"Well, aren't you still hopin' to see him some time?"

Carmen was circling her table now as she sometimes did when she was restless or troubled. It helped her to think. "I hadn't even thought about him."

"You should give him a call. He's the one you were after to begin with, remember?" Alaura turned to a page in her magazine that carried a picture of a handsome, unclothed man sporting a couple of days' worth of beard growth. The man was getting his stomach tickled by the abnormally long eyelashes of an unclothed woman with large breasts. Alaura couldn't recall ever having tickled Drew's stomach with her eyelashes and didn't believe she ever would—even if he asked her.

"I can't think about Tie right now," Carmen said. "All I can think about is Euless."

"Honey, I get the feelin' you ain't never gonna hear from that Euless character again so you best be gettin' on with your life. Why don't you come over here? I just bought a Nancy Sinatra Greatest Hits C.D. I ain't even opened it up yet."

Carmen didn't really care for Nancy Sinatra, but she was growing very fond of her new friend Alaura. "Can you come get me? I think my car's been sold for scrap metal."

"I'll be right over, shug."

***

Euless had driven as far north as his gas tank would take him. Then he'd filled up, turned right around and headed back down south. His only other stop besides Shelty's Amoco in Corby, Tennessee was a full facility rest area on the Mississippi/Tennessee state line where he got out for a few minutes to stretch his legs and soon found himself discussing cholesterol with a paunchy truck driver from Savannah, Georgia.

Now he was back home, stretched out on his bed in his underwear, drinking malt liquor and watching a billiards tournament on TV. It was hard for Euless to keep his mind on the colored balls as they banked and caromed and dropped into their designated pockets. He kept imagining how Carmen's face must have looked when she returned to her living room and discovered he'd gone. Would it have been better, he thought, to remain there and assail her with a possibly unwanted romantic advance? Of course, he could have always asked permission first. Or he could have exercised a little damned self-control. What am I, Euless thought—some kind of wild jungle animal? What next? Peeing on trees and mailbox posts like a territory-marking dog?

Euless pulled himself out of bed, cranked up the volume on the television, then shuffled from his tiny bedroom into the living/dining/kitchen half of his trailer. As he passed the full-length mirror that hung on the door to his bathroom he took a good look at himself. Maybe he didn't resemble a dog, but there was definitely a wild and mangy look to him. All scrounge and scraggle. Euless couldn't even tell that he'd shaved that morning.

"I don't deserve six million dollars," Euless said. "I don't deserve shit." He sat down on the combination couch and dining banquette, and started to make a mental list of all the people he was going to give a portion of his fortune to. The IRS was at the top of the list, and, of course, he thought it might be a good idea to give some of that money to the bank to pay off his mobile home. Then came Carmen. Yes, he was positive now that she'd be getting a big chunk of his inheritance for her probable mental suffering. Next came his mother, because she'd put up with a lot out of him over the years, and also because he was always forgetting her birthday. Then he thought he'd maybe give a few thousand dollars to

Saul to say thanks for loaning him money whenever he was strapped. After that, he'd give a few hundred to young Wayne Biddle who'd been trying for almost a year to save up to buy himself a used Harley and was making little progress. The rest of the money he'd donate to some good and worthy cause; after serious thought he was sure he'd come up with just the right one. Nothing too political or controversial—but the money definitely had to go to help people less fortunate than himself.

The billiards tournament was over by the time Euless made it back to the bedroom. The fat man on the screen was exuberantly pumping the hand of the not nearly so happy skinny man. Euless could have told them that the fat man always wins these things. He closed the blinds, switched the channel to an old western he didn't remember having seen before, and climbed into bed. He was asleep within a few minutes.

Sometimes Euless would leave his TV on all night long. The flickery glow from the screen served as a pretty good night light. Although he'd never tell anyone, Euless had always been a little afraid of the dark.

53

Should a man full of talk be justified?
Job 11:2

"Excuse me—is Officer Tomley here?"

A young female police officer with a tightly curled strawberry blond perm and a pronounced overbite looked up from her paperwork and shook her head.

Nancy Leigh didn't recall seeing the woman on her earlier visit to the station that afternoon. "How about Officer Reese?"

"He's out too."

"Would you happen to know what case they're workin' on right now? Like could they possibly be out tryin' to find my sister?"

The officer set down her pencil. "Who's your sister?"

"Talitha. Talitha Leigh."

"That name sounds a little familiar. Does she have anything to do with vans? Avis and Ray said they were gonna go look at vans. No, I take that back. Avis was gonna look at vans. Ray was goin' over to the Pomeroy Lumber Yard."

"What's Officer Reese goin' over to the lumber yard for?"

"He said a prime suspect in a kidnappin' case worked there."

Nancy Leigh groaned. She'd never hear the last from Bowmar now.

"What's that in your hand?" the officer asked.

"I think it's some kind of message about my sister, but I can't make much sense out of it." Nancy Leigh handed the officer the small slip of paper that had Carmen's hieroglyphics on it.

"Thanks." The officer held out her hand to shake. "I'm Officer Garland, by the way. I'm still kinda new to town. You can call me Julie if you like."

"I'm Nancy Leigh. Your name is Julie Garland?"

"Yeah. And don't go makin' a joke or anything because I have a short fuse."

"All right."

Officer Julie Garland produced a package of Big Red gum. "'Care for a stick?"

Nancy Leigh shook her head.

Julie studied the little picture for a moment or so while unwrapping two sticks of gum and popping them into her mouth. Nancy Leigh found a stray chair, pulled it up to Julie's desk, and sat down.

"So what do you think?"

"Well, these round things look like little beer cans to me. And of course a heart usually means love. So I'd say what you got here is somethin' like 'I love beer' or 'beer makes me happy." Somethin' along those lines."

"But that doesn't have anything to do with my sister."

"Well, who says the message has to have somethin' to do with your missing sister?" Julie had looked at the piece of paper all she cared to; she handed it back to Nancy Leigh.

"I just thought —"

"Well, maybe you were just jumpin' to conclusions."

Nancy Leigh crossed her arms. She let out a very audible sigh of displeasure. "You're awfully rude."

"You asked for my opinion. I gave it to you."

"I don't think those look like beer cans at all." Nancy Leigh was angry now, and saw no need to hide this fact. "I think they look like ... like *tin* cans. Thank you very much, Officer Garland, but I believe I have just solved the riddle without any help from you."

Julie eyed Nancy Leigh curiously. "What is it you think it says?"

"Now the heart—that stands for Hartley. Hartley Road. And the two tin cans is actually this person's way of sayin' twenty —"

"How do you figure that?" Julie interrupted.

"Two 'tins'—same as two 'tens,' like the number ten. It's an address, you see—or part of one. Twenty-something Hartley Road."

Nancy Leigh walked over to the large wall map and studied it for a moment. "An address that starts with twenty—that would apply to half the houses on that street."

"Hey, at least it's a start."

Julie mulled this over. "Here, better give that piece of paper back. Avis may want to have it dusted for fingerprints later."

Nancy Leigh surrendered the little piece of paper to Julie Garland.

"Well, I guess I'll be goin' over to Hartley Road now," Nancy Leigh said, getting up from her chair.

Julie shook her head. "You sit yourself right back down, Missy, and wait for Avis or Ray."

Nancy Leigh registered her exasperation over this suggestion with a loud snort. "I most certainly will not. No tellin' when those two'll get back here. Especially Officer Reese who'll probably be pesterin' my boyfriend with his stupid questions for God knows how long, just like he's done before—all on account of Ray havin' it in for ex-cons."

"At least wait until Officer Shippers gets out of the bathroom and I'll go with you."

"Really?"

Julie nodded, her jaws still working over the now flavorless cud of gum. A moment later Officer Dan Shippers appeared holding a toothbrush in one fist and a tube of Crest in the other. The two women were out the door before he'd even had a chance to formally introduce himself.

***

Bowmar Stambler and Tie Gibbons, having both clocked in very late that morning, were still hard at work in the north section of the Pomeroy Lumber Company lot as Officer Ray Reese, toting his billy club, sauntered up at about five minutes past five o'clock. The air conditioning had been out for over a month in the alternate patrol car, and with Avis using the primary to check out vans, Ray had a sticky and steamy ride from the police station. He had sweat blotches under both arms of his summer uniform shirt. A third blotch was getting started over his budding beer belly.

"Mr. Stambler, a word with you please," Ray said, drumming the club against the open palm of his free hand.

Bowmar, who had been teaching Tie how to use the forklift, now excused himself and walked over to Ray. Rolling his eyes, Bowmar said, "I don't understand why every time a crime gets committed in this town you have to come and bother me. Don't you have anything better to do?"

"Hey, Ray," Tie called out from the seat of the forklift. "I see you recovered from last night."

"Is that you, Tie?" Ray couldn't look right at Tie due to sun glare bouncing off the lift.

"Yeah. You really put 'em away last night. I'm amazed you're even up and around."

"I can hold my liquor all right," Ray said, yanking up on his belt and pants, which had been riding much too low on his hips for the fashion statement he wished to make about himself. Turning back to Bowmar, Ray said, "I gotta ask you a few questions. Just part of the job."

"Can you maybe ask your questions without poppin' that stick against your hand like you're fixin' to knock me upside the head with it?" The heat of the day had given Bowmar's voice a raspy, scratchy quality; he sounded a little like Louis Armstrong.

"Fair enough. Mind if we move to a shady spot? I'm dyin' in this heat. I was born in Canada, you know."

"No, I didn't know that," Bowmar replied.

"Yup. I think I got some eskimo blood."

Bowmar led Ray to a nearby storage shed. Tie continued to practice picking up two-by-fours and transferring them to the bed of a hauler parked a few yards away.

"I don't know why I'm cooperatin' with you, Ray. You've been a thorn in my side ever since I got out of prison."

"Like I say, I'm just doin' my job. Now, take a good look at this picture. You ever seen this woman before?"

Ray handed Bowmar a xerox of the photograph Nancy Leigh gave Avis. It had been enlarged to fill the entire sheet; in the process Talitha's features had become badly distorted.

Bowmar shook his head. "Nope. Doesn't look like anybody I know."

"Now that's pretty interestin'," Ray said, palming away sweat from the back of his neck.

"What's pretty interestin'?"

"That you'd deny knowin' your very own girlfriend's sister."

"That don't look anything like Talitha. It looks like the Hulk. The Hulk in a big wig."

"It's Nancy Leigh's sister all right. Are you standin' here denyin' you know her?"

"I'm not denyin' nothin'. Damn it, Ray, you sound like somebody's gone and scooped all the brains right out of your fool head."

Ray double-folded the xerox and returned it to his shirt pocket. "You watch that attitude of yours, Mr. Stambler, or I'm liable to escort you right down to the station. I know all about you. I know exactly the kinda things you're capable of doin'."

"And just what is it you think I'm capable of doin'?"

"Stealin' valuable artifacts. Breakin' necks."

"If you got cause to arrest me, Ray, then go ahead and arrest me. Otherwise, I gotta get back to work."

Ray took a long, deep breath. "All right. But just remember ..." Ray shifted into a poor Clint Eastwood impression: "I got my eye on you."

Tie was now standing in the doorway, chuckling. "Oh Ray, shit, go ticket some jaywalkers and leave the poor man alone."

"I got no beef with you, Tie," Ray said, thumping the billy club again. "But this one here better keep his nose clean."

Bowmar sighed exasperatedly as Ray marched past Tie on his way out of the shed.

As Tie and Bowmar were walking back to the forklift they noticed Ray stealing peeks into a couple of the other sheds. Bowmar, trying to ignore this, said, "So, Tie, this Marci Luck—you gonna start seein' her, you know, on a regular basis?"

"Maybe. I don't know. I think she likes me a lot. But tell you the truth, she ain't really my type."

"So what type you go for?"

"I like 'em with a little meat on 'em. Go figure."

54

Against whom do ye sport yourselves?
Against whom make ye a wide mouth,
and draw out the tongue?
Isaiah 57:4

After what happened in the dental office Marci had been feeling a little shaky, not to mention achy and sore. Upon her return to the State Farm Office she had promptly informed agent Jory Adams that she had cramps and should probably spend the rest of the afternoon in bed with her heating pad. Jory agreed that this sounded like the best course of action and hoped aloud that she'd be better by tomorrow. Jory, who was single and had been raised by two bachelor uncles, wasn't all that educated when it came to menstrual cycles, and therefore didn't find it odd that Marci had been having feminine discomfort one day a week for the previous five weeks, coincidentally on days when there was a sale on at Cathy-Oh's or when fellow residents of the apartment complex where she lived decided to have a impromptu midweek fun-in-the-Mississippi-sun pool party.

After a long bath and an even longer, fitful nap, Marci settled into her granny rocker. She was quickly joined by her calico Falana, who was in need of a few minutes of affectionate attention. Marci didn't have to wait long for the second round of Motrins to kick in. She also discovered that she had now calmed down enough to call Naomi Sailor. She intended to ask Naomi for a loan of about a thousand dollars so she could move to another town where not a single soul would know her or have heard of her soon-to-be-infamous assignation in an abandoned dental office.

But first Marci had to go to the bathroom and check her mouth in the mirror. Once when she was a little girl she fell out of a swing and didn't learn that she'd chipped a prominent tooth until her younger brother happened to mention that she was starting to look like Count Dracula. This time her teeth looked fine—although there was a dark spot on one of her bottom molars that she thought might be the beginning of a cavity.

After changing into a comfortable, oversized muumuu, which her aunt had given her following a trip to Kauai and which Marci favored whenever she wanted something flowing that would allow her body to breathe, Marci sat down and picked up the receiver of her phone, only to discover the absence of a dial tone. She tapped the mouthpiece on the table a couple of times. She was pretty sure the trouble wasn't in the line. She'd gotten this phone as a free gift with a magazine subscription. It had gone out on her a couple of times before; on both occasions she had been exchanging strong words with her mother. It had taken an oath on her father's grave for Marci to convince her mother that she hadn't hung up in a senseless fury.

After cursing the phone for about a minute Marci got up from her sofa, changed into jeans and a teal cotton blouse, which she liked but hardly ever wore, and walked about a half block from her apartment to Chicken Dandy, where she'd remembered seeing a pay phone in the vicinity of the public rest rooms.

There was a police cruiser parked out front. A middle-aged officer was talking to a skinny, pimply-faced teenaged boy stationed behind the service counter.

"Where do you keep your van?"

"Usually out back, Officer Tomley, unless we're makin' deliveries."

"You got a picture or anything painted on the side of it?"

The boy nodded eagerly, happy to be of assistance. "Yeah. There's this picture of two chickens shakin' hands or feet or whatever it is chickens have down there."

"I see." Avis jotted this piece of information down on his pad. "Thank you for your help, son. You make a pretty good chicken sandwich here."

"Thanks. We use only farm-fresh poultry."

As Avis was returning to his patrol car, Marci, who was on hold, waiting for Naomi to get off another call, let her hips sway a little to the music she was hearing through the phone receiver. After a moment or so Naomi came back on the line. "I can't believe those people. They won't look at anything but stucco. I felt like tellin' 'em to move the hell to El Paso."

"What am I gonna do, Naomi?"

"Do about what?"

"You know what."

"Are you talkin' about the expensive damage you two did to that dentist's office or are you referrin' to your topsy-turvy love life? Excuse me just a mi— BOY! BOY! I'VE TOLD YOU THIS BEFORE: WE DON'T WANT ANY OF THAT MEXICAN CANDY. NOW JUST GO AWAY, YOU HEAR ME!"

"Naomi, you're not listenin' to me."

"Yes I am. There's just this nuisance of a Mexican boy who keeps— oh I don't know what he's even doin' in Higby anyway."

Marci glanced over at the service counter and caught the gaze of the gangly teenager. He was staring at Marci's tight-fitting jeans. Marci gave the boy a disapproving look and quickly pivoted her back to him.

"I know now who I want to spend the rest of my life with."

"You do?"

"I guess I've never stopped lovin' Stewie. I just didn't know it."

"So besides the fact that you're probably makin' the biggest mistake of your life goin' back to that choirboy, what's the problem?" Naomi was now trying to keep her voice low; her employer Vanity McElroy had just come out of her private office arm-in-arm with a new commercial client whom she was escorting to the front door. Vanity didn't approve of personal calls at the office unless necessitated by dire circumstances.

"The problem is, I just said good-bye to him. We both agreed that it was over between us. He's got this Jeannie Plough person he likes now. She has a large chest and she's —"

"Yeah, yeah. You told me. Listen—Tie Gibbons doesn't seem to mind the size of your chest. Tie thinks you're gorgeous." This was said in a whisper, followed by a stentorian, "YES, MRS. POTTER, PRIVATE MORTGAGE INSURANCE COULD BE ELIMINATED ALTO- GETHER WITH A TWENTY PERCENT DOWN PAYMENT."

Vanity gave Naomi a hard look. "Naomi, I have asked you before not to dispense real estate advice. You are not a trained and certified broker."

"I'm sorry, Ms. McElroy. But that wasn't advice. I was just statin' fact."

Vanity didn't want an argument with one of her employees right in front of her new client; she ended the exchange with a dismissive flit of the hand.

"I'm not in love with Tie Gibbons," Marci said despondently. "And from now on whenever we have sex it won't be honest and pure. Why can't things be the way they were back when Stewie and I first met? Everything was so uncomplicated then. I loved him and he loved me."

"For one thing, Stewie's got religion now. For another, I think you two got into a major rut. Now I have to get off the phone before I lose my job. Give me Tie's number. Do you have it?"

"He's still roomin' with Stewie. Bye, Naomi. Oh—don't call me. My phone's broken. Bye."

Marci hung up slowly, thinking about how much she loved Stewie and how screwed up her life was at the moment. She turned back around expecting the teenaged boy to still be looking at her, but he was busy filling a food order for a woman and her three young children. All three wanted Kiddy Kluck Packs, and the mother was insisting that each contain identical prizes so her kids wouldn't fight over them.

55

Thine eyes shall behold strange women,
and thine heart shall utter perverse things.
Proverbs 23:33

Nancy Leigh made a little clucking sound with her tongue as she considered what to do next. The fingers of her left hand played pianist-like against her lips. Julie watched her impatiently.

"I've got it!" Nancy Leigh suddenly exclaimed. The two women were seated in the front seat of the unmarked Plymouth Reliant, which served as patrol car of last resort when the two officially marked patrol cars were in use.

"What?"

"Okay, we drive down Hartley one more time ..."

Julie let her head drop to the steering wheel and remain there as she exhaled a loud sigh of frustration.

"... really slow, of course, and over the loudspeaker I say in a very low, authoritative soundin' voice: 'We know you've got Talitha. Let her go or we come in shootin'.'"

"You're kiddin'."

"Well, how else are we gonna find out which house she's in? You refuse to go door to door like I asked you."

"I didn't refuse. I was just hopin' if we patrolled the street for a while, maybe that van might drive out of one of those garages. Or some woman wearin' a sari might come out to water her lawn or somethin'."

Nancy Leigh fanned herself with Julie's clipboard. Blank offense report forms fluttered under the clip. "Okay, we tried it your way, and except for those folks comin' home from work and that woman leavin' in the big green station wagon to go get her hair done, there's been hardly any activity on this street at all."

Officer Julie Garland blinked a couple of times, then said in an almost contentious voice, "Now just how do you know that woman was drivin' herself to the beauty parlor?"

"Well, I can only hope that's where she was headin'. Did you get a good look at that train wreck of a hairdo of hers?"

Julie didn't reply. She just picked up the mike and radioed Avis. Avis's voice crackled from the speaker: "Yeah. Go ahead."

"That ten-eighty-six—you got a proper i.d. van registered on Hartley? Over."

"I've already checked out Hartley, Julie. What are you doin' on Hartley? Over."

"Chasin' wild geese. Over." Julie gave Nancy Leigh a dirty look.

"Well, get on back to the station. Ray and I are already on the case. Over."

Julie was about to respond when Nancy Leigh suddenly snatched the mike out of her hand. "Officer Tomley, this is Nancy Leigh. Over."

"What are you doin' in Officer Garland's patrol car?"

"I'm tryin' to find my sister. Now listen, I found a note on Bowmar's refrigerator. I think it's connected to the kidnapping."

"What does it say? Over."

This time it was Julie who seized the microphone. She used a bit more force than Nancy Leigh had. "It says 'I love that beer, yum yum.' We're headin' back to the station, Avis. Ten-four."

At first Nancy Leigh was too angry even to speak. When she finally found her voice, everything came out in a low growl: "And you call yourself an officer of the law. I tell you this, Ms. Judy Garland—if anything happens to my sister I'm gonna hold you personally responsible."

"Julie. Not Judy," Officer Garland snapped, revving the motor of the Reliant in a show of profound annoyance.

Avis, radio microphone still in hand, tried to figure out what love of beer had to do with the Talitha Leigh religious cult-kidnapping case. It was an impossible task. Sometimes Avis wished he'd never given up teaching criminal justice at Natchez Trace Community College. Upholding the law was a lot easier to do in theory than in practice.

56

Why doth thine heart carry thee away?
And what do thy eyes wink at?
Job 15:12

"Sheila Billows is here to see you, Clint."

Oren waited a moment outside Clint's bedroom door. Then, thinking that Clint hadn't heard him, he knocked a second time. Seconds later the door creaked open. Clint had a sleepy look. His room was dark, the curtains drawn.

"Are you goin' to your Bible class?" Clint asked.

Oren shook his head. "I decided to cancel tonight. I need to visit with someone who's interested in our church."

Oren told lies so infrequently he just knew this one was written all over his face. But Clint wasn't looking at his face. Clint's eyes were fixed on the floor.

"I don't need a baby sitter," Clint said softly.

"I wouldn't exactly call it baby-sitting, Clint. Ms. Billows would just like to visit with you for a while. You don't have to be sociable if you don't feel up it, but I'd feel better if she hung around until I got back, this being your first night home from the hospital."

"Where is she?"

"Waiting in the living room."

Clint considered this for a moment. "I'm gonna put some clothes on. I don't want her to see me in my P.J.'s."

"All right." Oren backed away from the door. "So I guess I'll be going now." Clint nodded and closed the door.

"Well, I'll be leaving now," Oren said to Sheila Billows as he entered the living room. Sheila was sitting in an armchair Oren's wife Alice had inherited from her parents.

"Johnny wanted to come too but it's inventory week at the store."

"I understand."

Sheila rubbed her palms along the arms of the chair, feeling the smooth texture of the upholstery fabric. "I brought a couple of movies and some microwave popcorn. We'll do fine." After a pause she said,

"You do have a microwave, right?"

Oren nodded. "Well, good-bye."

"Good-bye, Reverend Cullen." Oren left through the kitchen. As he was closing the door that led out to the carport, he could hear Sheila greeting Clint. Oren couldn't tell what Clint was saying in response, but from the tone of his son's voice, it didn't seem that he was all that unhappy she'd come.

On the drive out Table River Highway to Desiree Parka's Far East House of Massage Oren began to regret not having called ahead. What if this wasn't a typical Tuesday evening for her? What if some massage emergency had required her presence elsewhere? Oren would have abandoned his son and disappointed seven diligent students of the Bible for nothing. As it was, he was beginning to feel guilty over what he was about to do. He didn't want to even consider how God might be assessing his actions of the moment.

As Oren brought his car up the gravel drive that led to Desiree's slightly neglected yet still somewhat cheerful-looking Victorian gingerbread house he noticed that the porch light was on. This was a good sign. Lights also seemed to be on in one of the upstairs rooms. Even better, Desiree's mobile massage van was parked out front.

Oren got out of his car. He was greeted by Desiree's three-legged dog Bubbles who'd been let out earlier in the evening to go to the bathroom. Desiree usually allowed Bubbles to sniff and pee around her property for a leisurely while before calling him in for the night.

"Hello, fella," Oren said, patting the little dog on the head. Bubbles yipped a friendly hello of his own.

Desiree, hearing a car door opening and closing in her drive, put down her romance novel and walked over to the window of her bedroom. She could see the dark figure of a man standing next to an unfamiliar vehicle. The man was petting her dog. "Oh damn," she said to herself. She opened the window. "NO CUSTOMERS TONIGHT!" she called down. "NO MASSAGES ON TUESDAYS!"

"IT'S ME!" Oren called up. "OREN CULLEN."

"OREN?"

Oren nodded, but thinking that Desiree wouldn't be able to see the movement of his head in the dark, he shouted, "YES, OREN CULLEN."

"Oh my God. COME UP TO THE PORCH AND I'LL LET YOU IN."

Oren mounted the steps to the front porch and waited for Desiree to unlock the front door. Bubbles hung close beside him, licking his wrist.

"You came," she said. "I can't believe you came."

"I wanted to see you," Oren replied with a sheepish grin. Desiree threw her arms around him and gave him a big hug. Oren thought Desiree felt soft and warm against him. He was also aware of how nice she smelled; it was partly a perfumy smell and partly a clean, soapy smell like she'd just stepped out of the tub. He allowed his hands to touch her back. He could feel her shoulder blades. He rubbed her skin a little, then gave her a couple of hearty pats, similar to the way men slap each other when embracing to mask any feelings of excessive affection between them.

Desiree pulled away but held on to Oren's arms. She smiled. He couldn't help smiling too. She held the screen door open for him to come inside. "I heard your car pull up. I thought you were Officer Tomley. He called about an hour ago asking me questions about my van."

Bubbles was now sniffing Oren's shoe. "You must have stepped in somethin' interestin'," she said. "Go away, Bubbles. Go lie down." Desiree closed the front door behind them and led Oren into what she liked to call her "come-a-callin' parlor."

"What did Officer Tomley want to know, if you don't mind me asking?" Oren watched the little dog trot off into the next room.

"How it was painted. Whether I ever leased it out to strange religious cults. That sort of thing."

"Oh."

An awkward moment passed with neither Oren nor Desiree saying anything. Finally Desiree spoke up: "I'd like to offer you some wine. Do you drink wine? I hope you don't mind me asking."

"I'd very much like some wine."

"Good. You sit yourself right down. I'll be back in a jiffy. We don't keep a lot of liquor in the house as a rule because if we serve it to the customers they get bold and unruly. But this is different. This is a special occasion."

"A special occasion," Oren repeated with a nod. Desiree's yellow-orange vinyl couch squeaked as he sank into it.

Desiree returned a few minutes later with two wineglasses each almost filled to the brim. Handing one to Oren, she said, "I've had this sassy Merlot tucked away for about a year." She clinked their glasses together. "Drink up. I also found a nice Cabernet in the cleanser cabinet. You do know that I was serious when I offered yesterday to give you a massage. It'll relax you, I guarantee it."

"Thank you. I'll certainly consider it."

Desiree sat down next to Oren on the couch. "Oh my God!" she suddenly cried out. "You're gonna think I'm the rudest, most insensitive person who ever—Your son—how's your boy doin'?"

"Much better. He's home from the hospital."

"So soon? Oh, he isn't alone, is he?"

"No. One of the neighbors is with him."

"And he's gonna be all right?"

"Dr. Humphries thinks it'll take a couple of weeks for the bruises to heal, but after that he ought to be fine."

"That's good. That's really good." Desiree took a sip of her wine. "So why do you think he went up to the top of that old tower in the first place?"

Oren shrugged. "I can't figure the boy out."

Desiree moved a little closer to Oren, took his hand, and began absent-mindedly massaging his fingers with her thumb and forefinger. "He probably hasn't gotten over losin' his mother. You know it's hard when a boy's mother dies at such a young age. There's a special bond between a mother and a son. I used to have a little boy. Did I tell you that?"

Oren shook his head.

"He died of spinal meningitis when he was two. His name was Zedekiah. I called him Zed."

"Zedekiah's a biblical name."

"Yes, I know. I wanted him to have a name out of the Bible so about two months before he was born—I didn't know whether he'd be a boy or a girl—I sat down with my grandfather's old Bible. It had beautiful leather bindin' and thin tissuey paper that made this nice crinkly sound when you turned the pages. I sat right down and started lookin' through that Bible for a good name. Started right at the beginning. By the time

Zed was born I'd read almost all of that book. I really hadn't meant to but I did. I couldn't get through Revelation though. It was like readin' somebody's LSD diary or somethin'."

Oren laughed. He couldn't help himself. "Sorry," he said.

"No. I like to hear you laugh. You have a very sweet laugh."

"I'm sorry about what happened to your little boy."

"It was a long time ago. I was only eighteen. To be honest with you, I don't even know who the father was. Don't that beat all?" Desiree took another sip of wine while thinking about all the teenaged boys she'd slept with at the time who could have been little Zed's father.

Oren was now almost halfway through his glass. He was really enjoying the wine; it tasted decadently expensive to his tongue. Of course, Oren didn't really have anything to compare it to.   Desiree licked a little drop of the Merlot from one corner of her mouth and said, "I have a friend who lives over by Shiloh—Delci Maypole. She has this theory that Jesus was actually a woman, and that her name was Jesette. She believes that whoever wrote the Bible got it all wrong. What do *you* think?"

"I think Bible scholars are fairly certain that Jesus was a man."

Desiree nodded and thought about this for a moment. Then she said, "You know, maybe Clint's a bird watcher. Maybe he can see a lot of pretty birds from up there."

"Could be," Oren said, but without much conviction. "Or maybe — " Oren stopped himself.

"Maybe what?"

"I was going to say maybe he just wants to get as far away from—well, from *me* as he can. Maybe he climbs up to the top of that tower and pretends like he's hundreds of miles away. From up there I'll bet it doesn't look much like Higby anymore. Just a blanket of green with a few church steeples poking through." Oren couldn't believe he was talking so much. Something—Desiree, perhaps, or the wine, or maybe a combination of the two—was making Oren feel very relaxed and gabby.

"I don't think it's *that*," Desiree said.

"I wish I knew. I wish I could talk to him. I wish a lot of things."

Desiree set her wine glass down on the old sailor's trunk that served as her coffee table, then stood up. Rubbing her palms briskly together she said, "I'm ready to give you that massage now, Reverend Cullen."

"You can call me Oren."

"I know. I was just bein' funny. So what do you say—a full-body massage—head to toe? You'll be so relaxed by the time I'm finished, I'll have to drag you out to your car."

"Well, I think I just might. I came prepared with clean and tasteful underwear."

"You won't need any underwear, Oren." Desiree said this without even a hint of a smirk. Seeing a look of worry suddenly register on Oren's face, she quickly added, "In a full body massage nothin' must be covered. A good masseuse will permit nothin' to come between the customer's stiff muscles and her magic hands."

Oren hadn't even thought about the possibility that Desiree might ask him to remove all of his clothes. No woman had seen him naked since Alice, and he'd doubted that any woman would ever see him that way again.

"Don't chicken out on me, Oren. You're gonna love it, I just know it. And it'll be my pleasure to give it to you. Please, now, you just sit here and think it over for a minute. Think about how nice it'll be."

Oren thought about how nice it would be, and after three more glasses of wine, followed Desiree upstairs.

57

And he drank of the wine,
and was drunken;
and he was uncovered.
Genesis 9:21

For about an hour Sheila Billows and Clint Cullen sat quietly watching back-to-back syndicated episodes of *The Cosby Show*. Sheila hadn't said much except to marvel at how much the youngest Huxtable daughter had grown from one episode to the next. Clint had thought a commercial with singing cats was funny and said he hoped they'd run it again, which the station did, two more times.

When the shows were over Sheila asked Clint if he'd like to play a game. "What about that Stratego game Johnny got you?" Sheila, who had sat with her legs tucked under her for most of the previous hour, now gave them a good long stretch and wriggled her toes.

"Do you know how to play?" Clint asked from his spot on the sectional sofa.

"Not really. But you can teach me. Is it hard?"

"No. But there's a strategy about where to hide your flag. Oh, and your bombs. And your miners. Oh yeah, and your spy."

"It sounds complicated."

"Not *that* complicated." Clint went back into his bedroom and got the box. He was still tearing off the cellophane wrapping as he entered the living room. "I hadn't opened it up, you know, because I already knew what the pieces looked like."

Clint looked up to see that Sheila had now crossed her legs in a not necessarily provocative but still interesting way. Clint stared at the legs for a moment—a long enough moment, as it was, for Sheila to take notice.

"Do I have a run?"

"Huh?"

"A run. Do I have a run in my pantyhose?"

"No, I don't think so." Now Clint felt embarrassed. He had been staring at Sheila Billows' shapely legs without any good reason except that he liked the way they looked. Sheila gave her hose a cursory inspection, then got up.

"You wanna play over here at the dining room table?" she asked.

"All right." Clint carried the box over to the table.

As he was taking out all the pieces and unfolding the game board, Sheila said, "I'm so glad you fell into my pool. Just think, if you hadn't landed in that pool we wouldn't be havin' such a nice visit right now."

Clint wasn't sure whether this meant it was good that he hadn't died in the fall or it was good that he'd happened to fall into her particular swimming pool. It didn't matter; he enjoyed listening to Sheila's voice. It had a musical quality he found very soothing to the ear. Clint wished that his guest would just keep right on talking.

"Which is better—a low number or a high number?" she asked, examining the game pieces in front of her.

"The low numbers mean high rank. I guess it's opposite from what you'd think." The good thing about playing Stratego with Sheila, Clint quickly decided, was getting to sit right across the table from her where he could look at her whenever he wanted to; it's important through the course of a game, he told himself, to be able to read your opponent's face for revealing clues and reactions. The bad thing: he'd no longer be able to see her legs.

"Like number one —" Clint went on animatedly, "where is it?—okay, see—this marshal—nobody can take this marshal but a spy."

"What about a bomb?"

"Yeah. That can take a marshal. But I'm just talkin' about human beings right now."

Sheila looked at all the game pieces piled in front of her and said, "Can I have red? Red's my favorite color."

"Sure. I like blue."

Sheila smiled. Clint smiled back. Whoever it is that Dad's gone to see, Clint thought, I just hope they keep him there for a long time.

***

Five minutes into the massage Oren was still so tight and tense that Desiree wasn't sure she could go on. "You're makin' my hands very tired, Oren, and I've hardly gotten started. You have simply got to relax!"

"I'm sorry," Oren said. "I'm trying."

"You aren't supposed to try. The wine should be making you relax naturally."

"I do feel pretty good, if that helps any. Oh, and I feel kind of light-headed."

Desiree stopped karate-chopping Oren's gastrocnemius muscles, stepped away from the massage table, and folded her arms. "Well, this just doesn't make any sense at all. How can a man who feels good and light-headed still be tense?"

Oren shrugged his shoulders. Then, thinking that Desiree wouldn't understand the meaning of this gesture because it was executed while he was lying flat on his stomach, he shook his head.

"Oren Cullen, I'm gonna ask you an honest question and I expect an honest answer: why are you so tense?"

Oren finally gave in to the desire. The desire to tell the whole naked truth. A desire that had been burning within him—growing stronger with each additional glass of wine he'd drunk. "It's because—it's because of all the effort I'm having to put out. To fight the urge —"

"What urge?"

"The urge to ask you something."

"There's somethin' you wanna ask me?"

"Yes."

"Well, silly Billy, just ask me. The worst that can happen is I'll say no."

Oren took a moment, tried to swallow, found his mouth suddenly very dry, panicked, reminded himself that he was supposed to be in a state of calm and happy inebriation, relaxed, then said, "I want to make love to you, Desiree."

"That isn't a question."

"It isn't?"

Desiree shook her head and grinned. Then she picked up a folding chair from across the room, brought it over to the massage table, and sat down. Taking hold of Oren's hand she said with soft tenderness, "Are you fallin' in love with me, Oren?"

Oren didn't have to think of how to answer. Desiree wanted him to be honest and so he would be honest. Honest with her. Honest with himself. He nodded. He was still on his stomach, but now his head was turned so he could look right into Desiree's soft, mocha-brown eyes. His right hand was stroking the smoothness of her palm. His left hand still held a half-finished glass of wine. He looked to Desiree like a party guest too afraid to put down his wine glass lest he do something gauche and ill-bred with his idle hands.

"I love you too, Oren. From the first moment I saw you out on that highway with that broken-down bus and all those rambunctious kids."

"But I thought in your letter you said you just wanted me for a friend."

Desiree now reached up and patted Oren on his bald spot. "I've learned never to expect too much from people, Oren. I figured I'd never be so lucky as to have you for a lover, so I just decided to work on makin' you my friend."

Having said this, Desiree leaned over and gave Oren a long, passion-filled kiss. Oren not only relaxed; he dissolved—disappearing inside Desiree's caress. When the kiss was over, sooner than either of them would have preferred, he said, "It's been a long time since —"

"I know."

"All the time Alice was sick, we didn't —"

"It don't matter, sugar. Don't matter one bit."

"There'll be a scandal at my church. I could be removed from the pulpit."

Desiree grinned. "From that sweet little church of yours? Now why do I doubt that, honey?" She tweaked Oren's nose. "And let's say you *are*—how do you put it—*defrocked*? Well then, we'll just have to go off and start our own church. One where a widower preacher is allowed to fall in love again, with whoever he pleases, and not have to feel even the tiniest bit guilty about it."

As Oren lay, drowsy and content, among Desiree's collection of exotic, hand-embroidered souvenir pillows, waiting eagerly for Desiree to emerge from her bathroom, and thankful for being able to feel romantic love again, he used this time to do something that in his present alcohol-affected mental state didn't seem inappropriate or incongruous at all: Oren Cullen rededicated himself right then and there to God's service, renewing his commitment to the ministry—although admitting that it was going to be a very different kind of ministry from the one he'd practiced before. One based on simple truths. Of which the greatest was now self-evident.

58

Sing unto him a new song;
play skillfully with a loud noise.
Psalm 33:3

"What's your pleasure: wash or dry?"

"Huh?"

"It's our night. There's a schedule. It's hangin' on the door to the pantry."

Talitha was raking rice and black beans around her plate with her fork, making little black and white designs with her uneaten dinner against the midnight blue of the glazed ceramic. Very little of the meal had left the plate; she wasn't all that hungry.

"Wash or dry? I promise you, this ain't a trick question." Pud, who had been in the process of clearing the table, now stood across from Talitha impatiently tapping a bean-caked serving spoon against a large glass fruit bowl. This produced a pretty, musical sound.

"I'll wash," Talitha finally said, pulling herself up from the table. Dutifully, she removed her plate, eating utensils, and blue anodized aluminum drinking glass, which still had a little guava juice left in it, and followed Pud through the swinging door into the "galley." "Where is everybody?" Talitha asked, suddenly noticing that she and Pud were alone.

"They're all in the music room. Valor's written a new song of praise which they're gonna work on. Hope plays the piano. Valor's on the guitar. We'll probably be hearin' 'em any minute now."

As Talitha filled the sink with hot water and suds, Pud leaned casually against the counter, the dish towel draped over one shoulder in the manner of a wine steward. "So, I guess your sister'll stop worryin' now, huh?"

"Like hell she will," Talitha snapped.

"Hey look, I'm not the one who brought you here. And I'm certainly not the one who signed your name to that piece of paper. So don't you think you're howlin' at the wrong moon here?"

The water was getting much too hot; Talitha added a little from the cold tap, and swished the dishrag around to build up the suds. "I was not in my right mind when I signed that contract. It'll never hold up in a court of law. I have been kidnapped pure and simple, and if you don't want to see yourself hauled right off to jail with the rest of 'em, I'd advise you to help me figure a way to get out of here."

Now the sound of song began to waft its way into the kitchen from the music room at the other end of the house. Valor's voice was the loudest of the trio: a booming baritone. Hope's, Talitha thought, sounded like the chirp of an annoying bird that wakes you up in the morning.

Pud began to twirl the dish towel like a propeller. He seemed restless and fidgety; his right foot tapped out the beat of Valor's song. "The night I came here I felt the very same way you're feelin' right now."

"And now you're a religious zombie." Talitha pulled her hip out of the way of the flapping dish towel. "I swear, Pud, if you accidentally hit me with that thing I'm gonna crack you over the head with this mixin' bowl."

Pud took a step back. "I'm not a zombie. I've got a mind of my own, same as you. Like I told you, it's my *choice* not to leave."

"I cannot believe you really like it here."

"I told you earlier—I'm treated very well."

Talitha handed Pud the bowl she'd just finished rinsing. He dried it diligently and placed it in the cupboard.

"And I guess you're as content as can be to eat tofu and fart-beans seven days a week, and never touch sirloin again for the rest of your life."

"I can get all the steak I want when I go into town on errands."

"And just how often is that?"

"Well, they haven't actually started lettin' me, you know, go on the errand runs just yet. But it's bound to be any day now, I'm pretty sure of it."

Talitha shot Pud a look of exaggerated disbelief. "You're either crazy or retarded or the most gullible person I ever met."

"You have a soap bubble on your nose."

"Don't talk to me. Just don't you even talk to me."

There was a brief silence during which Talitha and Pud could hear Valor singing the special solo section of the song: "Christ the King of all He surveys / Helps us change our woeful ways."

After putting away the big wooden serving spoon he'd just patted dry, Pud sidled up to Talitha and said in a confidential half-whisper, "Valor feeds the dogs at about nine-thirty."

"So?"

"So this: at nine-thirty you go to your bedroom. You can jimmy open the window in there pretty easy. I know because that used to be my room, and I got out that way one time."

"What about the dobermans?"

"This is what I'm tryin' to tell you. Those dog's'll be eatin' come nine-thirty. They aren't gonna come after you while they're gobblin' up their dinner."

"I get out the window—then what?"

"You run as hard and fast as you can in the direction of the highway..."

"Which is —" Talitha was all turned around.

"Straight shot from the window. You'll pass the garden, you'll pass some fruit trees, then you'll meet the fence which runs alongside the highway. That fence isn't too hard to get over, you know, unless you've got a big dog or two nippin' at your butt, tryin' to pull you back down."

Talitha's heart was racing. She was frightened and excited at the same time. "Thanks for the advice."

"I would've told you sooner but I thought you might start to like it here and then maybe you and I could ... you know."

"You're not my type, Pud," Talitha said as gently as she could.

"You mean because I'm not black?"

"Black *or* white, Pud—sorry." Talitha didn't add the fact that she usually wouldn't even date the brothers of men as goofy as Pud.

"Well, say hello to the outside world for me—that is, if you make it."

"Would you like to leave with me—I mean when *I* do?" As Talitha said this she handed Pud a plate that still had a little food stuck to it. He handed it right back, pointing to the spot.

"No, I believe I better stay here." Pud considered what he'd just said for a moment, his eyes tracking a roach as it crawled across the kitchen ceiling. Then with a nod he added, a little wistfully: "Yeah. I suppose this is the place for me."

The trio was now singing Valor's song for the third time. Without even realizing it, Talitha started to hum along with them, the catchy tune having successfully burrowed its way into her subconscious. Pud smiled, but he knew this wouldn't be enough to keep her around.

59

Her sins ... are forgiven;
for she loved much.
Luke 7:47

Clint wasn't sure if he was in the mood for another game. Although it had been kind of fun trying to guess Sheila's very unorthodox battle-field tactics—like trapping her poor general behind a barrier of bombs or placing her flag right there on the front line with only lowly sergeants for protection—what he *really* wanted to do at the moment was get out and take himself a long walk. And he wouldn't mind one bit if Sheila wanted to come along too.

"Why don't we do somethin' else?" he asked.

"You sure you don't wanna lay down or somethin'? You haven't had a Tylenol in over two hours."

"I'm fine. I'm really feelin' pretty good right now."

"All right." Sheila breathed an almost audible sigh of relief; military strategy games she just didn't find all that entertaining. She began to put the game pieces back into the box. Clint watched her hands as they plucked up each of the pieces, her long red nails clicking against the hard plastic.

"We could pop some popcorn and watch a video," she suggested.

"I have a better idea," Clint replied. "Why don't we take a hike around the neighborhood?"

Sheila was fairly certain that Oren wouldn't approve of this idea. After all, Clint was supposed to be recuperating from a terrible fall.

"Aren't your legs still pretty sore?"

"Yeah. But that's how you get the soreness out. It's good rehab."

"Won't your father be comin' home soon?"

"I don't know when Dad'll be home. Hey, we'll leave him a note."

Sheila was torn. A nice walk would give her the perfect opportu-nity—under quiet, starry skies—to try to form some kind of bond with Clint. She had made real progress during the board game; even though most of the conversation had centered on the game, she still felt the two of them were growing fairly comfortable with one another. Soon, she hoped, Clint would really begin to trust her and open up to her, and then she'd be able to find a way to help him adjust to life without his mother.

On the other hand, she just knew that Oren wouldn't be happy to return and find his badly contused and discolored son roaming about the dark streets of Higby rather than resting safe and sound at home and taking his Tylenol.

"Just a quick trip around the block," Clint said. "We'll only be gone a few minutes."

There was a pleading quality to Clint's voice that was too much for Sheila to bear. She consented to a short walk. A very short walk. Chances were, they'd probably be back long before Oren got home; she didn't even need to leave a note.

***

"I better go. If we fall asleep again we may not wake up for hours and then Clint will really start to worry."

Desiree was buttoning up Oren's shirt. Oren had tried without much success on his own. "You're drunker than a skunk, Oren. I'm not gonna let you drive back to town in this condition."

"You're tickling me."

"Sorry."

"No. It felt good."

"Look, why don't you call and tell him you're gonna be late? Maybe that Ms. Billow could look after him for a couple more hours."

"I'd hate to ask her to do that."

Desiree and Oren were sitting at the foot of Desiree's bed. Desiree affectionately twirled what little there was of Oren's hair around her right index finger. "I wish you could spend the night. I'd love to have you next to me all night."

"I'd like that too, but I really have to go home."

"Well, not until I get some coffee into you, and even then, I'm gonna do the drivin'."

Oren fell back against the mattress and took a deep breath. The whole room smelled of lilac-scented bath powder and Giorgio perfume. Oren imagined that this is what Heaven smelled like.

"Then how will *you* get back home?"

"Don't worry about me. I've got some friends in town who'd be happy to give me a lift."

"I love you, Desiree."

"And I love you too, Oren."

"I mean I really love you."

"And I really love you." Oren pulled Desiree down and started kissing her all over her neck, her face, her shoulders. She released tiny pleasure-sighs.

Oren opened his eyes so he could gaze at Desiree's face, but he couldn't get a good fix. In fact, the whole room seemed to be spinning. "I guess I've got to go throw up again," he announced. "I'll be right back."

Desiree watched Oren stagger into the bathroom. While lying on her bed alone, feeling warm and happy and loved, she wondered what Bibi and Ling Sue would think about her new boyfriend. My *last* boyfriend, she would hasten to add. The last man I shall ever love, for I have finally—yes, girls—I have finally gotten it right.

Desiree closed her eyes and summoned up still-warm memories of Oren and her making love. She played these back in her head, concentrating hard to block out the sound of Oren vomiting in the bathroom. Being with Oren had made her feel good about herself. And no, it wasn't a seduction, no matter what people might think. Didn't he just say that he truly loved her?

It was now, of course, official: Desiree had turned over a new leaf. And that leaf had someone's name written all over it. Never in a million years would she have guessed the name would belong to a Bible Methodist minister.

Life was, Desiree had to agree, pretty unpredictable.

60

How dreadful is this place!
This is none other but the house of God.
Genesis 28:17

Gordon was now over an hour late, and Stewie was fast running out of interesting things to read in the church office. Old church newsletters had held his attention for a while, as had a generously illustrated book of Bible stories for children that someone had left on the Xerox machine. But most of the thick volumes of Bible commentary that lined the office's bookshelves looked unapproachably scholarly. Why did the church's Board of Stewards meeting have to run so late on *this* particular Tuesday night? Stewie wondered as he checked his watch for the twentieth time since his arrival.

"A thousand apologies," Gordon puffed as he bounded into the office with several overstuffed manila folders tucked under one arm.

Stewie, who had popped up from his chair when he heard the footsteps, now reached out and with stiff formality shook Gordon's hand. "Good evenin', Reverend Wedgerly. No problem at all."

Dumping all the folders onto his secretary's desk, Gordon said, "Stewie, the air conditioner in my office isn't working properly and it's very warm in there. Would you mind if we had our talk in the sanctuary?"

"No, not at all." Now thinking himself too formal, Stewie tried to relax a little, and inquired with imposed casualness, "So how did the Board of Stewards meeting go?"

Gordon led Stewie out into the hallway. "We're debating the need for a bell choir. Claywayne Poole thinks it would be great for outreach. Randy Nutt would rather spend the money on liturgical dancers."

"I see." Stewie made a mental note to ask someone later what a liturgical dancer was.

Gordon opened the nearest door to the sanctuary. Calvary United Christian Church's sanctuary was much cooler than the rest of the building. With its dark wood and stone, and partially vaulted ceiling, it had a slightly cavernous feeling to it.

When plans for the new church building were first drawn up, many

257

in the congregation had worried that the structure would be too big, too ornamental and far too ostentatious for a small town like Higby. To many of the church's members it seemed out of scale even for its denomination. Gordon had ignored the naysayers and held fast to his vision, eventually investing seven years of his life to seeing it realized. Few knew that Gordon had been raised a Roman Catholic, and although he now found himself at odds with many of the tenets of the church of his youth, there was one thing in his mind that Catholics would always have over Protestants: houses of worship so grand and stately and beautiful that a person couldn't help taking proper notice. Gordon wanted people to take notice of *his* church. And he'd been very successful. Since the new building went up, membership in the Calvary Church had grown by nearly two hundred percent. Calvary, Gordon could boast, now had the second largest congregation in Higby, eclipsed only by Higby First Southern Baptist.

Gordon led Stewie down the darkened center aisle to a pew about a third of the way from the front. "Here's a good spot," the older man said, seating himself a few feet in from the aisle. The sun was going down; the last rays of the day were now percolating through the abstract designs of the stained glass windows on the west side of the room.

After Stewie settled in, Gordon clicked his tongue a couple of times in thought, then asked Stewie if he remembered what the Apostle Paul had to say on the subject of fornication. He posed his question in a very hushed and earnest voice—the kind of voice he usually reserved for public prayer.

Stewie nodded, then quoted First Corinthians, Chapter Six, verse thirteen (part two): "Now the body is not for fornication, but for the Lord; and the Lord for the body."

"And did Paul have anything else to say on the subject?"

"I'm sure he did but that's the only verse I remember from Bible study."

"'For it is the will of God, even your sanctification, that ye should abstain from fornication.' First Thessalonians, Chapter Four, verse three."

"I'll try to remember that one too."

"Those verses tell us what, Stewie?"

"That fornication is wrong."

Gordon leaned in a little closer to Stewie. "And do you believe this to be true, Stewie?"

Stewie nodded.

"And yet I understand that you and Marci Luck have been engaged in habitual fornication for the last thirty-two months."

Stewie stirred uneasily in his spot on the pew. "I really hadn't added it up, you know, in terms of months."

"You'll find that to be the correct number."

"We were plannin' on gettin' married."

Gordon gave Stewie a long, probing look, then asked, "Are you *still* planning to get married?"

"Well, actually, to be honest, we've been talkin' about breakin' up."

"Is this how a man and woman conclude a long-term romantic relationship—by having such a wild and reckless sexual encounter that they end up destroying dental office furniture?"

Stewie didn't know how to respond. He stared down at his shoes and socks. At that moment he realized that in his haste to get himself dressed back at the dental office he'd put on a sock that wasn't even his. Apparently, it had been left there by one of the former tenants. Now the thought of wearing a stranger's dirty sock started to make him a little queasy.

"Stewie, when you accepted Jesus into your life last October, we talked about the importance of your making certain lifestyle changes. There were things you did before, activities you willfully engaged in before your baptism and profession of faith that we both agreed God would not wish you to continue. I understood that you would make every effort to abstain from this sort of behavior. And when I heard a few months ago that you were continuing your intimate relationship with Marci Luck outside the bounds of holy matrimony, I'll admit I was disturbed. But I didn't say anything. For I knew how difficult it would be for you to stop having sexual relations with someone you've loved for so long. Yet after what I witnessed this afternoon, I can no longer keep silent. You were having her in a chair, Stewie—a chair which did not even belong to you. There was some level of perversion at work in that room, let there be no doubt about it. In addition to which your desire for sexual excitement appears to be growing at an alarming rate. I am disturbed because as a born-again Christian you should not be giving in to such a desire in the first place. And you certainly shouldn't be allowing it to consume you as it has. I must now ask you some important questions, Stewie, and I trust you will give me honest answers."

Stewie nodded. Now he imagined tiny foot lice invading his right foot from the foreign sock.

"Do you plan to see Miss Luck again?"

"I don't know. I mean, we were supposed to be sayin' good-bye. But I don't know if I want to say good-bye now."

"So there exists the very real possibility that you will continue to fornicate with this woman?"

"Yes. I mean, I think I love her now more than I ever have."

"I see." This encounter was starting to make Gordon very depressed. Stewie had been one of his most promising converts, and now the young man seemed to be backsliding all the way to hell. "Stewie, since we're being very honest here, please permit me to ask: have there been any others, I mean, besides Marci?"

Stewie started to shake his head, then sensing the presence of God in the beautiful, darkened sanctuary, he said, "Yes, last night I slept with a girl named Jeannie Plough who has long brown hair and works as a cashier supervisor at Mammoth Mart."

"This was an assignation of sorts?"

"You mean a one-night type-a-deal?"

"Mmm hmm." Gordon's ample brows were now knitted together just above his nose. His eyes narrowed in deep, serious thought.

"Yes. But I didn't think at the time that it would be a one-night thing. We had a very enjoyable evening."

"Fornicating."

"We also had some pleasant dinner conversation."

Gordon's voice dropped to the level of a loud whisper: "So I want to get this straight: you are now engaged in carnal relationships with two women—two women, neither of whom you are bound to in holy wedlock."

"Well, not exactly—I mean —" Stewie thought this might be a good time to try to explain to his pastor as best he could how such a thing could happen to a born-again Christian man like himself. "Pastor Gordon, I know I've probably broken a lot of commandments. I've tried to live the kind of Christian life which God would want me to but —"

"Temptation has overtaken you," Gordon interjected.

"Right. I don't have a lot of practice fightin' temptation. As you know, I wasn't raised in a very religious ... environment. My mother and stepfather just aren't really church-goin' kinds of people."

Gordon nodded. "I remember you telling me this."

"And I just—well, the thing is—I just think it's gonna take some time. I really want to do right by the Lord, Pastor Gordon, because I really do intend to keep my promise ..."

Gordon interrupted for clarification: "You're talking about the promise you made to God the night your boat capsized out on Silver Dollar Lake?"

"That's right. And I do—I really do intend to live a good Christian life and do as He wilt have me to do. But it's gonna take some practice."

"I understand that," Gordon said softly. The sanctuary was growing very dark now. The only illumination seemed to be coming from a narrow strip of light under the door to the corridor which led to the church offices and Sunday School rooms, and from the three eternal candles that burned on the wooden stand near the pulpit—one for the Father, one for the Son, and one for the Holy Ghost. Gordon tried to get a fix on Stewie's shadowy face before he said, "But I think, son, that it might be best for you to leave us for a while. Spend some time thinking very hard about how you can turn your life around. Have some good heart-to-heart talks with the Lord."

"I can't have talks with the Lord while I'm a member of this church?" Stewie had been nervous, then distracted by the strange sock. Now outright fear was setting in: fear mixed with strong feelings of rejection.

"To be honest with you, Stewie, I'm also concerned about your negative influence on other members of this congregation."

"What other members?"

"Tie Gibbons for one. That young man, I believe, given proper positive reinforcement and Christian encouragement, could be a pillar of this church one day."

Stewie was hurt, stunned ... and angry. He'd always thought that besides being his minister, Gordon was also his friend. Now his friend was turning his back on him. And at the very worst possible time.

Stewie stood up and held out his hand for Gordon to shake. Swallowing the anger that welled up inside him he said evenly, "I'll do whatever you think best, Reverend Wedgerly."

Gordon rose and shook Stewie's hand. It was a good, firm hand-shake—a proper good-bye handshake.

As Stewie started down the aisle toward the narthex and the front door, he could hear the clacking sound his shoes made on the slate floor. Gordon could hear those shoes too as he stood quietly beside the pew in which the two men had just spoken. He could almost detect an echo. This had always been his dream: to have a church so big your feet could make an echo.

61

Ye did run well.
Galatians 5:7

Hope liked to recite things, and this is exactly how she'd spent the better part of the hour which followed the Tuesday evening devotional: sitting Indian-style on an old ranch oak sofa in the communal farmhouse's knotty pine-paneled fellowship room, reading aloud passages from one of her favorite books of inspirational thoughts while crunching wheat nuts and suctioning lemon tea through a broken straw. Across the room Talitha and Pud, hunched over a card table next to the room's rustic fireplace, attempted to work a jigsaw puzzle of the Last Supper. They hadn't gotten very far, though; Hope's constant chattering had made it difficult for them to concentrate. At one point Talitha had futilely resorted to wedging a couple of the little puzzle pieces stopper-like into her ears.

Even with her eyes focused on the decorative mantel clock a few feet away from her, Talitha jumped slightly as it chimed the half hour. Pud waited for the chiming to stop, then looked up from the puzzle. "Where's Valor?" he directed to Hope. "Don't you think he oughta be feedin' those two hungry dogs out there?"

"Is it nine-thirty already?" Hope glanced over at the clock, then at her watch. "I'm a little slow." She put down her book and slid off the sofa.

"I think I have Judas," Talitha announced, pretending to be absorbed in the puzzle, and oblivious to mention of the dobermans' feeding time.

"I'll remind him," Hope said. "I think he's in his room." Hope excused herself and quietly withdrew from the fellowship room, its hardwood floors scarcely emitting a creak under her moccasined feet.

Alone with Talitha for the moment, Pud whispered, "I'm goin' to my room now. You stay with the puzzle. When you hear the sound of the can opener comin' from the kitchen —"

"Is it an electric can opener or the old-fashioned kind?"

"The old kind. You hear that sound, you go straight to your room. Don't run or anything. Just walk very slowly and calmly, shut the door, then hightail it out the window."

"Okay. I really don't know how to thank you for this, Pud."

"No need to thank me. I'm supposed to do three Christian good deeds a day. I still have two more to go."

"This should count for all three. You know, I think I could have really gotten into this puzzle if she hadn't been jabberin' so much over there. See—I was making little piles: brown beards, gray beards, red vestments, dark blue vestments."

"I'll finish it for you later," Pud said a little sadly.

"Thank you. Oh my God, I think I hear it."

Pud and Talitha got very quiet. Valor was in the kitchen now. He had just started on the first of the two cans of Ken-L Ration.

"Okay. Change of plans," Pud said quickly. He was almost as jumpy as Talitha. "I stay here with the puzzle. You go."

"All right. Good-bye, Pud." With forced composure Talitha rose from her folding chair and started out into the hallway. She walked with a brisk, yet deliberately nonchalant gait, her arms swinging in a carefree manner. She looked a little to Pud like a trendy model on a fashion show runway.

Halfway down the hall Talitha ran right into Joy, who was coming out of the bathroom wearing a terrycloth robe and drying her reddish-orange hair with a fluffy bath towel. "Hitting the hay so early?" she asked brightly, a couple of beads of bath water trickling down one cheek. "Usually after Valor feeds the dogs we play a couple games of Bible Lotto."

"What's Bible Lotto?" Talitha asked in what she thought was a convincingly relaxed and conversational tone.

"It's like Bingo but with pictures from the Bible. I bet you'll like it."

"It's been a long day for me. I think I'll go on to bed if nobody minds. Maybe tomorrow night."

"Sure. Good night, then." Joy went into her room directly across from the bathroom. Talitha continued down the hallway; her bedroom was through the door at the very end.

Once inside and with the door closed behind her, Talitha clutched her chest and took a couple of quick deep breaths in an attempt to get herself calmed down a little. Then she went straight for the window above the headboard of the bed. Standing on her nicely plumped pillows, she yanked back the ugly yellow-green curtains. From her right hip pocket she pulled out a metal shoehorn that Pud had given her earlier in the evening to pry the window open with. The casement slid easily to the right. She pounded on the screen a couple of times as Pud had instructed; it fell right off. Kneeling on the headboard she started to climb through.

Valor was outside now, calling the dogs: "Come on, Jezzie! Come on, Ahab! Supper time!" This made her feel better until she remembered Pud saying that the two dobermans were ravenous eaters, and she had at best about three minutes to execute her escape.

Halfway out the narrow window Talitha felt something catch on the window frame. A belt loop. She pulled it free. Then she felt something snag. A button from her blouse. She pushed forward and heard it pop free. Now, staring down at a drop of about five feet, the disturbing possibility that she might land on her head and break her neck gave her momentary pause. And yet there's no other way out, she thought. I can't back up and go feet first because the window's too high. Oh shit, I'm either gonna sever my spine or those frothy-fanged dogs are gonna have me for dessert.

Or ... there was a third possibility: she could go back and live the rest of her life as a pious Sister of the Blessed Redeemer. This, Talitha could safely say, would be the worst fate of all.

As she positioned herself to make the plunge, Talitha thought she heard a knock. She held her body very still and listened. Another knock. Someone was definitely outside her bedroom door. "Who is it?" she called out without considering that her voice might sound altered coming from outside the house.

"It's me: Hope. I was wondering if you'd like some sleepytime tea."

"No thank you. I'm sleepy enough as it is."

"May I come in?"

"I'd rather you not. I'm doin' somethin' private right now."

"What are you doing, Blithe? Are you praying?"

"That's right. I'm prayin'."

"Your voice sounds funny. You sound like you're in the closet or under the bed."

"Yes. I'm under the bed. I like to pray under my bed. Don't ask me why."

"You don't have to hide from the Lord, Talitha."

Any second now she's gonna come in, Talitha thought in a panic. It's now or never. And with that, Talitha dove headlong for the ground below the window. Her fall was cushioned somewhat by a large patch of soft green moss. But the impact still smarted.

"I'm coming in," Hope announced, opening the door. Seeing the window open and no Talitha in sight Hope began to shout as loudly as her diminutive vocal cords would allow, "VALOR—COME QUICK! VALOR! JOY! PUD! BLITHE HAS LEFT OUR BOSOM! BLITHE HAS LEFT OUR VERY BOSOM!"

The sound of Hope's voice grew fainter and fainter as Talitha tore through the darkness. There was little moonlight and it was very difficult for her to see where to put her feet. She stumbled twice and half-twisted her ankle, but she kept moving forward. She passed what seemed like a small vegetable garden and caught the fleeting scent of tomato and okra plants. She approached what at first appeared to be a ghostly-looking tombstone, but which turned out to be merely the box-like casing over the commune's well pump. She glanced back over her shoulder at the house and could see Hope's teeny face framed by her former bedroom window. She passed the fruit trees. Apples and peaches and plums.

And she heard the dogs. They were barking. Dogs can't eat and bark at the same time, she thought.

She picked up her pace. Her lungs hurt. Her ankle throbbed.

Then through the pitch black, a fence suddenly appeared—almost as if someone had plopped it right down in front of her. Pud was right: it wasn't that high. And it was chain link and not barbed wire, just as Pud had described it—quite manageable for a former student of Miss Neenee's School of Dance and Acrobatics. She vaulted over it with ease. She was free. Free.

Unless they had a mind to come after her.

Talitha kept running.

62

I sought him,
but I could not find him;
I called him,
but he gave me no answer.
Song of Solomon 5:6

Stewie ran.

He felt foolish, his gangly legs awkwardly slicing the air, his large feet flopping noisily against the sidewalk, but he didn't care. Stewie needed to put some distance between himself and the church to which he was no longer welcome. Running seemed the logical thing to do.

Stewie Kipp had never had a crisis of faith before. It wasn't until the night of his near-drowning on Silver Dollar Lake, only eleven months before, that he'd even had any faith to be in crisis over. Until then Stewie had never really given the concept of a Supreme Being much thought. *If there is a God*, he used to tell himself on those rare occasions when he'd allow himself to get philosophical, *then I suppose I'll be all right, because I'm a pretty good guy overall—and if it turns out there isn't one, then I guess I've made the best I can out of my short time on this earth.*

But that night in October as the rain lashed in rippling sheets, and powerful winds tossed him about in the black lake water, as Stewie grabbed for his capsized boat and was flung off like a rag doll—that very night Stewie Kipp found God, discovered prayer, sought and received deliverance, and afterwards made a solemn promise to honor and serve his deliverer in thought and deed for the rest of his days.

Stewie had never expected to go back on his word. *I suppose I can pretend that there's still something connecting us*, Stewie thought, as he now slowed to a stroll beneath the hazy streetlamp light of Oren and Tula and Sheila and Johnny and Carmen and Bowmar's neighborhood. *I can pray and hope I'm still getting through. I know a lot of people who do this. Or I can just thank Him for what He did, go back to the way things were before the accident, and hope He won't hold it against me. Because if you don't know the rules it's really a nearly impossible kind of promise*

267

for a person to try to keep.

The more Stewie thought about it, the more sense this second course of action began to make. I did my best, but I'll probably just keep falling short, and I'd rather not spend the rest of my life feeling like I'm disappointing the Lord Almighty on High. It'll be better, I'm sure, for me just to call it quits right now and return to a life where I'm not disappointing anybody.

He even knew exactly how he'd like to close this chapter of his life: he would return to Silver Dollar Lake and, standing on its marshy banks, engage the Lord one-on-one, thank Him appropriately, and say good-bye.

It was a perfect plan except for one thing that hit it almost immediately: the access road through the bog to the lake had just two weeks earlier been closed to all automotive traffic. A section of a large oak tree, split down the middle by a bolt of lightning, had come crashing down width-wise across the narrow gravel lane at a point about half a mile from the lake, thereby effectively blocking any vehicular passage. Since the road lay on private property owned by Conwell Pomeroy, who had other more important things to attend to during his last days on earth, the partial tree trunk still hadn't been removed. Stewie might have made the half mile on foot but not in the dark of night with all the wild creatures of the bog prowling for their supper.

So I'll just have to say farewell somewhere else, Stewie thought. He now found himself standing at the corner of Park and Post, about three blocks from the Calvary United Christian Church. The church was still in view, at the end of a long row of ginkgo trees. Tall and majestic, it stood boastfully among its small bungalow and frame house neighbors, its brick facade and steeple dramatically lit by several outdoor floodlights positioned about the front grounds.

Stewie turned and fixed his gaze elsewhere. His eyes fell upon a far less aesthetically pleasing Higby landmark: the old, dilapidated, several times-condemned wooden Higby water tower, the second tallest structure in town after the new pump tower. Unlike its more respected younger brother, the old tower had no electrified security fence around it. In fact, there wasn't any fence at all.

"I'll talk to the Lord from up there," Stewie resolved, "where I'll be a little closer." As for the risk involved in making such an ascent, Stewie rationalized that he was a very careful person, comfortable with heights, and unlike the unfortunate Cullen boy who must surely have been on crack or something when he went up, Stewie would be approaching the tower with all his wits intact.

It was almost as if the tower were beckoning him. Its north face—the side nearest where Stewie now stood, transfixed—had, it appeared, succumbed to so much weathering over the years that all that was left of the town's name on its tank were the letters "H" and "I".

"Hi yourself," Stewie said. Then he gave the tower a friendly little wave.

***

"I don't know where he could be, Tie. His truck is still parked over at the church but there's nobody there. The lights are all off. It looks like everybody's gone home."

"Maybe his battery's dead and he had to go look for a jump."

Tie had stepped out onto the porch so that he and Marci were now sharing Stewie's rubber welcome mat. It had little pieces of dried mud tamped down inside the two large "e's" and the fat, round "o" of the word "welcome."

"I don't think it's automotive trouble," Marci said. She was worried and didn't see any need to hide the fact. "I think he heard some things from that high and mighty ol' Reverend Wedgerly—things that upset him. And I know Stewie; whenever he gets upset, like when we used to get in a fight or somethin', he'd just walk out the door and keep on goin'. He says he can think better with his legs movin'. So where do you think those legs took him? It's really late."

"I don't know. I'm sure he's all right. You want a beef pot pie? It's the good brand that doesn't leave a film on the roof of your mouth."

"No, I'm not hungry."

"Well, come inside anyway, and we'll wait for him. Your hair looks kinda wet from sweat. You should come sit in front of the air conditioner vent and let it dry out."

Tie touched Marci's perspiration-dampened hair with his free hand. The other was holding a can of Coors.

"I guess I'm just bein' silly. It's just that I saw that truck sittin' there and nobody around and suddenly terrible thoughts came into my head."

"You have a very wild imagination, Marci Luck. I actually kinda like that about you." Tie put his arm around Marci and drew her up next to him. Then, holding her tightly against him, he began to kiss her on the neck.

"Stop it, Tie!" she said, pushing his face away. "I don't want to kiss you right now."

"But I wanna kiss *you*." Tie tried to meet Marci's lips with his own, but she was squirming and twisting around so much that he ended up licking her chin.

"I said to stop it!" Marci barked, shoving Tie backwards, and completely displacing him from the welcome mat. "You're spillin' beer all over the back of my blouse and you stink with B.O. and I'm not in love with you. I'm in love with Stewie."

"That's not what you said last night."

"I was confused last night. I was all mixed up. Let's just forget about last night."

Tie stretched his shoulders back, then deeply inhaled the clean night air. "I wanna go swimmin' with you naked in that pool. I've been thinkin' about it all day. I know where to turn off the lights if you'd be worried about anybody seein' us."

"I don't wanna go skinny-dippin' with you, Tie. I just wanna go inside and eat somethin' light but high in protein like peanut butter and crackers, and wait for Stewie to get home."

"Can I put little dabs of that peanut butter on your nipples?"

"Forget it. I'm goin' home. When Stewie gets in, please have him give me a call." This said, Marci turned and left.

Tie drained the last drop of beer from the can, crumpled it with one hand, and pitched it behind the scraggly privet bush that grew just below Stewie's living room window. No sooner had the can left Tie's hand than he began to feel guilty about having disposed of it in such a reckless manner. He vowed to retrieve it as soon as he sobered up. On the way back inside the apartment he sniffed his underarms and without much internal debate agreed that Marci was right when she indicated that he wasn't, at present, smelling his best. After watching the Cardinals game which he'd taped earlier he'd take a good soapy shower, then call it a night.

Marci, while sweet and spunky, really wasn't his type anyway. With his good looks and winning personality it would only be a matter of time before he'd find—probably without much effort—a girl who *was* his type. And coincidentally, there were already at least two girls out there who wanted to meet him: Carmen Valentine, and this new girl who'd just that afternoon left him a message on Stewie's answering machine. Her name was Naomi Sailor, and if her looks were half as inviting as her sultry, sexy voice, Tie was pretty sure he was going to have at least one hot date come Friday night.

63

Wherewithal shall a young man cleanse his way?
Psalm 119:9

"I call to order this emergency meeting of the Administrative Council of the Brothers and Sisters of the Blessed Redeemer, Magnolia County Chapter. Madam Secretary, are all council members present or accounted for?"

"All present or accounted for, Council President."

Valor was pacing, circling the dining room table, then doubling back in the opposite direction while nervously cracking his knuckles. Joy, the Council secretary/treasurer, and Hope, the Council vice-president, remained seated. Pud was in the galley but not all that removed from what was taking place in the dining room, as the shadow he was casting through the crack in the open swinging door between the two rooms would attest.

It was Joy, seated nearest the door, who detected the shadow first. She addressed Pud, her voice bristling: "Pud, this is a meeting to which you are not welcome."

"But I'm not even in the room."

"You're still eavesdropping. That's as good as attendance. You seem to forget that you are not a member of this administrative council."

"Well I oughta be," Pud grumbled. "You promised me that after I'd been here six months I'd be invited to join." Pud spoke through the crack in the door, not wishing to violate the terms of his temporary exile by coming fully into the dining room.

Valor, like his secretary/treasurer, didn't think this was the proper time to be discussing Pud's eligibility for membership on the administrative council. A more important matter was now before the three officers; the very future of the Brothers and Sisters of the Blessed Redeemer's Magnolia County Chapter. "Please remove yourself from the vicinity of that door, Pud, and make yourself useful. You could start by brewing us some strong tea; we may be in emergency session all night."

Reluctantly, Pud backed away from the door, allowing it to close all the way. He had first wanted to hear if Valor was planning to go after Talitha and return her, by force, to the fold. When the council members unanimously agreed that this course of action would probably prove counterproductive, discussion then shifted to the possibility of a visit to the communal farm by local law enforcement officers. Given her unhappiness during her brief stay at the farm there was a strong chance that Talitha would swear out some kind of troublesome complaint. This topic interested Pud as well.

It was a critical moment in the two-and-a-half-year history of the Magnolia County Chapter of the Brothers and Sisters of the Blessed Redeemer (at present the organization's only chapter, though Valor had hopes of an eventual national or even global fellowship). It was a moment in which Pud wanted badly to be an active participant. Unfortunately, as of the last vote on his eligibility taken three weeks earlier, Valor and Joy still weren't convinced that Pud displayed sufficient emotional or spiritual maturity to join the decision-making inner core of the group. Hope had given Pud the benefit of the doubt, but hadn't been able to make much of a case in his favor.

"I don't even know what I'm doin' here," Pud muttered to himself as he rattled and clanked the pots and pans and tea kettles that shared space in the cookware cabinet—a not so subtle effort, he hoped, to demonstrate to his brother and sisters in the next room his intense dissatisfaction over not being included in this crucial, all-important meeting of the council. "I should've just followed Talitha/Blithe right out that window and never looked back."

Of course Pud had no idea where he would go. Prior to his arrival at the BSBRMCC farm, he'd pretty much been living the wandering wayfarer's life, hitchhiking from one town to the next, working odd jobs, making very few friends, drinking a little too much; a "rudderless, itinerant loner" was how Joy had described him in her initial evaluation, "with no moral center to his life whatsoever."

"And Talitha looked pretty damned sincere when she said I wasn't her type." Pud was now addressing the tea tin in his hand as if it were a person. "I guess I must make a terrible first impression on folks."

"PUD, QUIT TALKING TO YOURSELF," Valor called in. YOU'RE DISRUPTING OUR VERY IMPORTANT STRATEGY MEETING OUT HERE!" Valor's voice had an impatient edge to it.

"OH YOU CAN ALL JUST GO TO HELL!" Pud bellowed back. He

picked up a tea kettle and hurled it across the kitchen. It missed hitting the hanging spice rack by just a few inches and continued on into the canning room. From the sound of it, Pud guessed that the kettle eventually made contact with a couple of jars of recently put-up vegetables, knocking them right off their shelves. Within seconds, the swinging door to the dining room flew open and Valor, his face flushed with rage, burst into the kitchen. As the door whooshed back it smacked Joy in the forehead.

Valor was too focused on Pud to notice what had just happened to his secretary/treasurer. "Pud, you will kindly pack your suitcase and leave. You are no longer welcome here." Pud could tell that Valor was trying very hard to rein in his temper. He guessed that the commune leader's outburst in the dining room had probably elicited looks of surprise from both of the other members of the administrative council.

Pud, however, saw no need to bridle his own temper: "I can't wait to get out of this place!" Then he added, noticing that Joy was now tottering about the kitchen with both hands on her head, bumping into various pieces of furniture and labor-saving appliances, "Watch out for that counter. It has a sharp edge."

"Thank you, Pud. I'm sure she got that," Hope said with uncharacteristic sarcasm. Hope was busy trying to catch Joy before further damage could be done to a room that she had worked so hard to decorate.

Turning back to Valor, Pud said, "I can't believe I ever thought this was a good place to live! I can't believe I ever thought any of you liked me. You never liked me. You just needed somebody to help with the chores. You used me like an unpaid servant is what you did!"

"That's not true!" Hope said dispiritedly. Her arms were now locked around Joy's torso from behind in a vise-hug. She was trying to deposit her Christian sister into one of the kitchen chairs.

"Lookee, lookee! It's raining blue glitter," Joy exclaimed, reaching out and trying to touch some of the sparkly things that floated in front of her eyes.

"Yes, yes, blue glitter," sighed Hope, finally forcing Joy down. Looking over at Pud, Hope said, "We love you, we do, but if you really, truly believe that we should all be in hell, then you haven't learned very much in the time you've been here. And that probably means you're never *going* to learn anything. We aren't giving up on your soul, Pud, but we just can't permit such dark, angry thoughts to blacken our bright and happy Christian home."

Pud noticed that he was still holding the tea tin in his hand. He flung it blindly at the counter, where it clattered into a ceramic rooster cookie jar. "First of all, my name ain't Pud. It's William Edward Labey. I hate the name Pud. I've always hated that name. Second of all, you don't have to worry no more about my dark, angry thoughts blackening your bright and happy Christian home because I'm already out the goddamned door."

Hope gasped, clapped her hands over her ears, turned and fled from the kitchen. Joy didn't seem aware of the offensive remark; she was still off in her own world—pinching imaginary blue glitter out of the air and collecting it in her bathrobe pockets.

"You think I don't know what this is all about?" Valor said in a low, menacing tone, his eyes reproachfully narrowing on Pud. "You think I'm *stupid*? It's that Talitha. You're mad because she didn't choose to stay here and fall in love with you."

"Ha! That's all *you* know. I was the one who helped her escape from this Jesus-freak farm!"

"Don't tell me you wouldn't have preferred it if she'd stayed. I've seen how happy and accommodating you've been since she got here. Compare this to the time we took in that emotionally disturbed teenaged hitch-hiker with the club foot. You said it wasn't right that we keep that boy here against his will. You said it was kidnapping. So why wasn't it kidnapping this time, huh?"

"It *was* kidnapping."

"Why haven't you said so until now?"

"I thought it."

"You wanted Talitha to be your girlfriend."

"So what if I did? *You* have a girlfriend. Two in fact."

Valor was getting red-faced again. "Hope and Joy are not my girlfriends. They are my sisters in Christ."

"Sisters indeed!" Pud said with a wry laugh. Not thinking of anything to say next he repeated, "Sisters indeed!" Then he turned and marched out of the room through the swinging door.

Five seconds later the door swung back open and Pud reappeared, determined to have the indisputable final word: "I hope Talitha has you all arrested. I do. And I hope they throw the book at you—and it would serve you right if it was a big book—big as a fat, ten-pound coffee table Bible!"

64

Oh wretched man that I am!
Romans 7:24

The Cullen boy notwithstanding, there were, Stewie decided, only two kinds of people who climb all the way to the top of rickety, ramshackle, old wooden water towers in the dead of night, mocking danger and ignoring the potential for serious personal injury: certifiable lunatics—a category to which he was pretty sure he didn't belong—and those otherwise sane and sensibly minded people suddenly emboldened by alcohol or any of its narcotic cousins. Stewie didn't know where he could get his hands on any narcotics but he was quite aware that the Catfish Bar and Grill was only about three short blocks away. And he recalled seeing an ad in the *Star* which stated that Tuesday was two-for-one drink night.

Stewie had been a frequent visitor to the Catfish Bar during his heavy drinking and partying days. But those days had long passed. He had, in fact, become disenchanted with the tavern long before his religious conversion, following an unfortunate food poisoning incident involving a whole plate of under-refrigerated oysters.

Now he was prepared to give the Catfish Bar and Grill another chance. Because a good stiff drink would be just the thing he needed for emboldening, just the ticket to get him up to the top of that tower to meet his maker, in the short-term sense. If he was lucky, he might, during his stopover at the Catfish, even get to hear Veronique DuBois sing her locally famous Randy Newman medley, which he'd been told by Veronique's husband Eldridge DuBois, a coworker at the lumber company, was just about as good as anything you'd hear in one of the Beale Street clubs up in Memphis.

"A late supper, sir?" the woman who greeted Stewie at the door with menus under her arm inquired. She had a tight cap of curly black hair, dark skin, and twinkling brown eyes.

"No, I think I'll just visit the bar. Is Veronique DuBois performin' tonight?"

"No, I'm afraid she isn't with us on Tuesdays." The maitresse d'

277

smiled apologetically. "This is amateur night, though. Who knows? You just might get to hear a Veronique-in-the-making."

"Then maybe I better just stick around for a while," Stewie said cordially. Around the corner he found the doorway that led from the grill and restaurant to the bar. The passage was draped in fisherman's netting. Shells and starfish and colored, blinking Christmas tree lights had been deliberately tangled inside it. Stewie stroked one of the smooth conch shells as he passed through.

The bar was decorated in much the same nautical motif as the restaurant half. There was a thin and delicate-looking teenaged boy up on the stage. The boy was wearing flared lime green pants and a rose-colored shirt. He was singing "She's Out of My Life."

Stewie sat down at an empty table in the shadows not too far from the stage. The boy stopped singing when he reached the end of the second verse and began to do an interpretive dance. A cocktail waitress wearing a yellow fisherman's coat and matching hat walked up and asked for Stewie's drink order. He requested the first drink to pop into his head: Scotch and soda.

The bar was crowded with, it seemed to Stewie, mostly friends and relatives of the amateur performers. When the effeminate boy's number was over, a middle-aged woman with big, over-sprayed hair and two teenaged girls sitting on either side of her applauded loudly. The more raucous of the two girls whistled. Stewie imagined that she was also the person who had a few moments earlier yelled, "Sell it!" when the boy had belted with feeling, "It cuts like a knife. She's out of my life."

Stewie glanced around the room to see if there was anyone at any of the tables he knew. None of the faces looked familiar to him. This wasn't all that odd; the Catfish Bar and Grill was a popular night spot that attracted a lot of people from outside of Higby. It had a fairly good reputation for a night club that didn't exclusively feature country singers. Earlier in the summer a saucy and sophisticated Stephen Sondheim cabaret act even got reviewed in the *Memphis Commercial Appeal*.

Stewie was on his second Scotch and soda and was starting to feel comfortable and relaxed when the emcee for the evening, a lanky young man wearing a rumpled tuxedo and sporting a flat-top, introduced the next to last performer for the evening: "A honey-sweet songbird from right here in Higby: Ms. Jeannie Plough."

It wasn't until Jeannie was well into the second verse of a song which Stewie had never heard before about a woman who was torn between twin brothers that she noticed him. He had broken into a sweat the moment her name had been announced and had briefly considered leaping up and making a mad dash for the door. But he decided that this would only draw attention to himself, so he just sat where he was, hoping that she wouldn't be able to identify him given the bright blue mood light that was surely shining right into her eyes, and especially given the fact that he had turned his body sideways in his chair and now had one hand covering half his face.

A squint. Then a smile of unmistakable recognition. Then an abrupt change of expression as it hit her that this was the same Stewie Kipp who hadn't responded to a single one of the messages she'd left for him at the lumber company that afternoon.

When she was finished, and while people were still clapping politely, she stepped off the stage, walked straight over to Stewie's table, and sat herself down right across from him.

"Did you come to hear me sing, or is this just an accident of fate?" she asked.

Stewie wasn't feeling sharp enough to fabricate a convincing lie. "I didn't know you'd be here, Jeannie. I didn't even know you could sing."

"I mentioned it last night. But you must have been too busy thinkin' about how you were gonna dump me after our evenin' of carnal pleasure was over."

Stewie didn't have time to respond; the waitress had returned to check on things. "You two doin' all right here? That was a real pretty song you sang, honey, but I didn't much care for the grisly way it ended."

"I'd like two more Scotches," Stewie said without even looking up from his glass.

"I'll have a light beer," Jeannie said.

"It's two-for-one night, honey," the waitress offered, adjusting her hat, which was slipping down one side of her head. "Would you like both of 'em now?"

"No. One'll be fine. Are you tryin' to turn your patrons into alcoholics?"

"Why, of course not." The waitress left the table.

Jeannie furrowed her brow. She began to shake her head slowly and despondently.

"I didn't mean for it to be a one-night stand," Stewie said, still not wishing to look up. "I liked you. I mean I still like you."

"So why didn't you return any of my calls to that lumber yard?"

Now Stewie raised his head. Jeannie's face seemed a little fuzzy around the edges. Two Scotch and sodas on an empty stomach were definitely doing the trick; he was getting drunk all right. "Because I came to realize that I'm still in love with Marci. And I think that she still loves *me*. We thought it was over. But maybe it isn't."

"You weren't even gonna call? You didn't think I deserved even a 'good-bye and good luck'?"

"I don't know *what* I was thinkin', Jemmie."

"My name is *Jeannie*, you drunkard."

"I'm sorry."

"I can't believe I thought you were different. You know, this just makes me sick to my stomach. I don't even know if I want to sit here and continue this conversation."

"A lot has happened to me today, Jeannie. I know if you'd just given me enough time I would have done the right thing by you. I don't use women. I'm not that kind of guy."

The last performer was a balding man in his fifties who did impressions of famous people yelling at their children. It was becoming hard for Stewie and Jeannie to hear each other.

"I'm sorry if I hurt you, Jeannie," Stewie said, almost shouting. "I really mean that." He said this very fast because he noticed that the waitress was on her way over with Jeannie's beer. Jeannie looked down at her hands. They were clinched into tight fists in her lap. The waitress set her mug on a cocktail napkin and quickly departed.

"That's the way it always is." Jeannie said this so softly that Stewie had to lean almost all the way across the table to hear her. "You men—you think you can make everything all right by apologizing, and then just go on and forget all about it. I was really startin' to feel somethin' for you, Stewie Kipp. And I thought you were startin' to feel somethin' for me too."

"I was."

The comedian on the stage was now doing a convincing impression of Kirk Douglas chastising son Michael for not putting his dirty clothes in the Douglas family laundry hamper.

"I don't believe it anymore. Because if you felt anything for me you wouldn't have treated me like this. You would have shown a little interest in other parts of my life that don't involve rollin' around naked in a bed. You would have shown me some goddamned respect, that's what you would've done." Jeannie's angry voice was now quite audible ... and not just to Stewie; several bar patrons seated nearby seemed to be bending an ear in their direction. "You know, I thought this mornin' that that Marci person was a little bit kooky, but you know, for her to stay with you and put up with all this shit out of you for as long as she has, hey, she's gotta be Number One Crazy Woman of the Year. I guess you two deserve each other."

With this Jeannie got up, took one long swig of her beer, tossed a couple of crumpled dollar bills onto the table and left. On the stage the comedian was still yelling away, this time doing a passable Lyndon Johnson. Stewie let his eyes go out of focus. The colors of the room melted together, soft and hazy like an impressionist painting.   "Lynda Bird! Luci Baines! Get in here—I'm out of toilet paper!"

Stewie felt miserable, and kept on drinking.

65

Go not from house to house.
Luke 10:7

Nancy Leigh had just finished working her way door to door down the west side of Hartley Street, and was sitting on the curb, resting her feet before returning to her car. Unknown to Officer Garland, she had returned to Hartley in hopes of visiting every house on the street with addresses in the 2000's—she counted twenty-four in all—before the evening was out. Unfortunately, it was now past eleven o'clock, and even though her task was only half finished, the last five Hartley Street families she'd visited had seemed so unhappy having their bell rung at such a late hour by an alleged magazine subscription salesperson that she decided to call it a night.

Nancy Leigh had suffered the additional misfortune of ringing the doorbell of her high school archrival Bunnyjean Gibbs, who Nancy Leigh had lost touch with over the years but who, it turned out, possessed a very sharp memory for every single detail of Nancy Leigh's successful campaign to be voted head varsity cheerleader of Higby High School. "You know I deserved to be squad leader much more than you did," Bunnyjean had railed. "After all, *I* was the one who could do the full aerials. You couldn't even pull off a simple frickin' cartwheel."

Bunnyjean had answered her door wearing a powder blue satin nightgown and clutching a filled martini glass. When she spoke, some of her words came accompanied by a spray of vodka and vermouth. "You're a pretty nervy one," Bunnyjean had continued, her eyes searing Nancy Leigh with naked disdain, "comin' to the door of my happy home after what you did to me."

"I didn't come here to dredge up the past, Bunnyjean. I just thought you'd like one of these colorful and highly entertaining women's magazines."

"I've got all the magazines I want, Nancy Leigh, but thank you for showing me how far you've slipped since high school."

"What's that supposed to mean?" Even after all these years Bunnyjean still knew how to get under Nancy Leigh's skin.

"Look at you, selling magazines subscriptions at such an ungodly hour. Why, you just drip success. Good night!" With this, Nancy Leigh's high school nemesis had slammed her front door with such force that the glass casing over her porch light slipped out of its groove, and Nancy Leigh had to grab it to keep it from rattling right off and shattering on the cement porch.

Thinking about how bitter Bunnyjean had become since the two of them graduated from high school made Nancy Leigh a little sad. The only good thing about it was that it got her mind off Talitha for a minute or two. Nancy Leigh was happy that *she* hadn't spent the last fifteen years of her life drinking martinis all alone late at night and holding grudges, and being an assistant county clerk wasn't such an inconsequential thing to be. And combined with her tutoring and her work with the Feed the Shut-ins program she helped to found, she didn't see how her life could be any fuller or more satisfying than it was.

Provided, of course, she got her sister back.

Nancy Leigh was up now and walking back to her car. She passed the unmarked rear entrance to Bethany Oaks Apartment Village, then was seized with a thought. She stopped, turned around and stared at the inconspicuous gravel drive. Although the apartment complex's official address was on Market Street, there was always the chance that the author of the mysterious refrigerator note may have been directing her to enter the complex through its back entrance on Hartley. This possibility at least seemed worthy of investigation.

A few moments later Nancy Leigh was rewarded for her side trip into Bethany Oaks by the discovery of a white van parked in front of one of the fourplexes nearest the Hartley entrance. Although the words "David Davis Hardware" had been stencil-painted in big black letters on both sides of the van, one could also discern vestiges of color beneath a sloppily applied coat of white paint. It was a long shot, to be sure, but Nancy Leigh wasn't about to dismiss even the tiniest possibility that this might indeed be the same van she had seen speeding away from the courthouse earlier that day. And so, despite the late hour, Nancy Leigh reconsidered her decision to postpone her search until the morning. Tomorrow morning, she decided, might be too late.

"You don't feel *anything*?"

"Of course I feel somethin': a painful burnin' sensation in my throat..."

Drew was standing in the doorway to the master bedroom watching Carmen and Alaura sitting on the bed sharing tokes on a marijuana cigarette which Alaura had gotten from her friend Tony Ruberi at the catfish processing plant where the two worked part-time in the filet department. Drew had an amused look on his face. "Maybe you ain't inhalin' deep enough," he offered. "Lemme show you."

"You're not gettin' any of this good weed, Drew, until you take that van back," Alaura said sternly.

"I was on my way, but I just had to see if Carmen was floatin' yet."

Carmen shook her head. Alaura started to pass the clip back to her, but was waved away. "Maybe I better stop," Carmen said. "I'm just wastin' it."

From the stereo speakers at the other end of the room Nancy Sinatra could be heard singing "These Boots Are Made for Walking." Alaura liked this song and had already played it six times since Carmen's arrival.

"Breathe in deep like Drew says," Alaura said, forcing the joint back into Carmen's hand.

"Why do I want to get high anyway?" Carmen asked. She was leaning back in bed, propped up by her left arm, which was partially sunk into the soft plumpness of Drew's pillow. Drew thought Carmen looked relaxed and regal—almost like some painting he'd seen but without the slave girl fanning her with ostrich feathers and dropping grapes into her mouth.

"You want to get high because Euless Luddly walked out of your life today and you need to escape his memory." Alaura was already high; she was having a hard time trying not to laugh at inappropriate moments or throw herself at Drew and kiss and nibble on his big fleshy ears.

"His name isn't Luddly," Carmen replied. "It's Ludlam. Oh my God, I'm startin' to float."

Drew chuckled. "See, I told you."

Alaura took her turn. Holding the marijuana smoke deep in her pulmonary passages, she pushed the words out as best she could: "Will you please go now, you big handsome, lovable man." She let the smoke go; it escaped in two hacky puffs. "And take that van back to the hardware store. They're gonna arrest you!"

"All right, all right. But I was havin' fun watchin' you two." Drew turned and started for the front door. At that moment someone rang the doorbell. Drew stopped, frozen in his tracks.

"Oh shit," he said to himself. "Shit, shit, shit!"

"It's the police!" Alaura cried out with alarm. Jabbing an index finger at the joint, which was now back in Carmen's possession, she yelled, "Put that out! Put it out!" Then she began to wave her arms through the thick cloud of pot smoke.

Carmen, though still floating, was now seized with fear. "I don't wanna be arrested for drug abuse. Why didn't you tell me something like this could happen?"

Alaura was flapping her arms harder now. It looked to Carmen as if she might be trying to fly around the room. "I'll bet they came to arrest Drew for stealin' that van. Let's hide in the bathroom."

Drew took a guarded look out the living room window: he saw no police car. In fact, he saw no car at all. He walked to the door. Without opening it he said in a booming and, he thought, somewhat intimidating voice, "Who the hell is it?"

"My name is Nancy Leigh."

"Nancy Lee what?"

"Just Nancy Leigh. Are you a member of a magazine-reading household?"

"Yes I am."

"Mind if I come in and speak to you about a special money-saving offer?"

Drew opened the door. "Do you know what time it is?"

"Yes, I am quite aware of the hour, but I was told that day-sleepers lived here." Nancy Leigh craned her head to get a good look inside. She continued in a casual tone of voice: "Has anyone told you what a lovely home you have?"

In the master bathroom Alaura's right ear was pressed against the door. Carmen was sniffing little rose-shaped soap medallions. "It sounds like a woman," Alaura whispered. "Maybe it's a female police officer. Uh-oh, what if it's that Judy Garland-woman Drew had a run-in with one time? We better make sure he's all right." Alaura opened the door and led Carmen out. Carmen had now become acutely aware of how much pressure her feet were applying to Alaura and Drew's shag carpet as she walked. This fascinated her.

Drew was completely relaxed now and even feeling mildly conversational: "Well, if it's mostly women's magazines you're sellin', maybe I oughta get my wife. I don't much look at 'em myself except for them lingerie ads."

Drew winked. He turned and found Alaura standing behind him. "Hello," Alaura said cordially to Nancy Leigh. She took Nancy Leigh's hand and shook it for a very long time. Nancy Leigh had to retrieve it in an awkward manner.

Carmen, nearly hidden behind Alaura, decided that it was important at the moment to closely examine the weave of her friend's knit blouse.

"As I was tellin' your husband, my name is Nancy Leigh and I'm sellin' subscriptions to various magazines."

"I'm gonna take that van back," Drew said. "Good-bye, Ms. Nancy Leigh with the dark gypsy hair." Drew ambled on past Nancy Leigh and down the concrete walk to the van. He had a big grin on his face. Drew liked to compliment other women in front of Alaura to make her jealous, but at the moment Alaura was too stoned to take notice.

"Please come in," Alaura said, ushering Nancy Leigh into the apartment with an expansive sweep of the arm. "I just got a subscription to *Vanity Fair*, which I consider one of the best purchases I ever made. You got anything like *Vanity Fair* on your list?"

As Nancy Leigh fumbled toward an answer, Carmen stepped out from behind Alaura to get a better look at Nancy Leigh's hands. Nancy Leigh was nervous and pulling at her fingers; this activity drew Carmen's sudden interest.

"Is that *you*, Carmen Valentine?" Nancy Leigh's expression suddenly changed to one of pleasant surprise.

"Yes. Who are you?"

"I'm Nancy Leigh. Your next-door neighbor."

"Yes. I know you! You live next door to me! Oh, I didn't know you sold magazines."

"Oh, well, I —" Nancy Leigh could now hear Drew revving up the engine of the van and driving away. It was quite obvious that Talitha was not being held hostage in this apartment, and although she was tired, and a part of her wanted to go home, the odor of marijuana which hung in the air made Nancy Leigh extremely curious about what other illegal activity might be going on here. She wondered if Carmen Valentine might be leading some kind of double life.

"It's late. I shouldn't have disturbed you." Nancy Leigh said this without conviction as she slowly began to back herself out the door.

"You weren't disturbin' us," said Carmen, who was now in a partying kind of mood. "We were smokin' pot and listenin' to Nancy Sinatra."

"Is Nancy Sinatra here?"

"Of course not," Alaura laughed. Carmen was glad that Alaura had answered. In her present disoriented state of mind Carmen wasn't sure if Nancy Sinatra was with them or not.

Nancy Leigh felt embarrassed. "What a stupid question. I must be tired. My sister was kidnapped by a religious cult last night and I just don't think I'll be able to rest until I get her back."

"Oh no!" Carmen exclaimed. "I didn't even know you had a sister, and now to learn that she's been kidnapped!"

"Come in and have some bourbon and relax," Alaura offered. "Tell us all about it."

Nancy Leigh considered this offer for a moment. Remembering how much she liked the taste of bourbon, she had no other choice but to accept the invitation.

66

Why stand we in jeopardy every hour?
I Corinthians 15:30

"I think we're okay," said Sheila. "That is—if we hurry. How are your legs doin'?"

"They're all right."

Clint hadn't been satisfied with a stroll around the block—or even *three* strolls around the block. "I'm not ready to go back to that house yet," he had adamantly replied when Sheila had suggested as gently as she could that perhaps it was time for him to go home and get some rest. In semi-desperation she'd offered up a compromise: they'd walk over to *her* house. Clint could just as easily rest there. Clint found this alternative much more to his liking, especially after Sheila mentioned the possibility of homemade hot fudge sundaes and a few minutes of her favorite movie of all time, *In Search of the Castaways*.

A few minutes turned into 100 minutes. Sheila just couldn't get enough of her childhood idol Hayley Mills, and besides, it was hard, given the succession of natural disasters depicted in the movie, to find just the right spot to turn it off. So the two had ended up watching the entire film, Sheila bouncing up every fifteen minutes to phone Oren and Clint's house to make sure that Oren hadn't gotten home yet.

"So what *didn't* you like about the movie?" Sheila asked as she and Clint reached the halfway point between their two homes.

"The rear-screen projection was a joke," Clint replied matter-of-factly. "And that French guy Maurice Chevay laughed too much. He got under my skin." Contrary to what he'd told Sheila, Clint had to admit to himself that his legs actually were starting to ache a little. But he'd bear any amount of pain for the privilege of getting to walk alongside a woman as attractive and attentive as Sheila Billows.

"Listen to all those crickets and cicadas!" Sheila remarked. The two had stopped for a moment by a kudzu-blanketed vacant lot. Clint bent down to inspect what he thought was a frog. "Reminds me of this movie I saw once," she continued, "where this cloud of grasshoppers descends on this farmer's wheat field and has it almost totally digested in a matter

289

of minutes."

"I think I saw that movie," Clint said. Sheila was squatting right next to him now. Clint was right; it was definitely a frog although only the average garden variety. As it hopped away, Clint said, "Hey, I dissected a grasshopper last year in biology. He was really big. Bigger than what you'd see around here."

"Oh Lord, I hated biology for that very reason. I just didn't see the point of learnin' how to cut up animals unless you were plannin' on becomin' a vet or somethin'."

"It's to see how they're put together," Clint said. "Same reason you take a car apart." Sheila's face was very close to Clint's now. She watched the bony-legged frog as it disappeared beneath the carpet of kudzu. She thought about the meaty fried frog's legs she'd enjoyed at a restaurant in Mobile the summer before. At just this moment Clint reached over and kissed her right on the lips. The kiss took Sheila so much by surprise that she lost her balance, fell backwards, and landed flat on her seat.

"What was *that* all about?" she blurted out.

"I don't know—I —"

"Honey, I think we need to talk," said Sheila, looking up at Clint from her spot in the bed of kudzu vines.

"I'm sorry. I—I'm really sorry." Talking to Sheila was now the last thing in the world Clint wanted to do. There was only one imperative on his mind at that moment: getting away—getting as far away as possible from what he had done, from the mortification of it, from the sheer bone-headed stupidity of it.

He backed away, then broke into a trot.

Sheila pulled herself up and started after him. "Clint, honey, now, your house is in the other direction. Where are you goin' now? Clint!"

But Sheila needn't have even asked. She knew exactly where Clint was headed. And it gave her chills to think about it.

***

"CLINT? SHEILA? SHEILA BILLOWS? I don't understand this, Desiree."

"Maybe they went out for some ice cream or some of that frozen yogurt with all the toppings."

"But it's almost eleven-thirty."

Oren closed his eyes. Things weren't spinning around so much now, but the living room was still out of focus, and this made his head hurt.

Desiree, standing in the dining area of Oren's combination living/dining room, noticed the telephone though the kitchen pass-through. "I don't see a note anywhere. Where's your answering machine?"

"In the closet. It's broken."

"Well, you want me to call this woman—this Sheila? Maybe Clint's over there."

"Why would he be over there?"

"I don't know. Maybe the two of them wanted a change of scenery. What's her number?"

"It's in the phone book under the phone. Billows, John and Sheila." Oren suddenly got a picture in his head of Clint lying on a gurney in the Presbyterian Hospital emergency room, hanging on to life by a slender thread thanks to internal bleeding, massive seizures, and a host of other catastrophic medical problems the doctors hadn't previously detected or predicted. But if Sheila had rushed Clint back to the hospital why wasn't there a note? Oren just couldn't think of any other reason for the two of them to be gone at such a late hour. Now he was wondering how he could have ever left in the first place, deserting his son on the boy's very first night home after the accident. Only a bad father would do such a thing. A terrible father. Within seconds Oren had convinced himself he was the worst father in the world.

"Hello, is this Sheila Billows?"

"No. It's Johnny. Sheila's voice is lower." Johnny Billows had just come in from spending a few minutes in the backyard feeding little Milk-bone dog biscuits to Muffin. He had only been home for a couple of minutes when he heard her whimpering for company.

"This is Desiree Parka. I'm a friend of Oren's—*Reverend* Cullen. Are Sheila and Clint—are they over there by any chance?"

"No. Have you tried over at the reverend's house?"

"I'm *at* the reverend's house. They aren't here."

"Maybe they just went out for a hamburger or somethin'. Although I'll admit it is kinda late." Johnny looked out the window into his back-yard. He wanted to see if Muffin had gone back into the little dog house he'd built for her earlier in the summer. She'd pretty much avoided it most nights until Johnny installed a miniature ceiling fan.

"So you haven't heard anything?"

"Nope. Where's Reverend Cullen?"

"He's here. He isn't feelin' well."

"Well, no wonder. That fella's been to hell and back. It was just a matter of time before things started takin' their toll on his health."

Desiree could see Oren through the pass-through. He was gripping the back of his sofa, and seemed to be fighting off a new wave of nausea. His digestive system, she decided, had a definite aversion to red wine—especially one and a half bottles of it. "Well, thank you, Joey."

"Johnny."

"Yeah. You be sure and give us a call if they show up over there, okay?"

"All right. Hey you're not that massage—whatchacall—*masseuse* with the place out Table River Highway, are you?"

Desiree began to tap her foot with growing impatience. "Yes I am."

"Small world. I was one of your clients a while back. Six, no, seven years ago. You probably don't remember."

Agitation began to creep into Desiree's voice. "No, I wouldn't remember a customer that long ago."

"You were pretty good. You were actually *very* good if you catch my drift. It was the night of my bachelor party. I guess the guys paid you pretty well, huh?"

"For your information, I don't perform those particular services any more. Just in case you were considerin' a return visit."

"Hey, I'm a happily married man, Ms. Parka." There was a momentary silence. Desiree was just about to insert her "thank you" and "goodbye" when Johnny exclaimed, "Holy Jesus! There's somebody up on top of that water tower!"

"What? Are you sure?"

"Of course I'm sure. It's dark but it sure as hell looks like somebody movin' around up there."

"What is it?" Oren called from the living room.

"Johnny says there's somebody up on the water tower."

There was no doubt in Johnny's mind about what he was seeing: somebody—he couldn't tell, though, whether it was a man or a woman—

skulking around the catwalk like a thief in the night.

"Holy shit! The guy's gonna—Half the rail's gone, you know."

"Does it look like Clint?" Oren was now on his way into the kitchen. "Ask him if it looks like Clint."

"Does it look like Clint?" Desiree obligingly inquired.

"I can't tell. Could be. I'm gonna call the police. Tell Reverend Cullen, if it's Clint—sorry, but I gotta call the police for the boy's own good."

Johnny hung up. Desiree hung up too and turned to Oren. "He said it could be Clint. He isn't sure."

For a few seconds Oren just stared at Desiree, stared at her face, trying to make some sense inside his wine-clouded head out of what she was telling him. Then he said quietly and without emotion, "I've figured it out, Desiree. My son wants to kill himself."

Desiree shuddered. Oren took her hand. The two were almost to the door that led from the kitchen to the carport when Oren suddenly felt weak and dizzy. He stopped and grabbed onto Desiree for support. "I think I'm going to—going to —"

"Uh-oh." Desiree braced for the worst. As Oren went down, Desiree went down with him, cushioning his body from hard impact with the kitchen floor.

"I was wonderin' how long it was gonna be before you passed right out on me, sugar," Desiree said, addressing Oren's head, which now rested in her lap. "I'm so sorry I got you this way." She began waving her hand back and forth in front of his face. "Wake up now. We gotta get over to that tower."

Desiree Parka wasn't much of a praying woman. But she did believe this was a good time to start.

67

He lieth in wait secretly as a lion in his den.
Psalm 10:9

Avis stamped the brake pedal of his cruiser. There was somebody in the middle of the road—a young woman, it looked like—bobbing up and down, waving her arms in the wash of white light from the car's high beams.

"Oh boy, am I glad to see you!" the woman exclaimed, running around to the driver's side of the car.

"Step back from the car, ma'am," Avis directed, his voice even and authoritative.

"Sure. Okay." The woman took a few steps back. She was wearing a faded, flower-print dress over frayed blue jeans. Careful not to take his eyes off of her, Avis climbed out of the car, but left the door open behind him. As an extra precaution, he kept one hand close to his holster.

Avis took a moment to scan the surrounding terrain for ambushers. "Did you had a breakdown?"

The woman shook her head. "Although I came pretty close. You wouldn't believe what I've just been through."

"I beg your pardon?"

"Oh, you meant—" Talitha suddenly found herself giggling uncontrollably. It took a moment for her to will herself to stop.

"Are you havin' car trouble, ma'am?"

"Oh no. I don't even own a car. I sold it. I got my license taken away for gettin' too many speedin' tickets, so I just got rid of it. I believe *you* gave me a few of those tickets yourself, Officer Tommy."

"*Tomley,*" Avis corrected Talitha with a frown. This wasn't the first time he'd been called Officer Tommy. He didn't much care for it. "So may I ask what a young lady like yourself is doin' way out here all alone at night and without adequate transportation?"

"I was kidnapped."

Avis had been studying the woman's face. "Are you, by chance, a Miss Talitha Leigh?"

"Yes, I am." Talitha's eyes grew big. "Were you out here lookin' for me?"

"Yes, I was." Avis allowed his body to relax. He retracted the hand that had been poised over his service revolver.

"My sister made the report, right? I guess I owe her big time now."

"Did they let you go?"

"No. I escaped."

"How?"

"I got out through a window and outran the dogs. I'm so glad to see you. I keep thinkin' they're gonna come after me."

"You're safe now. Why don't we go on back to the station house?"

"All right."

"You'll need to decide if you want to press charges."

"I understand."

"And would you have any objection if we drove by the place where they held you so I can note its location?"

"No. I'll feel pretty safe in your car. But don't stop: that farm gives me the creeps."

"All right."

Now Avis heard his P.D. number being paged on the patrol car radio. He excused himself, ducked into the car and got a priority report from Melody Jenkins, the dispatcher, on the newest trespasser atop the old Higby water tower.

"Somebody really oughta tear that damned thing down," Avis grumbled before signing off.

Talitha, who'd been listening in, slid into the front seat on the passenger's side. "I don't mind if you wanna stop there first," she said.

"Good," Avis replied. "Because whoever's up there's liable to break his fool neck, or worse. And as usual, that idiot Ray Reese is nowhere to be found."

***

Ray was sure he'd picked the perfect spot for his stake-out: Tula Gilmurray's old backyard pump house. Even though the well hadn't been used for many years, Tula and her late husband Theo had kept the tiny structure intact because it continued to serve as a good, dry place to store firewood for the winter. For Ray's purposes the pump house offered an excellent vantage point for undetected observation of the comings and goings of one ex-convict by the name of Bowmar Stambler. Through its little window Ray had a clear, unobstructed view not only of Bowmar's carport and backyard, but also of about half the rooms in the Stambler residence, since Bowmar and his live-in girlfriend and literacy tutor Nancy Leigh usually left all their curtains wide open, even late into the night.

Ray took out his cigarette lighter and used the flame to illuminate the fine print on the side of the can of Diet Pepsi from which he'd just taken a sip. He wanted to make sure that it didn't contain any saccharine which he'd heard was deadly in large doses; Ray had already consumed six Diet Pepsis that day—a record even for him.

While keeping the lighter ignited in his hand—the warmth and light of its tiny flame making poor but undemanding company for an officer of the law engaged in a lonely nocturnal stake-out—Ray squinted through his police-issue binoculars. Bowmar came into easy focus through the lens. He was stretched back in his Barcalounger in his wood-paneled den watching television and eating little orange snack-food pellets from a plastic bag.

Ray wondered when Bowmar would make his move. He could get up at any minute now, Ray thought—get up, go out to his truck, drive straight over to wherever it was he was surely holding Talitha hostage, and then transport her to a new location. Because just twenty minutes earlier in a falsetto voice which Ray was fairly certain disguised his identity, he had phoned Bowmar and said the following: "Mr. Stambler, I know that you kidnapped your girlfriend and literary tutor's sister Talitha. Don't ask me how I know—I just do. And don't speak. I'll be doin' all the talkin' here. Of the ransom money which you're plannin' on askin' from whichever rich relative she's got down in Jackson or over in Tupelo, I would like precisely half. If this arrangement ain't acceptable to you I will go to the place where you're holdin' her—don't ask me how I know where that is—I just do. I will go with a police escort to that place and your goose'll be cooked. I will call you again with instructions as to where you may leave my half of the ransom money. I would advise you to stay put until you hear from me again." This last part, Ray felt sure, would be just the thing to get Bowmar out to wherever it was he was keeping Talitha; and Ray would, of course, tail him all the way, then promptly arrest not only Bowmar but all of his Children of the Holy Jesus or whatever weird, religious, crazy-head accomplices he'd enlisted for this particular job.

"It's a perfect plan. Even Avis would admit it!" Ray had declared to himself as he strode proudly over to the patrol car from the pay phone at Zachary and Brita Brownweather's Texaco Station on Old Post Road.

"What a loonball," Bowmar had marveled aloud as he hung up the phone in his kitchen and started rummaging through the pantry closet for the Cheetos. Bowmar had recognized the voice immediately. I oughta call Avis up right now, he thought to himself, and have that Ray son-of-a-bitch Reese's badge stripped away from him this very night. On the other hand Bowmar had really been looking forward to a certain *Star Trek—the Next Generation* episode that was due to be broadcast in less than a minute, because it was one he'd missed while he was in prison. For the moment, seeing Whoopie Goldberg in her funny hat meant a lot more to him than seeing Ray lose his job.

Ordinarily, Bowmar wouldn't have taken Ray's call in the first place, but he'd been getting a little concerned about Nancy Leigh; the message she'd left on the answering machine had ended prematurely when the "incoming calls" cassette tape ran out. What he got was, "Hi, honey. Sorry I'm not home. I'm gettin' ready to go out with one of the officers to look for Talitha. I think we have a le—" Bowmar mulled the incomplete last sentence over and over in his head. The closest he could come was "I think we have a leak." Which didn't make any sense at all.

Inside Tula's laundry room, which used to be a patio but was now glassed in and serving as a partial greenhouse for her succulents, Hank squatted next to the dryer and listened to his sneakers bumping around inside. He was wondering if they were doing irreparable damage to the metal drum. Tula had assured him just a few minutes earlier that there wasn't a problem—she dried sneakers this way all the time—but the loud thuds seemed to Hank to indicate otherwise. He touched the top of the dryer to see how much heat was being generated—he was just curious— then hearing a night bird whose song he didn't recognize he took a look out into the darkness of his sister's backyard. His eyes were drawn to a faint spark of light in the window of the pump house. "Somebody's in the wood shed stealin' all our firewood!" he exclaimed. Without hesitating, he pushed open the laundry room door and rushed out into the night.

Ray heard footsteps in the grass. He snapped the lighter shut, set the binoculars down, and drew his gun.

Louder footsteps, then silence. Hank stopped right in the doorway of the pump house. To Ray he appeared as a large dark silhouette framed against the dim ambient light of the back yard. "Come out of there, you wood thief!" Hank commanded, keeping the pitch of his voice low so as to sound appropriately threatening. "Come out of there at once!"

"I have a gun," Ray replied, a high, frightened tenor. "I won't hesitate to use it if you don't back off."

Ray had no idea who this hulking stranger was, menacingly blocking his only means of egress. His prep work had shown that the property belonged to an elderly widow, a Ms. Tula Gilmurray.

Hank, not being too fond of guns, stepped back and away from the door. "Now, I'm comin' out," Ray announced. "No funny business." Ray edged slowly toward the door. "I must remind you again that I am in possession of a loaded firearm."

"I understand that," said Hank, stationed off to one side just out of Ray's line of vision. He clutched a stray stick of kindling with both hands, holding it high above his head, poised for assault.

68

And he shot out lightnings,
and discomfited them.
Psalm 18:14

Stewie had already lost his footing once, and had come perilously close to slipping right through the gap in the broken wooden railing and plunging to his death fifty-five feet below. Now he stood quiet and still, his back and shoulders pressed safely against the curve of the tank. He wondered as he gazed down at all the twinkling lights of Higby if it might have been wiser for him to have postponed his summit with the Lord until some night when he could be completely sober. Stewie's thoughts were interrupted by the sound of creaking wood below. "Looks like I'm about to get myself some company!" he whispered incredulously to himself. He cocked his head. The creaking was now replaced by the rumble of distant thunder. He scanned the sky. A flash of light lit an area of grayish rain clouds just west of town.

Sheila was too short of breath to speak, let alone call up to Clint, who was now several rungs up the wooden ladder that led to the tower catwalk. She had run the last two blocks to the tower, and shouldn't have; she wasn't in very good shape.

Clint temporarily halted his ascent and glanced over his shoulder to find Sheila standing almost directly below him. He wished that she would just go on home and leave him alone. He advanced another two rungs, then was stopped again. Someone was speaking to him from above: "This catwalk's already occupied. You'll have to go on down and wait your turn."

Clint tipped his head back. He could just barely make out the dark outline of a man crouching on the wooden planks above. Clint couldn't tell what the man looked like, though, and wasn't sure if he ought to be frightened or not.

Not receiving a reply, Stewie snapped, "Hey, I'm talkin' to you!" He leaned wobblingly forward in an attempt to get a better look at the unwelcome visitor. Too far forward, in fact. Suddenly Stewie felt himself losing his balance for a second time. As gravity began to pull his floun-

301

dering body downward he reached blindly for what was left of the rail and found only air. He felt his knees make contact with the wooden planks of the platform. His arms flailing, one hand finally caught—almost by accident—one of the balusters from behind. He felt something pop in his shoulder. Pulling himself back up was a painful endeavor.

"You don't own this tower," Clint declared, oblivious to the battle Stewie had just waged to keep himself from toppling right off the catwalk. "This is *my* tower."

Sheila had now regained her voice: "Clint! For God's sake, honey, get yourself down here before you fall —"

"Again." A voice Sheila readily recognized had finished the sentence for her. She turned to find her husband Johnny negotiating his way toward her through the tall Johnson grass and ragweed. As he sidestepped a suspicious-looking dead branch in his path he said, "You know there's snakes out here, honey, and you don't even have your boots on."

Sheila glanced down, noting that Johnny did have *his* boots on.

"I can't get him to come down," Sheila explained, pointing out Clint who had now made it almost all the way up the ladder.

Sheila began dancing in place a little to discourage any snakes from dropping by. "He just won't listen to me."

"Maybe whoever's already up there'll have better luck," Johnny said. He tried to get a fix on the dark figure now squatting on the catwalk, but without a searchlight directed right at this person, it was impossible to make an identification.

"Oh, I hope he's not somebody who'll do harm to the boy. Lord, Johnny, what if that person's up to no good? What if he decides to throw Clint right off?"

"I better go up," Johnny said.

"You can't go up. You're afraid of heights."

"I like that kid too, Sheila. I wouldn't want anything to happen to him, and the police seem to be taking their sweet time gettin' here." Johnny now tramped purposefully over to the tower leg that supported the access ladder, and began his ascent.

Fifty-five feet overhead, Clint had just completed his own climb. Stewie greeted him with a cold, suspicious glare. "I told you already: there isn't room for two of us up here. I was here first. You go on down."

"I'm not gonna take orders from you," Clint said. He stood almost nose to nose with Stewie. The climb had made Clint's arms and legs hurt. He didn't feel like stretching those achy muscles for a descent any time soon.

Stewie, who was a little slow on the uptake from all the alcohol in his system, now realized who his companion was. "Wait a minute— you're that kid—you're that Cullen kid who fell off this thing yesterday."

"So what?"

"So you, if anybody, should know how unsafe it is up here. Why don't you just go on down now before you fall off again?"

"First of all, I don't intend to fall off again. Second of all, I have somethin' up here I gotta do. Third of all, you stink like liquor. So why don't *you* go on down? You're in my way."

"Well, it just so happens that I have somethin' I gotta do up here too." After a short silence Stewie added, sounding very much like a fractious child, "And I was here first."

While grabbing hold of the twenty-first rung, Johnny was overwhelmed with acrophobic terror and became paralyzed.

"Oh honey, I knew you couldn't go all the way up," Sheila said, still bobbing from foot to foot. "Come on down."

Johnny nodded and began his descent. As he transferred the weight of his right foot from rung number sixteen to termite-rotted rung number fourteen, the second rung snapped completely in two, and Johnny suddenly found his right foot dangling. He yanked it back up and hugged the pylon in terror.

Sheila called up to him, "Are you okay?"

"The step broke. I can't get down." The fearful sound in Johnny's voice made Sheila feel uneasy.

"Then just reach a little farther for the step below it."

"I can't. I'm afraid it might break too."

"What are they talkin' about?" Stewie asked Clint.

"I think Sheila's husband wants to come up here and get me. But I'm not goin' down."

"Neither am I," Stewie said, parking his seat on the wooden-planked floor of the catwalk.

Clint did likewise. Four legs now dangled over the edge. A moment passed. Then Stewie said, almost casually, "So what are you doin' up here?"

"I don't know if that's any of your business."

"Suit yourself." From his shirt pocket Stewie removed the pack of Marlboros he'd bought on his way out of the Catfish Bar and Grill. He had been surprised at how much the price of cigarettes had gone up in just the short period of time since he'd declared his body a true temple of the Lord and stopped smoking. After three unsuccessful attempts to light one of the cigarettes, he handed the matchbook to Clint. "Here, will you light this for me? The wind isn't bein' very cooperative. Plus, I'm about as piss-drunk as a person can be right now."

Clint took a few stabs at it and was finally able to keep one of the match flames alive long enough to make contact with the end of Stewie's cigarette. Stewie thanked Clint, sucked the aromatic smoke into his lungs, hacked a couple of times, then smiled contentedly.

"Can I have one?" Clint asked.

"Do you smoke?"

Clint shook his head.

"Then I'm not gonna be the one to get you started."

Clint sighed. He had been kneading his sore legs off and on although this didn't seem to make them feel any better. Thinking about his achy legs reminded him of the accident, and thinking about the accident made him think about Sheila and Johnny Billows. He wondered what had happened to Johnny. He peered down and could just barely make out Sheila's husband wrapped around one of the tower legs. Sheila, who had earlier been trying her hardest to coax him down, was now pacing and shaking her head.

Stewie examined the restless sky. The storm was closing in. White zigzags of lightning flashed in the west. The wind was growing fierce, the air turning cool, almost cold. "I don't think this is the best place to be during a thunderstorm," he remarked to Clint as he put out the cigarette.

"Then climb on down," Clint said matter-of-factly.

"I couldn't if I wanted to," Stewie replied. "That frightened man down there is blocking the way. I guess he just plans on hangin' there all night."

Stewie was feeling a little less drunk now, but no less happy. It was nice sitting in the dark—a brisk, clean wind brushing past his face and arms. He could smell the approaching rain. It was one of his favorite smells in the world. He even had a new friend: a teenaged boy who, though somewhat contentious and probably very troubled, was, at least when it came to climbing about the tops of water towers, a shining example of determination and daring. You had to admire these qualities in a young man.

"So I guess if I don't tell you why I came up here, you're not gonna tell me why *you* came up here," Clint said. Clint had stopped rubbing his legs. It wasn't helping to ease the pain that much and was actually starting to make them a little chafed.

"That sounds fair," Stewie replied. "And anyway, when you come to think of it, sometimes a person's reason for doin' a certain thing is only gonna make sense to the person doin' it. You understand?"

Clint nodded. He understood too well. "Tell me anyway."

"Why?

"Because I'm wonderin' if you're up here for the same reason I am."

"And what would *that* reason be?"

Clint didn't answer. He just grinned—the custodian of a big secret that wasn't going to be divulged that easily. Stewie returned the grin.

Headlights shone on the weeds at the foot of the tower as Avis Tomley maneuvered his patrol car up through the adjoining vacant lot and over to where Sheila was standing. Avis was out of the car first, then Talitha. "Looks like we got *two* folks up there," he said, staring up at the tower. He took out his bullhorn.

"Actually *three* if you count my husband Johnny," Sheila volunteered. "He's kinda stuck on the ladder."

Hearing his name, Johnny sheepishly executed a tiny wave with the fingers of his right hand.

"The mystery guy—what's he doin'—tryin' to talk the boy down?"

Sheila shook her head. "I don't know. Apparently he was already up there when Clint got here."

Now Avis spoke into the bull horn: "ATTENTION PLEASE— THIS IS AVIS TOMLEY, HIGBY POLICE FORCE. WHOEVER'S UP THERE WITH YOUNG CLINT, PLEASE IDENTIFY YOURSELF IMMEDIATELY."

"Should I?" Stewie asked Clint. "As long as I stay anonee— annomena —"

"Anonymous," Clint said, trying to be helpful.

"Yeah—that. As long as I stay that, then nobody'll think I've gone

305

completely crazy, you know, because they won't even know it's me up here."

"Are they thinkin' that about *me?* That *I'm* crazy?" Clint and Stewie had scooted back away from the edge of the catwalk and were now sitting cross-legged against the wall of the tank. Clint had been tearing open the inside of one of Stewie's cigarettes to see how it was put together. Now he looked anxiously over at Stewie.

"Oh, they don't think you're crazy, Clint. They probably just think you're remote."

"What does that mean?"

"That you prefer not to have much to do with other people."

This troubled Clint even more than people thinking he was crazy. "But that's not true! I like people. I like people a lot. It's just that I have certain feelings. I have these feelings that I don't know what to do with."

"YOU ARE BEIN' REQUESTED BY A UNIFORMED OFFICER OF THE LAW TO IDENTIFY YOURSELF. YOU MUST COMPLY OR BE SUBJECT TO ARREST AND POSSIBLE PROSECUTION."

"I'd rather not," Stewie whispered to Clint.

"Then don't," Clint whispered back.

"Okay, I won't."

"Do you have a searchlight or somethin' in your car?" Talitha asked Avis.

Avis shook his head and let out a heavy sigh that seemed to empty all the air out of his lungs. As he considered for a moment what needed to be done, he allowed his gaze to drift down to his shoes. He was still looking down at his shoes, making a little nick in the dirt with his right foot when he said, "Well, whoever's up there with Clint's gotta come down too, so I guess I better go up there and get 'em both." Avis excused himself and walked over to where the ladder met the ground. He threw his head back and addressed Johnny through the bullhorn: "YOU COME ON DOWN NOW, JOHNNY, SO I CAN USE THIS LADDER."

Johnny's ears were throbbing. "You don't have to use that thing on me, Avis. I'm not in the next county."

"Then come on down like I ask."

"I can't."

"How come?"

"I can't move. I can't get my body to move a single muscle."

Avis was losing patience. "You want me to pull you down by force?"

"I told you, Avis. I am immobilized. I have a palpable fear of falling."

"You have a what kind of fear?"

"Palpable. Don't ask me what it means."

"Find yourself some guts, Johnny, or I'll have to arrest you for trespassin' and obstructin' justice."

"Like I said, Avis. I can't move. Not to mention the rungs on this ladder, they're old and full of termite holes. It's a wonder none of them broke off on Clint or that other guy up there."

"Oh for the love of —" Avis found a small rock to take out his frustration on, and kicked it across the field. Then he returned to the cruiser to call for backup.

Up on the catwalk Clint felt the first drop of rain. It served only to remind him that the tin-woodsman hood which topped the water tank wouldn't offer much in the way of shelter. A major storm was approaching, and the two would soon find themselves exposed to whatever the angry winds might bring.

And yet, for the moment, it wasn't the weather that weighed heaviest on Clint and Stewie's minds. There was another matter—the reason they'd climbed the tower to begin with.

69

Thou shalt beat him with the rod.
Proverbs 23:14

"Get up off the ground. I barely tapped you."

"You cracked my skull open."

"I don't see any blood. All I see is your hair with a little bit of this here bark in it." Hank offered a hand to help Ray up. Ray didn't take it. He was feeling a little dizzy from Hank's blow and thought it might be best to sit on the wet lawn for a moment longer and try to get his vision realigned.

Hank was still holding the stick of kindling wood. He honestly hadn't thought he'd hit Ray all that hard, but apparently the blow had been forceful enough to knock the officer right to the ground. Hank was now in possession of Ray's gun too, Ray having let it slip carelessly from his hand while he was busy collapsing.

"I desire my gun back if you please."

"You can't have your gun back," Hank said resolutely. "You'll only make more mischief with it."

"I'm not makin' mischief! I got no desire for any of your stupid firewood! I'm on a stake-out! A botched-to-hell stake-out thanks to you." Ray fingered the growing lump on the top of his head and wondered if there'd be long-term brain damage. So far he was thinking fairly clearly, but there was always the possibility that he might wake up the next morning with the mind of an infant.

"Who are you stakin' out?" Hank asked, looking about the murky back yard.

"I'm not gonna tell you that, you crazy old man."

Tula took slow, cautious steps across the damp lawn toward Hank and Ray. She was protected from the drizzle by her favorite umbrella—a salmon-colored antique, with petite bows sewn into the fabric. A few yards from the pump house she could barely make out the bodily forms of her brother and a stranger sitting at his knee. "Hank? Hank? Who are you talkin' to back there so late, honey?"

"He says he's a police officer," said Hank.

"Of course I'm a police officer," Ray muttered. "You think I got this badge and uniform from some damned costume shop?" Ray thought he might get up now. Using the faucet spigot projecting out of the side of the pump house for support, he pulled himself to his feet.

Drizzle was fast turning to hard rain. Tula walked over to Hank. She held the umbrella up high so that it might cover them both. "What are you doin' in my backyard, officer?" she asked. Without an umbrella Ray stepped back under the eaves.

"Police business, ma'am.

"What kind of police business?"

"He says he's on a stake-out, but he won't say who it is he's spyin' on," Hank offered.

"Is that why you hit him over the head with that stick, honey?"

Hank looked first at the kindling, then at his sister. He thought about the question for a moment while rubbing his chin with the barrel of Ray's revolver, then replied, "I don't exactly remember *why* I hit him."

"Hank, dear, give the officer back his gun. What's your name, young man?"

"Reese. Officer Raymond Reese."

"I don't believe I know you. Have you been in Higby for very long?"

"A couple of years. I came up from Crowder. I was born in Canada. He isn't giving me back my gun."

Reluctantly, Hank surrendered the revolver to Ray. Tula's umbrella arm was starting to get tired. She said, "We're gettin' all cold and wet out here, Hank. Let's go inside and get warmed up. You come too, Officer Reese."

"Thank you, ma'am, but I best be gettin' back to the station."

"I think I heard your teeth chatter. You follow us inside and let me fix you somethin' hot to drink."

Ray didn't feel like arguing. Besides which, his head was in need of minor medical care—which he felt sure Ms. Gilmurray could provide— and it certainly wasn't a bad idea for someone who'd just been assaulted in this manner to wait a little while before getting behind the wheel of a motor vehicle.

Ray had made up his mind to go with Tula and Hank when Bowmar appeared from around the corner of the pump house. He was wearing a wet denim jacket over his T-shirt and had a combative expression on his face. As soon as Ray made eye contact, Bowmar said, "This is for accusin' me of kidnappin' my girlfriend's sister!" Then he drew back and delivered a sideways punch to Ray's jaw.

Ray staggered backwards a few steps and quickly lost his footing in the wet grass, his legs flying out from under him, his arms sawing the air as if fending off further blows. Bowmar watched as Ray's body met the ground. Calmer now, Bowmar added, "And you know I oughta wop you a couple more times for all this other stuff you've accused me of the last couple of years. But I won't. Because I just now noticed that Ms. Gilmurray's gettin' heart palpitations."

Tula, whose free hand was now pressed to her chest, shook her head. She stammered a little as she said, "I'm not havin' heart palpitations, Bowmar. You just startled me, that's all."

Ray didn't know which hurt more—his jaw or the top of his head. He worked his jaw a little to see if it was broken, then said, "I happen to believe that you *did* kidnap her."

"If you believe a fool thing like that, Ray, then you've got the mind of a retarded monkey. Now I've had about all I'm gonna take out of you. I have a mind to —"

"Bowmar did his time, Officer Reems," Hank interrupted. "You leave him be, now, and let him live a good Christian life without intrusion."

"Hey, y'all quit gangin' up on me," Ray whimpered. "I'm just tryin' to do my job to the best of my ability."

Tula had begun to feel a little sorry for Officer Ray. She renewed her invitation for him to come inside her house and have something warm to drink. Bowmar received the same invitation.

"Thank you but I better start callin' around to find out what's become of Nancy Leigh," Bowmar said. "It's pretty late and she's still not home yet."

"All right," Tula said, watching with interest as Ray struggled to get to his feet. Although he seemed to be having a fairly difficult time of it, part of Tula felt that Ray had certainly asked for it, and so she decided not to offer any assistance. This wasn't a very Christian attitude, she admitted, but she couldn't help herself.

"Yeah, I oughta go on back to the house," Bowmar said. "I wouldn't even be out here except that I saw Ray with those binoculars and figured I'd better come over and sock him in the mouth."

"Bye, Bowmar," Hank said. He had just relieved Tula of umbrella-holding duty, but wasn't doing such a good job it; water was dribbling right down one of the spokes and onto her shoulder.

She shivered as the thunder and lightning closed in.

70

The voice of thy thunder was in the heaven:
the lightnings lightened the world.
Psalm 77:18

"Okay, so tell me: what sorts of feelings do you have that you don't know what to do with?"

"It's kinda hard to explain."

Clint and Stewie were definitely being rained on. The drops were big and fat, and stung a little when they struck the skin.

Talitha and Sheila had sought shelter in the patrol car. Avis stood in the rain, midway between the car and the ladder. He glowered up at Johnny Billows, infuriated with the human obstruction set before him. "Johnny Billows, you're the biggest ass fool I ever saw in my life!"

"I'm sorry!" Johnny hollered back. "We all have our fears."

"Then why the hell did you go up there in the first place?"

"I thought I could beat it. I just didn't know how strong it would be." The rungs were wet now and Johnny was beginning to fear that his fingers might slip, dropping him to his death, or at least to very serious injury.

"You know you can't live the rest of your life on that ladder. You know that, don't you?"

"Yes. Logically, I know that."

Feeling totally powerless, Avis trudged back to his patrol car. Talitha rolled down the window a few inches.

"Did you get through?" he asked.

"No. All I'm hearin' is static. I guess it's the storm."

"It's also a dime store radio. I've been after Chief Howell for months now to install new ones in all the vehicles."

"You want me to keep tryin'?"

"No. Let's give it a rest. Move over. I'm gettin' drenched out here for nothin'." Talitha and Sheila slid over as Avis ducked into the car. It was a tight squeeze for the three of them.

Up on the catwalk Stewie couldn't stop laughing. "Look at us! We're soaked to the gills!"

"You're right about that," Clint said through a grin. He pointed to Stewie's hair, which was now plastered straight down against his forehead, and exclaimed, "Hey, you look like Moe."

"Well, you look like all the Stooges got together and beat you silly."

Clint thought this was a pretty weak comeback but laughed anyway. Together they laughed—loudly and raucously, their voices rising, then breaking and scattering into the wind.

There was a definite chill in the air. Both felt it, and both realized that the glow of good feeling wasn't going to last much longer.

Clint shivered, then said very softly, "My mother died about two years ago."

"Oh—I'm sorry. I guess that's a tough thing, losing your mother when you're still pretty much a kid."

Clint nodded.

"I guess you must still miss her lot," Stewie went on.

Clint nodded again. Then in a voice still soft and small he said, "I don't *want* to miss her anymore, though. I mean, it hurts too much."

"You never said good-bye to her."

"No."

"Why can't you tell your mother good-bye, Clint?"

"Cause I'm not so sure she wants me to. I keep thinkin' she's sittin' up there somewhere worryin' that once I say good-bye I just might stop thinkin' about her, that all the love I have for her might just go away."

"Do *you* think that's gonna happen?"

Clint shrugged. "I don't think so. But sometimes I wonder if it isn't hard tryin' to keep lovin' somebody who isn't around anymore."

"Maybe you learn to love 'em in a different way," Stewie said. Looking right at Clint, he added, "You don't think you have the right to get on with your life?"

"Your teeth are chatterin' like a cartoon character."

"Yeah. I'm cold."

"Yeah, so am I."

"Did you come up to the tower to say good-bye to your mother, Clint?"

"I did." Clint let the ground-up tobacco leaves from the cigarette he'd been disassembling drop into the palm of his hand. He watched as the wind whisked up the bits of leaves and carried them away. "I know they say Heaven's not in any particular place, but I feel closer to it when I'm up here. I guess it's because of the clouds and all."

"That's why you came up here yesterday?"

"That's why I *always* come up here. But Mama and me—we usually just end up talkin'. Well, actually, I'm the one doin' all the talkin'. I know she hears me, though."

"What do you tell her, if you don't mind me askin'?"

"Just everyday kind of stuff. Stuff I think she might be interested in. Nothin' big, though, or all that important."

"You mean, important like how much you miss her?"

Clint nodded, then looked away.

"You want me to help you, Clint?"

"How?"

"I'll think of somethin'. Let's stand up for a while. I'm gettin' stiff sittin' like this." As Stewie and Clint were pulling themselves to their feet everything suddenly lit up: the water tank behind them, the partially railed catwalk, the treetops, the rooftops, the weed field and police car below. It was as if some giant camera were taking a picture of the scene using an enormous flash cube. A brief moment later came the explosive sound of thunder. Inside the patrol car, Talitha shrieked and threw her arms around Avis. Sheila, thrown into a panic, flung open the door to the car to see if Johnny was still hanging onto the ladder; he was—still trembling, his eyes shut tight, his face pushed so hard against the pylon that he no longer resembled himself.

Clint swallowed hard. The thunder and lightning had left him with a very unsettled feeling. Stewie took his hand and said, "Now I guess we better be quick about this, and I guess we better hope that what's-his-name perched on the ladder there —"

"Johnny Billows."

"Yeah, that Johnny gets the hell out of our way once we finish what we gotta do up here."

Clint nodded and let out a nervous little laugh.

More thunder. Clint squeezed Stewie's hand. Stewie closed his eyes, then felt dizzy and had to open them. Turning to Clint, he said, "Okay, now you have to repeat everything I say."

Clint nodded. The rain pricked his skin. He could hear the wind whistling past his ears.

Looking skyward, Stewie spoke in a loud, booming voice, "DEAR GOD IN HEAVEN, HEAR THIS OUR HUMBLE PLEA."

"Dear God in Heaven, hear our humble plea."

"Louder. You gotta say it louder."

"HEAR OUR HUMBLE PLEA."

Talitha's hand flew to her mouth as she let out a choked gasp. "My God. They're fixin' to jump!"

"Goddamnit!" Avis threw open the car door and stepped out into the mud-sogged field. He stood there by the car in the middle of the torrent, thinking terrible thoughts about Johnny Billows. He wanted to shoot that Johnny—wanted to take out his service revolver and shoot that stupid coward right between the eyes for impeding his rescue effort.

"WE BESEECH YOU OH LORD TO HEAR WHAT WE HAVE COME YEA TO THIS MOUNT TO SAY UNTO THEE."

"WE BESEECH—My throat hurts, Stewie. Maybe I can just nod?"

"All right. You just nod."

Clint nodded. He didn't stop nodding.

"FIRST, KINDLY PUT ... What was your mother's name?"

"Alice."

"FIRST PUT ALICE ON THE LINE. ALICE, THIS IS STEWIE KIPP. I DON'T THINK WE EVER MET, UNLESS MAYBE I HELPED YOU WITH A LUMBER PURCHASE THAT MONTH I WORKED IN SALES AT THE LUMBER YARD. ANYWAY I HEARD YOU WERE A GOOD WOMAN AND A GOOD MOTHER. WELL, YOUR SON HERE WHO LOVES YOU VERY MUCH AND WILL ALWAYS LOVE YOU WOULD LIKE TO SAY GOOD-BYE. Say good-bye now, Clint."

Before Clint could say goodbye to his mother, the world lit up again. The flash was quickly succeeded by a volley of thunder even louder than the one before. Johnny Billows now launched into a recitation of the Lord's Prayer. Sheila, sliding and stumbling her way through the slippery mud to reach her husband, began to cry, the salty tears mingling with the raindrops that converged in jagged trickles on her face.

"Hallowed be Thy name ..."

"Good-bye, Mama." Clint, who had been fighting the urge to cry for some time now, finally let go. "You know how much I love you, how much I need you, Mama, but we all know you're not comin' back."

Sheila was touching Johnny's right boot. "I've got you, babe—I won't let you fall, uh-uh."

" ... on earth as it is in Heaven. ..."

"Come on down, honey. I'm right here behind you."

"... Give us this day ..."

"GIVE THIS BOY HIS LIFE, ALICE. GIVE HIM A HAPPY LIFE. HE DOESN'T KNOW WHAT TO DO WITH THESE FEELINGS. A PERSON CAN'T GROW OR MOVE ON WITH FEELINGS LIKE THESE, YOU UNDERSTAND."

" ... As we forgive those who trespass against us ..."

"Can't you even hear me, Johnny?"

"Yes, I can hear you."

"Then stop prayin' and come on down. I'm not gonna let you fall."

Johnny could feel Sheila's hand on his right calf. Slowly and gently she guided the leg down past the missing rung. "I can't get a grip. My hand's slipping," Johnny said, his voice quivering.

"You're almost there."

"We're gonna wave now, Clint."

"Why?"

"We're gonna wave good-bye, and I know your mother'll be wavin' back."

Desiree now inched Oren's Duster up to the curb. Through the thick sheet of rain it was hard to see the tower. It was hard to see anything. "Maybe we should wait in the car until the rain lets up," she said to Oren. "If the police are here, I'm sure they've already gotten him down."

"I can't just sit here not knowing anything, Desiree," Oren said, opening the passenger side door.

Water was now streaming down both sides of Stewie's face. He turned to Clint. He had to blink a few times to see him. "Okay, now it's *my* turn."

"Who do *you* have to say good-bye to?"

Another flash of lightning suddenly turned Clint and Stewie's faces ghost-white. The boom of the accompanying thunder sounded as if a bomb had just leveled all of Higby.

"I'm not a good person, Clint. I let people down. I hurt people. I thought I could get my life back on track, but I can't. So I've got to apologize for takin' up the Lord's time. I've got to tell Him I won't be both-

317

erin' Him anymore. Then I plan to return to my previous Godless life."

"You think that's gonna make Him stop carin' about you?"

"I don't know. I don't know about anything. I'm not a damned preacher. It's all a major mystery to me."

"It isn't a mystery, Stewie," said Clint, his eyes still filled with tears. "It's just love. That's all it is."

"One more step. There you go." Johnny made it down. Sheila gave him a big hug, squeezing him tightly, while waving Avis over.

"I'll never live this down," Johnny said, his head bowed in shame. "I'll spend the rest of my
life —"

"Excuse me, ladies," Avis barked as he began to clamber up the ladder. The rungs were slick; his hands slipped and slid, but he didn't stop.

Seconds after Avis began his climb, lightning finally made contact with the old Higby water tower. The bolt struck the northeast pylon, splintering it at about a forty-five-degree angle. It took a moment following impact for the leg to split not-so-cleanly in two. With a deep, unearthly creak and groan the tower, buckling from its lost footing, began to tilt—almost in slow motion—downward in the direction of the severed pylon. Avis, spread-eagled on his back in the mud, gaped up at the wooden structure, which rasped and shuddered as if it had suddenly come to life only to keel over dead. Smoke from the charred tower leg drifted into his view. Encountering the rain, it had begun to produce thick white steam.

As the tank drew Clint and Stewie backwards, their hands clawed the air in search of something to grab hold of. What was left of the railing broke off and fell completely away; planks from the catwalk snapped in two and began to disappear beneath their feet. Clint's right leg slipped through one of the gaps. Stewie lost his balance and tumbled to his knees as what was left of the catwalk ceased to be level plain. Stewie began to feel himself being pulled downward. He felt for a brief moment as if he were on the deck of a sinking ship and was about to slide right off into the wet darkness. Clint, his leg now wedged between jagged remnants of catwalk flooring, latched onto Stewie's arm. Stewie gratefully reinforced the link with both of his arms, wrapping them tightly around Clint's shoulders.

The tower continued its convulsive slow-motion list. Stewie began to feel his whole body being tugged toward the earth. He tightened his hold on Clint. Clint tightened his hold on Stewie.

Shedding its age-loosened bolts and fastenings like beads spilling from a broken necklace, the tin hood of the tower began to slide off. It somersaulted a couple of times in midair, and crashed to the ground. The tank, somehow, held fast—coming to rest at an awkward and precarious angle, just a few degrees past the Tower of Pisa.

Oren watched from a spot just behind Johnny and Sheila. When it appeared that the tower wasn't going to carry his son all the way to the ground, he allowed his lungs to take in oxygen again.

For a moment the only sound anyone could hear was that of the still steady rain. Its assault on the tin hood lying in the weed field made a high-pitched hiss.

71

Hast thou seen the treasures of the hail?
Job 38:22

Euless liked to lie back and listen to the rain as it drummed the aluminum roof of his mobile home. The sound almost always put him in a relaxed and sleepy mood. But not tonight. Tonight the rain was loud and pounding. It reminded Euless of the way the water sounded as it raced through the release gates at nearby Arkabutla Reservoir—like a thousand-horse stampede. And with the rain came the thunder that boomed and crackled like close-range cannon fire, shaking Euless's walls and rattling the cologne bottles on his small dresser. Trailing above everything else was the wind: shrieking and wailing and, Euless felt sure, giving serious thought to whipping itself right up into a tornado and flattening his flimsy little trailer house right into the ground.

With the first report of thunder Euless had been jolted awake from a dream in which he'd driven Carmen up to Tennessee and then callously left her at a rest stop among a group of truck drivers discussing triglyceride levels. As he was accelerating back onto the highway he could see her through his rear-view mirror standing at the water fountain lapping at the water with her tongue like a thirsty young deer. She seemed totally unaware of the fact that she'd just been abandoned. Euless remembered thinking in the dream that it was not possible for him to go back and get her, but he might be able to send her some expensive bottled water after he'd returned to Higby, just in case the water fountain accidentally got turned off.

The dream made Euless feel guiltier than ever. It was clear to him now that Carmen deserved some form of explanation, and so he decided that come morning he would drive straight to her house and tell her exactly why he had run off just as she was about to show him her macaroni paintings. If she never wanted to speak to him again, that would be okay; at least his conscience would be clear, and he could return to more palatable dreams such as those involving automobiles and bikini-clad calendar models.

Euless was out of bed and pacing from one end of the trailer to the other as the rain suddenly gave way to hail, and the icy marbles began to dimple his roof. For the moment, he didn't even notice. He was too busy thinking about Carmen. And about his inheritance. He didn't want all that money. He really had no use for it. After all, he wasn't one for pleasure boats and expensive trips to the Orient. And as much as he'd always liked flipping through the automotive magazines to check out all the new models, Euless really couldn't picture himself behind the wheel of anything that would look out of place parked in front of, say, Teena's Western Lounge or the Grogan Family Cafe.

Euless stopped by his kitchenette window. The pellets had formed an almost solid white sheet over the ground in front of his trailer. It sparkled and glistened under a nearby post light. Euless thought about braving the elements, dashing out and scooping up a handful of the hailstones to keep in his freezer and marvel at now and then; it had been quite some time since he'd seen hail this big.

The wind was making very strange sounds: low moans and high-pitched squeals, and a few odds noises in between. Euless thought he heard a bassoon. He studied the windswept landscape outside his window, trying to detect any sign of the only bassoon player he knew. It seemed improbable after what had happened to Hank the night before that Tula would allow him to go out into this night alone. Unless she was asleep, and he'd wandered out without her knowing it. He listened for the bassoon again, and decided to call her to make sure that Hank was safe and sound.

"Hello, Tula?"

"Yes?"

"This is Euless Ludlam."

"Hello, Euless. Is anything wrong?"

"Nothing's wrong. Did I wake you up?"

"Oh, of course not. Hank and I are watchin' the hailstorm destroy my beautiful clematis."

"Hank's with you?"

"Well, not at this very moment. He just went out with a bucket to bring in some of those hail balls to put in the freezer."

"Just now?"

"Yes. I can see him standin' on the porch. I guess he's tryin' to get up his courage. I'd imagine those big stones don't feel too good when they hit you. Excuse me, Euless. Officer Reese, would you like some more soup?"

Ray, who was sitting at Tula's kitchen table slurping soup, nodded.

"How's your head?"

"I think the swelling's gone down."

"And your jaw seems to be all right. You don't seem to be havin' any trouble chewin' those little clam cubes."

"No ma'am."

Back into the phone Tula apologized to Euless for the interruption and said, "What are you thinkin' about Hank for so late at night?"

"I thought I heard his ba— oh, it don't matter. Ms. Gilmurray, did you know that I'm about to inherit a very large sum of money?"

"Yes. Your mother told me."

"Well, I'd like to spend some of it on Hank."

"On Hank?" Tula went over to the kitchen table and sat down next to Ray who was wearing an ice pack like a hat. "What is it you want to buy for him, Euless?"

"I was thinkin' he might like to have a valette."

"A valette?"

"It's like a butler, Saul says."

"You mean *valet*."

"You'll have to speak up, Ms. Gilmurray. It's gettin' real hard for me to hear you with these golf balls hittin' the top of my house."

In a voice similar to the one she used to employ whenever she had to talk to her hearing-impaired gynecologist Tula shouted, "I SAID, YOU PROBABLY MEAN *VALET*."

"No ma'am. This wouldn't have anything to do with the ballet. Maybe I better call you back later. I just wanted to let you know that I'd like to hire somebody to look after Hank. I'm not sayin' you're doin' a bad job of it, but he probably needs somebody else around too, you know, who can give him some pretty close attention. You just think on that for a while, okay? I'll talk to you later."

Euless hung up before Tula could even say good-bye. She couldn't believe what she'd just heard, and sat for a moment in a minor state of shock, just staring at the phone receiver. Ray gave her a puzzled look. He was very curious, but didn't want to pry.

Outside on Tula's front lawn, Hank had just finished shoveling up about half a bucket of the largest hailstones he'd ever seen. Next door Fred Cowls, who was wearing a motorcycle helmet, and his two young sons, Fred Junior and Thu Minh, who were both wearing bicycle helmets, were braving bruises to do the same. Seeing Hank, Fred Senior waved, then motioned for Hank to cover his head. Hank laughed and crunched his way back to the protected front porch. Tula was waiting just inside the door. She wore a big smile on her face.

72

Use hospitality one to another
without grudging.
I Peter 4:9

Carmen Valentine and Nancy Leigh and Alaura Trumble had spent most of the previous hour sprawled out on the thickly carpeted floor of Alaura's den, drinking bourbon with just a little splash of Coca-Cola, listening to Fleetwood Mac and Barry Manilow and the sound of the elements as they attacked the mansard roof of Alaura and Drew's apartment building. The three women had been discussing lost or, in the case of Carmen Valentine, unrequited love. Carmen had done most of the talking, her tongue having been loosened by too much marijuana and too much bourbon and the opportunity to unbosom herself of the almost unbearable indignity of having reached her early thirties without having had anything that so much as even approached a torrid love affair.

Alaura had listened with polite attention to most of the story of little Joey Fisher who had broken Carmen's heart in the fourth grade when he stopped sitting next to her in the school cafeteria because she had made an offhanded remark about his new Frankenstein wallet. But now as Carmen began for yet a third time to describe how Euless had run out on her, Alaura's thoughts began to drift to Drew, whom she could faintly hear snoring in the bedroom down the hall. She wondered if he was planning to look for a new job in the morning, or would he end up spending the whole day wandering aimlessly about the apartment, sulking and eating Cap'n Crunch right out of the box?

Nancy Leigh was just waking from what had been a pleasant little nap. "You have such a comfortable and cozy den," she remarked in a tiny, contented voice to Alaura, whose sock-covered toes were tickling her in the side.

"Thank you," Alaura said. "This is Drew's favorite room. It was supposed to be the baby's room but we've chosen to be childless."

"I want to have Euless's baby," Carmen said out of the blue.

"I know you do," Alaura replied. She stroked Carmen's hair as if she were petting an affectionate little dog. Carmen smiled. "But Euless is no

325

longer a factor in your life so you have to get his behind."

"She means get him behind you," Nancy Leigh corrected. The carpet was plush and soft and made Nancy Leigh think she was lying on top of a big furry animal hide.

"I don't want him behind me!" Carmen exclaimed so loudly that Alaura worried that Drew might have been awakened. "I want to see his handsome face." For a brief moment Carmen felt the urge to cry. But the bourbon and the friendly company had put her in too good a mood to give in to abject despondency so she laughed instead. Nancy Leigh laughed along with her while slithering slowly across the floor on her stomach and elbows in the direction of the telephone.

"I have to call Bowmar. I don't want him to worry that something's happened to me," she said, fumbling for the receiver. In the process, she knocked a wooden outhouse miniature off the table; it landed right next to Carmen, its teeny door springing open to reveal an embarrassed little plastic boy who seemed to be in the process of urinating.

"Oh did I break it?" Nancy Leigh inquired, concerned.

"No. It was already like that," Alaura said. "See, when the door opens, the little boy is supposed to turn around and squirt pee pee out at you, but nowadays he doesn't really do much of anything except look afraid."

"What time is it?" Nancy Leigh asked. Everything had turned fuzzy—her watch face especially—after she took out her contacts to Visine her itchy eyes quite some time earlier. "About midnight?"

"Where have you been, girl?" Alaura laughed. "It's almost two."

"Oh my God!" Nancy Leigh was so distraught over having lost all track of time and so shaky-fingered due to the large quantity of bourbon and Coke she had imbibed that she had difficulty punching the correct touchtone buttons on Alaura's phone and ended up waking Vivian Wallace, one of the tellers at the Magnolia County Bank of Commerce, whose phone number was three whole digits different from her own.

When she finally did punch in the correct number Bowmar answered on the first ring. "I've been pretty worried about you, Nancy Leigh. I would've called the police but I didn't know as if they'd be too helpful after I went over to Tula Gilmurray's house and beat up Ray Reese.

"Oh no, Bowmar, you didn't!"

"He had it comin'. Anyway, they found Talitha. Or she escaped, or somethin'. I don't have all the facts. Sheila Billows called to say she's all right and you can stop lookin' for her."

"Talitha's okay! She's not kidnapped anymore!" Nancy Leigh informed her two drowsy drinking companions, who reacted with alcohol-muted enthusiasm.

"I guess you haven't been listenin' to the news on the radio," Bowmar said. He was sitting on the floor of the den nuzzling Monty. "That old water tower got struck by lightnin'. The preacher's boy was up there again. Another guy was up there too."

Nancy Leigh relayed this information to Carmen and Alaura. "Who was the other guy?" Carmen asked anxiously. "It wasn't Euless, was it?"

"Who was the other guy?" Nancy Leigh asked Bowmar.

"Fella named Stewie Kipp. We work together at the lumber yard."

As Nancy Leigh repeated Stewie's name, Carmen gasped. "I know him! He goes to my church!"

"Are they all right? What happened?" Nancy Leigh was now talking so fast that Bowmar could hardly understand her.

"Have you been drinking?" he asked.

"Yes, a little. Will you please tell me what happened?"

"Like I said, that water tower got hit by lightnin'. Then it just kinda buckled over, but that preacher's boy and Stewie, they hung on, and an engine company from Devane is out there right now tryin' to pull 'em down."

"Why didn't Talitha call? Was she up on that tower too?"

"Baby, why don't you come on home and go to bed? You're not makin' any sense. Where are you, by the way?" Monty had tired of the attention. Bowmar watched as the large cat waddled off, his plump belly dragging along the floor. Bowmar guessed that he was going to the kitchen to see if more cat tuna had appeared in his food bowl.

"I'm at Alaura Trumble's house. We're listenin' to Barry Manilow singin' 'Mandy.' You know I never get to put on this song when you're around because of how much you dislike it."

"Come on home, baby. There's some words in this magazine article I'm lookin' at about endangered species I can't figure out, and it's robbin' me of all readin' pleasure."

"All right." Nancy Leigh wanted to dance around the room. Talitha was safe, and on top of this, it was quite obvious that Bowmar, the love of her life, was missing her very much at the moment. "I adore you, Bowmar," she said softly.

"I adore you too. Do you want me to come get you?"

Nancy Leigh glanced over at Carmen and Alaura. Both women were still awake, but neither seemed capable of operating a motor vehicle. "Yes. I'm over at Bethany Oaks. Apartment ..."

"258," Alaura shouted over a crescendo in the music. Then, having completely forgotten about Drew and his need for ten hours of sleep a night she began singing loudly along with Barry: "Oh Mandy, you came and you gave without taking, but I sent you away."

"Sent you away," Carmen joined in.

A few moments later Alaura and Carmen were asleep. Nancy Leigh moved into the living room and propped herself up next to the front window to watch for Bowmar's truck. "Thank you, God, for making everything turn out all right," she whispered, and then as an afterthought, added, "And spirit Bowmar to my side. Thou knowest how much I love him."

73

My son, give me thine heart.
Proverbs 23:26

It took over an hour and a half for Stewie and Clint to touch soggy but solid ground. The firemen called over from nearby Devane had been concerned that any sudden shift in body position by the tower's two occupants just might tip the structure over. So the whole rescue operation had to be carried out in cautious slow motion.

As the ladder was being swung into place, a wooden support beam beneath what was left of the catwalk snapped in two and fell away. Sheila Billows, who had just returned from calling Bowmar, covered her eyes. Oren, who was pacing in the mud beside the patrol car, froze and held his breath. But the catwalk didn't collapse. The tower didn't even budge.

For a brief time the hailstones were so large that impact with the skin became painful. But the rescue operation had continued without pause. And Oren and Desiree, and Sheila and Johnny, and Talitha and Avis kept their vigil in the weed-covered vacant lot. They were soon joined by curious neighbors, and then, as the two summitters began their climb down the fireman's ladder, Marci Luck, who had noticed the searchlight from several blocks away, and had followed it, thinking that Stewie just might have followed it too.

The hailstorm was over now, and even the rain had moved on, although Higby was still blanketed by a drizzly mist, as if a cloud had descended over the town. Clint was the first to make it down; Oren was waiting for him at the foot of the ladder. Without speaking, Oren reached out and grabbed hold of his son's shoulders, worked his way down the boy's arms, finally taking hold of both hands. He held his son's cold hands for a long time, squeezing them, rubbing warmth into them.

Clint stared into his father's eyes, not knowing what to say, but hardly troubled by the silence that passed between them. Because for the first time, without a sound being made, things were being said—everything that needed to be said—clearly articulated by the heart. Oren loved him.

And it was at that same moment that Oren came to know why his son had climbed to the top of the tower, and he broke the silence by asking in a whisper: "Did you say it?"

And Clint nodded yes.

Stewie was just stepping down from the ladder when Marci spotted him. It took a little longer for Stewie to notice Marci. At first she had been hidden behind a large cluster of happy and relieved people standing near the fire truck. Then he caught sight of a familiar teal blouse. He had given Marci that blouse because she had once declared teal to be her favorite color. This was the first time he'd ever seen her wearing it. He wanted to say something to her as she reached him, but for the moment his feelings had no words to go with them. He smiled, then laughed, then reached out for her.

"I was so worried about you," she said. She kissed him on the cheek, then pressed her head up against his chest as she often did late at night when she wanted to feel him breathing as he slept. The fabric of the shirt was cold and wet. "I've been lookin' all over for you. Is this where you were?"

He nodded, stroking her wet brown hair. "You don't have to tell me why you went up there, Stewie. Just promise me you won't ever do it again."

"I couldn't if I wanted to. Which I don't," Stewie said, glancing up at the contorted tower.

"Can I get my old Stewie back? Just tell me I get my old Stewie back."

Stewie nodded, but deep down he knew he'd never be the way he used to be. Because these last few hours had changed him forever. In the company of a fellow traveler Stewie had found God—a different God— one he had never known existed. A God removed from clumsy human projections and self-serving interpretations. A God unfathomable beyond the one simple truth acknowledged by all the religions of the world: God equals love. A generous love. A love without specifications. This is what Stewie Kipp came to realize. And it was at this moment that he started to like himself again.

Marci didn't want to let go of Stewie. "I've never stopped loving you," she said. "I want you to know that."

Stewie smiled, then kissed her, holding her face delicately in his hands.

Ponce arrived, carrying his medical bag and holding the hand of his six-year-old daughter Donnakaye, who, having been dressed in a hurry, was wearing her dinosaur T-shirt inside out.

"Hello, Ponce," Oren said.

"Hello, Oren. Maxine called me from the hospital. She said she got a report that everybody was okay, but I thought I'd better come over and check things out anyway. How are you feeling, Clint?"

"I'm pretty sore. But part of that, I think, is from the hailstones." Ponce led Clint over to the fire truck and opened his medical bag. Oren and Desiree and Donnakaye followed, Donnakaye hopping onto the running board to stand next to Clint. A pipe-puffing middle-aged fireman took off his hat and placed it jauntily on her head.

"Higby sure took a few hits tonight," the fireman remarked to Oren.

"What's that?" Oren's thoughts were of Clint.

Desiree took a firm grip of Oren's hand, interlacing her fingers with his. Clint noticed.

"Clint, this is Desiree. Desiree, my boy, Clint." The two exchanged a nod and a smile. Oren's expression seemed to indicate to Clint that a fuller explanation was forthcoming.

"What I mean," the fireman continued, "is that this tower ain't the only thing that got zapped this evening." The tiny puff-clouds from the man's pipe hung in the thick moist air about his head, the redolence of the smoke blending with the aroma of Desiree's amply applied perfume to produce a sweet and pleasant fragrance all its own. "Lightnin' struck a couple trees in the park, I understand, along with the steeple of that big church up the road."

"Which church do you mean?" Oren had never heard his church referred to as big, but knew he wouldn't rest easy until he was positive it wasn't Bible Methodist the fireman was referring to.

"Calvary United Christian," offered Avis, walking over from his patrol car. "You finished with that boy, Doctor? I gotta talk to him and his Dad about this trespassin' problem he has."

"Just the steeple?" asked Ponce, who was feeling the lymph nodes in Clint's neck for evidence of infection.

Brendan Grove, a cub reporter from *The Higby Star*, while scribbling away on his reporter's pad and hardly looking up at all, responded,

"Didn't hurt the church. Just knocked the steeple off, about a third of the way up from the base. Speared the ground, it did, landed point-down right into the front lawn like a Heaven-chucked javelin. Got some pictures. Gonna send them to the wire services. Now, I'd like to ask the kid a few questions. And where's the other guy that went up on that tower— Stewart Kipper?"

Stewie was at that moment being questioned by Officer Dan Shippers, who had just arrived on the scene after Ray Reese was reported missing in action. Dan thought it pretty unlikely that charges would be filed against Stewie and Clint, and although he tried very hard to impress upon Stewie what a reckless act he'd just committed, the officer couldn't resist relating the incident to the time he himself had climbed to the top of his hometown water tower in central Arkansas and spray-painted in big red letters, "BOBTOWN GIRLS GOT LITTLE BOOBIES."

74

And they that dwell upon the earth shall…
make merry, and shall send gifts one to another.
Revelation 11:10

At 8:15 the next morning Euless Ludlam showed up at Carmen Valentine's door with a big bouquet of yellow coreopsis clutched in one hand and a greeting card in the other. The card had a picture of a contented-looking young couple strolling hand-in-hand along a sandy beach. There was no printed message inside. This was fine with Euless; he was happy to write his own:

> Dear Carmen,
> I'm sorry for running out on you yesterday. Please give me another chance to win you with my charm. I will also in a few months have a lot of money to give you too if that will help.
> Your friend,
> Euless
> PS I believe I am in love with you.

After two doorbell rings and little heavy knocking, Euless concluded that Carmen was probably still in bed, and was in all probability a very heavy sleeper. He considered for a moment sitting himself down in her porch swing and waiting until she came out for her morning paper. He wouldn't have cared how long it took; it would be worth any wait just to see her happy morning face. Unfortunately, the worn pressure plate in the transmission of Tina Louis Sperly's Grand Prix still needed to be replaced and Euless hadn't even gotten the cover plate off yet.

Carmen had wanted to walk home, but Alaura wouldn't hear of it: "Considerin' how much you drank last night, I'm amazed you're even able to stand up this mornin', and I certainly don't want you steppin' out in front of a truck or somethin'."

So after taking three sips of black coffee, which turned out to be three sips too many given the queasy state of her stomach, a very hungover Carmen Valentine allowed a slightly less hungover Alaura Trumble to drive her home. The trip took about five minutes. Their arrival couldn't have been any better timed for Euless's purposes.

"Oh my God! It's Euless!" Carmen screamed while punching Alaura excitedly in the arm. Euless's face brightened as he recognized Carmen. She grinned and waved. Euless Ludlam had returned. And had even brought flowers!

"I went over to that spot north of town where we had the accident," he said, helping Carmen out of the car. "There was a field nearby with all these yellow daisy flowers."

"They're beautiful!" Carmen exclaimed. "I love wildflowers."

"Oh—and here's a card."

As Euless handed Carmen the card, Alaura looked on happily from beside her car. She knew she was intruding on a private moment but she didn't care. It was so nice to see things working out for Carmen, who was overdue for a little good fortune.

Carmen pulled the card from its envelope. A puzzled look came over her face. "What is it?" Euless asked, concerned.

"It's a very pretty card, Euless, but I don't understand." Euless took a look at the picture on the card. What he hadn't detected in the early-morning darkness of his mobile home was now quite evident: the happy beach-strolling couple were both ... men.

"I'm sorry," he said. "I guess I didn't look at it carefully enough." Euless didn't want to admit that he'd gotten the card out of a box of old stationery and blank greeting cards Conwell Pomeroy had asked him to toss out a couple of months earlier but which he'd taken home instead.

"It's still a very pretty card," Carmen said. She paused to read what Euless had written inside, then added, "That is so sweet. Euless, you are so sweet."

As Carmen stood on her tiptoes to kiss Euless on the cheek, Alaura sighed contentedly and got back into her car.

"Good-bye, Alaura," Carmen said, with a glance over her shoulder. "Thank you for everything."

"Anytime, honey."

A moment later Alaura was gone. Carmen and Euless stood alone on the dewy grass of Carmen's front lawn.

"What about Tie Gibbons?" Euless asked.

"I don't think Tie and I would have hit it off," Carmen said. Euless now had his arm around Carmen's waist, holding her close to him. "We passed him just a couple of minutes ago outside the lumber yard. He looked very handsome in the early mornin' light, but he was pickin' his nose in a disgustin' way. Suddenly, all my feelings for him just disappeared."

Euless didn't know whether to tell Carmen that like every other man he knew, he also had certain unsavory habits. Maybe it would be best not to spoil the moment. And habits can always be broken.

Euless looked into Carmen's eyes, which were now slightly rheumy from her night of heavy drinking. "There's a lot we need to talk about, Carmen. I wanna tell you why I walked out on you yesterday. It's kinda weird when you think about it."

"That's all right. I do weird things. I talk to angels. Well, just one angel actually. She's my guardian angel. My physician says I imagine her. If that's true, I suppose I have a very well-developed imagination."

Carmen didn't want to let go of Euless. She didn't even care what her neighbors might think. Tula certainly wouldn't have minded seeing young love blossoming right in her very own neighborhood. And Bowmar and Nancy Leigh wouldn't care at all. It was only two weeks ago that Carmen had surreptitiously observed her next-door neighbors trying to pull off each other's bathing suits during an afternoon of amorous lawn sprinkler play.

75

And it fell:
and great was the fall of it.
Matthew 7:27

At 8:47 that same morning, arrest warrants were served by Avis and Ray on Gerald McNair (a.k.a. Valor), Heather Stemmons (a.k.a. Hope), and Kimberly Willis (a.k.a. Joy). Avis wasn't carrying a warrant for William Edward Labey (a.k.a. Pud), who wasn't on the premises of the Brothers and Sisters of the Blessed Redeemer, Magnolia County communal farm anyway. William was sound asleep in one of the less expensive unrenovated rooms of the Dollar Econo Motor Court, dreaming of Talitha Leigh, imagining in his fantasy-nurtured subconscious what life with this beautiful young woman of color might have been like.

When he awoke about an hour later he felt rested and rejuvenated. In the bathroom as he showered and shaved, he sang made-up songs with wandering tunes and coarse, irreverent lyrics. William would never have been allowed to sing such songs at the commune. Now he could be as vulgar as he wanted to and no one would even care. Sometimes William Edward Labey had feared that Valor could read his thoughts. He was glad to be gone.

It was a short hike over to Table River Highway where William was able to hitch a ride with an extrusion hauler to, just for the hell of it, Birmingham, Alabama. Magnolia County, Mississippi, would soon be no more than a memory, and Talitha Leigh, the one nice part of that memory.

About a half hour out of Higby, William took his eyes off the scenery and glanced over at his trucker-chauffeur, a tubby man wearing bib overalls and loose-fitting false teeth. "Hey—we gonna be stoppin' for some grub a little later?"

"I reckon," the truck driver said, adjusting his dental plates.

"Could we maybe go to someplace that serves steaks? I'm really feelin' like a great big juicy T-bone right now."

"Sounds good to me."

"I haven't had me a steak in months. Hell, I haven't even had a hamburger."

"Where you been, son? The planet Mars?"

William chuckled to himself, shook his head, closed his eyes, and then began to hum—so softly that his companion couldn't hear ... Valor's last song of praise. He had to admit it had a catchy tune.

At 9:32 that morning Ricky Day parked his boyfriend Greg's silver Taurus in front of Brannigan's Funeral Home and climbed the steps to the front portico. Although he'd driven most of the night he didn't feel tired. Which was good because Ricky wanted to spend this day before Conwell Pomeroy's funeral getting to know the deceased's hometown a little better: soaking up the local color, sniffing the fresh fruit and vegetables from the tailgate stands lined up by the local farmers around Courthouse Square, and visiting some of Higby's dusty antique stores. Ricky also wanted to pay a visit to Conwell's beautiful old Victorian mansion, which he'd never been able to get enough snapshots of on his previous trips to town, and which he understood would be soon be passed into the hands of a local arts organization that specialized in unusual media. But first he had to see Conwell.

The funeral director was appropriately respectful and soft-spoken as he led Ricky Day into the flower-bedecked anteroom.

"Are you kin to the departed?"

"No, we were friends." Ricky adjusted his bolo tie.

There were several men and women seated about the room. A couple of old men wearing stiff suits eyed him as he moved toward the viewing alcove. The lid to the casket was open. Conwell looked very much like himself, Ricky thought, although a little paler, and very, very still.

"You did a good job," Ricky said, then turned to discover that the funeral director had disappeared. Ricky was alone now.

The hushed voices of the men and women were now barely audible over an instrumental recording of "How Great Thou Art" drifting through the funeral parlor. Somebody coughed, a thousand miles away.

"Thank you for making me your personal barber," Ricky said in a soft, sad voice to the body of Conwell Pomeroy. "And thank you for laughing at my jokes and coming all the way down to New Orleans just to see me do my cabaret act. You'll never know how much that meant to me. And thank you for leaving me all that money. I promise to do good things with it. And I swear to you, Connie, that I have no regrets about the fact that our friendship never developed into something truly wonderful. I know we both wanted it to. But you were afraid. I know. I've been there. It's a rotten world, if you ask me, Conwell Pomeroy, where people have to be afraid to show their love for one another. I say to hell with them all." With this, Ricky reached down and kissed Conwell's cold cheek. "And to heaven with *you*."

Ricky knew that he was being watched as he left the anteroom. He knew that people were thinking things about him, asking themselves the same question that people had been asking about Conwell Pomeroy for most of his life. But Ricky didn't care. Not one tiny little bit.

At 9:58 that same morning the old Higby water tower, finally yielding to gravity and the ravages of structural trauma, collapsed into a mangled wooden heap in the weed field that separated the tower from Sheila and Johnny Billows's backyard. Neither Sheila nor Johnny was home at the time. Muffin, initially frightened by the noise, soon forgot all about it and went back to clawing up Sheila's surprise lilies.

Only one person witnessed the tower's demise: Jeannie Plough. Jeannie had been on her way to Holmes Food Village to buy milk and Tampax and instant coffee, and had stopped out of curiosity; the tower incident had been all over the local morning radio shows. More curious, though, than the fact that the structure was still standing after all it had been through, was that she was, at this critical moment, totally, completely alone.

Careful not to go beyond the yellow crime scene tape strung around the property by Dan Shippers and Julie Garland a few hours earlier, Jeannie found herself a spot with a good view of the tower, framed by the branches of two old pines.

As the tower heaved forward and breathed its last, Jeannie gasped, then screamed with delight. Two blue jays screeched overhead, fleeing the scene. A whoosh of displaced air blew past her face, caressing her cheeks. She laughed. She yelled, "Wham! Bam! Goddamn!"

She applauded.

Then she returned to her car and headed for the supermarket.

She hoped it wouldn't be too crowded.

Let all the people say, Amen.
Psalm 106:48